My Sweet Haunt

BAKER CITY: HEARTS & HAUNTS 1

JOSIE MALONE

MY SWEET HAUNT
Copyright © 2019 by Josie Malone

ISBN: 978-1-68046-768-0

Published by Satin Romance
An Imprint of Melange Books, LLC
White Bear Lake, MN 55110
www.satinromance.com

Names, characters, and incidents depicted in this book are products of the author's imagination or are used fictitiously. Any resemblance to actual events, locales, organizations, or persons, living or dead, is entirely coincidental and beyond the intent of the author or the publisher. No part of this book may be reproduced or transmitted in any form or by any means, electronic or mechanical, including photocopying, recording, or by any information storage and retrieval system, without permission in writing from the publisher except for the use of brief quotations in a book review or scholarly journal.

Published in the United States of America.

Cover Design by Caroline Andrus

MY SWEET HAUNT is dedicated to my grandmother, Bernice Josephine Maloney-McMahon who shared stories of the "haunts" in the tavern she operated below First Avenue in Seattle, Washington and always said to open your eyes to "seeing things that aren't there." The best grandma ever, she always believed in me and encouraged me to follow my dreams.

PART I

"This is my home and no haunt is taking it away…"

CATRIONA O'LEARY MCTAVISH

PROLOGUE

Snohomish, Washington

"And now a human-interest story for all you dreamers who love to write."

Cat cracked eggs into a bowl as she listened to the news anchors on the kitchen radio talk about two men determined to sell their dilapidated family farm in an unusual way. They wanted someone to restore it as a guest ranch so they were running an essay contest.

"So, all you have to do is describe the way you'd save the place, toss in a hundred bucks for the entry fee and you're good to go. You could be the new owner of Cedar Creek Guest Ranch. Of course, the catch is you can't sell it."

Cat froze, staring first at the bowl where she was supposed to be creating French toast batter for her eight-year-old daughters and then at the radio as the babbling continued.

Oh my Gawd. I remember that place. We visited every summer until it closed when I was fourteen. It was pure heaven.

Memories floated through Cat's mind of camping trips on horseback, square dancing in the rec hall, movies shown on the barn wall, swimming in the mountain snow melt-off of the icy river and long cozy conversations with Aunt Rose over cups of hot cocoa.

It's mine, she thought with staunch determination. *Well, it will be when I write the winning essay. What can I say? How can I tell strangers how wonderful it was to have a perfect place, a place where nothing and no one could ever hurt me?*

Horse lunch fed, her collie-mix pup tagging behind, Catriona McTavish strolled toward the two-bedroom trailer, planning the rest of her day. She had three horses to work before her eight-year-old daughters arrived home from school and of course her intern had chosen today to do the 'no-show' routine which meant Cat had to groom and saddle for herself in addition to riding. Vestiges of the argument she'd had with her husband this morning still clouded her mind. She felt like one of the twins must feel when being dragged to a doctor's appointment.

No, no, no! I don't wanna go to Louisiana. Listen to me. I want to stay here where I have a great boss, friends, a job I love. I'm finally making it as a natural horse trainer. I've followed you for nine years. Why can't our lives be about me for once?

She'd had to throttle down the impulse to yell at him this morning. Frazer claimed he couldn't talk to her when she was angry. He'd fled to the 'safety' of the casino where he worked as a pit boss, knowing she had to get the twins off to school and wouldn't stay up till the wee hours to confront him when he reluctantly returned home.

The landline rang, interrupting her silent rage. She hastily closed the door behind her before going to pick up the receiver. "Hello?"

"Is this Catriona O'Leary McTavish?"

"Yes."

"Oh, good. I'm Ed Williams. Did you enter an essay contest my brother and I held?"

"Yes." Cat caught her breath, recalling the day last spring when she'd heard the announcement on the radio. "You were awarding your family dude ranch to the person who wrote the winning essay. Did I—?"

"Yes, we picked your essay. It stirred a lot of good memories."

"I won?" Cat asked in a whisper. "I really won?"

"Yes. You still want the ranch, don't you?"

"Oh, my Gawd. Yes! Of course, I want it." She resisted the urge to dance around the kitchen. "Are you serious? Do you mean I have a home? I finally have a 'real' home—the perfect home."

"It's not perfect. The place needs a lot of work. The ranch is just a few miles outside of Baker City."

"I know," Cat said. "I used to visit my grandmother there."

"We thought you might be one of those O'Leary women. Glad to hear it. Welcome home, Catriona. Do you have time to meet with my brother and me tonight so we can discuss the details?"

"Of course, I do. Thank you so much. You won't regret this, Mr. Williams. I'll make the Cedar Creek Guest Ranch shine again. I promise."

"We're counting on you. We're so happy you entered our contest."

"Me too. You don't know what this means to me. I'm so lucky. I feel like I just won the lottery."

He chuckled. "Actually, you don't know how long the town and we've been looking for someone like you, Catriona O'Leary. We're the lucky ones."

CHAPTER ONE

*Cedar Creek Guest Ranch,
Baker Valley, Washington*

"If a man's been dead more than forty years, he ought to be able to enjoy peace and quiet."

Hearing the crunch of tires on the gravel driveway, the spirit of Rob Williams floated toward the picture window to see who dared come onto his land. A battered pickup stopped in front of the house. An equally ancient horse-trailer was hitched to the four-wheel-drive. Two little girls got out and raced around the rigs followed by a young black and gold collie, not much more than a puppy.

Not again. What was it going to take for his family to stop renting out his home? This was his place. He'd died for it at Hamburger Hill back in '69 during the height of the Vietnam Conflict. He bought the farm with his blood. Well, actually his parents had used the money from his military insurance to pay off the last of the mortgage on their home. Rob had no intention of passing on to what was considered a 'better place.' Now, he had a new bunch of strangers to haunt and send away. He supposed he could call it a favorite hobby in what was supposed to be *his* after-life.

Suddenly, a copper-haired woman strolled into view from the far side of the truck. As he watched, she knelt and caught both girls in a hug. The pup flopped down beside them in the dust, panting. Rob may have been dead, but nothing said he couldn't enjoy the sight of a woman who looked like one, instead of a scrawny hippie with no bosom, no waist, no hips and flowers in her long hair. That was the fashion back in the 1960s, but he'd never cared for it. Besides, curiosity had always been his downfall.

Rob drifted through the window and out onto the rotted deck of the wrap-around porch. The woman glanced toward the house and he glimpsed the emerald green of her eyes, as green as the needles on hemlock trees. Her head would have just reached his shoulder when he was alive. For a moment, he admired the voluptuous curves that filled out her lacy white western shirt and faded tight-fitting Levi's. He could have fit both hands around her waist if only he could touch her. Rob moved closer. What was he doing? This woman was nothing to him and she would have to go, taking those kids and the dog with her.

He'd send them away, but not just yet.

Cat McTavish released her daughters and stood. "Okay, let's settle down a little. I've got to convince Dynamite and Skyrocket that they're safe and need to calm down. They can't unless we do."

"How come Dynamite's so mad, Mommy?" Samantha asked, following her mother toward the trailer.

"He just is," Sophie said, tagging along.

Cat smiled over her shoulder at them. She unlatched the hook on the back of the hauler. "He's scared. That's all." The palomino hammered the rear panel with his hind feet, kicking the door open.

She whirled to check on the twins, but the girls carefully stayed out of reach. She breathed a sigh of relief. This horse had been the only one at the last Quarter-Horse auction within reach of her skimpy finances. She'd made progress with him during the five months she had him and he'd started to trust her, or maybe it was all the carrots she fed him. Treats might not be a popular strategy during the socialization process for some trainers, but they worked for her.

"Where are you gonna put them, Mommy?" Samantha asked, interrupting her thoughts.

"In the barn?" Sophie asked. "Or in a paddock?"

"The round pen for now," Cat said. "We have to fix up stalls for them, but first we have to check out the barn and make sure it's in good enough shape for them."

"What's wrong with it?" Rob demanded. "It's a dang good one. I should know. I helped my dad and grandpa build it."

Cat swung around. She didn't see anyone but could have sworn she heard a man speak. No, she didn't. She knew better. She'd finally learned that lesson when she was thirteen.

Don't make up stories, Catriona. Don't say you see things no one else does, hear voices nobody else hears or you'll wish you hadn't. Nobody will say my daughter is as crazy as her Grandma O'Leary.

"Can you hear me?" Rob asked. "Nobody's heard me talk since I passed. Usually, I have to throw things to get a reaction."

"That's naughty, mister." Samantha shook her head, strawberry blonde curls bouncing. She pointed her finger at him. "Tantrums get you time-outs."

"Or you have to stand in the corner if you're real bad," Sophie added.

"Who are you girls talking to?" Cat glanced at the empty yard once more. Only she and her daughters were here. The lawn sloped down to the creek. Maples, cottonwood and alder trees, bright with fall leaves framed the open yard. She didn't see anyone watching from the nearby grove of evergreens, but she thought she'd heard someone. "Who?"

"That man." Samantha moved her hand a little but continued to point toward the house.

Cat frowned. "What does he look like?"

"He's taller than you, Mommy," Samantha said.

"But not as big as Frazer," Sophie chimed in.

"Terrific," Cat muttered, and gave both girls a steady look. "I call your daddy by his first name. You don't. Got it?"

Samantha nodded in mute acquiescence.

Sophie's lower lip stuck out the proverbial country mile. She planted small hands on childish hips, narrowing summer-sky blue eyes, adopting one of her father's poses. "But, Mommy—"

"I mean it, Sophia Gale. No being rude to your daddy or about him."

Sophie continued to scowl, but finally nodded.

Cat counted her blessings. She wanted the girls to have a good relationship with their father, but it would be easier if he met her halfway. Instead, Frazer either ignored them or favored one over the other or pitted the two of them against each other. And now, she had to deal with another imaginary friend. The twins always seemed to find one whenever they moved to a new place.

It was the last thing she needed. Well, it shouldn't cause any problems here. There wouldn't be anyone else on the farm. She wouldn't have that much company, just customers who wanted their horses trained and they rarely talked to the girls, much less listened to the eight-year-olds. Of course, things would change when she reopened the guest ranch next spring.

She opened the trailer door and checked Dynamite. The palomino had calmed down and stood quietly eating hay out of the net. She'd still be wary of darting hooves. "You girls stay back. I don't want you hurt."

"We'll wait here," Samantha said.

Rob frowned when one horse began kicking again as the woman approached the trailer. The nearest phone wouldn't be much help since he couldn't use it. The girls were too little. He'd have to save the woman. He floated to the trailer and between the gal and the horse. She shivered. Did she feel his presence?

"It sure is cold today. Easy, Dynamite. I won't hurt you." Murmuring reassurances, she eased into the trailer next to the palomino gelding. "Steady, son. It's all right."

Dynamite shifted and stomped a rear hoof. Rob moved closer. "Settle in, horse. I have no patience for bad-tempered critters. I'll feed you to the dog. Hear me?"

"I bet he did, mister." Sophie patted the collie pup at her feet. "He's not kicking at Mommy no more. Watch out that he doesn't kick you." The little girl tipped her head to one side. "Are you a stranger, mister? We're not *s'posed* to talk to them. It's okay when we talk to Mommy's nice customers, but not the nasty ones. Who are you?"

"I guess you could call me a ghost," Rob said. "This is my place. I've lived here most my life."

Samantha wrinkled her nose, blue eyes curious. "I'm Samantha and she's Sophie. What's your name?"

He scowled at the children, but he didn't really want to scare them. They weren't frightened yet and he wasn't going to change that. He'd sent a lot of trespassers running over the years. He saved his worst tricks for adults, not small fry, and especially not little girls. Most adults called him Rob. However, he'd heard his brothers refer to him as Robbie when they talked to their kids. "I'm Robbie and I don't want company."

"Your eyes don't look mad," Sophie pointed out.

"And you're smiling," Samantha informed him.

"You can see me?" Rob wished he could move nearer to the girls, but he had to stay close to the trailer to keep their mother safe. Why did he suddenly feel like it wasn't the first time he'd protected her? "What do I look like?"

"Don't you know?" Sophie asked.

"Don't be rude." Samantha elbowed her twin. "You got curly black hair and dark brown eyes, Mister Robbie."

"And bushy eyebrows like Santa, only yours are black too," Sophie said, "but you sorta disappear sometimes. You're wearing a soldier suit and we can see through you like a window."

"It would be nice to have company that can see me, but you're not staying here."

"We're living here," Sophie said, "and we're not company. Mommy told us so. She won the essay contest and we're starting our own guest ranch."

"We're not working at other people's places no more," Samantha added.

"That's right," Sophie agreed, twining a strand of strawberry blonde hair around one finger. "Mommy said."

"Well, you're not doing it here," Rob announced. "This is my place."

"You'll just have to share." Sophie lifted her chin and narrowed her eyes. "You *gotta* be nice to us, or Mommy will get you. She doesn't take no pris-ners. That's what she tells Frazer, our daddy, all the time."

"Who are you girls talking to?" Cat asked as she backed Dynamite out of the trailer. "For once, he's behaving like a real horse. He's not biting or kicking today."

"Mister Robbie told him to be good," Sophie said, "so he is."

"Mister who?"

Samantha frowned. "Can't you see Mister Robbie, Mommy? He's a ghost."

"He's funny," Sophie added. "Can we keep him, Mommy?"

"Nonsense." Cat petted the nervous, sweating horse's neck. "There are no such things as ghosts, girls."

"How come Mister Robbie says he is one?" Sophie's face filled with concern. "Is he fibbing?"

"I don't lie, especially to little kids." Rob snapped. "Woman, you'd better not call me a liar again."

Cat flinched. Had she heard him? That was odd.

Over the years he'd learned he had to really raise a ruckus, or most people didn't know he was around. Of course, raising hell and putting props under it had never been something he shied away from when he was alive, and his fiancée had chewed him up one side and down the other for it back in the day. He had to reform to get her to consider dating him. He still counted the moment she agreed to marry him as the luckiest in his life. Only he died before they could marry, much less have the houseful of rug-rats she promised him.

"Mister Robbie doesn't like being called a liar," Samantha said. "He's getting mad."

"Well, I don't like him scaring poor Dynamite." When the horse snorted, Cat petted him again. "Easy, son. This horse is spooked enough from the trip in the trailer. He doesn't need to be scared witless. Tell your new *pretend* friend to behave himself, or he'll be standing in a corner until supper time."

"I'm not imaginary or a *pretend* friend," Rob said, "I'm real."

At least, he was as real as a man could be who had died in a war most people didn't remember nowadays, not with the one in Afghanistan that showed up on TV most nights. It wasn't like she didn't hear him, even if she refused to see him. She had to be sensitive to him. If she wasn't, she'd never know he was here. "Are you listening to me, woman?"

"Hush, Mister Robbie." Samantha looked worried. "Mommy only gave you a little *what-for*. It can be worse."

"A hissy fit," Rob grumbled. "Woman calls me a liar. Then she says I'm scaring her horse when I'm the one standing between his hooves and her. Who does she think she's talking to?"

"Quiet," Sophie whispered. "You keep being mean, Mister Robbie and Mommy's liable to get annoyed. She can't help it. Like she says, her red hair keeps coming out. She don't suffer fools at all." She trotted off to stand next to her mother. "Mommy, can Mister Robbie stay? We think he's fun."

"And he's nice to us," Samantha added.

Cat turned the horse toward the line of fruit trees, between the house and the barn. "Okay, girls. Let's go through this again. Ghosts aren't real, not like you and me. I've never stopped you from having *pretend* friends. If you want a new one in our new home, that's all right. If his name is Mister Robbie, that's okay too. But he can't sass me any more than you two can. As my granny used to say, if he wants to live here, he'd better mind his 'P's and 'Q's."

"And 'member his fetchin' up," the twins chimed, "since the O'Learys have good manners."

"Now you're talking." Cat laughed. "Let's go. It's time for us to get Dynamite squared away. We still need to get Skyrocket out of the trailer."

Cat stood in the center of the round pen watching the flashy bay gelding dart and dance around her, playing in the September sunshine. Skyrocket had been the soul of patience while she groomed and saddled him. He didn't fuss when she bridled him, even allowing her to slide the snaffle bit into his mouth without tossing his head.

All of that changed when she led him out of the barn to the round pen. He'd circled the ring, galloping to the left, then the right for nearly an hour. She wanted to ride him now, before she had to drive to Lake Maynard and pick up her daughters at their new school, but today might not be the right day. She could end up in the dirt. If she was hurt, who would do her chores? "Well, Sky. What do you think?"

The horse tossed his black mane and snorted. Then, he tore off again. He leaped into the air, twisted and uncoiled like a ballet star. One jump led into the next. His hooves slammed into the dirt. Then he reared up on his hind legs. What did he think he was? A movie horse?

Cat sighed and tossed her long rope at him. So far, he'd trotted and cantered both directions of the corral, but he wasn't licking or chewing or flicking his ear at her. He didn't want to join her in the middle of the pen. He was his own herd leader and he was large and in charge today. He figured he pleased her with this act, because he certainly wasn't afraid of her.

"Well, there's always tomorrow," Cat told him. "We have all the time in the world."

He snorted again, as if he wanted to share in the conversation. She laughed, then sauntered toward the fence. He didn't try to trample her. He'd never showed any inclination to hurt her. She'd let him wear the western saddle and bridle and run around. Sooner or later, the fool had to give up. At least, that was the theory in natural horsemanship. She was pretty sure the gelding hadn't read the same books or watched the trainers on the RFD channel the way she had.

Force wasn't an option in the horse-training world anymore. The two of them were supposed to be a team and trust was the foundation, according to current theories. Somehow, she didn't think Skyrocket believed all the new-age horse handling theories she practiced, but he was certainly fond of the carrots she fed him.

She unbuckled her equestrian helmet and removed it before climbing through the metal corral gate. After she checked the latch, she headed for the three-story Victorian house. She'd have a cup of coffee on the wrap-around porch and watch the young horse in the corral at the same time. As she mounted the first step, the scent of roses drifted toward her from the garden. For a moment she remembered the old lady who tended the flowers and cooked fabulous meals so many years before. Once upon a time, the Williams family's guest ranch had been a destination resort and it would be again.

The next afternoon, Cat lay on the ground in the round pen, tasting dirt. Her entire body ached from the force of the fall. She rolled over to eye her nemesis. Skyrocket lowered his head to look back at her. He snorted and jumped sideways.

She jumped to her feet, brushed off the dirt and started walking toward the bay. "I'm getting too old for this crap," she said aloud.

The gelding trotted to meet her. He nudged her in search of a carrot. She fed him a piece, stroked his white blaze, petted the arched neck and smoothed the tumbled black forelock. "What's your trouble, Bubba?"

Skyrocket pricked up his ears and nickered softly, as if he wanted to answer the question, but she didn't have the right vocabulary to understand him.

Cat gathered the reins, slipped one up on each side of his neck. "Didn't you ever hear that song? There isn't a pony who couldn't be rode. You're about to find out, you bugger."

She put her boot into the stirrup, eased up into the saddle. She sat deep, pushed down her heels and tightened her grip on the young horse's reins. Hopefully, Skyrocket wouldn't throw her this time. She wasn't counting on it. Her pride got her into this fiasco. The Madisons, the gelding's owners had told her they'd been through three other trainers with this horse. All of those would-be experts agreed the bay was a natural bucker.

Cat didn't believe it. Somehow, somewhere, this youngster learned to buck. He didn't have the streak of mean that a few horses did who hated people and wanted to throw them. He never tried to stomp her when she hit the ground. Instead, he carefully avoided her prone figure and waited for her to leap up and play with him.

He plunged forward, then twisted like a cat as he leaped into the air. Hooves slammed into the dirt. He soared into the air again, sun-fishing, swapping ends and bucking across the pen. One jump cascaded into the next, an equine dancer on stage in the round pen.

She glimpsed a strange shimmer of sunlight in the yard but was a little too busy to analyze it at the moment. She concentrated on keeping her balance and sticking in the saddle. Sliding her gloved hands down the reins, she yanked hard. Damn! She hadn't gotten his head up. If she could, he'd be able to rear, but couldn't continue bucking. He uncoiled into the next bucking frenzy.

For some reason he avoided the side of the corral next to the front yard, leaping from the right side of the pen to the left. He kept his head down. It allowed him to twist his body like a snake. Every jump ended with hooves thudding into the dirt. He spun, twisted and rose into the air again. The landings jolted her.

The stirrup slipped off her right foot and she knew she was headed for a fall. *Not a bad one*, she thought. *Please, not that.*

As if he read her mind, Skyrocket slammed down and froze in the center of the corral.

"Bail off!" a deep voice rumbled.

What the—?

Cat looked around the empty corral. Empty, that is, except for her and the horse.

Sunlight shimmered off the lawn. This time she stared at the spot. She blinked at the haze in the corral. A dust devil whirled through the round pen. She hadn't hit her head. Why did she have trouble seeing clearly?

She blinked hard.

"Hit the ground. *Now!*" Impatience filled the bass tones.

What the—? Again, nobody else was in the ring. Nobody except her, and Skyrocket.

Oh, this was not good.

Getting out of the saddle seemed like a good idea, especially since she was imagining things, or was it people? No, not people. Just one person. A man. Mario? Was that it? Was she hearing Mario for some reason?

Her mentor never liked riding a horse that bucked. He always said it meant more work until the animal learned the rules. No wonder she thought she heard him. Straight out of high school, she'd trained with the old man for three years before going out on her own as a certified trainer. He'd have had a fit and fell in it if he saw her try to ride

Skyrocket when the horse obviously wasn't ready. Her mind must be telling her what Mario would have.

She kicked her left foot free and vaulted out of the saddle in a fast dismount. She backed away, watching the bay warily. He stood rock still, until she was about ten feet from him. Then, he spun and galloped off, crow-hopping in a series of baby bucks and leaps. She could have ridden him through those without half trying.

Cat headed for the corral gate, cautiously glancing over her shoulder at the horse. "What am I going to do with you?"

"Dog food," a man's voice answered.

What?

She looked around the round pen. No one here. Again, it was just her and the colt. She didn't recall Mario ever saying that a horse should be fed to dogs, but then again, she didn't speak Italian. That could have been what all his cusswords were about.

"Of course, I might have a guardian angel too," Cat said. "Well, thanks a lot."

Did she hear a low, masculine chuckle or had she gone totally nuts?

CHAPTER TWO

An hour later when Cat returned to the corral, Skyrocket met her at the gate. She eyed the set of reins hanging neatly on a nearby fence post. She didn't remember unsnapping them from the bit, much less taking care of them when she left the corral after the gelding's bucking fit.

She'd comforted herself with a cup of coffee and two homemade chocolate chip cookies while she sat on the front porch. She had a good view of the corral. There was no way anybody could have entered the round pen without her seeing the visitor.

She patted Skyrocket's neck. "I know you're a smarty-pants, but how did you take these off?" She picked up the reins and snapped them onto his bit. "Come on. Let's get you ready for the shoer. And remember what we've worked on. There's no biting, kicking, stomping or acting like a jerk. You've done enough of that for one day."

Skyrocket nuzzled her and walked beside her to the barn.

"Like I believe all this charm." Cat petted him again. Her busy day started early in the morning with chores, breakfast for the girls, and taking them to their elementary school twenty miles away. She'd returned to the farm and unpacked the twins' clothes, arranging them in the closet and dresser drawers. Then, she'd started the debacle with this silly horse. She sighed. "Well, if you behave yourself, there will be carrots in your future."

Zeke Knight showed up fifteen minutes early for their appointment. She never had to worry about being late to pick up the twins when Zeke was her shoer. He'd arrive on time, zoom through what had to be done, and leave. And he didn't believe in do-overs, so he never lamed any of the horses she trained.

"I don't believe you, Catriona McTavish." Shaking his long gray hair, Zeke stood outside the stall while she haltered Skyrocket. "How on earth did the Madisons talk you into taking on this monster? Who do you think you are? Gunga-Din? Jane Wayne?"

Cat eyed the small, wiry man. "Sky isn't a monster. Spill your guts, Zeke. You know horses the way a good used car salesman knows what's on the lot. What didn't the Madisons tell me about this guy?"

"Well, I'm betting they didn't tell you he's one of Angelica's rescues." Zeke propped his elbows on the stall wall, watching the horse. "She got him at the rodeo a couple years back. The bucking string was loose in a big stock trailer and this guy got knocked down and trampled. He damn near bled to death. Would have died if some 4-H kids hadn't seen him and ran for Angie. She stopped the bleeding until the vet arrived to suture him."

"We both interned with Mario O'Rourke and she's even better at breaking horses than I am." Cat stroked Skyrocket's brown neck and fed him a carrot. "Why didn't she train him? Come to think of it, I didn't see her around the Madison's barn. Is she still teaching at some school in Seattle?"

"Hell no! She's in Afghanistan with her Army Reserve unit. She'll be home next spring, and her old man wants the horse trained for her. Bet he didn't tell you that the last fella who tried to ride this boy is still in the hospital."

"Sounds like there are a lot of things he didn't tell me." Cat clipped a lead line to the halter. "But beggars can't be choosers, Zeke. I may wish people who hire me would just be straightforward and give me the whole history of their animals instead of keeping secrets, but I can't afford to turn away the few clients who still want me to train their stock. Are you comfortable trimming him?"

"I'm willing to try," Zeke said cautiously. "But, I'm not willing to be stomped into hamburger. I'm not Nick MacGillicudy. He doesn't mind busting horses when he trims them, but I don't have anything to win and a lot to lose."

"Do I want to know what he did to Sky?" Cat unlatched the stall door and slid it open. "Or is that another secret?"

"Ran a rope around his rear legs, threw him, belly-kicked him a few times, then hobbled him and trimmed his hooves. When he was turned loose, the horse attacked Nick."

"I don't blame Sky." Cat led the gelding to the barn entry and the concrete apron in front of the building. It was built in the shape of an upside-down capital L. She'd put the horses in the first half of the long arm until she finished repairing the other stalls. "Now you know why I will never call Nick to shoe horses that I train. He's too mean."

"Well, the apple doesn't fall far from the tree, and his old man, Herman, is a real son of a buck." Zeke buckled on his leather chaps and pulled on a pair of gloves before picking up a hoof knife. "Let's see what this fella does when I trim him."

"Better be absolutely nothing if he ever wants another carrot." Cat stepped to the left side, so she and Zeke would be together when he headed for the first hoof.

Skyrocket nosed her vest pocket and flicked an ear. She hummed along with the classic country song coming from the radio in the tack room. The gelding always enjoyed music, but—

That was odd. She didn't remember leaving on the old stereo, let alone turning it on. Maybe, she *was* losing it. Her memory was shot today.

It only took twenty uneventful minutes for Zeke to trim the excess growth off Skyrocket's hooves. After he had finished and fed the young horse a couple carrots, he glanced around. "Been years since I worked here. It surprised me when you called and said you'd moved in. What are you going to do to the place?"

"Restore it," Cat said. "That was one of the conditions when I entered the essay contest last March. Whoever won had to promise to stay and work it for ten years."

"And then what happens?" Zeke asked.

"I get clear title to it. I can sell it if I want, but only to someone who continues to run it as a dude ranch. I had to promise to call it the

Cedar Creek Guest Ranch and hire any of the Williams relatives who wanted to work here."

Zeke nodded. "Think that's likely?"

Cat frowned thoughtfully and stroked Skyrocket's neck. "I don't know. When I met Ed and Adam Williams and their wives, they told me that their kids and grandkids only wanted to sell the property to the developers. I couldn't bear to have that happen."

"Old man Williams used to hire me to help bring in the hay and wrangle dudes when I was in high school," Zeke said. "That was almost fifty years ago, one of the best times of my life."

"Closest to heaven I ever got." Cat straightened Skyrocket's black forelock. "My aunt used to bring me to stay every summer when I was a kid. I swam in the pond, pitched in the baseball games, kayaked on the river, rode all of the horses and went on the camp-outs. But I don't remember you being one of the cowboys, Zeke."

"Oh, I was before your time, honey. Got drafted and did my senior trip in 'Nam' as the old song goes." Zeke rubbed his chin thoughtfully. "Going to put together a riding string?"

"You know it," Cat said. "I'm planning to open next spring in time for the summer season. I'll need about twelve more head before then. Dude-safe horses, nothing real spirited."

"Got that right." Zeke smiled. "Mr. Williams always swore a horse didn't have a brain before it turned fifteen and he never wanted anything younger than that for the guests. You don't want to winter them if you can get out of it. The nutrition will be out of the grass next month when the ground starts freezing."

Cat nodded. If she had to feed a dozen head for the next six months, they'd eat her out of house and home before they started bringing in money. "I want to get them in by March so I'll have time to refresh whatever training they need."

"I'll start looking for you now, Cat, but we won't buy them until folks run out of hay in February," Zeke said. "You can always put down a deposit if you run into a hard-case who wants you to take one early."

"Works for me. Thanks, Zeke."

"It'll give me an excuse to run the roads." Zeke grinned at her.

"And it'll get me out of the house before Donna shoots me. Now, when do you want me back to trim this fella?"

"Six weeks," Cat said. "Then, he'll be on the same schedule as Dynamite. If I get any more in that need trims before that, I'll call you. And if you come across a good horse, call me."

"You got it." Zeke held the gate so she could lead Skyrocket back to his stall. "Good training, Cat. He was a lot better than I expected when I first saw him."

"Not as good as he's going to be. He pulled his right rear leg away twice. We'll work on that before you see him again."

"I'll look forward to it." Whistling Lynn Anderson's signature song, Zeke sauntered toward his truck.

She locked Skyrocket in his stall and checked the manger. He still had leftover hay from lunch, so he could munch on that while he waited for his supper. She hung the halter and lead-line on the hook by the door, then paused by Dynamite's stall next door. He was out of food, so she fetched more grass hay. On her way out of the barn, she stopped at the tack room to turn off the lights but decided to leave on the music to keep the horses company.

She stopped when she saw the old radio on the corner shelf. Cobwebs covered the black plastic stereo and the cord hung free, dangling a good three feet from the plug-in.

Still Lynn Anderson sang, *I beg your pardon. I never promised you a rose garden...*"

It must run on batteries, Cat thought, but she didn't have the courage to look and see. What if she was wrong? She took a deep breath. Why wasn't she annoyed or having a sudden case of the heebie-jeebies?

Something she'd heard as a child suddenly flashed in her mind. A man's deep voice. *Nothing and no one at Cedar Creek Guest Ranch will ever hurt you, kitten.*

Who was it? Who had tried to comfort her when she was frightened? She took a deep breath. It hadn't been her father. He'd never reassured her and by the time her aunt married, Cat was too old to trust the new addition to the family. That came later.

She eyed the radio again, shook back her long braid and forced a laugh. "Good taste in music, but that doesn't mean you've won me over."

Turning, she picked up her brushes and went to groom Dynamite. Afterwards, she led him out for a turn in the round pen. He enjoyed the opportunity to graze, but of course, he immediately rolled in the grass. Smiling, she left him to enjoy a few hours of freedom while she went to do her errands.

She needed to visit the post office and arrange for mail delivery, open a new bank account, and buy groceries. With any luck at all, she could complete those tasks before she had to pick up the twins at school. By next week she hoped they'd be comfortable with their peers and ready to ride the bus.

On the way back to the ranch from town, the girls talked about their adventures in second grade. "I got all my spelling words right," Samantha said, a sunshine smile lighting her face. "Sophie missed a word."

"And the playground teacher couldn't tell us apart," Sophie finished. "She kept calling me, Sam."

"I think we need name tags for her," Samantha said. "Can we make some tonight, Mommy?"

"It sounds like a good idea." Cat carried bags of groceries to the kitchen, speaking as she walked. "This is a new school, so what if you wore different colored shirts? Would that help?"

As they headed for their room to change clothes, Cat heard the twins discussing what colors would be best to wear to school the next day. While they were in the other room, Cat put away the groceries and prepared a snack for the girls. She heard the stereo come to life in the living-room. This time, it was Loretta Lynn threatening to take some floozy to the proverbial cleaners for chasing her man.

Cat frowned. Had she even unpacked the stereo? She didn't remember doing so, let alone tuning in a country station, or sorting through her CDs or albums to find the classic *Coal Miner's Daughter* album. Maybe she'd hit her head and hadn't noticed. This was starting to worry her more than a little. And it couldn't be the twins, because she still heard them in their room.

She headed into the living room. The stereo was still in its cardboard carton, but the flaps on the box had been opened and

Loretta continued to sing about her man throwing trash away, not dating it. Cat eyed the box. How could the stereo work without electricity? It must have back-up batteries, which she didn't remember reading about when she bought it in the first place.

She went to the box—and the music stopped. Her grandmother used to say there were often things seen and unseen in new homes and old, so maybe this was one of the unseen. Shrugging, Cat closed up the box and headed back to the kitchen.

Sophie met her in the hallway. "Mister Robbie wants to know what kinda music you like. He says if it ain't country, it ain't worth singing."

Cat stopped and stared at her daughter. "Mister Who?"

"Mister Robbie," Sophie said. "This is his house."

"No," Cat said. "It's our home now."

Sophie's blue eyes widened as she shook her head. "Can't you see him yet, Mommy? He's a ghost. He's been here forever."

"I see," Cat said. And she did. There was something strange about the house and farm, but she certainly didn't believe in ghosts. The girls had obviously made up this story because they missed their father, but once they became accustomed to their new home, the mischief would end. Granted, she hadn't seen one of them sneak into the living room, but that didn't mean it hadn't happened. And she wasn't making a big deal of it or punishing them, not when everything was so new and different in their lives.

Ruffling the child's strawberry blonde curls, Cat said, "Come eat your snack. After this, I need your help in the barn. We have to get more stalls put together for the next bunch of horses that come in for training. You girls have to stomp on the floors and see if we need to repair any of them."

Cat struggled to hide her amusement as the twins told their new friend about school with the same intensity they used when they talked to Lad, their puppy, and even Dynamite. Where had the twins gotten their imaginations? She'd never been much of a dreamer. After her grandmother died, moving back and forth between her divorced parents every week had been one long-running lesson in reality after another. So, why hadn't she seen through Frazer?

His life revolved around the casinos where he dealt cards or worked as a pit boss. He moved from one fancy gambling place to another whenever he got bored. She'd had to tell the dealers at this casino that he was her husband, not her boyfriend. He hardly ever spent time with the girls and sometimes, she could have sworn he couldn't tell the twins apart.

It was difficult to remember he was the same man who wined her, dined her and charmed her into a quick trip to Reno nine years before. He swore he'd love her forever, but forever didn't last too long for him. The longer he stayed away, the better. Maybe, she'd finally get over her addiction to him. If the twins needed a *pretend* friend to help with the transition from a two-parent household to one with a single mother, it was okay. She could handle it.

Later that evening she wasn't quite so confident. She'd already fed both horses and they were settled for the night. However, the same couldn't be said for her and the girls. The bulbs in the kitchen went out whenever Cat walked away from the switch. What was happening here? She'd been told the house was rewired a year ago and it passed inspection before she moved in. Was the place going to burn down around her ears?

What could she do? Where would they go? Frazer hadn't left any money in their bank accounts and since she left her last job, she didn't have the funds for them to move to a shelter. Plus, how would she find one that took not only her and the twins, but also two horses and a dog? She glanced at her daughters. They giggled together at the kitchen table.

"Mister Robbie's playing with us," Sophie said. "He wants to see if we're scared of the dark."

"We're not." When Cat lit the candles she found on a shelf by the woodstove, the white tapers went out too. The girls laughed harder.

Cat studied her daughters. There was only so long that she was going to humor them with their claims of an invisible friend. "You'd better tell him to stop the tricks, or you two will have cold soup for supper."

She tried to keep her voice even and hoped her own apprehension didn't show. How much would it cost to hire an electrician to straighten out the wiring? That's all it was. It had to be. She took a deep breath and pasted on what she hoped was a confident smile.

"And until I can figure out what's happening to the wiring, I can't use the electric range or the microwave so our dinners are going to be pretty simple. I don't want to light a fire in the woodstove until the chimney has been cleaned."

"Mommy's getting mad, Mister Robbie," Samantha said, turning her head and speaking into thin air. "You'd better stop blowing out the candles and being so naughty."

"Or she'll make you do a time-out. Those are awful. You *gotta* sit real still for eight whole minutes," Sophie said. "You can't talk, or read a book, or play or nothing."

They weren't taking this seriously. "Okay, you two have to sit eight minutes right now." Cat rested her hands on her hips. "How old is your new friend? It's one minute for each year." She looked around the room. For a moment, she thought she saw a man standing near the light switch, then changed her mind. "I'm waiting."

"He's old, Mommy," Sophie said.

"Older than you," Samantha agreed.

"Then, he should have better manners." Cat shook back her long red hair. Was she losing her mind? The twins were still giggling up a storm. The girls wouldn't be so worried or upset if they camped in the barn until an electrician arrived. She swung around to look at the light switches again.

For an instant, she almost caught a glimpse of a tall, broad-shouldered silhouette in some sort of Army uniform again. She blinked. Her eyes were definitely playing tricks on her. Maybe she needed glasses. Maybe she needed to have her head examined. "All right, Mister Robbie. I've had it. Go to your room."

It didn't take her daughters' laughter to tell Cat their invisible friend protested the punishment. As a mom, she knew immediate obedience was the exception, not the custom. "Don't you squabble with me. Guests in my house follow my rules. Fun isn't fun unless it's fun for everyone. Now, scat. I don't want to hear from you for a whole hour. If you can't behave yourself then, you'd better just stay in your room until you can."

"Mommy, he's not *that* old," Samantha said, in shocked tones. "Nobody is."

Cat raised her chin. She'd overreacted and she knew it. She didn't dare back down now. The twins would think it was okay to break rules and then not accept the consequences. "He deserves it. He forgot the number one rule."

Silence prevailed while the girls waited and listened. Then Samantha heaved a sigh and shook a finger in the air. "You're old enough to know that rule. It's 'Mommy's the Mommy'."

"And what she says, goes," Sophie said. "If you don't want major trouble, you'd better mind her, or she'll make you wish you had."

Cat didn't know whether she wanted to laugh or cry. She recognized some of Frazer's feelings in what the twins said. He thought she was the worst kind of control freak. Someone had to take charge, or she and the girls wouldn't survive thus far.

Taking a deep breath, she narrowed her gaze. "Does your Mister Robbie want two hours?"

"No, ma'am!" Samantha waved to the kitchen door and the staircase beyond it. "Go quick, Mister Robbie, or Mommy will make it three hours."

"You'll never be able to leave your room again," Sophie announced. "Mommy sent Frazer, I mean our daddy clear to New Orleans 'cause he let us eat candy and watch monster movies all day."

Cat studied her daughters, concern mounting. Why had the girls started referring to their father by his first name and stopped calling him Daddy all of a sudden? "Do you want to talk to your dad?"

"No. We have other things to do." Honesty shone in Samantha's eyes. "Daddy is lots of fun, but he never does real work. When you were at that big horseshow, he never cooked us nothing to eat."

"Wait a minute, girls." Cat gave up on the notion of punishment for the imaginary friend to focus on this problem instead. "Why aren't you calling your father Daddy?"

"He told us not to," Samantha said.

Cat stiffened. "What did you say?"

"It's okay," Sophie said. "We told him that he wasn't a very good daddy anyhow."

"Then he said, he didn't like being our daddy and he was gonna stop," Samantha said. "So, we told him, 'Bye and see ya later.' Then we went to ask Miss Peggy for a peanut butter and jelly sandwich 'cause we were hungry."

And her ex-boss Peg Lawson stepped up to take care of the twins until Cat returned from the four-day horse show in Colorado. The older woman could have called the authorities and had the girls removed from such an unfit parent. Still, she must have made some comment to Frazer or he wouldn't have gone on an all-out campaign to drive away all of the people who trusted Cat to train their horses. Frazer could be devastatingly persuasive when he turned on the charm. Lord knows what he'd told the clients at Evening Gold.

Those clients moved their stock out of the barn, leaving Peg with empty stalls and the hefty financial loss of fifteen boarders. To keep Peg from going bankrupt because of her husband's shenanigans, Cat started looking for a new place to live and a new job. She had no luck at all until things suddenly changed two weeks ago and she'd won the dilapidated dude ranch in the essay contest she'd entered last spring.

She blinked away the tears. She couldn't show how upset and hurt she was by what Frazer had done to their daughters. Not yet, not now. She'd cry later when she was in the shower and the girls couldn't hear. "That was pretty smart of you. Good job, twins."

"It's okay, Mommy." Sophie hugged her.

The twins appeared to be listening to their new imaginary friend again. Cat sighed. "All right, what does your Mister Robbie think?"

"That boys got to be 'sponsible too," Samantha said. "And Daddy wasn't when you were working."

Sophie nodded agreement. "It's bull-hockey when they're not. Mommy, what's bull-hockey?"

"Probably a way for Mister Robbie not to get in trouble for cussing in front of you," Cat said. She took a deep breath, then purred in her sweetest tone. "I'm so glad he admits I'm right. He'd better get started on his time-out. Remember, it's a punishment, Mister Robbie. No television. No games. No chapter books. No talking and definitely no whining. You sit and think about how naughty your actions have been today."

"Mommy, you didn't say the part about how you're glad he's being 'sponsible for what he did," Sophie chided.

"Or about how you love him, just not what he did," Samantha reminded her.

Cat went across the room to the light switch. "Girls, I say those things to you because you're little and you need to hear them. Isn't your Mister Robbie a grown-up?"

The twins nodded. "Is he s'posed to know what's right all the time?" Samantha asked.

"Yes. He also knows when to do what's right. He knows better than to do what's wrong." Cat flipped the switch. To her amazement, the overhead kitchen lights came on and the room stayed lit. "If you ask him, Mister Robbie will tell you so, especially since he says he's not a liar. He's being powerful tacky today. His own momma wouldn't be happy with his manners."

"He's lucky he only got timed out for an hour then," Sophie said. "You always say there's nothing worse than tacky."

"Unless it's being rude." Samantha lowered her voice to a whisper that was louder than she obviously thought. "If Mommy finds out you're dragging the same cotton sack too long, you'll be in big trouble, Mister Robbie."

"Really? People who waste my time also waste my patience." Cat checked the pot of water on the stove. It wasn't boiling yet so she couldn't add the macaroni. "Is he still here? Okay, Mister Robbie. That's it. I'm done. Two hours." She glanced at the twins and saw shock on two small faces. "Is he still sassing me? Does he want three hours or is he waiting for something worse?"

What could she do to an invisible friend? She hoped she didn't have to think of something.

"Mommy has to be minded," Samantha said to nothing in particular.

"That's right, Mister Robbie," Sophie chimed in. "Or else!"

The worry on their faces changed to surprise and then awe.

"Okay," Cat said. "What's he done now?"

"He floated through the wall," Sophie marveled, blue eyes wide.

"But only 'cause he had to, not 'cause he wanted to," Samantha said. "He told us he was afraid if he didn't, you'd be really mad. There's nothing worse when it comes to mad than a red-headed woman. That's what Mister Robbie says, at least."

"Oh, really?" Cat planted her hands on her hips, ready to tell off one arrogant man.

Hastily, she remembered that this particular male didn't exist outside of her daughters' imaginations. She was starting to worry, not only about her children's insistence on an imaginary playmate, but what was going on with the house.

She struggled to regain her composure. She walked over and smoothed the twins' strawberry blonde hair. "Well, he's in big trouble then, isn't he? There are three redheaded women in this house."

CHAPTER THREE

He debated breaking the bulbs in the ceiling lights on his way out of the room, but he didn't really want to hurt anyone in this family. It sounded like they had a hard-enough row to hoe with a worthless dad who enjoyed hurting his daughters' feelings. If he'd met the fellow, Rob knew he'd have cleaned the other man's clock. Granted, he'd have had to answer to either the law or his fiancée, Rosie for it, but sometimes kicking tail was worth the cost.

Besides Cat and her daughters were different from the other renters who'd lived here since his relatives moved off the ranch. Rob couldn't recall if the other tenants ever did anything to improve the farm. They'd simply thrown trash everywhere, indoors and out. He paused on his way upstairs to admire the sparkling windows in the living room. Cat had swept down the cobwebs and vacuumed the carpet. When she unpacked, she covered the old couch with a crocheted gold and brown blanket. The collie pup lay on a rag rug in front of the sofa. For the first time in years, the room looked and felt like a home. Could the way she worked be the reason he had difficulty driving her away?

Rob floated up to the attic room he claimed as his own. Why did he care about the woman and her children downstairs? He was dead. Didn't he want them gone? Of course, he did. He hadn't wanted another girl since he fell in love with Rosie back in first grade. He'd followed her all through grade school, junior high and finally caught her attention in high school when he won the championship ribbon at the county fair in the pulling contest with his draft team.

Still, it didn't matter how hard this gal tried to make the place a home for her and the twins. *She's not family*, Rob told himself again, *I'll send her down the road.*

When he entered the dark kitchen on his next visit, he wondered if it would be necessary. Had they left while he was gone? He glanced around the room. The dog lifted its head, wagged a plumed tail, then snuggled down again outside the bedroom the kids shared. Rob glanced inside and saw the little girls sleeping in the bunk beds. He'd miss them when they left. They were spunky sweethearts.

He went across the kitchen. There was a bedroom at the back where he remembered a porch in his youth. His parents had converted it when they grew too old to climb the stairs and he still didn't like entering the room. He hadn't forgotten the night he'd heard a noise, gone inside and startled his mother. He wasn't sure if she'd seen him or not. She'd said his name and then began to cry.

Tonight, the bedroom had a new occupant. Face buried in the pillow, blankets over her shoulders, Cat slept in a queen-size bed.

He leaned in and yelled. "Wake up. Get out of my house!"

No reaction. She just snuggled deeper in the bedding.

"Dang it!" He could find a handful of logging chains to rattle. That would do it, but it meant a trip to the tool shed and dragging them to the house. He'd use up all his energy and would have to wait until tomorrow or the next day before he made a real racket. He glanced around the room and eyed the boxes and suitcases. For now, he would toss around some clothes, books and such. That wasn't much of a challenge for a ghost with his experience.

The thunder rolled. A bluish-white light flashed outside the bedroom window. Cat squirmed deeper into the blankets, knowing what would come next. The next rumble of thunder sounded like a train in the sky. It thumped and banged as it grew closer. Soon, it would run over her and the bed. She yanked up her covers. The cabin shook. The train roared in the midnight sky.

She reached out, grabbed her pillow. *It's a storm,* she thought. *That's all. I'm 'mostly seven. Daddy says I'm too big to be scared.* She buried her head in the pillow, then huddled under the blankets. Would it be quiet now? *Please, please, please. Make it go 'way.* She didn't dare wake up her aunt. That would mean big trouble, even if Auntie Rose was always nice and gave lots of hugs.

Before he left today, Daddy told Auntie Rose to call him if Cat acted like a baby. If she whined or complained or cried or didn't eat her veggies or ran in the house or made too much noise, he'd come get her. He'd take her back to Seattle. She'd have to stay there for the whole summer with his new wife and her boys since Mommy was on a hon-moon with a new husband.

But I don't like them, none of 'em. Cat knew better than to say that to anyone. They weren't mean to her, not like her last step-mama had been, with the kids she knew hated her. These new ones never hid her books or broke her dolls or told Daddy bad things about her. They just didn't like being stuck with a little kid, not even the woman Cat was s'posed to call Mama. *Only she isn't my for real mama. My mama is in Hawaii with Papa Ol-ver.*

Another loud slam overhead, a bang as the train rattled through the clouds, right behind the lightning. Cat squeaked, clutched the pillow tighter over her ears, trying to block the noise. She slid further down in the bed. It was only scary when there were big storms after bedtime. They hardly ever happened in the day time.

She wanted to be here at the ranch with Auntie Rose. Tomorrow, the sun would shine. There would be ponies to ride, kittens to play with and the tea party for all the little girls at the big wooden house that looked like a castle. She even had a new dress to wear, a white, ruffled one with a green sash that matched her eyes.

"Hey, kid. You're making me nuts. Come out from under those covers."

It was a man's deep voice, but not her daddy. He'd be mad. He wouldn't sound sorta nice. He'd yank away the blankets, the pillow. He'd yell at her for being such a—

"Stop thinking so much. Your dad's an idiot. So what?

Everybody meets at least one. You should have seen some of the guys in boot camp. My drill sergeant said the Army should have issued brains to 'em because they were too dumb to think on their own."

Why did she hear him? He wasn't as loud as the thunder that rumbled overhead, that sounded so much like a train. Who was he? Where did he come from?

She slowly peeked out, ready to duck under the blankets again. A large, shadowy shape sat in the old rocking chair by the foot of the bed. She managed to whisper, "Hi."

"Hi, yourself." He sounded like he was smiling. "I'm Rob."

"Why are you here?"

"Are you joking, kid? Your screams could wake the dead. Lucky I'm the only one who lives here now."

"I wasn't yelling. Not out loud."

"Doesn't mean I didn't hear you hollering on the inside," Rob said. "It's why I'm here. What's wrong?"

Cat held the pillow tight, eyeing him cautiously. "Noisy bad girls get locked in the pantry."

"Hmmm. Anything good to eat there? My momma always hid the cookie jar behind the canned beets."

"I don't know. I'm too scared to look. It's dark."

"You need to stash a flashlight in there. Then when you get locked up, you can hunt for chocolate chip cookies or potato chips."

Cat peered harder at him. He wore some kind of suit, but it wasn't a dark one like her daddy's. No, Rob's suit looked green with the pants tucked into lace-up boots. She saw the gleam of his white teeth when he smiled. "I'd get in trouble for snacking, wouldn't I?"

"If you're locked up already, why does it matter?"

Twining a strand of red-gold hair around one finger, Cat considered the question. Her visitor wasn't coming any closer. Suddenly, she realized he didn't make the chair move. Even when she barely sat on the edge, it rocked. She took a deep breath. "You're one of Gramma's special friends, aren't you?"

"Special? How?"

"You came 'cuz I had loud thoughts," Cat said. "At Gramma's house, her friends come when I have bad dreams. Gramma says that there are things all folks see, but not us. We see the *unseen* too. That's you, huh?"

He nodded, smiled again, another flash of teeth. "It's nice of them to visit you."

"Daddy says they're not real. Little girls who tell lies 'bout people who aren't really there get locked in the pantry or the closet after a whipping with his belt."

"Then, you need to keep your grandmother's friends a big secret."

Cat nodded vigorously. "That's right, Rob. If Daddy doesn't know when I'm bad, he can't hit me."

"What does your mommy say about that?"

"She said no more hitting ever. Else, she'll tell the judge and he'll take me away from Daddy forever."

A flash of light outside the window lit the room. In that moment, Cat saw the wooden back of the chair through Rob. He was special, a ghost, but not the scary kind like in the movies or the bloody, burned ones she'd seen in Seattle. Thunder rolled overhead. She flinched, wishing she still had her stuffed, toy puppy to hug, but Daddy had thrown him away because he was ragged and dirty.

"Talk to me," Rob said. "No more letting your thoughts race like puppies chasing balls. What's your name?"

"Catriona Rose O'Leary. I like Cat best. That's what Gramma and Auntie Rose call me."

"Okey-dokey, Cat. Know what?"

"What?"

"Nothing and no one at Cedar Creek Guest Ranch will ever hurt you, kitten."

"Really? Are you sure?"

"I promise, kitten. Now, I have two stories about thunder and lightning. Which one do you want to hear first? The real one? Or the one about thunder being the hoof-beats of horses in heaven?"

"The horse one."

The next morning, she was the first to awaken.

No surprise, Cat thought. The twins still weren't sleeping well after the overdose of junk food and monster movies last month when their father was in charge. Normally, if they were frightened or had bad dreams, the girls climbed into bed with her. They must not have needed her last night. Odd that the electrical storm hadn't awakened them and brought them rushing into her room to climb into bed with her.

Cat stretched. Slowly, she looked around the large bedroom. After working around the ranch all day, she must have been exhausted last night as well. She hadn't heard the thump when a box of clothes hit the floor. Jeans, shirts, panties and bras lay scattered around the room. What could have caused it to fall? She could have sworn she'd placed the carton securely on top of the bureau.

But, had she actually left her suitcase open? No, she knew it'd been closed and stored in the closet when she went to bed. She had been too tired to unpack anymore and figured the rest of her belongings could wait. She eyeballed her socks thrown everywhere. Two hung from the curtain rods. It wasn't just the clothes. Her riding boots, running shoes and two pairs of heels perched on top added to the mess.

What had happened last night? She'd been too tired to move, even when that storm rumbled through in the early, dark hours of the morning. She'd had the strangest dream about her grandmother and her aunt and someone, a man, telling her a story of horses in heaven.

She didn't have a cat. An animal might have knocked over the boxes, but it wouldn't be Lad. The twenty-pound puppy couldn't climb up on the dresser, much less drag out her suitcase from the closet. And she hadn't felt an earthquake, certainly not one strong enough that would have knocked everything around. Something was definitely going on, but what?

Slowly, she tossed the blankets aside and rolled out of bed to her feet.

Cat started from the room. Something sharp poked her bare toe. "Ow!"

Hopping on one foot, she looked down. "What on earth?"

She bent down, picked up a boot shaped earring. What was it doing out of her jewelry box? She stopped, looked again. The rest of her costume jewelry was scattered on top of the piles of her clothing.

There wasn't any earthly reason for her jewelry to be anywhere except in the wooden jewelry box that her uncle carved for her.

Shaking her head, Cat left the bedroom, and made her way to the room the twins had chosen for their own. The girls slept soundly, two small lumps in matching bunk beds. And that was odd too, she thought. Her daughters hadn't stayed in separate beds since the misadventure with their father.

Cat glanced around the room. The three of them were alone in the house, but why did she feel as if someone else watched her? For a moment, she thought she caught a whiff of lime aftershave. It wasn't a leftover from Frazer—he always wore a pine scent though she wasn't sure why he wanted to smell like someone who just walked through a Christmas tree farm when he preferred urban to country life.

Huh?

Was that a man?

She blinked. She thought she'd glimpsed a male silhouette in the rocking chair in the corner. No, she was imagining things. Frazer was long gone to Louisiana. She'd filed for divorce and he wouldn't be back. She crossed the room to smooth the blankets over her daughters.

When she tucked in Sophie, the little girl shifted. "Mommy?"

"That's right." Cat stroked the curls on the pillow. "Go back to sleep, honey. It's too early for you to get up."

"Don't be mad," Sophie murmured. "He had to do it."

The child had to be referring to Frazer's cruel words about not wanting to be a dad. "I'm not mad." Cat dropped a kiss on her daughter's forehead. "Now, sleep."

She was lying, but the girls didn't need to know how angry she was with their father. Most people wouldn't consider a total lack of discipline, too much junk food and monster movies to be child abuse, but she did. And she was the mommy, as the twins said, so that made her the final authority.

Even if he was out of the picture, she still wanted to nail Frazer's hide to the barn wall. He could have made an effort to be a good father, but her soon-to-be ex didn't. And that pissed her off!

Rob leaned back in the rocking chair. The little girls had interrupted him in the middle of his activities. He hadn't wanted them to be the ones who woke up their mother. The woman refused to admit he existed, but he couldn't ignore her. Wearing the loose purple t-shirt she slept in that skimmed her thighs, she was a sight to behold with long red hair everywhere. He longed to tangle his fingers in it, but he couldn't. She finished tucking in the other child, then sauntered toward the kitchen.

Slowly, he rose to his feet and followed her. He'd promised the twins he wouldn't let any monsters in the house, and he hadn't. Of course, some folks might consider a ghost a monster, but what did they know? What would it take for this woman notice him? Well, he'd find out before he sent her down the road.

She took a deep breath, shook her head. At six in the morning, she needed to get moving. There was a lot to do today. She plugged in the coffee pot and waited for it to brew. The house might have come mostly furnished, but it needed more cleaning. She had horses to feed, stalls to muck, breakfast to fix, lunches to pack, girls to take to school. Despite it all, she enjoyed having a place of her own.

A real home! A forever home! Woo-hoo! She did a little dance on the way to the cupboard to get a coffee cup.

They'd landed on their feet, as her grandmother used to say. A hundred-acre farm with a sturdy, almost fully-furnished house, that hadn't been vandalized in spite of being empty for more than a year still astonished her. The living room held an entertainment center complete with a television and VCR, along with couches, chairs, coffee and end-tables. She'd had to make room for her stereo yesterday. The dining room had an antique, elaborately carved oak table with six matching, intact chairs. An oak hutch filled with a set of china stood against the far wall. Not one dish was missing, much less broken.

As for the twins' bedroom, the bunk-beds were built into the wall. It would have been hard to dismantle the bed, but not impossible. So, what had happened here?

Maybe, it was the mile-and-a-half curving driveway that wound through the trees, past the guest cabins, along the creek that could overflow during the rainy season that scared off potential owners. The long gravel road leading up to the house did lend an eerie feeling to the place. It might have kept would-be thieves away. She didn't know. She poured herself a cup of coffee. "I do know one thing. I don't believe in ghosts. There's no such thing."

Was that a man's low chuckle? "Oh, I'll change your mind, sweetheart."

There it was again. Something that could have been a voice. No, it couldn't be. She knew better than to admit she had unseen company.

Don't say you see things no one else does, hear voices nobody else hears or you'll wish you hadn't, Catriona O'Leary. Go get my leather belt from the closet upstairs.

Carrying her coffee, she headed for her room to grab clean clothes on the way to the shower, before she started her busy day. "La, la, la," Cat sang. "I can't hear you. It has to be the acoustics in this old house."

"Want to bet?"

CHAPTER FOUR

After breakfast, she stacked the dishes on the counter while the twins collected their backpacks for school. "Did you girls sleep well?"

"After Mister Robbie got done making a mess," Sophie said.

"Excuse me?" Cat eyed her daughter. "What are you talking about?"

"He has to haunt us," Samantha explained. "It's his job. He didn't want us to get timed out for having our toys all over, so he threw your stuff around."

They were either going to get over this fiction or she would definitely have to start worrying about her kids. "We could have slept through an earthquake," Cat rationalized, ushering the girls toward the front door. "The box might have fallen off the dresser."

"It was Mister Robbie," Samantha insisted.

"We'll talk about it later." Cat held the door for the girls and locked it behind them. "Come on, now. We don't want to be late for school."

"But, Mommy. He's real," Sophie said.

"No, he's not. I don't believe in ghosts. If your new pretend friend doesn't want to be grounded past forever, he'd better stay out of my room."

She saw the worried glances between the twins and nodded in

satisfaction. Maybe, they'd stop acting out and everything would be settled for once and for all. The stories of Mister Robbie would end, and she could get on with the work she needed to do on the ranch.

Once she dropped the girls, she headed south toward Snohomish and Evening Gold Stable where she used to train horses. She needed to pick up the rest of their belongings and her last paycheck.

Cat drew a deep breath. Facing Peggy Lawson wouldn't be easy especially after hearing about Frazer's stunts during the August Expo. But it needed to be done, and she could handle it. That had been her mantra since she was ten years old and she wasn't changing it now.

As she pulled into the circular drive, she spotted the two-bedroom mobile home sitting adjacent to the indoor arena. It'd been her home for more than a year. Their home—hers, the girls', Frazer's.

She took a moment to recall that last morning. She remembered Frazer coming down the front steps after she'd loaded up the ten horses to go to the show in Colorado, along with everything they'd need, a week's supply of hay and grain, gallons of apple juice to add to water buckets so they'd hydrate. Saddles, bridles, blankets, pads, vet supplies…

Her suitcases had been safely stowed in the dressing room of the fancy trailer. She'd just had to hug the twins one more time before she left that day. Of course, she'd be checking in with them every morning and night, but as it turned out, Frazer had other plans. The way he'd stomped toward her that morning should have been a clue, as if she hadn't expected as much after nine years of marriage.

Six-foot-six, thick black hair that curled down to broad shoulders, narrow-hipped, he radiated pure sex in the black suit he wore as a pit boss for Black Raven Casino. Strong features, but rugged, not pretty, a warrior's face, she always thought, although he was more likely to call for Security than confront anyone except her.

That morning she'd wanted to placate him, so she had pasted on a smile and tried not to wish that the heart of the man matched the gorgeous exterior. "Hey, handsome."

He wasn't buying it. He scowled, black brows drawing fiercely over coal-black eyes. "I want a divorce."

"Really? Just as I'm leaving for a week? How convenient. Why doesn't this surprise me?"

He'd glared at her and jerked car keys out of his jacket pocket. "A divorce, Cat. I mean it this time."

The words had still struck her like a blow. She'd shaken her head. "No. We're not going there today. I'll deal with this crap when I get home."

"Fine. But don't say I didn't warn you." He'd stormed toward his red Corvette. Tires spitting gravel, he'd raced down the drive toward town and the casino although it wouldn't open for three hours.

She'd known then he was cheating on her again. She could feel tears burning her eyes, but she didn't let them fall. Instead, she'd promised herself a trip to the doctor to make sure she hadn't gotten an STD from his latest skanky girlfriend.

Back in the present, Cat shook her head. Parking the pickup, she headed for the office in the barn. Two of the stalls made up the room and she found herself studying it with new eyes, wondering how much of the setup she should imitate on her own ranch.

A dark brown carpet that didn't show dirt covered the wooden floor. There was a couch along one wall and a table with four chairs in the far corner where instructors and staff ate their sack lunches. Bookshelves lined two of the walls. Large picture windows on the arena side revealed the indoor ring. Glass display cases held trophies interspersed with ribbons and photos of champion horses. An old wooden rolltop desk took up the center of the room. Cat made a mental note to visit local estate and garage sales to find furniture for her own office. She certainly didn't want the public in and out of the house where she and the twins lived.

At the desk, Peg sat, surrounded by stacks of paperwork. For as long as Cat could remember, she could always find Peg there on Thursdays, surrounded by paperwork.

Today, she glanced up from the stack of paperwork in front of her. "Cat!"

The professional smile warmed to a friendly one. Peg stood, came around the desk to give her a hug. "Hey, stranger. How's the moving?"

"It's going well." Cat leaned into the embrace, glad to see the slender, older woman who had given her a job when no other barn owner would. "How are you doing? Did you find a trainer?"

"I'm interviewing another one tomorrow. You're a hard gal to replace." Peg went to the coffee pot and filled two cups, passing one to Cat. "How do the girls like the dude ranch?"

"They tell me we have a ghost. He was apparently there when we unloaded the horses and moved them to the barn. I think they miss Frazer more than they're willing to admit."

"Maybe." Peg leaned against her desk. "Or you could really have Casper living with you."

"I hope not." Cat laughed. "I already gave him a time-out and threatened to ground him."

Peg grinned, and ran a hand through her gray-streaked, brown hair. "The girls are lucky to have you. Most mothers wouldn't be so understanding."

Cat shrugged. "I've gotten used to their imaginations. They've been talking to the animals forever. And they've always had pretend friends. I'll be glad when this one disappears, though."

Peg nodded. "Maybe a distraction would help." Hazel eyes narrowed, she said, "I could use a couple extra stalls here if you didn't mind boarding Lucky and Stormy for me."

"Why on earth would you ask me to do that? They're two of your most reliable lesson ponies."

"Who are pushing thirty." Peg studied the dark coffee in her mug. "You'd really be helping me out, Cat. My instructors always want to use whips and spurs to make them go. It doesn't matter to most people that those ponies have worked since they were youngsters and have earned the right to a decent retirement."

"You told me you've had them over twenty years," Cat said.

"Longer than any of my husbands," Peg agreed. "And they're smarter too. The trainer I'm interviewing tomorrow wants to buy in as a partner and I'll need to ease out some of my old-time ponies and horses. I can't look like a softy."

"Is that all?" Cat eyed the older woman. There had to be more to the story. "The girls would love them." Granted, the twins wanted ponies, but they'd never expected to get the ones Peg let them ride here.

"It'll be a safe retirement home for them," Peg said. "And I'll pay board because I'm not selling them to you. When my daughters finally marry and have kids, we might need them back here in a few years."

Ah. That was it. "And you don't trust me to get that divorce from Frazer," Cat said.

"Nope." Peg's smile faded. "My last husband was just like your Frazer. He lied, cheated and stole from me. He had a violent temper and terrorized my children. And he kept charming me into taking him back."

"Not me." Cat shook her head. "It's over. He's been served. I've got the lawyer working on the custody issue."

"In that case, I'll be happy to tell the judge what happened when you were out of town." Peg crossed to the coffee pot and topped off her cup. "I've got some money here for you."

"It can't be much." Cat sipped her coffee. "I owe for utilities and the phone in the mobile."

"Not really." Peg took a deep breath. "Before you started training here, I always included those in the rent, but I didn't trust Frazer from the start. I hoped you'd come to your senses. So, I held back on your wages, bonuses and extras." She opened the top drawer of the desk and removed a check. "Spend it quickly because you don't want him getting his greedy hands on it. Besides, you'll have to declare all your income during the proceedings."

Cat's jaw dropped when she saw the amount on the cashier's check. It'd be enough to help get the basics started on the guest ranch. And she could pay the rest of the retainer to her attorney. "I don't know what to say."

"You earned it." Peg pulled out a file folder. "I've run off copies of the contracts I use for boarding and training horses. I've got a list of my suppliers along with their phone numbers. I already gave you a reference at Summer O'Neill's feed store in Baker City. She'll help you set up an account with her and her delivery charges are the most reasonable in your area."

"Wow. I really appreciate the help."

"It's the least I can do," Peg said. "A lot of people helped me over the years. It's time to pass it on. I'll follow you up to Baker City and deliver the ponies. Then, the girls will have them when they get home from school."

"And like you said, maybe it will make them forget about their ghost."

MY SWEET HAUNT

For the next two days, when the girls were at school, Cat focused on starting the business. She opened a new bank account under her own name with the money from Peg. She changed her business license to one with her current address and information. She ordered a sign for the dude ranch, bought pink and purple paint for the fences to the twins' delight and arranged for a glass company to replace the broken windows in the guest cabins. She needed to do more to ready them for the winter, but first and foremost, she had to deal with her house, the barns and fences.

She still needed to place advertisements in magazines, especially those that catered to people who traveled in the summer. Hay, grain and shavings had to be ordered. The best part about all the errands was she didn't hear about Mister Robbie's adventures. She refused to admit to herself how much she missed his opinions, as told by Sophie and Samantha.

On Saturday morning she fixed breakfast, the twins' favorite French toast. Mentally, she listed what she hoped to accomplish through the day. She had to start building paddocks for the horses. She could put Stormy and Lucky out to graze on stake ropes, but the only time that Skyrocket and Dynamite exercised was in the round pen. She had to muck stalls too, finish organizing saddles, bridles, brushes in the tack-room, and she should give the house some attention. She flipped the egg-soaked bread in the frying pan.

"Mommy, can we ride today?" Samantha asked.

"It's been three whole days since we got ponies," Sophie added, "and they're used to our home now. They said."

"Honey, unless those ponies started talking, they didn't say," Cat corrected gently. "Horses don't speak like people."

Samantha sighed. "Mommy, they think at us. In pictures. We've told you lots of times. You have to listen."

"I do listen to you girls." Cat slid two slices of French toast onto a plate. "I always listen." She didn't always believe the lengths their wild imaginations went to, but it didn't stop her from listening. The girls deserved that much respect.

"You listen," Sophie said. "You just don't hear."

Samantha nodded. She concentrated on buttering her French toast. Sophie followed suit.

Cat sighed and refilled her coffee cup before she sat down to eat. Sometimes, she felt as if she were the eight-year-old and the twins were the adults. Did all mothers feel this way? She wished there was someone she could ask, but it certainly wouldn't be their new imaginary friend. How on earth had the girls learned about ghosts, spooks and things that went bump in the night? Was it from other kids? Books in the school library? Had Frazer told them horror stories?

"I don't believe in ghosts," Cat murmured. "I don't. I don't. I don't!"

After breakfast, they headed for the barn. Rob followed the girls. A faded strawberry roan stuck his head over the first stall door and nickered at the twins.

Samantha went to him, holding up a carrot. "Good morning, my pony. Mommy says we can go riding today."

Next door, a gray Arabian/Welsh snorted impatiently. Blue eyes shone as he bobbed his head up and down. Sophie hurried to give him his treat. "Stormy is the bestest pony."

"No, Lucky is."

"I think they both are," Rob drawled.

"We love them," Samantha said. "Some ponies don't like riding together, but they always do."

"Because they're best friends forever." Sophie broke a carrot in half and shared out the pieces. "Just like us."

The two old duffers were nice and patient, perfect for little girls, Rob thought as he watched the twins feed treats. Even if she refused to admit he existed, the girls' mother was smart about horses. She'd selected trustworthy mounts for the children, not half-wild ones.

He glanced down the row of double stalls, remembering the Friesian stud he raised from a colt. They'd cleaned up in several show rings and he planned to breed, raise and train some of the best draft teams in Washington State after his hitch in the Army. Of course, he hadn't counted on his life being cut short, but who did for that matter?

"What are you thinking about, Mister Robbie?" Samantha asked.

"How pretty your ponies are," Rob said. He certainly wouldn't share all his memories with the little girls.

"Miss Peggy says we can keep them till she has grandkids," Samantha explained. "They're not really ours forever."

"But we're never mean to them," Sophie added. "They don't go so fast anymore. And we don't want to go fast anyhow."

"When you're ready to trot and gallop, they will," Cat said, coming from the tackroom carrying a small Western saddle. "You have to build up your skills first."

"They're helping us learn." Samantha petted Lucky's blaze. "They never buck or run away like the horses Mommy rides."

Cat frowned, then hung a saddle on Lucky's door. "Who are you girls talking to?"

"Mister Robbie," Sophie said. "You still don't see him, do you, Mommy?"

"Only because he doesn't exist." Cat turned and walked away.

Rob chuckled and raised his voice so it would be heard in the saddle area. "She is one stubborn woman, but I know she hears me."

"Why doesn't she say so then?" Sophie asked.

"Because she won't admit he's here," Samantha said.

"Okay." Sophie nodded. "Don't worry, Mister Robbie. Mommy will see you someday. Come on, Sam. Let's get our brushes. We got to groom before we can ride."

Samantha turned to follow her sister to the tackroom. "They like brushing, Mister Robbie. They never bite or kick at us and we can make 'em all shiny."

"What about hoof picking?" Rob asked when the girls returned with buckets of grooming equipment. "Some ponies won't pick up their feet for little kids."

Samantha frowned up at him. "Don't say we're little. We're eight. They don't know how old we are. And we always clean hooves by ourselves."

CHAPTER FIVE

While the girls rode in the round pen, Cat paced around the big outdoor arena nearby. Once she repaired the fences, she could use it as a paddock for the horses. When they finished mowing the high grass, she'd be able to teach patterns to Skyrocket and Dynamite. It was all a part of their training. They needed to learn to do transitions from the walk to the trot and gallop and back down to the walk again.

She glanced at her daughters. It was Samantha's turn to lead the way and Sophie's pony followed Lucky. "I'm going to look around a bit," Cat called. "Are you girls all right without me?"

"Yes. Mister Robbie says he'll stay and watch us," Sophie said.

"Mister Robbie," Cat muttered. "What a bunch of malarkey."

She thought she heard a man's low laugh and ignored the sound. The memory of her grandfather caching posts under cedar trees came to mind and she headed toward the grove of evergreens on the far side of the yard. She couldn't build fences without supplies and there hadn't been much time to explore the dude ranch in the short time they'd lived here. Maybe, she'd get lucky and there would be posts, fence wire, tools and other things she needed to fix up the place.

Two hours later when the girls finished riding, Cat had a good inventory of what was on hand. There were several hundred posts stored under the firs, pine and cedar trees at the base of the ridge behind the barn. A search of the tool room revealed an assortment of rusted hand tools, hammers, saws, shovels, rakes, old fashioned posthole diggers, wire cutters and even a fence stretcher. She'd even found two rolls of farm and field mesh.

After she and the twins had lunch, she would start the repairs on the big outdoor riding arena. By the time summer rolled around and they had their first guests, Cedar Creek Dude Ranch would be restored to its former glory.

"Mommy, where did Mister Robbie go? It's almost noon."

"I have no idea where he is, Samantha." Cat opened the front door. "It wasn't my turn to watch him."

"You mean you can see him now?" Sophie asked, excitement on her small face.

"No, sweetie. That's an old joke my aunt used to tell when I visited her and my grandma." Cat led the way to the kitchen. "Wash up, girls. I'll make lunch."

"But, what about Mister Robbie?" Samantha asked. "Is he on time-out again?"

Puzzled, Cat eyed her daughter. "Why would he be? What has he done?"

"He did sass you when we were riding," Samantha said, "but only once."

"That's because we told him he had to be good or he'd get grounded," Sophie said. "Come on, Sam. Let's go get him."

"Where is he?" Cat asked.

"In his room upstairs, of course." Samantha followed her twin.

Cat sighed and shook her head. Imaginary friends. What would it take to get rid of this one? She headed for the kitchen and washed her own hands. Then, she pulled out the peanut butter, jelly and bread and started making sandwiches.

"We woke him up, Mommy." Samantha returned a few minutes later, Sophie at her heels. "He says we do so much stuff, we wear him out so he needed a nap."

Sophie pulled out a chair and sat down at the table. "We told him that you needed him, and it was time to rise and shine."

"Why on earth do I need him? I like doing my own work."

"You told us you were going to build a big riding space. We're not big enough to carry posts or dig really deep holes," Samantha said as she started to eat. "Mister Robbie will. He's the only other grownup here. And then he won't get timed out for being naughty."

"I see." Cat filled two glasses with milk. "I appreciate the thought, girls. But, there's a lot to do before we open for guests. And there's no time for do-overs."

"Mommy, how do you know that he can't help?" Sophie took a bite of her sandwich.

"He said he wasn't wasting his morning to make you mad," Samantha chimed in. "And he has to haunt us. It's his job. Else he could get fired like Frazer always does, couldn't he?"

"I'm sure Mister Robbie could." Shaking her head, Cat decided to humor the girls. She put away the milk carton and poured herself a cup of coffee. "Everybody else has to worry about being fired, so probably your ghost does too. But it doesn't matter because we aren't going anywhere. We're staying right here. Deal?"

"Deal," Samantha and Sophie chimed.

Suddenly, Samantha turned her head and smiled in the direction of the doorway. "Hi, Mister Robbie."

Sophie waved and kept chewing. When she swallowed, she said, "You're going to help Mommy, aren't you?"

"I'm fine on my own," Cat protested. "Your little friend can watch cartoons with you while I put up string lines for the arena."

The ringing of the landline in the living room caught her attention and she left the twins to eat while she answered the phone. Perhaps when she returned, something else would have caught their attention and she wouldn't have to listen to any more nonsense.

Rob eyed the two girls at the kitchen table. "What does she think she's doing? Building any kind of fence is man's work."

"There aren't any men here," Samantha pointed out. "Except you."

"I'm a ghost. I don't work anymore."

Sophie frowned at him. "You've been making noises at night even if Mommy can't hear you all the time. And you made a big mess in her room even if she does say it was an accident. If you don't want to get timed out or grounded, you'd better help her."

Rob scowled at the twins. To think he'd been glad that someone could finally see him. It made all those long years by himself even lonelier. "I do as I please."

"You better please to help Mommy." Samantha glared at him through narrowed blue eyes. "We don't need no lazy folks here."

"I'm a ghost." Rob tried to reason with the pair. "That means I don't have a body. I can't dig postholes or build anything."

Silence took over the room.

Finally, Sophie asked. "How do you turn out lights? Or blow out candles? Or make the fire go out in the woodstove? Or throw clothes and books around?"

"By thinking about it. I use my ghostly energy."

"Okay." Samantha propped her chin on two small fists. "Then you can *think* posts over to the corral so Mommy doesn't have to carry them."

By the time they finished lunch and the girls watched an hour of cartoons, the three of them were ready to head back outside. With the twins and their puppy trailing behind her, Cat led the way to the tool room. She needed the posthole digger, a steel bar to loosen any rocks and a pointed shovel. With her daughters' help, they toted the tools toward the arena she planned to repair.

Halfway there, Cat froze. In the middle of the field was a pile of cedar posts taller than the knee-high grass. Why hadn't she seen them earlier? Because they hadn't been there. *But they must have been*, she told herself. They certainly couldn't have lined up and marched to where she needed them.

"Look," Sophie pointed to the hand-split posts. "Mister Robbie did it! He brought 'em here."

"I knew he could," Samantha said, beaming. "Good job, Mister Robbie."

"Girls, I'm sure the posts have always been there." Cat drew a deep breath. "The grass is so high that I just didn't see them this morning."

"Mommy!" Sophie looked shocked. "Mister Robbie did it. You gotta say, 'Thank-you,' or it's not fair."

Samantha nodded agreement. "You have to remember your 'fetching up' too."

"You can't be tacky either," Sophie concurred.

When Lad plonked his furry backside down by the twins as if they needed his allegiance too, Cat surrendered. "All right. I can't fight all three of you. What do you want me to tell your pretend friend?"

"Just say thanks," Sophie said.

"And you 'preciate his help," Samantha added firmly.

Cat glanced around the empty yard—vacant except for her, the girls and their puppy. "Okay. Thank you, Mister Robbie."

She waited. For what? An answer from the breeze? She felt like a complete fool.

"Go on," Samantha urged. "Say you like what he did for you."

"This is ridiculous," Cat muttered and deliberately mimicked the eight-year-old's tone. "I really appreciate you bringing the posts over here. I like having your help."

"Liar." A man's deep voice seemed to speak directly into her mind. "You'd rather do everything yourself, than have to admit you need a hand once in a while or be grateful to anyone."

What was that?

Glaring, Cat looked around the empty field, the round pen and across the yard toward the house. Nobody, at least no one besides her family and the dog was anywhere to be seen. That voice had to be her imagination. It had to be. "And stay the hell out of my room!"

Now, she *knew* she heard the masculine laughter she'd imagined before. "Damn it."

"Mommy, you can't say bad words." Samantha scowled at her. "Now you got to say you're sorry to Mister Robbie."

"In his dreams." Cat dragged the steel bar toward the big outdoor arena. "He's an arrogant, egotistical jerk and I'm not apologizing to him. And he isn't here, not really, anyway. He's just pretend."

Sophie and Samantha exchanged a look. Sophie sighed. "He says it's okay, Mommy. He shouldn't have teased you. And you're welcome for the posts."

"Good to know." Cat shook her head. Why was she arguing with a man who simply didn't exist, much less with her daughters about him? But, why did she hear him sometimes? Or at least she could have sworn that she did. *I can't*, she decided. *I'm just going along with the girls' stories.*

An hour later, she'd set new corner posts on the first line. Then, she started digging more holes. With the kids' help, she managed to set four more cedar posts before five o'clock when she stopped. It was time to clean stalls and feed the horses. She took the tools with them to the barn. Tomorrow, while the girls rode their ponies, she could continue repairing the big outdoor arena.

After supper, the girls watched a Disney movie. Cat made phone calls to previous clients. She avoided the ones who'd left in a huff from Peg's barn due to Frazer's shenanigans, but there were others. They still seemed interested in having her train their stock. She arranged for two more horses to be delivered the following week. Yes, she had work to do to bring the dude ranch up to speed for next summer, but she also needed money coming in from different sources. And horse training provided a good income.

At seven-thirty, she ran warm water into the bathtub, rounded up her daughters and their clean pajamas. "Let's go, ladies. Bedtime in a half hour."

"But, it's Saturday," Sophie complained. "Why do we have to go to bed so early? It isn't a school night."

"Church tomorrow," Cat said. "We want to make a good impression on the people who live in our new town. And that means we have to be there on time."

"So, we have to get up early," Samantha said. "Come on, Sophie. I bet we'll know lots of the kids in our new Sunday School class."

A smile slowly dawned on the other girl's face. "Yeah. I bet we will. It'll be fun."

"And you can introduce me to them," Cat said. It made sense to meet the other adults in Baker City through their children. Maybe, she could find some help. The guest cabins needed painting inside and out. And it would be nice to have somebody else dig the post holes on the new training arena. Her back protested from the heavy manual labor and she wouldn't be able to take a hot shower until the twins had their baths, they were tucked into bed and she read two stories, one for each girl.

As the girls undressed for her bath, Sophie asked, "Can we ride our ponies tomorrow?"

"Yes," Cat told her. "I'll work on the corral while you two ride in the round pen."

Samantha frowned. "Don't we have to go to Grandma's for Sunday dinner?"

"No, your grandmother is on a cruise to Mexico right now. So, we'll swing by the deli and get some fried chicken after church. Then, I won't have to cook supper."

"And potato salad too?" Sophie asked.

"Why not?" Cat smiled at her daughters, grateful it was so easy to entertain them. Ponies and a picnic and they totally forgot about their relatives. Yippee!

If only it was that easy for her. She dreaded telling her mother about the upcoming divorce from Frazer. In a television sitcom, her family would rally around and say the man wasn't good enough for her. But that wasn't life according to her parents. Her mother adored Frazer. She always claimed that he was such a hunk, far too handsome for her daughter, Cat. And the same went for her father. He loved the deals that Frazer got him at casinos throughout the country.

Both of them would be upset that he left her behind when he moved down south. Once they found out about the dude ranch, they'd try to convince Cat to sell it and give the money to Frazer for one of his crazy investment schemes. It wouldn't matter that the essay contest rules locked her into keeping the ranch for ten years. Her father would try bullying her until she quit, gave up on her dream.

I won't. Not this time. Aunt Rose used to bring me here and it was pure heaven.

CHAPTER SIX

The next morning, as she herded the twins to the pickup, she took a moment to glance around the yard and the wooden three-story Victorian house with its towers, bay windows and gingerbread trim. It needed work too. Loose shingles on the roof needed to be nailed back into place. The wraparound porch deck had to be replaced. And, of course, the whole structure had to be painted. Aargh! Too bad she hadn't won a million dollars to fix up the ranch when she won the place *'as is, where is'* in the essay contest.

After buckling in the twins, she climbed in, started the engine and headed down the long driveway. As she drove past the orchard, she glimpsed an apple tree loaded with ripe fruit. More work. For a moment, she remembered her grandmother and aunt making applesauce and apple butter. And the smell of cinnamon, sugar and nutmeg pervading the kitchen.

Okay, so it was time to dig out the ancient *Fannie Farmer* cookbook, the 1908 edition that had come down through the family forever, the one Aunt Rose saved to give to Cat after her grandmother died. Cat blinked hard to hold back the tears that pricked her eyes. She and the girls could pick apples this afternoon after church.

She glanced at the twins in the rear-view mirror. They looked half asleep. For once, Sophie didn't have much to say and Samantha hadn't started a conversation even in a whisper.

Actually, Cat thought, what she needed to do was lie down on a copy machine and run off a dozen copies of herself or else find a way to invent clones so she could get everything done. Either that or give up sleep for the duration. At the highway, she turned right and drove toward the small town of Baker City. Most of her errands had taken her the other direction toward Lake Maynard where the girls went to school.

Now, as they headed into the town, she spotted a large barn on the right-hand side of the street. A sign painted on the building proclaimed, "Summer's Feed and Tack." On the left, was another large structure, the Baker City Mercantile. Cat continued on past the café, two bars, and three blocks later pulled in at the church. This was pretty much the extent of the town, at least on the main east-west thoroughfare.

She parked in the lot adjacent to the church. After she helped the girls unbuckle their seat belts, the three of them strolled toward the over-sized carved wooden doors where a silver-haired elderly man stood waiting. He didn't wear the traditional dark suit that she associated with most preachers, but a plaid, flannel shirt tucked into faded jeans.

She studied him curiously. For some reason, he looked familiar, an older version of the man who preached here when she was a child. Was he the same one? How long had he been the minister in Baker City? Cat smiled at him. "Good morning."

"I'm Reverend Thompson." He beamed back at her, faded blue eyes friendly as he handed her a program. "Welcome to our services. Are you visiting the area?"

"No. We just moved into the dude ranch outside of town," Cat said.

"Are you going to fix it up or sell it?" Reverend Thompson asked cautiously.

"It's our new home," Sophie told him. "We're living here forever. Mommy said so."

"My goal is to have it fixed up by next spring so we can open for the season," Cat explained. "But we have a lot of work to do."

"Well, let me put on my thinking cap and maybe I can help."

Less than twenty people attended the service and it turned out there wasn't a Sunday School class for youngsters, at least not that day. Even if they poked at each other and looked around the church a little too often, the twins settled down once the minister headed to the front. They paid attention to everything the pastor said, and Cat was grateful the sermon was short, simple and the topic of loving one's neighbors, something her daughters could understand and appreciate. Afterwards, they followed the rest of the small congregation to a reception area for refreshments. The girls had chocolate doughnuts and milk while Cat had coffee and a bear claw.

Reverend Thompson brought over a woman about his age and joined them at their table. "Virginia, this is Cat McTavish and her daughters. Cat, this is my wife, Virginia. She runs our food bank and she knows everyone in town who wants work."

Cat smiled at the stately woman with silver streaked dark hair. "Would you like some apples for the food bank?"

"Sure. Where are they? In your car?"

"Actually, they're still on the trees. I need some help picking them," Cat said.

"Our ponies like apples," Sophie said. "Can we have some for them?"

"Yes, but remember we have to cut them into pieces for Lucky and Stormy," Cat told her daughter. "No letting them eat the apples whole."

Virginia frowned thoughtfully. "Let me see who I can round up. How does your tomorrow look?"

"I have time between ten and two," Cat said. "After I drop the girls at school and before I have to pick them up. I'm hoping to get them on the bus, but I haven't organized it yet."

"All right." Virginia nodded, then tilted her head to one side. "Have we met before? For some reason, you look really familiar. Did you grow up here?"

"No. My aunt and I used to come to the dude ranch when I was the twins' age," Cat said. "She actually lived in Baker City when she was a child."

"What's her name?"

"Rose Kathleen McTavish," Cat said. "Her maiden name was O'Leary." Glancing at her daughters, Cat lowered her voice. "She and her husband always go to Alaska for the summer and they should be headed this way soon. Aunt Rose and I were really close when I was a kid. And this was our favorite place in the world."

A smile lit Virginia's eyes and landed on her lips. "I remember Rose. I wanted to be her. She was so nice to everyone, but she wasn't afraid to speak up when she saw something wrong. She joined the Freedom Riders when she graduated from high school and headed down south to help people register to vote."

For a moment, Cat remembered the tall, slender, red-haired woman who always looked like the epitome of a 1950s actress in her low-cut blouses, tight pants, and open-toed, spike heels. Her bright red hair might come out of a bottle, but no streak of gray dared to erupt on Aunt Rose's head. She was the queen of the pithy comment, much to Cat's father's dismay, but it enlivened many a Sunday dinner.

"Yes," Cat said aloud. "I didn't know she'd gone down south, but I can see my aunt stepping up and stepping out of that box of what people expect women to do. My dad totally freaked when she demonstrated for the Equal Rights Amendment."

"She is a real hero." Virginia wrapped an arm around Cat's shoulders. "My hero. Come meet the other ladies who help me with the food bank. They'll love meeting Rose's niece."

When they left the reception hall a short time later, another memory stirred in Cat's mind. She glanced toward the rear of the church and saw the town cemetery. When she was a child, she and Aunt Rose used to take flowers to the graves of the O'Leary relatives. Cat hesitated, then guided the girls in the direction of the pickup. Next time she planned to come to town, she'd bring roses and visit her family. Her aunt would appreciate the respect.

On the way out of Baker City, Cat pulled into the parking lot between the mercantile and the town cafe. The general store had everything from groceries to hardware, along with two counters that served as the local deli. It didn't take long to pick up a box of fried chicken and luckily, she found a carton of homemade potato salad in the cooler. A bag of chips, a six-pack of cola, and a small watermelon finished up her shopping. They were good to go.

As soon as they arrived home, the girls charged into the house to change to clothing suitable for riding their ponies. Laughing, Cat followed them, her hands full with two bags of groceries. When she reached the porch, the front door swung open and remained that way.

"It's the wind," Cat said aloud. "I don't believe in ghosts. I don't. I don't. I don't!"

"A good thing you're pretty," she heard a deep voice say in her mind. "You're sure not very smart."

Cat shook her head. Even her own mind was saying disparaging things about her.

Samantha came out of her room in jeans and a t-shirt. "Be nice, Mister Robbie," she said to the air, "or you'll be in trouble with the folks in town."

Cat glanced at her daughter as they headed into the kitchen. "What folks, honey? Nobody seemed to know your 'pretend' friend. At least they didn't ask about him."

"Not the ones you were talking to, Mommy," Sophie said. "The ones at church and in the store."

Cat blinked. "Which ones? I didn't see you girls talking to any strangers."

"The ghosts. There's lots of them in Baker City." Samantha heaved a sigh. "I wish you would look at them instead of through them, Mommy. They were really excited to see you."

What had she done when she entered the essay contest? She'd been looking for a permanent home for herself and the girls and hoped to find one. Now, the twins were sure that they were surrounded by ghosts. Okay, so Baker City was a quiet, small town. That didn't mean it was inhabited by ghosts. There had certainly seemed to be actual living people there and she'd see to it that the girls made more friends. Once they settled into their new home, surely these figments of their eight-year-old imaginations would fade.

The next morning, she started a quick email to the feed store. If she got the order in before she took the girls to school, then Summer, the proprietor, could drop off the hay and grain this afternoon. Between fixing breakfast, packing lunches and approving what the girls wanted to wear, Cat typed in the list of supplies on her laptop.

She hit send, then hustled the twins through the rest of the morning routine.

When she returned home, she turned Skyrocket and Dynamite into the round pen to exercise together. Lucky and Stormy seemed happy to graze on their stake ropes, contentedly mowing the yard. Horses and ponies settled, Cat headed into the barn to muck stalls with Lad, the pup as her escort.

She'd just finished when two cars and a Chevy truck pulled into the drive. She recognized the pastor in one of the cars, but not the younger man in the other vehicle. A slender brunette in faded jeans and a red sweatshirt popped out of the pickup and waved a greeting. "Good morning. Are you Cat?"

"Yes." Tucking her leather work gloves into her belt, Cat strode toward her guests. The other woman looked as if she was in her late twenties too. "Summer?"

"That's me. Where do you want the feed?"

"In the barn." Cat approached and took the clipboard Summer offered, scanning the hard copy of the order. "Straw? I didn't want straw. I use shavings in the stalls."

"Got two bales here," Summer said cheerfully. "I can always take it back."

"No," a deep voice rumbled. "We need it for the apples."

That voice again. What was going on? Maybe she needed a one-way ticket to the loony bin! Cat glanced around the yard but didn't see a man. "Apples? Why would I use straw for apples?"

"For storage," Reverend Thompson said, obviously overhearing the question as he stepped out of his car, Virginia following him. "Hello, Cat. I haven't thought of that in years. My dad used to dig a hole near the orchard, line it with straw and then layer in the apples. They stayed fresh through the winter. They tasted like we'd just picked them."

Cat smiled at the pastor. "Hello, Reverend Thompson, Mrs. Thompson." She glanced toward the fruit trees. "I guess we'd better put the straw over there. What should we look for? I haven't seen a hole. The girls could have fallen into it."

"Not unless the wooden cover has rotted away," the pastor said. "I'll mosey over and see if I can locate the handle. It's probably rope."

He wandered in the direction of the orchard and Cat gestured toward the barn. "Okay, let's unload the feed."

"Sounds good." Summer hurried back to the truck, shifted it into gear and carefully maneuvered it so she didn't spook the ponies by getting too close.

A blond man in his twenties climbed out of the third car and headed over to open the tailgate and unload the bales of straw. He offered his hand to Cat. "Hello. I'm Jack Madison. You're training my sister's horse. How's he doing?"

"He's coming along," Cat said. "Did you want to take him home?"

"Hell, no! That fucking monster damn near stomped me half to death when we loaded him last time. My old man just sent me along to help with the apples when Mrs. Thompson called." Jack picked up the first sack of grain, slung it over a shoulder. "Where do you want this?"

"In here." Cat headed for the hay room that opened off the side of the barn, trying to think of a polite way to tell the young man to stop swearing. She didn't want to offend his parents or lose a client, but cussing wasn't appropriate on a facility that would be catering to families. She swung the door wide and gestured to the feed-room tucked in the front corner. "Grain goes there."

"Got it." Jack strode inside. He dropped off the first bag and went for the second.

Pushing the barn wheelbarrow, Cat went to help Summer with the bales of alfalfa-grass hay. "Guess I'm getting old when the potty mouth bothers me."

"Nah, it's just the mom in you," Summer said, with a smile in her friendly light blue eyes. "My kids always copy the wrong things, so I've told Jack that he can't be around them when he's sober. He's a very genial drunk, but last week he totaled his car and took out the flag pole at the Town Hall so he's back on the wagon again. His folks have threatened not to pay for a new rig unless he goes to AA."

"Wow. And now I'm up to date on the local soap opera." Laughing, Cat helped ease the hundred-pound bale into the heavy-duty plastic wheelbarrow. "All the things I've missed by living in Snohomish. Who knew?"

"That's nothing," Summer said with a grin. "Come to the BC

Business Association next Tuesday morning. We have coffee and decide what the town should do. Doesn't mean the town is going to pay attention. And of course, we talk about each other."

"I couldn't get there until after I take the girls to school," Cat said.

"That works. We don't meet till ten." Summer pushed the next bale closer to the end of the pickup bed. "And once you get to know us, you can join the carpool. We take turns driving the kids to Lake Maynard and picking them up. Otherwise, we'd all spend every day on the road and couldn't get anything accomplished. When you have your own business, it gets real tough being a taxi driver for the munchkins."

"The school secretary told me there was a bus," Cat said. "My twins just aren't ready to ride it yet."

"It leaves town before six and that's way too early for the elementary school bunch," Summer said. "They'd have to sit in the gym for almost two hours. If your kids are like mine, they won't enjoy it."

"You're telling me." Cat turned the wheelbarrow and pushed it toward the barn. She heard Jack muttering swear words as he stacked the bags of feed and wondered how to handle the situation. Well, she'd move hay while she considered her options.

Enough was enough, Rob decided. A guy might talk like a lumberjack when he was in the woods and no ladies were around, but as his dad used to say, there was a time and a place for everything. This wasn't it, not when the gals didn't like it, so Rob would do what needed doing. He stalked toward the feed room, eyeballing the young punk who was stacking bags of dry cob in haphazard piles. Rob slammed the door shut with just one glance. He looked at the string on the light bulb, mentally gave it a pull and plunged the room into darkness.

"What the hell?" The young man swung around.

"Punk, this is my place." Rob gritted out the words, making sure his voice echoed in the close space. "You hear me?"

"Yeah, dude. I can't see ya but I can hear ya." He took a step, stumbled to a stop.

"Then, man up and pretend you know right from wrong. No more swearing around women. Talk to them like you would your grandma."

"Come on. They don't care. It's no big deal."

Rob glared at the young man, then focused on the stack of full grain bags. They tumbled down, scattering like toys all over the floor, nearly knocking down the punk. "I care. Clean up that mess. And put away the feed right this time."

"All right. All right. You win. No more cussing." The young fellow fumbled around in the darkness. "Will you turn on the lights please? I can't see sh—squat in here."

"Remember my rules." Rob said. "And apologize to the ladies."

"Yeah. Okay. Whatever you say."

"Good. Because I'll be watching you." Opening the door, Rob turned the light on and went to help with the hay. Granted, he couldn't push the wheelbarrow, but he could give it a pull over the bumpy ground and make it easier for that danged fool girl to get the bales inside. Not that she'd thank him for it. She'd probably keep pretending he wasn't here.

Wasn't he supposed to send her down the road? How could he when she worked harder than most people who'd ever got near the place? And it wasn't a 'bass-ackwards' contingency as his father used to say. A person needed a place to go to, not just run from. And she didn't have anywhere else to take her daughters or those two unruly horses or those old ponies or that puppy who seemed to think that Rob had nothing better to do than provide tummy rubs in the middle of the day or night.

Once the hay was stacked, and the grain put away, the group meandered toward the orchard and Rob followed along. The old man, the pastor, had found the underground bin for the apples and already lined it with a thick layer of straw. Now, he organized his crew. As Rob watched, the old lady who had come in the car with the pastor approached Cat.

"I wanted to thank you again for helping out the food bank. People will love having home-grown fruit."

"I'm the one who really appreciates the help," Cat said. "Without you folks, the birds would be eating all these apples, pears and plums and making a total mess of everything. There's no way I could have done this alone."

"Doesn't mean you wouldn't have tried," Rob drawled. He saw her flinch, then look quickly around. Oh, she heard him all right, that was obvious. Now, what would it take to make her admit he was still here?

CHAPTER SEVEN

Cat sighed and stretched her aching back. She twisted to the right and left to ease her sore muscles. Then she pushed the wheelbarrow back to the orchard, ready for the next box of apples. As soon as she lowered the handles to the ground, Jack Madison put the carton of Red Delicious inside.

He glanced around warily. "Sorry about the language earlier, ma'am. I get used to talking in bars and forget my manners when I'm not drinking."

She nodded. "Thanks. I have kids so I have to remember to watch myself around them."

"Yeah, you should have heard my sister when she got home from her last tour in Afghanistan," Jack said. "As soon as she laced up her combat boots, she swore like a drill sergeant. My niece almost got kicked out of preschool for dropping the 'F' bomb."

Cat smiled. "I'll bet her language didn't make points with the high school principal or the parents when Ann started teaching school again."

"Nope, but the kids loved her." Jack looked around cautiously. "So, you'll tell your old man I shaped up, right? I don't want him kicking my um, my tail."

Cat gaped at him. "My what?"

"Your guy. Your partner. Your husband. Whoever it was that followed me into the feed-room and chewed me out for dissing you and Summer."

Cat managed to nod and watched him hurry back to collect another box of fruit. *What* man? Jack had been alone in the grain-room. Who had he heard? Or what?

She knew what the twins would say. It was Mister Robbie.

"Okay. Okay. Thanks for teaching Jack where the bear got in the buckwheat, Mister Robbie," Cat murmured. "Next time, just let me handle it. All right?"

She thought she heard a distant chuckle, then dismissed it as a figment of her over-active imagination. She so had to get a life and quit thinking there might really be a ghost lurking around the farm.

And not only that, she couldn't tell anyone she suspected there could be a ghost here. They'd think she was crazy. Besides she didn't want to look foolish or scare anyone away. She was just settling into a new place. Like the twins said, she was the mommy and that made her 100 percent right.

Later that afternoon, she parked the truck in front of the elementary school and waited for the girls. Reverend Thompson had rounded up his crew, so everyone left at the same time she did. He'd said they'd be back the next morning to pick the rest of the apples in the orchard. By the end of the week, all of the ripe fruit would be off the trees. That was good. She hadn't even considered it might attract wildlife and not just deer but bears as well.

Cat sighed and leaned back in her seat, closing her eyes for a moment. There was so much she needed to learn about living in the country. But first she had to do something about the apples she'd held back for them.

That evening after washing the supper dishes while the girls did their homework, she put a half dozen glass jars in hot soapy water to soak. Once she'd wiped down the counters, she carried a bucket of apples over to the table. She peeled them and listened as the twins drilled each other on their spelling words. Every mother knew how to multi-task. The apple peels and cores went back into the bucket for the horses. The sliced fruit went into a large kettle for applesauce.

The next three days followed the same pattern, horses fed, kids to school, home again to clean stalls and pick fruit. The only change was that she washed the stored jars from the pantry in the morning between breakfast and packing lunches, so the jars would be ready for whatever she cooked in the evenings after supper. Apple butter, pear jelly, pear butter, apple jelly, plum jam, the list went on and on. The girls delighted in making labels for each jar, occasionally asking their favorite pretend friend how to spell a new word like chutney.

Friday morning, while she put the next—and hopefully the last—batch of jars to soak, Cat remembered she had two new horses arriving that afternoon. She'd have to prepare stalls for them when she cleaned the barn. She'd ask Reverend Thompson if he knew someone who wanted part-time work, a man who could help with some of the repairs on the dude ranch. In order to charge for training, she had to work each horse at least an hour a day and that meant she'd have to use tomorrow to 'catch-up' rather than work on her new arena. Sometimes, it seemed the faster she went, the further behind she got, but it was a price she was willing to pay.

The day flew by. In no time, she was on the road to Lake Maynard to get the girls at school and of course as soon as they were home, they wanted to take apple slices to the new horses in the barn. Starlight, a coal black Morgan filly tossed her head nervously, then munched the treats. Gambler, her half-sister, a dainty bay with a diamond-shaped star and snip came forward and hung her head over the stall door, eager to visit with the twins.

"Do they know what to do?" Sophie asked, feeding an apple core to Starlight. "Have they been ridden before?"

"Not yet." Cat held out a treat to Lucky so he wouldn't feel slighted. "We're starting from scratch. They've been ground-worked, hauled and clipped, but nobody's ever hurt them so we're going to have a good time. They'll be here for at least three months."

"Can we help train them?" Samantha gave Gambler a long piece of red peel. "They like kids. They said."

"If they remember to be careful with you," Cat told her daughters. She wasn't going to repeat her lecture about horses not talking to people. She'd said the same thing for years and it obviously hadn't made an impression. The girls were positive they could converse with the animals, so there wasn't much use having a fit about it. And as long as everyone practiced what Peg called, "good safety," taking precautions and being sensible, things would be fine.

In spite of her best intentions, Cat slept late the next morning—well it was late for her, she thought, glaring at the clock. Most people wouldn't consider eight in the morning a horrible time to start, but she had a lot to do today, weekend or not. She scrambled into her clothes and hurried out to the barn to feed the horses.

Back inside, she made pancakes for breakfast and let the girls eat in their pajamas. While they watched cartoons, she ran through the housework, dishes, vacuuming, dusting, changing the sheets on all three beds and starting the mountains of laundry. At 10:30, she headed back to the barn with the twins.

It was a pretty day. A few puffy white clouds danced across the blue sky and a cool breeze brushed her face. Cat laughed as the girls raced by her in hot pursuit of Lad who barked and darted off in a series of short, collie dashes. She paused outside the barn and glanced toward the outdoor arena still waiting for the rest of the repairs.

And she froze.

Wire glinted as it stretched from post to post. *Wait a minute.* All she'd been able to do was set a few posts last weekend. She hadn't finished the job.

But someone else had. She slowly approached her new ring and reached out to touch the gatepost. The arena was restored exactly as she had planned, 300 feet square. The hand-split cedar posts stood approximately eight feet apart, again just as she planned. Wire mesh wove between the posts on the outside and three rails spanned the inside sections. She'd figured on two rails, one on the top and one on the bottom but whoever had built the arena, put a third one in the middle.

"The 'rena's fixed." Sophie hopped up and down beside her. "After we brush and saddle our ponies, can we ride in the round pen, Mommy? Can we?"

"Please." Samantha tugged on her arm. "Please, Mommy?"

"Sure." Cat rocked the gatepost or tried to, but it didn't move. It was real, not a fantasy. Somehow, her arena was finished, completely repaired. All it needed was a gate to fill this opening. She could order one from Summer and have it delivered today. But even if it had a gap here and another one on the back wall for the next aluminum farm gate, Cat could use it to train horses today.

"Who built this?" Cat asked the girls. "Who did it? When? Why didn't I see them?"

Samantha shook her head as if her mother's inability to grasp a simple point was beyond comprehension. "It was Mister Robbie."

"He did it," Sophie agreed, tilting her head to one side and listening to somebody else. "He says he fixed it after he made sure there weren't any monsters in our room at night."

Samantha giggled and poked a finger past her sister into the air. "You're silly, Mister Robbie. He says it was either this or he had to watch you make applesauce till midnight, Mommy, and you plumb wore him out. He can't haunt you when you're too busy to pay 'tention to him."

"Sorry I inconvenienced your friend." Cat shook her head and eyed her daughters. "For the last time, there are no such things as ghosts. And if there were, why would they build a fence, much less repair a riding ring? It had to have been Peg. She probably sent her hands up here to build a big corral for me."

"You just don't get it, Mommy." Samantha shook her head. "Mister Robbie did it. Why won't you say he's real?"

"Because he isn't." Cat lifted her chin. "I've never seen him, and he doesn't exist." She reached in her pocket and pulled out her cell phone. "Now, I'm going to call Summer and order two gates for the arena. If she gets them here today, we can hang them and then the horses will be able to graze down the grass in here. And after that, I'm calling Peg to thank her."

"What if she says she didn't do it, Mommy?" Sophie hurried toward her. "Then, will you believe in Mister Robbie?"

"No!" Cat pressed the buttons for the feed store number. "I'll know Peg did this and is keeping it a secret because—"

"There's no such things as ghosts," she heard that same disgusted male voice sound out of nowhere. "You're so stubborn you could give lessons to a mule. I'll make you admit you can see me. I know dang well you can hear me."

"No, I can't!" Cat spat the words, wondering why she bothered to argue with the voice in her head. And if she had to fantasize, why a man's deep tones? Why not a motherly woman's?

She blinked. For a moment, she thought she'd seen the shadowy shape of a man in green Army fatigues leaning against the round pen fence. Was her imagination becoming as wild as her daughters? "You don't exist. Nothing will make me think otherwise."

"I will. And the longer it takes, the worse it will be for your pride."

Later that afternoon, the twins rode their ponies in the round pen. When the stock gates arrived from the feed store, Cat hung them on the new arena, then put the geldings out to graze. They seemed to love the knee-high grass. She mucked their stalls and then did Lucky's and Stormy's as well. Once the barn was clean, she went out to watch the girls ride for a few minutes before she brought in Skyrocket and Dynamite, trading out their grazing time with the two young mares.

As she was taking a well-deserved break, an unfamiliar late model white Cadillac pulled up in the driveway. A stocky man in a three-piece suit climbed out of the car and headed toward her, the early autumn wind ruffling his silver blond hair. "Good afternoon."

Cat nodded. "Can I help you?"

"Yes. I'm Herman MacGillicudy." He held out his hand, a plastic smile appearing on his face that didn't touch pale blue eyes. "I own the Lake Maynard First Federal Bank."

Cat nodded and didn't say she'd chosen to do business with one of his competitors. "What can I do for you, Mister MacGillicudy?"

"Actually, it's what I can do for you, little lady." His smile widened and he focused on her chest, not her face. "I came to make you an offer for this place."

"No, you're not." Cat struggled to keep her tone civil, hating the way he leered at her breasts under her loose t-shirt. "We just moved in and I'm not interested in selling."

"You haven't heard my offer yet."

"I don't have to," Cat said. "This is my home and I'm staying here." She watched the words make their mark on his face and his smile fade. "Now, I'd appreciate if you'd leave."

MY SWEET HAUNT

He reached in his pocket and drew out a business card. "If you change your mind—"

"I won't." Cat didn't take the card, folding her arms instead. "Thanks, but no thanks."

"You don't understand. The place was promised to me. While I was away, it ended up for sale and you bought it. I want it back in my family." His tone oozed sincerity. "Now, what's it going to take to arrange that?"

"A miracle," Cat said. There was no way she'd escalate the situation and call him a liar. The Williams brothers had told her that they had tried various managers and renters for ten years before they decided to put the dude ranch up as a prize in the essay contest. "It's my home and I'm keeping it." She reached into her pocket, pulled out her cell phone. "Now, do I need to call the Baker City cops to make you leave?"

"Of course not." Herman glanced around the yard, then lowered his voice. "You're out in the middle of nowhere. You should think about that. Anything could happen here and—"

"Nothing will," Cat interrupted. "Do you want to bet on how long it takes for the cops to get here? We're less than five miles from Baker City. And it won't do your bank any good when I get a restraining order against you for sexual harassment. And if you think threatening me will win points, Mr. MacGillicudy, think again."

"I'm not threatening you." He held up both hands and backed away. "No need to get hysterical. I'm just saying you could have a better place closer to town."

"I don't think so." She watched him turn and hustle back to his car.

Moments later, he was driving toward the highway. She sighed, shook her head and tucked the cell phone back into her shirt pocket. She backed up and leaned against the round pen fence, grateful when her knees stopped quivering.

Sophie rode over on Stormy. "Who was that, Mommy?"

"No one important." Cat wasn't going to tell the girls anything that might frighten them. "He's a stranger who came to the wrong place."

"Okay, but Mister Robbie says he had your back." Sophie tilted her head. "What does that mean, Mommy? I didn't see him touch you. He just stood behind you."

"Well, thank him for me," Cat said. "And that's what 'having my back' means. Your imaginary friend was there to help if I needed him."

"Good." Sophie turned her pony and rode back to join her sister.

Cat drew in a deep breath of the cool September air and watched her daughters ride for a few minutes. Then she took out her cell phone again. She'd call Ed Williams and ask about Herman MacGillicudy. That way she'd know if there was any validity to the banker's story. "This is my home and I'm not going anywhere," she said aloud.

"We'll have to work on that," came a deep voice, "but I'd rather put up with you than a wanna-be land developer."

"Terrific," Cat retorted. "It's good to know the voice in my head is willing to let me stay."

CHAPTER EIGHT

The next morning, they headed into Baker City for breakfast before going to Sunday services. The café was on the opposite side of the street from the church so Cat parked on the street this time. She locked the rig, then guided the girls toward the small restaurant. The sign in the window read "Open" but when they stepped inside, it turned out they had the place to themselves. A spry balding man holding a stack of menus came to greet them. Cat smiled politely. "Good morning."

"Breakfast for three?" He ushered them toward a booth on the left-hand wall. "Does this one work for you folks?"

Sophie shook her head. "No, sir. That family already has it."

Cat sighed, eyeing the empty seats before she looked at the twins. "Girls, there's a time and a place for your imaginations."

"Tell you what, ma'am," the elderly man said, "we'll let the kids find the right place for you." He winked at Sophie. "Sometimes, I think I have company even when I can't see it."

"Because you do." Samantha led the way to a different booth. "We like this one and nobody else has it."

"All right. Now, how about some coffee?"

"I'd love some," Cat said. "And apple juice for the twins."

"And crayons and picture menus." He grinned at them. "I'm Pop MacGillicudy. I'm glad you're here."

Cat frowned. "Any relation to Herman MacGillicudy?"

"Oh sure, but I don't admit it in polite company." Pop waited while they slid into the booth and put a menu in front of Cat. "Yours has words." He winked at her. "You must be the folks who won the dude ranch. Reverend Tommy told me about you. It'll be good to have it back in operation. Brought a lot of business to town along with the tourists who used to come for the skiing and winter sports."

Cat relaxed as Pop carefully placed kids' menus in front of her daughters and handed each of them a new carton of crayons to draw pictures on their placemats. His face crinkled like a brown paper sack, wrinkled with the memories of past smiles. She liked him immediately.

"So, how are things going out there?" Pop headed for the counter and came back with a china cup in one hand, the coffee pot in the other. "Got everything you need?"

"Well, we could use a few more extensions for the landline." Cat opened her menu. "But I keep hearing that Baker City isn't a high priority and neither is having more phones in the house. Oh well, running to the living room keeps me from having to find a gym."

Pop filled the mug in front of her and returned the coffee pot to the warmer. He brought over two small glasses of apple juice and gave one to each of the girls. Then he ambled back to the counter and reached under it to pull out his telephone. He dialed a number and waited. "Is Ted there?"

Some answer must have come because after a few moments, Pop continued. "It's me. You know that gal who won the dude ranch has kids? Little ones? Reckon you all leave her without enough phones much longer and we'll be seeing how big a fit Chief O'Connell can throw when he gets back from his vacation tomorrow."

Cat stared at the old man as he hung up and put the phone back under the counter. "What just happened?"

Pop pulled an order pad out of his apron pocket. "You'll have your phone this afternoon, missy. Herman may think he's a giant frog in this puddle, but if you can't get the cops when you need one, the police chief won't be happy. And the O'Connells run the volunteer fire department too, so they're more concerned about keeping everybody safe than stroking egos."

"Well, thank you." Amazed by the result of what she'd considered a casual comment, Cat glanced at the menu and found her favorite western omelet, then looked at the twins. "Do you know what you'd like?"

"Pancakes with whipped cream faces," Sophie said.

Samantha nodded firm agreement, pointing to the picture on her menu. "They have strawberry eyes."

"That looks awesome," Cat said. "And maybe some scrambled eggs too?"

"Okay," Sophie agreed. "And more apple juice? Mommy, can you make juice from our apples?"

"That's a good idea," Cat said. "Let's try it at dinner time."

While she sipped her coffee, she found herself thinking about the phone issue again. It still amazed her that having more than one extension in the house was a harassment issue rather than simple bureaucracy. She'd just figured it would take time for the telecommunications company to fit her into their undoubtedly busy schedule. It had never occurred to her that someone meant to stop her from starting up her business. So, what other tricks did Herman MacGillicudy have up his sleeve? Perhaps, she was just suspicious by nature, but nobody else hassled her. Everyone she'd met in town had been friendly.

She gave their order to Pop and he headed for the kitchen. The bell jangled as the door opened and a plump brown-haired woman hurried inside. She nodded and smiled. "Good morning. Need more coffee?"

"No, I'm fine," Cat said.

Another friendly smile and the middle-aged woman went around the counter and into the kitchen. A low-voiced discussion and then Pop came back out to work the restaurant. He came over and topped the coffee in Cat's cup. "My daughter just got here and she's a much better cook than I am." He winked at the twins. "And she does a wonderful job with the whipped cream too."

The comment prompted giggles from Sophie, but Samantha continued her drawing. The café slowly filled up with other early morning customers. Silence fell when a tall man with a shock of tawny blond hair stepped inside. He shot a quick glance at Cat, then strode toward her and the twins. Cat judged him to be about her age or a little older, maybe in his early thirties. Now, what was his problem?

As he drew closer, his first reaction changed. He stopped and stared. "You're not—"

"Who?" Sophie asked curiously. "Who are we s'posed to be?"

"His fiancée," Pop said, making the rounds with the coffee. "Of course, since she's back in Afghanistan, that would be a bit hard, don't you think, Hawke?"

The comment earned the old man a dark-blue glare. "She's not in the Army anymore."

"You sure about that, Durango?" The question came from a young man sitting on a stool at the counter. "Heather said the recruiters kept calling and offering more money for her to go."

As Cat listened, the regular customers continued to tease Durango unmercifully. Clearly a good sport, he went along with the badgering, sitting at the counter and ordering a meal.

Meanwhile, Pop arrived with their food. After the girls oohed and aahed over their pancakes, they happily cut into them. Cat spread jam on her sourdough toast and bit into the slice.

Halfway through the meal, the bell rang as the door opened again and Herman MacGillicudy stomped inside. He made a beeline for the counter. "I've been looking for you, Hawke."

"Well, you found me, Herman." Durango picked up his coffee cup, took a swallow. "What do you need?"

"I know what you did. You stole the McElroy farm." Herman stormed toward the younger man. "Who the hell do you think you are?"

"The guy who's telling you to watch your potty mouth in public." Durango slowly lowered his cup to the counter. "There are folks here with their kids."

Pop approached the two men, keeping the counter between them. "Durango, what's this about the McElroy place?"

"Fenn didn't make it home," Durango said, "and he was supposed to inherit. The farm went to Heather when the trust ended and there's been no money to pay the property taxes." He shrugged one broad shoulder. "It's just money so I stepped up."

"And what happens when Heather comes home," an elderly woman asked from the far corner. "Do you give it back?"

"Yes, Mrs. Sweeney. It's her place."

That was obviously the answer people wanted to hear, Cat thought, watching as they returned to their meals and conversations. She had to admit that hearing a guy say he'd stepped up and looked after what belonged to his fiancée seemed new and different, but maybe being married to Frazer had lowered her expectations.

"I don't believe you, Durango Hawke," Herman snapped. "You paid four years of taxes to keep the place from being auctioned off and you're giving it to a woman? No way, you're that sentimental. It belongs to her family. And the McElroys are related to us."

Durango eased off the stool and took a step forward. "You calling me a liar, MacGillicudy?"

"Take it outside, boys." Pop hustled forward. "Take it outside. No fighting in here."

"I pay for my fun, Pop." Durango sauntered toward the banker who backed away. "If I break something with Herman's body, I'll cover it."

Laughter erupted as Herman scuttled out of the restaurant. Durango turned around, returned to the counter and his meal. "He's just mad because he intended to get the place instead of me."

"And then he'd plow it up for the gravel," Pop said. "Good thing you're looking after it. Now come meet Heather's cousin. She won the essay contest and will be reopening the dude ranch outside of town. You need to get those boundary fences in order and the trails so she can do overnights and such for the tourists."

Cat blinked as the two men approached her. "What cousin? As far as I know, I don't have any relatives living here."

"You're wrong about that," Pop said. "Reverend Tommy told me that your dad was an O'Leary, and the O'Leary girls have been marrying McElroy and Sweeney boys forever."

"And vicey-versy," old Mrs. Sweeney called from the back booth. "Rose was engaged to Rob Williams. The wedding was scheduled for the month after he came home from Vietnam."

"But, he didn't," Pop said. "And she left town. Years later, she married that nice McTavish boy from Georgia."

When Cat and the twins entered the church a short time later, her head was still reeling from Pop MacGillicudy's revelations. She'd never heard that she had any relatives. It wasn't something her father or mother had ever mentioned. Why not? She'd ask the next time she saw one of them. Why was it such a big secret? Why didn't her father want her to know she had cousins in Baker City?

There were a few more people in the pews than last week and partway through the service, Reverend Thompson encouraged the children to leave with Ginger Madison for their Sunday school class.

Samantha passed over her picture from the restaurant and Cat tucked the placemat neatly beneath her purse. Then the twins skipped off, happily joining other youngsters about their own age.

Cat listened to the sermon about having faith in all humanity and wondered if it applied to someone like Herman MacGillicudy. She decided that it probably did, although personally she didn't like the guy. Good thing she wasn't in charge of the universe.

Afterwards, she and the girls headed for the reception area and joined in the gathering. Virginia Thompson, the pastor's wife, came to join them at their table and thanked Cat again for the fruit she'd donated to the food bank.

"So, how is your weekend going?" Virginia asked, after the girls headed off to play with some of the other children. "Been busy?"

"A bit." Cat hesitated, then added. "I never knew that I still had family here in Baker City, other than my aunt and she doesn't live in Washington State anymore. Pop MacGillicudy told me that I have cousins."

"More than that," Virginia said. "The youngest of seven kids, your father has two brothers and one sister who never left town. They're still alive and they have kids. That wasn't all. In spite of the name, Baker City isn't that big. It was started by seven boys who met on the ship from Ireland during the height of the Potato Famine. They stuck together. Eventually, they emigrated here with their families in the late 1870s."

"I already met another MacGillicudy besides Pop," Cat said. "I guess Durango Hawke lives next door to the dude ranch."

"Durango isn't part of the town, not really." Virginia added cream to her coffee and stirred. "He's what we call a flat-lander from Everett.

He's always had an on-again, off-again engagement to Heather McElroy and she's your real neighbor. She's local even if nobody's 100 percent sure where she is right now. She and Durango had a big fight and she left the area, but she'll be back. It may take a while, but our folks always come home."

"So, who else is local?" Cat asked, watching her twins play with three other girls about their own age and one little dark-haired princess in a red velvet dress. "Besides, the O'Learys, the MacGillicudys and the McElroys."

"The Sweeneys, the O'Connells, the Garveys, the O'Neills and the O'Sullivans. The MacGillicudys are Scots-Irish and they didn't get here until the 1940s, so they don't count for much to some of the folks who live here."

"Definite newcomers," Cat teased, enjoying the small-town attitude.

"You know it."

"So, what about the Thompsons?" Cat asked. "Where do you come in?"

"I was a Fenwick before I married Tom," Virginia said. "We come in on the Sweeney side and the O'Sullivans. The first Sweeney hated being tied down and living in town so he headed into the hills with his Native American wife. That didn't stop their kids from marrying into the other families or bringing their new husbands and wives here. Everybody's related somehow, but nobody's too fond of some of the folks in the MacGillicudy clan."

"Why not?" Cat could guess.

"The first one stole cars, horses and cattle. A swindler and con artist," Virginia said. "He ripped off folks left, right and center. Herman's a throwback."

Cat tried not to laugh. She didn't like the banker, but the poor guy had a tough row to hoe if everybody still blamed him for things his ancestor did over eighty years before. "He offered cash for the dude ranch, but I told him it's not for sale. Even if keeping it for ten years wasn't a condition of the essay contest, I'd never leave it. I've loved the place since I was a kid and as the twins say, it's my 'forever' home."

"That's what I like to hear." Virginia finished her coffee. "Guess I'd better mingle. Tom's giving me that look."

"And I'd better round up the girls," Cat said. "Pop's arranged for me to get a few more extensions for the landline this afternoon, so we need to head home. I want to have my desktop computer hooked up so I can start putting together an advertising campaign for the dude ranch tonight."

Virginia might seem like a realist, but Cat sensed it was better not to let her know this was still a work day. And by keeping hourly status reports, Cat could let the respective owners know exactly what she'd taught their horses. The reports made it much easier to send out the invoices at the end of the month.

Cat smiled politely as she approached the children and saw Ginger Madison talking to the little princess. In her mid-fifties, Ginger was still slender in ironed jeans, a crisp western blouse and laced-up cowgirl boots. Her blonde hair came from the bottle now and didn't show a hint of gray.

"Hello, Mrs. Madison," Cat said. "How are you? Have you heard anything from Ann lately? How's she doing?"

"Angelique's fine. Thanks for asking." Ginger's own professional smile didn't touch her hazel eyes. "You're the woman training her horse, right?"

"Yes. He's coming along. Did you want to stop over and see him?" Cat asked. "We're heading home now, and we'll be there the rest of the day."

"I don't think so." Ginger took the little girl's hand. "But I'll tell Frank to swing by and take a look. He's the one who insisted on training the brute instead of putting him down."

Cat winced. She hated it when people talked about killing animals in front of children, especially when her own kids were obviously within earshot. Coming closer, Samantha stared at the older woman as if she'd seen a monster, instead of her Sunday school teacher.

"We feed Sky carrots all the time," Samantha said. "And he's not so scared anymore."

"But our saddles don't fit him," Sophie added, "so we can't ride him yet."

Cat rested a hand on each girl's shoulder and started them toward the door before the malarkey got any deeper in the church reception hall. There was no way she'd let them ride the flashy bay gelding, but she sure as sugar wasn't saying that. As they left the building, she asked, "Did you girls enjoy your Sunday school class?"

"Not really," Sophie said. "It's not much fun when the teacher has favorites. And Devon didn't like us so we didn't get to do any of the reading game."

"Maybe they do the reading game differently here," Cat said.

"Can we stay with you next time, Mommy?" Samantha asked. "We'll be good."

"Sure, you can." Cat paused long enough to hug her daughters. "I'm sorry the class wasn't much fun."

"It's not your fault," Sophie said, skipping beside her as they started toward the pickup again. "Maybe, Reverend Tommy could start another class, one for big kids."

Cat bit back an appreciative smile, amused at the notion that her daughters considered themselves 'big' girls. "We'll ask him."

CHAPTER NINE

Six feet away from the Ford, she froze. The truck squatted on four tire rims. What the—?

Her mouth dropped open as she stared at the rig. Someone had punched holes in each tire. She spotted the huge screwdriver hanging in the sidewall of the left rear one. Shocked, she felt a lump rise in her throat.

Who would do such a thing? Why vandalize her pickup? How was she supposed to get home? More important, how could she fix this when there wasn't a garage or mechanic in Baker City, let alone one open on a Sunday afternoon? And there was nobody she could call for a rescue.

She took a deep breath. Okay, she could cope. She had towing on her insurance policy. She'd return to the church, borrow a phone book and call the garage in Lake Maynard since her cell phone barely worked here in Baker City. They'd come get the Ford 150 and take it to the tire store thirty miles away. And she'd arrange for a rental car to provide transportation for the next few days. "Come on, girls. We're broke down. Let's go back inside for a few minutes."

Sophie tilted her head to one side and eyed the pickup speculatively. "Mommy, who broke our truck?"

"I don't know, sweetie," Cat said, shaking her head, "but we'll get it fixed."

Inside, she seated the girls at one of the tables and got each of them a carton of milk and a doughnut before she hunted down Reverend Thompson. He led her to his office and dug out a small gray pamphlet. The cover read "2007 Baker City Directory."

Cat blinked. "It's old."

"So's the town," Reverend Thompson said. "What are you looking for?"

"A tow truck," Cat said. "Somebody stuck a screwdriver into all the tires on my pickup. I need the rig taken to Lake Maynard."

"Sounds like someone is trying to 'nickel and dime' you to death," Reverend Thompson said. "Who's out to cost you money?"

"Nickel and dime? What does that mean?"

"It's when someone wants to hassle you, but not cost you more than your deductible," Reverend Thompson explained. "Your insurance company won't cover new tires because they'll be less than what your share is."

"Actually, I don't have vandalism on my insurance," Cat said. "It'd cost way more than what my truck is worth. So, I carry the minimum."

"Who doesn't in this economy?" Reverend Thompson ran a hand through his thinning silver hair. "Are you stuck on having a tow truck? Or can I have one of the loggers take it to the Tire Factory store in Lake Maynard? It'd only cost you gas money and they're bound to have some discount tires."

"That works," Cat said, "but how do I get home today? And it has to be soon. Pop arranged for me to have more phone extensions installed this afternoon."

"That's easy. I'll call Ted Fenwick and ask him to take you when he heads that way," Reverend Thompson said. "Why don't you pop over to the feed store and see if Summer will pick up your girls in the morning? She's scheduled to drive the rest of the munchkins to Lake Maynard tomorrow."

Cat bit her lip, hard enough to distract her from the tears that wanted to fall. She'd nearly said that this place was beginning to feel more and more like the home she'd never had. Since her grandparents passed away, nobody ever tried to help her. And now, the town preacher stepped up and offered solutions she hadn't even requested. "All right. Thank you."

"No worries." He patted her shoulder as if she was the same age as the twins. "It's what we're put on this planet for, Cat. I help you and then when you see someone who needs it, you pay it forward. Right?"

She nodded. "Right. Thanks, Reverend Thompson."

"Tommy." He swung around and headed for the phone on his desk. "Reverend Thompson was my dad. I'm Reverend Tommy."

"Good to know," Cat said.

The twins were happy to stay with Virginia and Cat seized the opportunity to stroll down the street and talk to Summer at the feed-store. She waited while the woman rang up a sale, then helped load three sacks of chicken mash.

"So, what's up?" Summer asked, slipping off her gloves and tucking them back into her belt, leading the way from the barn back to the front reception area. "I didn't even know you were in town."

"We came for breakfast at the café and church services," Cat said.

Summer wrinkled her nose. "Do I get burned at the stake if I say, eww?"

"Of course not." Cat laughed and lounged against the counter. "But you have to promise not to tell anyone that I only go because I want to meet people and get known in the community."

"That's probably a smart move." Summer poured two cups of coffee and passed a mug to Cat. "I have to warn you that gossip is a mainstay around here and I'm still catching hell for not marrying my kids' dad."

Cat blinked and sipped the strong coffee. "Where are your kids? I didn't see them here."

"My handy-man took them fishing," Summer said. "It's our Sunday tradition. I work and they play. When they get back, I grill the fish for supper. If they didn't catch anything, we go to the café for dinner. Then, if any of the O'Neills are around, Pop runs interference when they stick their noses in my business."

"That seems to be his thing," Cat said. "He told me I have relatives. I didn't know that so now I'll be looking for them."

"Really? Who are you related to? If you say you're an O'Neill, I'll try to be nice."

"Don't strain yourself," Cat teased. "All I'm certain of is that my dad is an O'Leary and he had more than the one sister I do know."

"That makes us cousins if we go back a ways," Summer said. "Got any questions about me?"

"Yeah, I guess. One, how old are your kids and the next is can you drive mine to school tomorrow? Somebody flattened my tires so I'll be without a rig for a few days."

"What the hell?" Summer narrowed her gaze and frowned. "Who did you piss off?"

"I don't know," Cat said, "but I have a feeling that things may get worse when I insist on staying."

Summer nodded slowly. "You may be right. I had my share of troubles when I bought this place from my aunt after my uncle passed. And it wasn't just about my family having issues with me being a single mom. They wanted the money Herman offered for the store."

"He's a banker." Cat glanced around the large room. Shelves filled with horse brushes, saddle pads and blankets, animal medicines, electric fence supplies, dog and cat toys lined the walls. "How on earth could he run it?"

"Oh, he has enough shirttail relations to put in one as a manager," Summer said, shaking back her long brown hair. "But he wouldn't have. He'd have shut the place down. He's closed all the businesses he's bought over the years. He's one of the reasons Baker City is a ghost town."

"Really?" Cat remembered the way the twins had chosen a different booth in the café that morning. "What are some of the others?"

Summer frowned, then asked. "Didn't your family share stories about this place?"

"My aunt only said she loved the dude ranch," Cat said. "She brought me to visit each summer for about five years. Whenever, my dad didn't approve of something she'd done, he wouldn't let me see her and my mom was the same way. Of course, it didn't help that Aunt Rose had issues with the way that the two of them had revolving wives and husbands. Every time my mom remarried, she demanded I use her new husband's last name and when I visited my dad, he'd insist I was an O'Leary. Both my folks were pissed when I turned eighteen and legally changed my name to McTavish, the same as Aunt Rose's."

"Gotta love the family drama." Summer sighed and then led the way out to the front parking lot. She pointed to the end of the main street and the mountains that rose behind it, gesturing to the highest peak. "That's Mount Carmody. Back in 1910, we had a harsh winter. The snow was ten feet deep and it didn't stop. On one particular day, a foot of snow fell each hour and it lasted into the night. A couple days later, it suddenly warmed up, began to rain and the avalanches started."

"How many avalanches?"

"Two that hit the town. They wiped out the train station, the hotel, the school, three shops and five homes. Sixty people died. It took months to dig out all the bodies. They're buried in the cemetery behind the church."

Cat struggled to remember if she'd heard about the avalanches before. A dim memory surfaced of her grandmother talking about different relatives. Had she ever mentioned the catastrophe? It would have happened long before she was born, but wouldn't someone in her immediate family have said something or told some kind of story?

Maybe not. Cat grimaced. She probably had to stop avoiding her father long enough to learn what he knew. "So, what does the history have to do with the town?"

"It's almost like the place still struggles to recover," Summer said, "even though it's been a few generations. Everything has been rebuilt, but nobody really forgets those who died although it's been more than a century. A lot of the old-timers claim the town is haunted and that's why we have a tough time making ends meet."

"Couldn't it just be the recession?" Cat asked. "Tourism has been on a downward spiral for years in a lot of places. People aren't spending as much. That's why I think reopening the dude ranch is such a wonderful idea."

"How do you figure?" Summer leaned against the hitch-rail in front of her store. "Didn't you just say folks are spending less on vacations?"

"Yes, but they won't have to fly or drive more than two hours from

Seattle to come to the ranch. If the costs are affordable, they'll love visiting it the way I did when I was a kid. Or if a family resort doesn't work, I could put together a resident camp for children."

Summer smiled. "And that's why I want to see you at the business association meeting on Tuesday. We need new blood. Otherwise, we forget to stay positive. There are enough negative people in the world. We don't need to join them."

"If my truck isn't fixed by that time, you'll have to pick me up," Cat said.

"I can do that."

After they finished making the arrangements for taking the twins to school the next morning, Cat returned to the church. She found the girls helping Virginia tidy the reception area. A bearded young man in jeans and a Huskies t-shirt ferried dishes to the small kitchenette. He greeted Cat with a friendly nod.

"Cat, this is Ted Fenwick," Virginia said as she finished wiping down a table. "Ted, this is Cat McTavish."

"So, I'm running you home, installing some phones, coming back to take your truck to Lake Maynard and then passing the word to the local malcontents to leave your rig alone, right?" Ted said as he finished loading the dishwasher.

Cat blinked. "Sounds like it. Who are the malcontents?"

"Pretty much the younger generation looking for an easy buck or two. Herman pays them for doing his dirty work."

"Now, Ted." Virginia shook a finger at him. "There isn't any proof of that."

"And that's why we know she and Reverend Tommy are a great team," Ted said with another smile. "They believe the best of everyone."

Rob heard the sound of a truck rumbling over the gravel in the driveway and went to see who it was. It wasn't Cat's rig. He knew the sound of its engine. As he watched, the girls and Cat climbed out, accompanied by a fellow toting a toolbox. Now, who was this guy and what was he doing here?

Sophie ran in first. "Hi, Mister Robbie. Our truck got broke at church." She dropped to her knees to hug the puppy. "And Mr. Ted brought us home and he's going to give us more phones. Mommy said."

"What happened to your mom's truck?" Rob asked. "Did it break down?"

"No." Samantha followed her sister into the living room, kicking off her shoes. "Someone hurt all the tires, so it has to have new ones."

"I see." Once again, he wished he could make their mother see and talk to him. There might not be much a ghost could do when she was in town and he was at home, but that could change. Like the girls had told him before, there were a lot of folks in Baker City who were like him, still hanging around long after their bodies were dead. If he asked one of the other ghosts, he would learn what happened to Cat's rig. She had enough troubles; she didn't need anybody harassing her.

"Have you girls taken Lad outside for a break?" Cat stood just inside the living room door.

"No, we were telling Mister Robbie about our truck," Samantha said. "We'll go now. Come on, Laddie."

"He says he'll be a guard dog when he's big and he needs to practice," Sophie said.

The growing collie wagged his tail and gave a friendly grin, then woofed at the stranger. It was a half-hearted attempt to sound brave.

Rob laughed. He'd never met anything less like a watchdog. "Go on, girls. I'll stick around."

Cat leaned down to pet the pup on his way out. "After he has a quick run outside, he can come back and practice being watchful. Ted, why don't you start in the den? Then, we'll hit the rest of the downstairs."

Rob glanced at the brown-haired man who was barely in his twenties. If he was a man grown, he wouldn't be trying to grow extra fuzz on his face. He had to be one of the Fenwicks. They had always worked in communications even when Rob was alive.

Whistling, Ted began looking around the room. He crossed to the far-right wall. "How many extensions do you want?"

"Several," Cat said. "The kitchen, the dining room, my bedroom, the den."

"Don't forget to check the upstairs," Rob advised. "If you get the bed and breakfast up and running again, the folks who come to stay here will want phones, and they can't always call out on their fancy pocket ones."

Did either of them hear him? Or would she pretend he still wasn't around? The boy was from the town. How much did he know?

The boy, Ted, had dropped to one knee and was unscrewing the cover on a phone jack. He looked up. "If you rent the upstairs rooms, you'll want extensions up there. We don't have many cell towers up here in the foothills and it can be hard to get a signal. You've probably found that out the hard way in town."

"I'd forgotten that guests actually stayed in this house with the Williams family," Cat admitted. "When I was a kid, Aunt Rose always arranged for us to have a cabin. It amazes me that the place is so big. Three full floors—it's almost a mansion."

"The first Williams was a timber baron," Ted said. "He wanted his mail-order bride to feel that her home was as good as the fancy ones back east. If you talk to Pop, he could tell you stories about the history of the farm."

"Either that or you could listen to me if you stick around and I'll tell you," Rob said. "They're my family."

At nine that night, the girls were sound asleep, and Cat finally had some time for herself. She checked the temperature of the water flowing into the tub. Nice and hot, so she added some of the girls' bubble bath. After the week she'd had she was ready for a nice long soak. She had a cup of chamomile tea and a new Dana Stabenow murder mystery. What could be better?

She coiled her hair into a bun and pinned it into place. She turned off the water. Oh yes, it was time to slide into the tub. She unsnapped her western shirt and slid it off her shoulders. Unfastening the front closure of her bra, it hit the floor next.

Just then, one of the bulbs flickered. And the lights went out.

"What the hell?" she said aloud, annoyed.

"We're both awake and I'm just doing my job, haunting you."

This time she *knew* she heard a man's voice. In her bathroom? "No way I'm putting up with this. I don't believe in ghosts," she snapped.

Cat wrapped a bath towel around her. She was the only one in the room. She'd locked up the house before she came in and ran a bath. The twins were sound asleep. *How* could a man *be* in here?

She flipped on and off the lights, then on again. She looked around. She was alone.

"Who are you?" Cat demanded, looking around the room again. "What are you? Where are you?"

"I'm right here, but I can be hard to see sometimes."

Cat glared. She clutched the towel tighter. With her free hand, she groped for the bottle of bath salts on the vanity. She couldn't throw things at a man she didn't see. "I don't believe in ghosts. There's no such thing."

"Keep talking and you're liable to prove you're prettier than you are smart."

"Show yourself, right now, you arrogant piece of—"

"Now, now. I do better in the dark."

The overhead bulb flickered again, went out. The only illumination in the room was the night light.

Suddenly, she saw something. *A man?*

At least, it looked like one. He was an insubstantial silhouette of broad shoulders, wide chest, narrow hips and long legs. How on earth did he do it? With a projector? Computer generated?

No, it couldn't be.

A ghost? A real ghost?

She could see the cedar panels of the wall through his body. He had to be a ghost.

"Who are you?" Cat asked, struggling to keep her voice calm.

"Robert Jacob Williams. Most folks call me Rob or Robbie."

"Mister Robbie." Cat gripped the towel more tightly. "My girls. They saw you."

"The day you moved in and they told you I was here, but you claimed not to believe them."

"If you hurt them, I'll—"

"What? Kill me? Too late. I've been dead longer than you've been alive." He grinned at her. "I'll admit I told them that you folks couldn't stay here, but they didn't take me serious. They laughed at me."

"Well, what are you doing here? You must have a reason."

"It's my home. Where else would I be?"

"I don't know. Wasn't there a white light or a door or something? Shouldn't you be in Heaven? Or…"

"Hell?" He shrugged. "I wanted to come home after I got killed at Hamburger Hill. I wasn't ready to die. I've been here ever since. I'm not leaving."

"Oh yes, you are. I won the place in an essay contest and I'm not having a man float around here. I'm in the middle of a divorce and my ex doesn't need the ammunition. Pack your ghostly bags and hit the road."

"You said I could stay." He winked at her. "You already told your daughters. If I tell them that you kicked me out, they'll figure you broke a promise and their feelings will be hurt."

She caught her breath. "Don't even try to start with me. I won't take it. No man's worth the powder it'd take to blow him to hell, not even a dead one."

"What a wildcat." He laughed. "And like I said before you don't know any *real* men. If you did, you wouldn't challenge me."

She stamped her foot, before she remembered she was standing in a bathroom with a towel around her chest. "Get out. We'll talk later. *After* my bath, not during. This is my home and we're not going anywhere, but you are."

"I wouldn't gamble too much on that card."

She adjusted the towel, then pointed with her free hand to the door. "Out. In case nobody has ever told you that it's inappropriate to interrupt a woman's privacy, I'm telling you now. Scat, Mister Robbie. I want to take my bath before the water gets cold."

He stared at her for a moment longer, then headed for the door. "All right, but don't ignore me anymore. It's annoying, especially when I know that you can see and hear me."

"I'll think about it."

Chuckling, he floated through the wall. "Take your time. I'll still be here."

CHAPTER TEN

She waited for a few seconds to make sure he was gone before she drew a deep breath.

He was real. And what was she going to do about him? She didn't know.

Keeping a wary eye out, she peeled off her jeans, panties and socks. So far, so good. He apparently intended to keep his word and leave her in peace.

What was she going to do? If she told the people in town that there was a ghost in her house, they'd think she was absolutely nuts. She had to keep him a secret.

Back to the original question. *How do I evict a ghost?*

No ideas came to mind. She sank into the perfumed bubbles. Much to her amazement, the water was still hot.

The encounter with Mister Robbie as the twins called him hadn't taken long. Had it really happened? Cat pinched herself. Ouch. She felt that, so she had to be awake. Her chat with him hadn't been a dream.

The ranch was haunted. No wonder the Williams had opted for an essay contest to find a new owner for the place. Who would put up with a ghost in these days of hundred-page real estate contracts? She was willing to bet most buyers wouldn't take the farm if they knew

Mister Robbie was part of the package. Even if they claimed not to believe in ghosts at first.

She leaned back in the tub. How had she managed to argue with him? Where did the courage come from? If anyone had ever told her that she'd confront a ghost, she'd have known better. She would have sworn she was the type to run from spooks, not carry on conversations with them. But it wasn't as if she had a lot of choices.

She didn't have anywhere to take the twins or Lad or the horses. She couldn't even pack up the truck since it was in Lake Maynard waiting for new tires. Thanks to Ted Fenwick, she had plenty of phones in the house. She could call and ask Peg to come get her, the kids and the critters.

What was the point? None whatsoever.

She had a deal to restore the ranch to its former glory and leaving wasn't an option. And if she insisted there was a ghost on the ranch, it would make her look as if she were crazy. Frazer didn't want custody, but he'd fight for it if it meant she'd have to consider reconciliation and suspend the divorce proceedings.

Nope, not going there. She was a convenience, nothing more to her soon-to-be ex-husband. He lied and cheated, but he liked having her to pay for his peccadillos. It meant none of his girlfriends could insist on marriage. And she planned to continue avoiding him until the divorce was final.

Men! You can't live with them and you can't just shoot them.

She still hadn't come to any decisions when she climbed out of the tub an hour later, the water tepid by then. She toweled off and put on a flannel nightgown, following it with her green fleece bathrobe. Okay, so she didn't look glamorous, but she lived in the Cascade foothills. She couldn't sleep if she was freezing.

On her way to the master bedroom, she paused to check on the twins. They were sound asleep in their bunkbeds, worn out by their activities on the ranch. Cat covered Samantha with her patchwork quilt, then bent to pick up Sophie's teddy bear off the floor and tucked it back under the covers. Where was their puppy? Lad usually slept by the girls when he didn't climb onto the lower bunk.

She found him in her room, a golden lump of fur beside the queen-sized bed. He wasn't the only inhabitant of the room. Sitting in the rocking chair in the far corner, Rob waited for her, a pile of logging chains at his feet.

She stopped. For the first time she could see him, really see him. Thick black hair curled around strongly carved features. He wasn't a pretty boy, more the brawny type. Heavy brows and long lashes framed coal black eyes. High cheekbones, a wide mouth, and a fierce line to his jaw that reminded her of someone, but she didn't recall who at the moment.

He was a hunk. Of course, he was. Why would she have a ghost who wasn't?

She laughed and the sound awakened the pup. She leaned down to pet him when he wagged his plumed tail. "Goodnight, Mister Robbie."

"Rob."

"Fine. Goodnight, Rob. You're not sharing my room. The door's that way."

"Now that you can see me, I'm going to haunt you tonight."

She shook her head and pointed to the doorway again. "No, you're not. I have a full list of work tomorrow and I need my sleep. If you get up in the morning, you can haunt me while I feed horses, muck stalls, train and start clearing out the upstairs so I can rent those rooms to college students like Ted suggested. And you can use your "ghostly energy" in a positive way."

"I never ran from a woman or a fight when I was alive."

"You may as well start now that you're dead. You won't win with me."

"Want to bet?"

Hours later, the scent of lime pervaded her sleep. She sighed and tried to slip deeper in the covers, then felt a teasing kiss trail across her forehead. "Come on, kitten. You know you want me."

"No, Frazer. I'm not going with you to New Orleans."

"Then stay with me." A kiss whispered across her lips.

Dimly she was aware of his long lean body lying next to her, but he didn't touch her, not really. Except for his mouth that teased and tormented hers in a series of soft kisses. She should be fighting him. He'd been cheating on her again, probably with another dealer at the casino. She turned her head for a moment and muttered, "I'm staying here to train horses."

He didn't answer, just kissed her again. She felt him shift as if he intended to leave and surrendered. She threaded her hands in his thick hair and brought his lips back to hers. This time the kiss grew hotter. His tongue slipped into her mouth, enticing hers into a duel that only lasted a heartbeat. She moaned when he unbuttoned the top of her nightgown. His hand slid inside to cup her breast.

Every move was so slow, so gentle—so calculated, but it didn't matter. If he'd rushed, she could have fought him. Instead, she pressed closer. His lips trailed down her neck, across her collarbone toward her breast. She caught her breath, waiting almost forever for him to find her nipple.

But, he didn't. He faded away. "Next time, sweetheart."

She reached for him. Gone. He was always gone when she needed him.

Cat opened her eyes, looked around the empty room. All that remained was the scent of lime and his deep, dark voice singing, *"I beg your pardon. I never promised you a rose garden—"*

Fragments of the dream lingered in her mind the next morning as she dressed. She'd been so busy on the ranch she barely thought of Frazer, much less missed him. And she didn't want him now. She was through with men. She had a ranch to restore, but right now she needed coffee.

She headed into the kitchen, plugged in the pot to brew. Lad ambled into the room to greet her. She petted the collie. "Come on. Let's go feed the horses," she told the pup. "Keeping me company is one of your jobs too."

The aroma of fresh coffee greeted her when she returned to the house. She poured a mug and went to wake the twins. Once they were stirring, it would be time to start breakfast and pack lunches. She glanced at the clock. It was barely seven and Summer wouldn't be here to take the girls to school for at least an hour. There was time for the twins' favorite French toast.

Sophie was the first to reach the kitchen, still in pony print pajamas. "Mommy, we did all our homework on Friday. Can we watch cartoons before school today?"

"We'll see." Cat cracked eggs into a shallow bowl. "What do you want to wear today?"

"Samantha says jeans and sweaters so we can play on the monkey bars at recess."

"Well, that makes perfect sense." Cat stirred milk into the batter. "Why don't you two watch cartoons now while I finish making breakfast?"

"Okay." Sophie spun around, then spun back, looking up. "Is it all right with you if we watch your TV now, Mister Robbie?"

"Since your mommy said you could, that makes it all right."

Cat glanced over her shoulder, waiting until the twins left the room. She wasn't quite ready to tell them that she could see their invisible friend too. She still wasn't ready to believe that the house came with a ghost, especially a drop-dead gorgeous one. That now, she had to admit she could hear and see.

In the autumn sunlight streaming through the windows, she saw Mister Robbie's faint image in an Army uniform, his harshly sculpted features, broad shoulders, wide chest, narrow waist and long legs, pants tucked into fancy combat boots. Of course, she also looked right through him and saw the pine countertop, but what guy had everything? Besides, it wasn't like she saw all that much last night.

"So, the dead have finally risen," she said. "Were you born lazy or did you just get that way after you died?"

Rob lingered by the coffee-pot, obviously assessing the brew. "I always heard the prettier the gal, the worse the java. Yours looks like tea."

"Pour yourself a cup before you condemn it." Cat sprinkled in cinnamon, added a dash of vanilla to the mixture in the bowl. "Or do you need a woman to do that for you too?"

He chuckled. "Spitfire. So, what are your plans today?"

"Horse training, mucking the barn, cutting down that dead apple tree at the edge of the orchard before it falls and hurts someone, weed-eating the orchard and trimming the rosebushes so I can take flowers to the cemetery in town." She slid the first two slices of egg-dipped bread onto the griddle. "After lunch, I'll start cleaning the upstairs."

"Do you ever slow down?"

She remembered last night's dream and shook her head. If she worked harder today, she wouldn't think of Frazer tonight. "I'll rest when everything is done."

"I can't wait to see that, ma'am. You've been going ever since you and the girls got here."

An hour and a half later, the girls were off to school with Summer. Cat wiped down the kitchen counters and returned to the sink to wash up the few breakfast dishes. Her grandmother always wanted the house clean before she went to work. Then at the end of the day, the place was ready when she arrived home to fix supper. It only took a few more minutes to vacuum, dust and tidy the living room. The girls had made their beds and put away their toys.

"Let's go hit a lick, Mister Robbie." Grabbing her gloves, Cat headed for the front door with Lad at her heel. "I'll put the horses out so we can muck the stalls."

"It's hard to hold onto tools. I'm dead, remember?"

"Didn't the girls say you repaired the big corral? How did you do that?"

"By thinking about it and imagining how it should look."

"Then, you can just imagine how clean a stall ought to be. Got any more questions?"

He laughed. "I wouldn't dare."

"Right answer."

Out in the barn, she haltered the ponies first. They were used to being together so she pushed open Lucky's door and led him over to Stormy's stall. The faded strawberry roan stood patiently while she opened the gray pony's door. "Let's go, guys."

They followed along, Stormy on her left and Lucky on her right. She turned them loose to graze in the big corral, then returned for Skyrocket and Dynamite. When she walked in the stable, she saw a training halter on the bay and Rob putting a second one on the palomino gelding. It wasn't the way anybody else would have done it. The thin green rope floated into place around Dynamite's face and the knot seemed to tie itself.

Okay, so that was a bit freaky. She took a deep breath and decided to lead out the bigger, younger horses one at a time. She paused in the tackroom to grab apples and then went to Skyrocket's stall.

"Okay, buddy." She hooked a lead onto the loop at his chin while he chewed on the treat. "Walk on."

He obediently walked beside her, flicking his ears as they headed into the morning sunshine. A breeze ruffled his mane and he snorted, prancing two steps before he settled back to a sedate pace. She heard hoofbeats and took a quick look over her shoulder in time to see Dynamite pacing beside the barely visible Rob.

She felt a smile start on her lips and bit it back. She hadn't really expected him to help her turn out the horses. Of course, she would never tell him that.

Unlatching the gate, she led Skyrocket inside the corral. She untied the halter and slipped it off his face. "Go have fun."

A battered blue truck pulled in and parked in the drive. Dynamite tossed his head, suddenly restless, so Cat stepped over to ease off his halter. When he was free, he trotted away. She latched the gate and went to see why Ted Fenwick had come to visit. "Good morning. What's up?"

Ted popped out of the driver's side while a dark-haired boy in jeans and a t-shirt climbed out of the passenger seat. "This is one of my cousins, Dray MacGillicudy."

The boy stared at her, dark blue eyes wide. "I've never seen anyone do that before."

"Do what?" Cat asked. "Turn horses out in a corral? It's not that big a deal. I do it every day when the weather's good. It makes it easier to clean the barn."

"No. Lead one and just have the second follow along." Dray continued to stare at her in obvious wonder. "You're an amazing trainer. I thought Heather could do miracles with horses, but she's never done something like that."

Rob was standing behind the boy, grinning in triumph. Cat ignored the ghost. Apparently, the boy hadn't seen the lead rope floating in the air since the horse was between Rob and their visitor. She couldn't admit she had help without appearing to be crazy.

She never had liked looking foolish, not even when she was a kid. But, of course, she'd also never been perfect enough to please her father. *Keep pretending you see things nobody else does and you'll beg me to stop beating you.*

She forced away the memory and shrugged instead. "Horses are herd animals. Dynamite likes being turned out with his buddy. Now, how can I help you guys?"

"I'm dropping Dray at the high school in Lake Maynard. He does a late start a couple days a week and you said you needed some help," Ted told her. "He's seventeen and he needs money."

"Who doesn't?" Cat turned to the younger boy. "So, what can you do?"

"Anything," Dray said.

"Well, come back when you can do something," Rob said. "No man can do everything and only a boy brags about it."

That was a good point, Cat thought, but obviously she didn't say so aloud. She coiled the lead lines around the halters and waited. When Dray didn't speak, she met his gaze. "Specifics, please."

"I can run a chain saw, chop wood, mow, build fences." Dray glanced toward the corral. "I don't know much about horses, but I can learn. Back when I was a kid, Heather let me muck stalls for her and feed the horses when she was out of town, so I know moldy hay from the good stuff. And when her horse colicked, I walked it all night till she got home."

"Did the horse live?" Cat asked.

Dray nodded. "After that, she made arrangements for me to be able to call in the vet whenever he got sick. Of course, she sold him when the Army sent her off to a combat zone since she didn't know if she'd be coming back alive or not and she didn't want him waiting for her. I don't have a number where you can call her for a reference, but Durango knows me."

"Dray is helping his mom restore their house," Ted added. "It always needs repairs so he knows how to put windows in those cabins for you, fix the roof and paint."

"Anything I don't know how to do, she does, and she tells me how to do it," Dray added. "I can put in toilets too, but I'm not a plumber. I don't know much about electricity, but if I help Grandpa at the café, he'll come when I need him and tell me how to do it."

"Pop MacGillicudy is your grandfather?" Cat asked.

"Yes, so I have to go to school because I don't want him hunting me down," Dray said. "I can work three mornings a week and on

Saturdays. I'm on the football team, so I can't miss practice or games."

"Well, let's try it out and see how we do," Cat said. "When can you start?"

"Tomorrow morning," Dray said. "I'll be here at seven if that's okay. I can work three hours before I have to leave for school."

"Is Ted going to drop you off or do you have your own wheels?" Cat asked.

"Oh, I'll drive my truck after I make enough money to buy a new starter," Dray said. "Meantime, Ted will drop me and pick me up."

"Sounds good. Do you have your own chainsaw?" Cat asked. "I have an apple tree that needs to come down and I was going to use the bow saw on it."

"I'll bring my tools." Dray stuck out his hand. "Thanks, Ms. McTavish."

Cat shook hands with the boy. "Welcome aboard. Maybe when school's out on break, you could have a few more hours each day."

A big grin was his answer. Then the two climbed back in the truck. With friendly waves and a quick U-turn in the drive, Ted and Dray were gone. Cat turned and headed for the barn. "Well, now I don't have to take down the tree unless he doesn't show up tomorrow."

"You'd kick if you were hung with a new rope," Rob said. "Why don't you give the boy a chance? He comes from a good family."

"Isn't he related to Herman, the evil banker?" Cat laughed. "Wait a second. That sounds like something out of vaudeville. As long as Dray shows up and doesn't try to slash my tires, I'll give him a chance."

"Well, Pop is a good guy," Rob said, "and his kids were always decent. I went to school with Kevin and Garrett. Dray's mom must be married to one of them or a cousin or some other kin."

"I've met one of the daughters." Cat walked into the barn. "I'll probably run into them at the business association meeting tomorrow morning. I can ask for a reference if I think I need one after I see the boy work."

"Taking down the apple tree should be proof enough that he can run a chainsaw and use a splitting maul."

"That's what I think, too." Cat slipped a halter on Starlight. "I'll put the girls out in the round pen. Once they're more comfortable with the geldings, I'd like all of them to pasture together. Since I don't own three of the horses, I have to be careful."

"Makes sense to me."

Cat grinned. "So, do I get to be a great trainer again and have Gambler follow me?"

"Definitely," Rob said.

By the time they broke for lunch three hours later, the barn was clean. Stalls had been mucked, dressed with fresh bedding, water tubs scrubbed and refilled, dinner hay in the mangers. She'd groomed one of the fillies while the second grazed. She'd heard hammering in the tackroom. Curious, she'd checked to see what he was doing. She discovered Rob in his ghostly way repairing the broken saddle pegs and hanging up the gear that was stored on the floor.

Then, she groomed Gambler. When she finished brushing the bay, she began working her on the longe line. It didn't take long for the filly to get the hang of walking and trotting around in small circles. Once she knew it, Cat switched to the black Morgan. Starlight was just as willing, so that meant both had positive experiences. Cat left them to graze in the round pen, contemplating where she wanted to build pasture fences. If she had some small fields, it'd save on hay. And it would give the horses the chance to have quality outside time.

She paused in the doorway of the barn. "I'm headed to the house for lunch. Are you planning to join me? Or continue to haunt the barn?"

"I'll be there." He came to join her.

To her surprise, he seemed more substantial than he had earlier. Somehow, he'd managed to change clothes, but she didn't ask how. This time a green Army shirt emphasized muscular arms and those magnificent shoulders. She refused to allow herself to look at those long legs in matching green pants or his rear end. Suddenly, she realized his booted feet didn't touch the ground. He literally floated when he walked, or rather didn't walk.

He's a ghost. Quit drooling over a dead guy.

CHAPTER ELEVEN

After a sandwich and a cup of coffee, she worked on her new website for an hour. Rob vanished and she didn't bother looking for him. He was bound to turn up sooner or later whether she wanted him or not and she intended to work the geldings while the twins were in school. Then if Skyrocket or Dynamite had fits, her daughters wouldn't see them.

She decided it would be a shame to waste the grass, so she staked out the two ponies in the orchard and reminded them that it was their job to mow. They seemed willing to do that. She led Skyrocket into the barn, locking him in his stall. Then, she brought in Dynamite. It was time for the two geldings to have their training sessions. Starlight and Gambler were up for a turn in the big corral. They could trot, canter, graze, roll and simply take care of whatever horsy business had to be done.

Cat picked up her grooming kit and eyed her saddle. Then she left it and the pads in the tackroom and opted for a bridle. The twins had been right about the ghost. Maybe, animals did communicate in pictures. What if she visualized riding Skyrocket? Would he understand that he had a different job now? He wasn't supposed to buck riders off anymore. As for Dynamite, he had so much difficulty with ground school, she hadn't progressed much beyond brushing and leading him.

She didn't take Skyrocket to the cross-ties in the aisle. She haltered him and put the lead over his neck, allowing him to chew on some of the hay in his manger. He wasn't really hungry after all the grass, but this gave him something to do. She started by picking his hooves, rewarding him with a piece of carrot as she finished each one. Next door, Dynamite put his head over the wall that divided the stalls to see if he could mooch a carrot or apple. She gave him a horse cookie, then focused on Skyrocket again.

She heard Dynamite finish chewing his treat but didn't stop brushing out Sky's black tail. "Wait your turn."

The golden horse snorted, tossed his head and pricked up his ears. He pawed the floor, but when she still didn't approach, he nickered at her.

"What?" Cat stopped and looked at him. "I don't believe it. You're talking to me?"

She knew that some trainers didn't encourage treats or vocal horses, but she wasn't one of them. She'd wanted to make friends with Dynamite from the start, but he'd been standoffish since she bought him. He always rolled his eyes and spooked at everything from bunny rabbits to butterflies. She gave him a second cookie, then returned to Skyrocket again, feeding the bay another apple core.

"You two are into snacks, aren't you?" She picked up the bridle. Between pieces of apple, she slipped the bit into Sky's mouth and eased the headstall behind his ears. "Let's go do some work."

"You're not planning to ride that critter, are you?" Rob stopped in front of the stall. "Didn't you get enough of a scare last time when I kept him from throwing you?"

Cat froze, remembering the bucking spree in the round pen. "I've been training horses for years and his owners want him broke to ride," she said. "He has to learn to be a pleasure horse. His days as a bucking horse in a rodeo are over."

"So, what are you going to do with him today?" Rob folded his arms and waited. "Ride him bareback?"

Cat petted the gelding's brown neck while he mouthed the bit. She really hadn't made a decision yet, but she knew better than to say so.

She wanted to try a few experiments on Skyrocket before she actually got on his back. He could send her flying again if she didn't have a saddle to help hold her in place on his back. "You could help me out."

"How?"

"Well, you led Dynamite out to the paddock for me. Can you hold Skyrocket?" Cat asked. "Then I'd do a few belly flops on him before I tried getting on him. We'd see how he feels about bareback riders."

"Probably about the same as he feels when you try to ride him with a saddle. Haven't you ever seen bareback bronc riding at the rodeo?"

"I don't go to rodeos. That doesn't mean I haven't seen bucking horses on TV." Cat straightened Skyrocket's black forelock. "Are you helping me or not? We need to get this done before the twins come home from school."

"I'm helping," Rob said. "Otherwise, you're pigheaded enough to try and do it alone."

The lovely fall afternoon was perfect for a ride to check out the remainder of the dude ranch facilities. There was plenty of time for Sophie and Samantha to do their homework after supper, not that they ever had much. Once they changed out of their school clothes, Cat helped them groom and saddle the ponies. Then, she tacked up Dynamite. He seemed to be willing to do some work today and he was supposed to be trained for riding.

She frowned when she noticed the wooden sign on his stall door had hit the floor again. "What is it with your name plate, buddy? I used six screws when I put it up last time. Do I need to use nails?"

"It won't do any good," Samantha informed her as she tightened her pony's cinch. "He wants a nice name, not a scary one. And he'll keep taking down the sign till you give him one."

"Honey, he's a registered Quarter Horse. The name on his papers is Adams' Dynamite Blast." Cat patted the gelding's golden neck. "Now, what am I supposed to call you? Adams or Blast?"

"He wants a pretty name," Sophie volunteered. "Can't you do

what Miss Peggy does and give him one for the barn? And he wants a forever home too."

Cat caught both sides of the bridle and held the palomino's head, leaning her face against his. He buried his nose into her chest. "What if I call you after that talking horse on TV? Would you like that?"

"No, because people might laugh at him, Mommy," Sophie said.

"I don't know what to do with you, buddy." Cat sighed, still snuggling with the horse. "But I'm going to need my own mount when we start the trail riding operation, so I'll keep you for always. And I'll think about a barn name for you."

"Want me to put the sign in the tackroom?" Samantha asked.

"Yes," Cat said. "Maybe, we'll be able to find a use for it later. Now, let's go riding."

Sophie went to open Stormy's stall door while Samantha carried off the sign. "Where are we going?"

"We'll start in the round pen and see how the horses do, since Skyrocket and the fillies are out in the big corral. Then, if Dyn—" Cat paused to think and collected her reins. "For now, I'm calling him Pal, until I come up with a barn name. If he's good with it, we'll ride around the farm and start getting the horses used to this level. Then, we'll ride up the ridge and check out the trails we'll be using when we have guests next spring."

"It'll be fun." Samantha came back to get her pony. "Let's go 'sploring, Lucky."

Once the girls were ready to lead their ponies from the stable, Cat started out with the palomino. She'd undoubtedly lost her mind. Why else would she try what her daughters said and 'listen' to the horses? Maybe, she could start a new training technique instead of 'whispering' to them.

She laughed and shook her head. "Well, let's keep it a secret between us, Pal. You don't tell anybody I'm ready for the nut-house and I won't either."

The palomino nosed her, and she patted his neck while she waited for the girls to walk their ponies through the gate to the corral. "Come on, Pal. Let's see how you feel about closing barn doors while I hold your reins."

"No need," Rob drawled. "I've got it. Once you get one of the others ready, I'll ride along with you."

"That ought to be interesting," Cat said. She shook her head. Was it her imagination or did he seem disturbingly alive for someone who actually died more than forty years ago?

In the corral, she checked the saddles on the ponies and helped the girls mount up, before she swung into her own saddle. Dynamite—no—Pal, turned his head to nose her stirrup and she leaned forward to pet his neck. "What's he doing?"

"Checking for spurs," Samantha told her. "He doesn't like 'em."

"Neither do I." Cat petted the horse again. "And I don't use crops either. I just ride the old-fashioned way, squeezing my legs. That's what I want you girls to do too."

"We will," Sophie promised.

"Okay, let's warm up." Cat started their usual riding routine to review the basics of equitation. "Who wants to lead a balance exercise?"

"Me." Samantha stood in her stirrups. "Cowboy jumping jacks. Everybody up and pat your thighs. Oh, and put your reins behind the saddle horn."

Cat laughed and joined in. After ten of the jumping jacks that Cat had adapted for riders, then Sophie led them in horsy sit-ups. They leaned back and forth in their saddles. Then, it was Cat's turn. She chose the twists that the girls called, "this-a-ways, that-a-ways." Once everyone was balanced in the saddles, it was time to practice stops, starts, left and right turns. Finally, they began circling the arena, first on the left track and then on the right. Through it all, the newly rechristened Pal performed as if he'd been riding for years.

When she thought the girls were ready, Cat rode over to the gate and unlatched it. Pal didn't quite have the concept yet of side-stepping or standing while she hooked the gate open, but he was willing and that was half the battle. She petted his neck again, then turned to the right and rode past the bigger corral.

Skyrocket trotted over to the fence, followed by the two young mares. He hadn't been upset when she sat on him bareback a few hours ago and had actually followed Rob around the ring a couple times. She hadn't wanted to push her luck so she'd dismounted then and turned him out with the fillies for a reward.

Cat glanced over her shoulder. Sophie rode Stormy a safe ten foot behind Pal and Lucky trailed his old buddy. Both of her daughters waved, sunshine smiles on their faces. Cat laughed again. "All right. Tally-ho!"

Rob leaned on the round pen fence. "You ladies are riding western. Shouldn't it be 'head 'em up, move 'em out?' Like my dad used to say, 'You gotta sell the sizzle, not the steak.'"

That was an interesting idea. She hadn't considered that she would need to market the trail rides to her customers. When she was a child, horseback riding had just been part of the fun experience of staying at the dude ranch. She swung left past the machine shed, circled the parking lot where guests left the cars. Mentally, she started a list. Somewhere along the way, she would gravel the lot and replace the cedar logs that framed the area.

She glanced over the rolling pastures to the creek that wound along the front of the place between the ranch and the highway. She would have to check the swimming pond and see if it was usable at another time. A short time later, she led the girls past the next building, a combination dining hall and party barn. Behind it were the tennis courts and baseball diamonds. She saw the tall grass from here and wondered if she could afford a riding mower. Otherwise, it would take forever to get the recreational areas back in shape. She hadn't even opened up the machine shed yet. Perhaps, she'd find a mower there and restore it to use.

Pal snorted as Lad loped past, tail wagging. The pup obviously figured this was a new way to take a walk. He flushed a rabbit and chased the bunny off into the weeds by the old dock where the Williams had launched rowboats in the past. Cat added another thing to her mental to-do list. Search the Internet and find used kayaks. Could Dray repair the rowboats they already had, or would she have to replace them?

A cool late September breeze rustled the trees when she crossed the driveway. They rode along the creek. On the far side, she saw the small guest cabins which not only required new glass in the windows, but also paint. When she was a girl, they always stayed in the red one, but the exterior of that one-room sleeping cabin had been the same white color as its six neighbors. The only difference was the trim. Talk about a smart way to save money, she thought, and she could do the same thing now.

She circled back through the picnic area, looking at the tables. More repairs. More new ones and definitely more paint. She checked on her daughters again. They were riding side by side, carrying on a conversation that probably included the ponies and the puppy that bounded alongside. Lad occasionally raised another rabbit, but more frequent prey were the butterflies that danced above the knee-high grass.

Cat frowned as she spotted a white car parked near the barn. "Looks like we have company, girls. Be sure you have control of your ponies and let's go see who came to visit."

"Can we 'splore more tomorrow, Mommy?" Samantha called.

"If the weather stays nice, we can." Cat leaned forward when she felt Pal tremble beneath her. "Don't blow it now, buddy. I won't let anyone hurt you."

As they neared the big corral, she recognized the blonde woman and the teenager feeding treats to the horses. It was Ingrid and Mandy Nielsen. "It's Starlight's and Gambler's family. We'll take these guys into the round pen to dismount. Come with me and Pal."

Rob held the gate for them, and Samantha beamed at him. "We rode a long way and I get to close the gate 'cause I'm last," she told the ghost.

Cat smiled. "Okay but let me turn Pal so he can see what Lucky does. Next time it won't be so hard for him." She nodded toward the other woman. "Hi, Ingrid. How's it going?"

"Fine. Mandy wanted to check on Gambler and I told her you said it'd be all right with you if we came often."

"They miss you." Sophie rode Stormy closer. "They miss you even if they're doing school now and we give 'em lots of carrots and apples."

Ingrid laughed. "I hope Star misses me as much as I do her, but I like the way your mom trains." She came closer to the fence. "Is that the palomino you bought at the last Quarter Horse sale? He looks good. I never thought he'd come back after that trailer wreck."

"He doesn't seem to like road trips." Cat swung out of the saddle, stroking the white blaze on Pal's face. "How did you know he was in an accident? They didn't mention that in Oregon when we were there."

Ingrid brushed a strand of light gold hair from her face. "I listened to all the gossip at the sale barn. I figure knowledge is something we all need to acquire. That's my deal. I know you hate snooping."

"I hate all the secrets in this business a lot more," Cat said. "I swear I spend more time playing detective than I do in the round pen."

"That's why Mom and I told you everything about our horses." Mandy watched Samantha still in Lucky's saddle successfully close and latch the gate. "Will you teach Gambler to do that?"

"If you want me to," Cat said. "It does come in handy when I'm riding." She flicked a glance at Rob. "You won't always have someone around to open and close gates for you so it's nice when your horse can help you out."

"Since I want to take her to the 4-H shows when she's ready, then she'll do better in trail class too," Mandy said.

"You got it," Cat agreed. "Let me unsaddle and I'll show you their stalls."

Ingrid and Mandy stuck around to help put their horses back in the barn and watch the young mares start eating supper. Chores quickly completed, the Nielsens left with promises to return soon. Cat headed past the orchard for the house. Sophie and Samantha charged in front of her taking turns to throw a frisbee for Lad to chase. The collie-heeler mix seemed to believe that was the only reason the girls played in the yard.

It'd been a wonderful day and she'd accomplished so much, Cat thought. She'd worked all four horses, possibly hired a part-time ranch hand and with Lucky and Stormy's help mowed the orchard. After supper, dishes, homework and bath time, she might start on the upstairs. At least she'd take a look at it and then leave it for tomorrow.

Gravel crunched and she glanced over her shoulder to see a late-model, black Lexus cruise slowly up the drive to a stop. She grimaced when the driver's door open and her father stepped out of the car. She hadn't seen him in more than a year, but he didn't look any different.

Tall, gray-haired, in an expensive dark suit, white shirt and tie, Liam O'Leary appeared the epitome of a successful businessman. The twins paused in their game with the puppy, then vanished into the rose garden. From there, they'd slip into the house.

Lucky kids. Smart too. She wouldn't scold them for the disappearing act. What was the point? Their grandfather didn't like them, any more than he liked her.

She walked toward him, pasting on a professional smile. "Hi, Liam." None of this 'Dad' business for her father, no sir! "How are you?"

"I can't believe you did something stupid again."

Cat kept the smile and counted to ten. "The appropriate response is for you to greet me and tell me how happy you are for me that I won this place. It's a dream come true."

He gave a disparaging look around, then sneered. "Tell me you've listed it for sale."

"That's not an option." Cat folded her arms, grateful her daughters were out of earshot. "So, if you're expecting me to invest in some get-rich-quick scheme of yours or Frazer's, it's not happening. This is my home and I'm staying here."

He narrowed his hazel eyes. "I'm an investment banker. I don't do Ponzi schemes."

"I don't have anything to invest," Cat said. "And even if I did, I wouldn't." Not with him, that was for sure.

"If you sold this place, you could live well."

"I can't sell it for ten years and then only as a dude ranch." Cat lifted her chin and met his gaze. "I don't have any money to give you, Liam. You may as well go."

Another sneer before he said, "You could try listening to Herman MacGillicudy. He's a smart man. He'd find a way to buy it from you."

"Not to him and not for you," Cat repeated. "Didn't you hear me? It wasn't in the rules of the contest I won. And that reminds me. Was there some reason you didn't tell me I had more than one aunt? Why keep your family a secret?"

"Family?" He glared at her. "A bunch of hillbillies looking for handouts."

Ignoring Rob when he came to stand beside her, Cat gazed at her father. "But they're your relatives and I loved being with Aunt Rose."

"They had nothing to give me. Why should I waste time on them?"

"You mean they turned you down when you tried to con them out of their money," Rob said. "And it about killed your father when you emptied the register in his hardware store and hightailed it for Canada instead of enlisting in the military like your brothers. He'd have given you the money if you'd asked. You didn't have to steal from him."

"You stole from your parents?" Cat caught her breath, staring at the older man. "And you judged me and found me wanting as a wife when I told you that Frazer cheated on me the first time, right after our honeymoon."

"If you were better to him, he wouldn't." Liam opened the car door. "It's your fault that you can't keep a man."

"Really? Was it each wife's fault when you kept trading one for another, until this last one who is younger than I am?" Cat asked in her sweetest tone. "Last year, when she told me she wanted kids, I told her that you'd had a vasectomy an eon ago. Has she swapped you off for a human being yet?"

By then, he was in the car and gone, not providing an answer. She watched him go, biting her lip so the tears wouldn't fall. She wasn't about to cry in front of a man, even a dead one. She had things to do.

She walked past Rob to the porch and climbed the stairs. When she reached the kitchen, she found the girls setting the table for supper.

Samantha put down the last fork and came to hug her. "I'm sorry your daddy is mean."

Cat nearly said that she regretted it too, but she couldn't. She bent and drew both girls against her. "I'm glad you two came inside. Keep doing that. I don't want you hanging out by him if he comes again. And always bring your puppy with you too."

Sophie nestled closer. "We need waffles and bacon tonight."

"We do?" Cat dropped kisses on the top of each head. "Why, baby?"

"To make the hurt in our hearts go away," Samantha said.

"Sounds like a wonderful idea." Cat hugged the girls one more time. "And we'll have homemade apple juice too. Let's get cooking, ladies. Find the waffle iron for me."

On her way to the cupboard to get a bowl and the box of pancake mix, she spotted Lad under the table. He'd cuddled up with an old toy bear that the girls had given him to sleep with when he first arrived. "Did you tell Laddie that he gets bacon tonight?"

"No, but I will," Sophie said.

"He'll be happy when he smells it," Samantha added. "And then he can have the extra grease on his dog food too."

"Then we have a plan." Cat measured the dry ingredients into the bowl. "This will be fun. After homework, shall we explore the upstairs?"

CHAPTER TWELVE

There were times when he missed having a body more than others. He hadn't liked Liam O'Leary when he was alive, Rob thought. And the guy wasn't any better many years later, now that Rob was dead and couldn't smack him up-side the head. The little snot always spied on him and Rosie and tattled to their respective fathers. Granted, she always cut her youngest brother slack, but the kid had received too many breaks. And he hadn't changed. An investment banker?

Obviously, he worked with Herman otherwise Liam wouldn't have brought up the man's name. Maybe that explained why Cat had been so wary when the other man attempted to buy the property. She'd learned not to trust at an early age. What had Liam done to her when she was young and innocent?

No point in asking her tonight. She was on edge and she needed time to gather strength. He'd leave her alone for a while. Tomorrow was always another day.

Cat yawned and leaned back against the pillows, making a list of what the second and third floors of the house needed. There were four furnished bedrooms, two shared bathrooms and a sitting or possible study area on the second floor. The top story had almost the same plan. They'd been able to get into three of the bedrooms, but the fourth one that opened into the tower rooms had a locked door. Sophie had told her that was Mister Robbie's room and since he hadn't invited them, they couldn't go inside.

Shaking her head, Cat sighed and put her pen and pad aside. She reached for her paperback. She was pretty sure that she didn't want to ask the ghost if she could visit his room. It sounded tacky at best and kinky at the worst. Maybe, she could just ask him if it needed repainting. Of course, it would wait until she finished refurbishing the others and she'd bring up the idea of renting rooms at the business meeting in the morning.

College girls only, she decided. And Mister Robbie would have to behave himself if there were guests in the house. She couldn't have her renters harassed by the resident spook. With a firm nod, she opened her book and allowed Dana Stabenow's writing to take her away to murder most foul in Alaska.

Two hours later, her eyes almost closed, she heard music. Country music. Lynn Anderson's signature song again. Cat put down her book and eased out of bed. She wandered through the house and came to a stop in the living room. "What's going on?"

Her resident ghost was almost substantial, here in the dark. He rose from where he sat a foot above the couch and floated toward her, holding out a barely visible hand. "Dance with me."

"You're dead, remember?" Despite herself, Cat felt a smile on her lips. He was such a hunk in his military uniform. She met his night-dark gaze. Her pulses raced. "How could we possibly–?"

"We won't know unless we try."

"Good point." She drifted forward, her cotton nightgown swirling around her ankles. She put up her hands so they would lie on his broad chest, if it were actually corporeal. She pretended she could feel the muscled arms he slipped around her waist. They slowly moved together across the carpeted floor to the song.

And they danced as Lynn Anderson sang. *"I beg your pardon. I never promised you a rose garden—"*

The scent of roses startled Rob. He hadn't realized the bedroom window was open. He heard a motor roar and recognized the sound of a chainsaw. The boy had arrived to start work. Did that make Cat happy? She'd talked about other tasks she wanted him to do, but she obviously hadn't believed the teen would actually show up this morning. Now, Rob had another question—one he'd wait to ask since it was bound to rile her. That might prove to be amusing. Would she continue to run herself ragged?

He went to the window and opened it a little wider. He smelled rain on the breeze and wet grass, but the sun shone bright today. The pup woofed in the rose garden and tussled with a stick. He wasn't alone. Nearby, Cat cut roses, from the looks of it carefully choosing buds that would last a while. Interesting. She hadn't seemed the type who filled the house with flowers, but what did he know? She'd lived here only a few weeks.

A short while later, he drifted downstairs. The aromas of pancakes and fresh brewed coffee filled the air. He paused. Why did the scents seem new and different today? *Because I've been dead for a long time.* At some point in the past forty-plus years, he'd lost the ability to smell, but his nose seemed to be back on track, oddly enough.

The twins sat at the kitchen table while Cat flipped pancakes at the stove. All three wore jeans and he wondered if that meant they weren't going to school. Then, he remembered that customs had changed since he was a boy. Back then, girls always wore dresses to class. He wouldn't have dared to even ask if he could wear jeans to school. His mother would have taken it as an insult that she didn't do right by her family if he and his brothers didn't have ironed shirts and slacks every day.

"Good morning." Rob spoke to the woman who'd taken over the house. He winked at the twins. "Looks like everybody's raring to go and can't go for raring."

Samantha giggled. "You're being silly, Mister Robbie."

"What else is new?" Cat murmured but didn't do more than flick a scathing glance at him.

"We're having hotcakes," Sophie intervened. "Want some?"

"Not unless he plans on helping out today." Cat turned from the electric range, pointed the spatula like a royal scepter at Rob. "I have a long list of chores to do today before and after the meeting."

Silence from the twins as they stared at Rob and then their mother. "Mommy, can you really see Mister Robbie?" Samantha finally asked.

Cat nodded, a flush seeping into her cheeks. "Yes, you girls were right about him being here and I'm sorry I didn't believe you right away."

"It's okay," Sophie said. "Most people don't think ghosts are real. We're just glad you can see him now."

"And we won't be in trouble for saying he's real," Samantha finished. "So, should I get you a plate for some pancakes, Mister Robbie?"

"Not today, princess." Rob winked at the little redhead. "Your mom's hotcakes smell nearly as good as my momma's, but I can't eat. I'm a ghost and I never get hungry."

"You got to work harder then," Sophie said. "Uncle Mac says that if a man can't eat, he needs to go back out in the fields and plant more cotton."

Cat laughed. "Next time I talk to him, I'll tell him you remember his words of wisdom." She scooped up two pancakes on the flapjack turner and brought them over to the first plate in front of Samantha. She returned to the stove, collected the next two hotcakes and put them on Sophie's dish. "Butter up, ladies."

"What meeting are you going to today, Mommy?" Sophie asked.

"The Baker City business owners get together once a month to discuss what they need to do." Cat poured out more batter on the griddle. "Since we'll be opening the ranch next spring, I need to connect with folks who work in town," she explained. "Reverend Tommy's wife will drop you off at school and then come back for me. The pickup should be ready today. Do you want me to pick you up after school or are you happy riding with the other kids?"

The twins shared a glance, then Sophie said, "We like the big kids in the carpool. We want to keep going with them."

"That works for me," Cat said. "I'll talk to Reverend Tommy and arrange to be included in the schedule." She glanced at Rob. "Are you working today?"

"I'll try but it's still hard for me to hold onto tools. I'm a ghost, remember?"

"It's a little hard to forget when I can literally see through you."

She'd finished cleaning up the kitchen and feeding the dog so she'd be ready when Virginia Thompson returned to take her to town. Cat walked out to the orchard where Dray cut the dead apple tree into 22-inch sections for the kitchen woodstove. "I'm going to a meeting in town. Are you okay here?"

"I'm fine," Dray said. "I'll split as much as I can and stack it in the woodshed tomorrow unless I can get back here after school."

Cat hesitated, then asked. "Do you have your license? My truck's at the tire place in Lake Maynard. I've already paid for it. If you want to pick it up, you could drive it back here and then I'll take you into Baker City later."

"That'd be great." Dray grinned at her. "Thanks, ma'am."

"He could swing by that big hardware store and pick up a new apple tree to replace this one," Rob suggested. "Or did you want to plant something else?"

Cat glanced around at the rows of trees. Rob was right. They needed a replacement here. "Could you bring out a Red Delicious or a Gala sapling too?"

"Sure. You make a list and I'll do the shopping," Dray said. "No point in making a special trip to Lake Maynard when I'm already there."

Cat smiled at him. "Sounds like a winner."

She struggled with the urge not to stare at Rob who seemed to be coming more and more solid each day, which seemed odd for a ghost. He wore the same clothes he had the day before, a green work shirt and green pants tucked into combat boots. His black hair curled around his face. His dark eyes held amusement. For a moment, she remembered dancing with him the night before. She'd almost felt the magic of his touch even when she couldn't feel the warmth of his skin. She'd breathed in the scent of his lime aftershave, but before she surrendered to the urge to kiss him, she had escaped to her bedroom. Thank heaven, he hadn't followed her.

She really needed to talk to her lawyer and see if the woman had heard back from Frazer. It wasn't like he'd fight for her or the girls. He didn't want any of them. She sighed. She wouldn't think about him right now. There were too many other things she had to do, and he wasn't on her list, not anymore.

It was another beautiful September day. She glanced down the drive to the bridge over Cedar Creek. Sunlight caused the dew to sparkle like diamonds on a grass carpet. The sky was a brilliant blue. A few fluffy white clouds floated overhead. Cat looked at her watch. "After I turn the horses into the paddocks, I'll go make a list for you, Dray. I need receipts from the hardware store. The fruit trees should be on sale at this time of the year and I already paid for the tires so don't let them sell you anything else for the truck."

"You got it, boss." Picking up the maul, the boy began to split chunks of wood into smaller pieces. "I'll get as much done as I can before Ted gets here to take me to school."

"Works for me." Cat headed for the barn, Lad at her heel. She pretended not to notice when Rob immediately followed and waited until they reached the barn before she spoke to him. "What do you plan to do today?"

He shrugged a broad shoulder, then winked at her. "Reckon, I'll try putting more stalls together."

"That's a great idea." She put a halter on Gambler. "I'd also like to rebuild some pasture fences so these guys and gals can spend nights out on the grass when the weather's good. I'm just not sure where the fields were. It wasn't like I ever saw them when my aunt brought me here years ago."

"I can show you when you get back from your meeting." Rob haltered Starlight. "Shall we go? That boy's going to be certain you're the best horse trainer in the world when he sees you play 'Follow the Leader' with these two fillies."

Cat laughed. "It takes so little to impress some people." She opened the stall door, then paused, eyeing him curiously. "Why are you being nice to me? I thought this was your place and you didn't want strangers here."

"It is my place," Rob said, "but you work a sight harder than the renters my brothers had here. That being the case, I can share the ranch for a while."

"Brothers? Who are your brothers? You're the only ghost I've seen here."

"Oh, Ed and Adam aren't dead yet. If they were, I'd be able to talk to them. Little punks barely listened to me when we were boys. I should have thumped their heads a lot harder when they were kids. I thought there'd be time when I got back from 'Nam to whip them into shape."

"But you didn't come home."

"Yes, I did. I just didn't come back alive." He gestured to the barn door. "Better get a move on if you want these horses out and to make your list before you run out of time, kitten."

The endearment lingered in her mind, sounding familiar. Why? She couldn't remember. She put it out of her mind for the time being.

Instead, she listened to Virginia chat about the upcoming meeting as they drove into town. There had to be a way to promote Baker City and bring tourism into the area if the locals weren't interested in selling off the gravel or the evergreen trees.

"What about a festival?" Cat asked. "Halloween's coming. Maybe we could do a haunted house. There are certainly enough empty buildings in town."

"And if we ask the old-timers, they'll tell us we have enough ghosts." Virginia laughed. "Why not? Then, we could do a Christmas town immediately afterwards."

"That's been done to death," Cat pointed out. "We ought to do a big thing about Thanksgiving. Nobody celebrates that – at least not in a commercial way. It would get the press out here and they're always looking for timely harvest-type stories."

"I hope you're writing down these ideas." Virginia pulled into the parking lot next to Pop's café. "We've needed someone enthusiastic like you for quite a while."

"That's just off the top of my head. When we start brainstorming, I'm sure other people will have better ones."

"We'll see. I hope so."

Inside, they found Pop pouring coffee for his daughter, Linda, Reverend Tommy and Summer. Cat glanced around while Virginia helped herself to a mug. "Where is everyone?"

"Maxine should be coming from the mercantile any moment,"

Pop said. "I called Frank Madison and he'll be along soon. He's the president of the Association this year. He owns several of the old buildings in town and the former school. Steve and Jasmine are always late because they don't close the bars till midnight."

"And that's everyone." Carrying her cup of coffee, Virginia led the way to a long table. "Cat has a lot of good ideas that will help us all make money."

"Well, let's hear 'em." A gray-haired man in a red plaid shirt that jarred with his orange suspenders leaned forward in the corner booth. "Time's a-wasting, girl. We don't have all day."

Cat blinked. Didn't anyone else hear him? Apparently not because none of the locals answered. Suddenly, she realized she could see the brown vinyl seat through his body. Another ghost? Where had she come to live? And why didn't she remember seeing anyone when she was a girl? Wait a minute. She must have or why would Liam have constantly threatened her with physical abuse?

"Hold your horses, Newt." This time it was a middle-aged fellow in a black suit that looked like something out of a museum or the 1940s. "We have to call the meeting to order and run through all the old business before we start anything new."

"I've been sitting around waiting for too many years, Mayor," Newt grumbled. "I got places to go and things to do, even if the rest of you don't. My hardware store doesn't run itself."

"Cat, come pull up a chair." Virginia interrupted the argument between the dead members of the business council. "We'll get started soon and I want to bring Linda and Summer up to speed on your suggestions for Halloween."

That afternoon while she bedded three more stalls with shavings and put hay in the mangers, Cat found herself thinking about the meeting. Her idea of a haunted house for Halloween had led to a long discussion. The ghosts had been unanimous in their support of the idea, but their comments didn't matter, as their living descendants hadn't been as willing to try to lure tourists to the town.

The spectral Newt O'Leary had even suggested they expand the concept to a haunted block and volunteered his store. The postmaster wanted them to include the old post office which was a derelict building now, since everyone living got their mail at the mercantile. The local madam and the original school teacher both of whom died in the avalanche almost came to blows in the middle of the restaurant. If they hadn't been called to order by the mayor, Cat was sure the living members of the association might have realized they weren't alone in the restaurant when she ducked from insubstantial blows.

But she personally thought Newt's idea was a good one, not just because he was related to her in some way so she was the one who brought it up to the living association members. When Frank Madison pointed out that most people wouldn't be interested in visiting a dying town, the tavern owner, Steve O'Connell, nearly had a fit and fell in it. It was Pop's turn to calm down the situation. He said the president was right. One haunted building wouldn't draw much of a crowd, but a haunted town could make some serious money. There was no arguing that.

When Frank finally called for a vote, all the Baker City business members were on board, alive and the unseen dead. Cat had struggled to keep a straight face doing her best to ignore the squabbling members of the deceased portion of the meeting and agreed to put together a website for the event as well as sending out promotional releases. Pop and Reverend Tommy promised to start rounding up people to work on the buildings that they would use. The first meeting would be next Sunday after church.

In all, it had been an insightful meeting for Cat. She just had to learn to ignore those who wouldn't actually have a vote.

A horn honked out in the driveway and Lad barked, startling Cat out of her reverie. "Okay, let's go see who is here," she said. She bent and petted the collie pup. "It's too early for the girls."

A long silver horse trailer was in the parking lot, pulled by a distinctive red and black pickup. The words, Majestyk Morgan Farm were scrolled along the sides of the trailer and painted on the truck too. Cat frowned as Frank Madison slid out of the driver's seat and came toward her.

"Hello, Frank. I didn't expect to see you again today," Cat said. "Did you come to pick up Skyrocket?"

"Nope. I brought you two more," Frank said, a smile lighting his pale green eyes. "According to Pop, his grandson says you're an old-time trainer and I haven't had one of those since Angie shipped out for another tour in Afghanistan. Didn't Sylvia call and tell you I was on the way?"

"No, but I don't have a phone in the barn yet," Cat said. "I was thinking about it, but Pal is such a smarty, I was afraid he'd be calling long distance."

Frank chuckled. "Shades of Mister Ed and his pencil on that old TV show. Well, come see what you think of these two. They're purebred Morgans, half-brothers to Ingrid's fillies, but they're both rowdy five-year-olds. I'm thinking it'll take you five or six months to train them if you don't rush things because they've had zip in the way of ground work."

"I don't like to rush any horse," Cat said, "especially not babies."

"And that's why they're here." Frank walked to the back of the trailer and unlatched the door. In western wear and low-heeled boots, he barely had two inches on her, but he carried himself like he was ten feet tall. "I really liked the idea you came up with to promote Baker City. It's a stroke of genius and it means we won't have to rebuild the place. We'll be able to capitalize on the town's mystique."

"You didn't seem that wowed by it at the meeting," Cat pointed out.

"No, because if I'm the bad guy, then everyone has to convince me, and they talk themselves through any self-doubts. I figure that's my job as president of the association." Frank eased into the trailer and came back with a gorgeous, black gelding. "Meet Tonka."

Cat took the lead rope, petting the sturdy Morgan's ebony neck. "Aren't you a beauty?"

The horse snorted and tossed his head up and down, agreeing with the assessment. He nosed her pockets and she silently promised him treats later. She didn't have anything to give him right now. She waited until Frank returned with a bay about the same size. "So, who is this?"

"Lucky Charm." Frank rubbed the horse's neck. "He's got a lot of potential and I can't wait to see what you do with them."

"Good thing I have stalls ready. We can put them inside for now and once they're used to being here, I'll start turning them out."

"You're the boss of them," Frank said. "Any chance I can see what you've done with Skyrocket? We're on for Angie to 'Skype' tonight and I'd like to tell her what he can do."

"You bet." Cat took a quick look around for the pup and spotted Lad over in the orchard. The collie had probably gone to supervise Rob and the firewood stacking. "Follow me."

Once they had the young Morgans settled, she stopped in the tack-room for a handful of apple cores and Skyrocket's halter. Then, she led the way out to the big corral where he grazed with Pal and the two fillies. Frank remained at the gate and she went inside. Pal was the first one to her, but the others weren't far behind. She shared out the treats, haltered up Sky and urged the rest to go back to their grazing. She led the golden bay toward the gate, his black mane fluttering in the afternoon breeze.

He stood quietly while she unlatched the gate and led him through the opening. She turned him and closed up the corral again. "Let's go to the round pen and show Frank what you've learned to do," she said quietly to the horse.

She loosened her hold on the rope until she held the end of the lead. She always thought of this as sending the energy down the line and Sky seemed to like the notion. He had freedom to move his head as he trailed her to the smaller ring. She'd groomed the fillies earlier, so her bucket of brushes was still there. She led Skyrocket into the pen, ground-tied him and began by hoof-picking him.

She was pretty sure that Frank didn't see they had company. Rob had come over to join them and he stood close enough to grab the lead line if Skyrocket moved from where she stationed him. She nodded at him but didn't speak. It was one thing to be considered a trainer with an ego as big as an indoor arena. She didn't want to look like a nut-case to the man who was rapidly becoming her biggest client.

"I like to feed treats." Cat glanced at Frank. "I got cleaned out when I was in the bigger corral. Did you see where I keep the bucket? Could you grab some more for me?"

"Be right back." He paused. "I should say that I'm already impressed. I've never seen him come up to anyone like that. And he's standing still while you groom him. I didn't think he'd ever do that. He tore out four different sets of cross-ties in my barn."

Cat waited till the man was out of earshot before she spoke to the horse. "Keep up the good work, Sky. We want more of his business."

"Are you going to ride him today?" Rob asked, leaning on the fence, the trees of the orchard visible through him. "He's been doing pretty good when I'm on him."

Her jaw dropped, almost to the grass of the corral. He was a ghost. What the hell was he doing riding *her* horses? She glared at him. "You and I are going to have a serious talk later," she hissed. "Nobody else rides the horses I train."

He shrugged. "I'm not having you hurt. You need to stick around and raise those girls of yours. Spit and scratch all you like, kitten. It won't do any good, but I'm willing to wait to teach you to purr."

CHAPTER THIRTEEN

While the twins rode Lucky and Stormy in the round pen, Cat headed for the garden to cut a few more roses. She could take the flowers to the cemetery later. She'd intended to do it this morning, but she'd been distracted making the arrangements for Dray to collect her truck. Then Virginia arrived to take her to the meeting. Cat clipped three more pink roses, pausing when she saw yet another vehicle on the bridge over the creek. She frowned. That wasn't her rig coming up the drive. So, who was the visitor?

She walked toward the front of the house with Lad trotting behind her, toting one of his chewed-up tennis balls. He probably hoped the visitor would be up for a game of 'chase' since his girls were busy with their other four-legged pets.

The dog was doomed to be disappointed. Cat grimaced when she recognized the white Malibu. Sighing, she put the clippers and two dozen roses on the bench on the porch before she went to do the meet and greet.

"Yoo-hoo, Catriona." Still a blonde, still slender in the clingy sky-blue dress, Camille O'Leary-Craig-Evans-O'Leary-Talbot-Abbott-Waller waved a perfectly manicured hand. "Come give me a kiss, sweetie."

In comparison to her much-married mother, Cat knew she had to look like a total hick in her jeans, boots and Washington State University sweatshirt. She wondered what would happen if she actually hugged the petite blonde who was barely five foot, four in her blue spike heels without bothering to brush the dust off her clothes. Camille would probably break into tiny fashion doll pieces and be scattered all over the gravel. Better not to risk it, Cat thought. How would she ever clean up the mess?

Instead, she exchanged air kisses with her mother and asked. "How was your cruise? What did you do with Dave?"

"Oh, he simply insisted on going to the hotel in Everett." Camille pouted, but the disappointment didn't land in china-blue eyes. "He wanted to be sure that everything was all right, as if he didn't call and email that new manager of his every day for hours when we were on the cruise."

"Well, that personal touch is what makes his hotel chain one of the best in Washington state." Cat actually liked this stepfather better than the others. She was careful not to praise him too much to her mother. Always suspicious, Camille was convinced that each of her husbands were on the prowl and a teenage girl was fair prey. None of them had dared to do anything inappropriate, of course, since even a birthday present for Cat was grounds for a raging tantrum followed by three days of sulking and it was never a pleasant situation for either husband or stepdaughter.

"You don't understand because you're so big and strong." Camille heaved a dramatic sigh and pressed a hand to her silicone chest. "A real woman wants her husband to put her first and she makes sacrifices to be sure that happens."

"Really?" Cat bent and took the soggy tennis ball from the puppy and hurled it into the orchard. *Save yourself, Lad.* The pup tore off, all collie in hot pursuit of his treasure. "Is that your subtle way of saying that I should have packed up the kids and followed Frazer to New Orleans for one more casino adventure and to wait for him to cheat on me with some skank from down South?"

"Didn't sound too subtle to me," Rob joined them. "What would a horse trainer do there?"

Cat ignored him. It was rapidly becoming a habit since she

couldn't say that a snoopy ghost wanted to be entertained by her life. "Well, Mother?"

"Oh, Cat, don't be nasty. Call me, Milla. 'Mother' makes me sound so old."

"And you can't be a day over fifty-five," Rob agreed. "You're just a spring chicken."

Cat coughed and kicked a spurt of gravel in his direction. He laughed and stepped aside. "Well, heaven forbid that I sound nasty," she struggled for a civil tone. "Come on over and talk to the girls. They've missed you."

"Oh no." Camille shook her head. "They'll be all dirty since they're riding those ponies and I don't want to get horse hair on my clothes. How on earth I raised a farmer, I have no idea."

Cat drew a deep breath. "I'm not a farmer yet, Mother. I don't have enough animals, just a few horses and a puppy. I'll have to wait till next year to add most of the livestock."

"Hopefully, you'll come to your senses by then." Camille looked around. "I can't believe that old house is still standing. Why didn't you take the cash when you won that contest?"

"Because there wasn't any cash, Mother." Cat folded her arms and tried to keep her voice calm. How many times was she going to have to explain this? "All I won was the farm and there are conditions. I have to restore it to its former glory as a dude ranch. I can't sell it for ten years and even then, it can only go to someone who continues to operate it as a destination resort."

Camille sniffed. "Well, Dave keeps a good lawyer on retainer. I'm sure he can do something to get you a better deal, to cash you out or something."

"I have the deal I want. We're happy here." Cat shot a glare at Rob, silently wishing he'd be quiet for at least a moment. She glanced down to meet her mother's eyes. "Now, why are you *really* here?"

Another big dramatic sigh. "Your father called. He has a friend who wants to buy this place and then you'd be settled. You and Frazer could have a decent place to live."

Cat counted to ten under her breath. "There is no Frazer and me. We're getting a divorce."

"Catriona, no! You don't throw away a perfectly good husband."

"Why not? You've thrown away six if I count Dad twice. And I'm not including Dave because you two are still married."

"Well, you don't toss one out like yesterday's garbage until you have a better one to take his place. And by 'better,' I mean one with a better-paying job and a better class of friends."

Enough was enough. Cat pasted on what she hoped was her sweetest smile. "That lets out Frazer then. He's never been able to hold a job for longer than a year. I don't need a new husband, Mother. I have the twins to nag me, the puppy to whine, the woodstove to smoke and an electric blanket to keep me warm."

"There's no talking to you when you're in such a nasty mood." Camille's voice trailed away as the twins approached. "Hi, girls. How are you?"

"We're fine," Sophie said, wariness in her tone, Samantha's expression echoing her sister's. "Guess what, Gramma? Miss Peggy gave us ponies to keep here and we can ride whenever we want. Come see them."

"I don't think so." Camille held up a hand to keep the girls from drawing any closer. "I have presents for you in the car. New dresses all the way from California and beautiful porcelain dolls. Won't that be fun?"

"We'd rather have another puppy," Sophie said. "Laddie wants a friend who can play catch with him."

"I'll bet he does," Rob grinned and moved close to the twins. "Most farms like to have two dogs so they can work together. We should keep an eye out for a companion puppy."

Cat struggled not to laugh. Sophie might have been the one to speak up, but Samantha headed off to throw the ball for her pup, a definite sign that dresses and dolls weren't what she considered a good time. "Thank you, Mother. It will be nice for the girls to have new clothes to wear to church. Let's go see, ladies."

Sophie scowled, but she didn't speak up when Cat put a hand on her shoulder and guided the girl in the direction of her grandmother's car. Samantha trailed along.

"Mommy, did you hear Mister Robbie?" Sophie asked. "He thinks Laddie should have a friend too."

"Who is Mister Robbie?" Camille looked over her shoulder. "Do you have a boyfriend already, Catriona?"

"No. He lives here too, but not everybody sees him 'cause he's a ghost," Samantha explained. "Mommy said if he minds his p's and q's, he can stay but he has to be good."

"That's one way of handling imaginative children," Camille said, wrinkling her nose for a second, "but you should just tell them that not everyone believes in 'pretend' friends and to keep them a secret. That's what I did with you and it worked quite well."

Cat blinked, then stared at her mother. "I don't remember having 'pretend' friends."

"All kids do, but they grow out of it," Camille opened the back door of the car, revealing the bags that filled the rear seat. "And I finally told you that I didn't want to hear about them anymore. Of course, when your father caught you telling lies, he spanked you, but I just said that you were too old to have 'pretend' friends and you stopped talking about them."

"How old was Mommy when she got too old?" Sophie asked. "We're eight. We like seeing Mister Robbie. He tells us stories and keeps the monsters away at night."

Samantha nodded in agreement and pressed close to Cat's side. "I don't ever want to get that old."

"Don't worry, honey." Cat bent down and whispered in the little girl's ear. "You won't. You both know I can see Mister Robbie just fine, but don't tell your grandma that."

"Okay." Samantha grabbed Sophie's hand and pulled her toward the orchard where Cat's rig was finally being delivered. "Look. There's our truck. Come on. We got to throw Laddie's ball and keep him with us."

While the twins scampered off, Cat focused on the matching white dresses that her mother drew out of the car. A sleeveless design with a scoop neck, an empire waist, full pleated skirt and the sequined details would make the girls look like princesses. "They're beautiful, Mother. Thank you."

"Really? You like them?" Camille's smile was genuine. "I bought dress shoes and white socks too. They'll look like little angels."

"They certainly will." Cat laughed, taking the dresses. "And I promise not to let them anywhere near the barn in those. You always think about hair ribbons. What color did you get?"

Another beaming smile and Camille dove for one more bag. It was so easy to make her mother happy, Cat thought. All she had to do was act girly and make her daughters do the same. There was a time and a place for that. It wouldn't hurt the twins to get in touch with their feminine sides.

As her mother hunted down the ribbons, Cat watched Dray pull up in her truck and park. The boy waved, switched off the engine. He came toward her with a handful of receipts and a cardboard beer box. "Thank you, Dray. What do you have there?"

Red crept into his young face. "I got the saplings in the back of the truck. They were on sale for cheap because it's the end of the season, so I bought the rest of the apple trees. And these people outside the store were giving away kittens so I got the litter and their mom," he said, holding up the box. "I didn't see any cats around here and you have a farm and—"

Cat grinned. "If I said no, what would you do?"

"Take them to Ted. His mom has a farm too and I didn't want the kittens taken away from their mother," Dray said. "They're too little."

"Catriona, you know you'll keep them," Camille said, rolling her eyes as she finally produced the ribbons. "Now, stop teasing the boy and introduce us. You always wanted cats when you were a child and your father never allowed pets. The girls will like them a lot more than the dolls or the dresses I bought."

Her mother was actually being nice and realistic for once. "Yes, but they can't wear kittens to church." Cat leaned down and kissed her mother's cheek. "I'm glad you buy nice clothes for them. They're so whiny when I want to get them something other than jeans."

"If they saw you in something other than jeans, they might change their minds," Camille said. "As it is, you have two girls who are just like you."

The twins dashed back, Lad behind them. "Hi. What's in the box, Dray?"

"A momma cat and her kittens. Where do you want them?" Dray asked as the girls squealed and started to jump up and down.

"In the kitchen. Leave Lad with me and go help Dray unpack the kitties," Cat told the twins. "They'll stay inside until they figure out this is their new home. You can pet the mom if she's friendly, but don't touch the babies until she tells you that it's okay."

"She's a cat," Dray said. "How will she tell them?"

"By showing us her babies," Samantha said, "and purring."

Cat waited until she was alone with her mother—well except for Rob. Since Camille couldn't see the ghost, it was as secluded as it was going to get. "Why didn't Dad allow me to have pets? He's not allergic, is he?"

"Of course not." Camille brought out more garment bags. "He had issues with his family, and he was extremely annoyed when you were like his relatives. The O'Learys are country folks. They always had all sorts of animals around their houses. You adored your grandmother and aunt. I finally got tired of all his tantrums and divorced him when he got rid of the puppy they gave you."

"What happened to the puppy?" Cat asked, struggling to remember it.

"I had to bail it out of the pound and return it to your grandmother. I know she thought I was a real witch." Camille forced a smile. "I couldn't let her give it back to you because I knew it would end up at the shelter again and I might not find it a second time. They killed animals in those shelters, back then."

"And they still do." Recalling the golden collie that followed her around when she visited her grandmother, Cat hugged Camille. This had to have been their first in-depth conversation in a long time. "Thanks for rescuing her. That took courage. Now, let me see what else you brought the girls. Even if I hadn't seen those bags, I'd still know you didn't stop at one outfit each."

"You may have to move the girls upstairs just to find a closet big enough for all those things," Rob drawled. "Next time your daddy comes to visit, I'll see to it that he falls down a lot. I never liked him when he was a youngster and now, I really have issues with that bully."

So did she, Cat thought, but she wasn't going to agree with him when her mother would overhear. Even if the two of them were getting along for the moment, it didn't mean that Camille had finished expressing her opinion about the divorce or Frazer.

When the older woman finally left an hour later, they were still in charity with each other, Camille clutching a bouquet of red, pink and yellow long-stemmed roses. Cat promised to come to lunch the next time she was in Everett.

While the girls oohed and aahed over the calico and multi-colored kittens, Cat went through the receipts Dray provided. She frowned at the one from the gas station. "Why did you have to stop there? I always top off when I'm in Lake Maynard because we don't have anywhere to fuel up in Baker City."

"The gauge showed empty at the tire store and I didn't want to risk driving up the mountain until I filled the tank." Dray rubbed his chin thoughtfully. "I'll bet it got siphoned while it was in town waiting to be towed. Sometimes, if a rig looks abandoned, it gets hit. You need a locking gas cap. I'll swing by O'Leary's hardware store and see what they have left."

O'Leary's? As in her relatives' store? "I didn't know it was still open," Cat said.

"It's not, but Aidan keeps a few parts on hand because the nearest auto supply place is so far away."

Cat hesitated. Rob had disappeared and her daughters were still busy with the kittens in the kitchen while Lad cautiously looked on from a safe distance. He'd already had his nose scratched by Momma Cat as the mother cat had been unceremoniously christened. "Is Aidan related to Liam O'Leary?"

"One of his older brothers," Dray said. "Why? Do you know Liam?"

"He's my father." Cat shrugged. "We're not close. I adored my Aunt Rose though, so when I turned eighteen, I took her married name."

"Well, don't tell folks in town that you're related to him," Dray advised. "A couple of the old-timers lost big bucks in a couple of his schemes. He and my cousin, Herman are really tight. Nobody trusts Herman, so if they're good buddies—"

Cat nodded. That was pretty much what she'd assumed. "I'll be careful." She looked at the receipt from the hardware store. Dray had gotten a good deal on the trees. "Wow, buy one, get one free. So, you got six trees for the price of three."

"And those three were discounted to half-price already. We made out. I should have worn a mask." Dray paused. "I noticed you stacked all the firewood in the shed. I would have done that tomorrow."

Thanks to Rob, but she wasn't going to mention that. "I know," Cat said, "but now you can check and see if there's a riding mower in the machine shed. If there is and it's in working order you can cut the grass after you plant those trees."

"Yeah, unless you work the night shift again and do it before I get back."

She smiled, unwilling to mention Rob working as her otherworld handyman. "Well, let me get my checkbook and we'll settle up," Cat said. "Then, I'll run you into town."

"Sounds good." Dray went across the room to kneel down by the beer box where, by the sounds of it, the kittens and their mother were making themselves at home. The twins were still looking at them, making cooing sounds. "Seems like these fur-folks found the best home."

"We like kitties," Sophie told him.

"But, Laddie still wants his own puppy to play with," Samantha added.

"Then we'll just have to see what we find," Dray told them.

Laughing, Cat headed for the den and her purse. With the teenager on the case, she'd better warn him that she would only have another collie on the farm. They were her favorite breed and now she knew it was because she'd had one as a child. She sat down behind the rolltop desk and reached for her calculator. Before she could total the receipts, Rob appeared in the room.

"You're settling in for the duration."

"Afraid so, Mister Robbie." Cat smiled at him. "And if you have a problem with that, you shouldn't have told the twins that a second dog was a good idea."

He leaned against the doorframe—or he would have, if he were solid. "It is. It will give the pup company and then he won't be as likely to chase a coyote over the hill and get torn to pieces."

She stared at him. He didn't look like he was joking tonight. She met his dark gaze. "Are you serious?"

"Yes. Seen it happen before and I don't want to see it happen again, not to the twins' pet even if the silly thing thinks I'm only good for tummy rubs."

Cat laughed. "Thanks for looking out for him. Now, I have to run Dray into town, and I'll take care of the horses when I get back. It won't hurt them to have a bit longer on the grass."

"You should have told me before I put them in the barn and fed them. I unsaddled for the kids. Kittens don't come every day and the girls usually look after their ponies."

Tears stung, but she couldn't let them fall. He was so much better to them than their own father and she sure as sugar wasn't saying that either. "I owe you."

"Don't worry." Rob winked at her. "I'll make you pay me back, sweetheart."

CHAPTER FOURTEEN

Since they didn't have to rush home, Cat dropped Dray at the café, then drove to the cemetery. She and the girls took the roses she had cut to the O'Leary section and put small bouquets on the various graves. Afterwards, they returned to Pop's and had dinner. Once they finished eating, they headed over to the mercantile to pick up kitty supplies.

Maxine waved at Cat as she entered the general store. "I'm glad to see you. I was telling Julie about your ideas and she wants to sign up to run the haunted—" The older woman closed her mouth when she saw the girls coming in behind Cat.

"What?" Samantha asked, her eyes wide. "The haunted what?"

"It's a surprise," Cat said hastily. "We're going to party hearty over Halloween, but the grownups are putting it together. Now, I need you and Sophie to go find food for Momma Cat. We need a tray for the litter too."

"Okay." Sophie pulled on Samantha's arm. "It's over where we got Lad's food last time."

After the kids ran off to accomplish their mission, Cat went to the counter where Maxine waited, the ghostly figure of the long-ago madam floating behind her. "So, who is Julie and what does she want to do for the festival?"

"She's the deacon's wife and Ted's mom," Maxine said. "And she wants to open up the bordello and wear a red dress cut clear to her navel. I said yes to the house of ill repute, but the dress—"

"Nothing nasty ever went on in my house and it's not starting now," said the madam. "I ran a high-class place. She can wear a low-cut dress, one that shows her legs but that's it."

Cat nodded at the ghost. "I agree with you, Maxine. We have to remember to keep this family friendly if we want to make money. She wears a knee-length dress that shows a bit of cleavage, fishnet stockings, high heels and has a feather boa around her neck. How many kids does she have?"

"Six. Her place is a zoo, most of the time. I know she really wants her husband to see her as a woman, not only a mom."

"So, let's give her a chance to dress up on her own," Cat suggested. "That should be the rule for everyone who participates. We need this to be fun all concerned so we can make money and do it every year."

"All right. I'm making a list of the buildings we can use. Herman told Frank that all of his are off-limits."

That figured. "Why?" Cat asked. "Does he have something else in mind for Halloween?"

"No. He claims he's afraid of being sued if someone gets hurt. Frank said that his insurance agent is taking care of a liability policy for the town, but Herman still refused to get involved." Maxine didn't sound too concerned. "And Pop said he was glad because then we don't have to worry about Herman ruining everything."

Cat glanced at the back of the store and saw the twins coming toward her, carrying a bag of chow, a scratching post, a plastic tray and toys. "Good thing Frank paid me for training his horses today. It looks like we're buying out your place."

"That's okay with me." Maxine beamed at the girls. "Did you find everything you need?"

"Yes. Did Mommy tell you about the kitties Dray brought us?" Sophie asked.

"No, he did when he came to get his grandpa's order." Maxine began to ring up the sale. "Herman tried to tell me not to take your check, Cat, and I told him that I don't owe him anything so I'm not listening to him."

"What business is it of his? I don't bank with him and he doesn't know anything about me, but he should be careful. There are laws against that sort of discrimination."

"He's a woman-hater." The madam twirled her pink boa. "You owning property and having money is enough to get his goat. I wouldn't let him in the front door of my place."

Cat ignored the ghost of the old prostitute.

"Mommy sent him away when he came to our house," Samantha volunteered.

"Well, that would do it," Maxine said. "I know Summer doesn't like him either, but some people do listen to him, Cat. I just wanted to warn you. Julie works for me part-time and you won't have any problems with her taking your money either."

"I appreciate it." Cat put away her debit card, deciding to keep a certain amount of cash in her purse whenever she came to town. Then, she definitely wouldn't have a problem. Very few businesses turned down cash.

Collecting their bags, she led the way from the mercantile to the pickup parked near the café. She helped the girls buckle up then slipped into the driver's seat. She slid the key into the ignition, turned it. Nothing. Not even a click. Strange. The truck usually started right up. She tried again. Nothing.

She pulled the release, climbed out, walked around to the front and popped the hood. She lifted it, propped it open. Had the battery died?

She gaped at the empty spot where the battery normally sat. Gone? Who would steal it? How? She had the keys. Had Dray made a copy for himself?

Think, Cat. Remember. Frazer used to drive the pickup when he had the late shift. He always lost his keys when he was gambling and drinking at the casino. He'd put an extra set in a magnetic case and stuck it under the truck, up from the left front tire. The case was still there and so were the keys, but it didn't mean someone hadn't used them.

She tucked the extra set into her pocket. "Come on, girls. The truck's broke again."

"Why? Who keeps hurting it, Mommy?" Sophie asked.

"I don't know, honey, but we'll find out." Cat guided the twins back into the café, grateful once again that Rob had done the chores so she didn't have to rush home to the horses. When the twins were settled in a booth with mugs of hot chocolate, she approached Pop. "Somebody stole my battery. Is there anywhere to get one in town?"

"I'll call Aidan," Pop said. "He may have one. Anything else?"

"A locking gas cap," Cat said. "My gas was siphoned when the tires were punctured."

"Okay." Pop headed for the old-fashioned phone on the wall. Before he reached it, the bell jangled on the door and Dray rushed inside. "What is it, son?"

"Is Cat…" He stopped. "You're all right?"

"Why wouldn't I be?"

"Because somebody broke all the glass out of your truck," Dray exclaimed. "Windshield, side windows, mirrors, the works!"

The pup yapped and rolled to his feet. Rob followed him to the picture windows, and they watched Ted Fenwick's truck roll to a stop in front of the house. "This is getting to be a bad habit. You reckon somebody messed with her rig again, dog?"

Lad woofed, but since Rob didn't speak canine, he decided he'd better wait for an interpreter. The collie trotted to the front door to meet the twins.

Samantha petted him, then followed the dog back into the living room. "Hi, Mister Robbie. We went to the store two times and we got stuff for the kitties."

"And a new toy for Laddie so he won't feel bad," Sophie added. "And somebody mean broke our truck again."

Rob watched Cat come in, carrying a litter tray and two dishes. Behind her, Ted Fenwick toted a sack of food and another of litter. They headed for the kitchen. Rob and the girls followed along, Lad a cautious escort.

Momma Cat had apparently made herself at home during their absence, because she leaped off one of the chairs at the table and came over to inspect the purchases. Two of her tiny kittens, a black one and a tabby, so young they barely had their eyes open, shadowboxed near the woodstove.

Cat laughed, scooped up the fist-sized felines and carried them back to the box where the others slept. "In here, you two. I don't want you stepped on by our big feet."

"They're awesome," Ted said, grinning. "If you decide you want homes for a couple, let me know. My sisters love cats."

"This place is big enough, I think we'll be fine," Cat said. "They may decide to move out of the house to the barns and that'd be okay too. I'll keep you guys in mind if I hear about more kittens. Dray brought us these so you may want to connect with him too."

"He knows where to bring strays when he finds them," Ted said, "so we always get our share." He glanced at the clock. "It's almost eight and I need to head for home. Aidan said he'd call when your truck was ready. Any ideas who did it?"

Cat shook her head and glanced quickly at the girls. "No, but I'll put my thinking cap on and see what I come up with before I talk to the police chief tomorrow. Maybe, he'll have a few suggestions too."

"What does your thinking cap look like, Mommy?" Sophie asked.

"It's an expression that my grandma used," Cat said. "Now, it's time for you girls to grab your jammies. I'll go start your bath water."

"I can do that while you send your guest on his way," Rob told her, straightening from where he leaned against the wall. "Then, I want to hear all about your truck."

She didn't say anything for a moment, but escorted Ted to the front door. Rob heard her thanking him for the ride home and then the sound of the lock being turned, something she hadn't bothered to do since she moved into the house.

She was spooked and not by him. When she came into the bathroom, she glanced around quickly for the twins. They hadn't come in yet.

She stepped closer to the tub, so the rushing water hid her voice and said, "Someone stole the battery out of my truck, followed that up by breaking out all the glass *and* siphoning a full tank of gas."

"Do you know who'd do something like that?" Rob asked.

"I'm suspicious by nature. I think it's probably Herman

MacGillicudy, but I don't have any proof." She shook her head. "It's just a truck. I'm not going to cry over it."

"Not now," Rob said. "You have two girls to round up and put to bed if you want them to go to school tomorrow and there are kittens in the kitchen undoubtedly distracting them."

"Good point." She left the bathroom and went in search of her daughters.

Rob hadn't left the farm in ages, but it didn't mean he couldn't. Some ghosts were locked into the locations where they died, but he'd always been able to move around the ranch, the Baker City area where he grew up and as far away as Seattle. Once the twins were busy splashing in the tub and their mom was supervising, Rob headed for town. The three bars were hopping with customers, both alive and dead. He headed for the back table in the one where the late mayor and his cronies could be found.

Newt O'Leary was the first to spot him. "Hey, young feller. You ain't been around for a while. How's your home place?"

Conversations faded while the rest of the men waited for Rob's answer. "Fine and dandy. I have company staying. And she and her girls can see me."

"And talk to you?" Newt elbowed the mayor. "Told you she knew we were at the meeting today. And you didn't believe me. She's one of mine, ain't she? And she has the O'Leary gift."

"What's the gift?" Rob asked, although he was pretty sure he already knew.

"Seeing the dead," Newt told him. "Not all of my kin have the sight, but quite a few do. She can help you move on if you want."

"No, I'm happy where I am." Rob leaned against the corner post of the booth. "She works really hard on the farm and is a fine mother to those girls of hers. So, any idea who busted up her truck tonight, left her and the twins to walk home?"

"It's a good stretch of the legs out to the dude ranch." The mayor frowned and looked around at his companions. "Who'd leave a woman and her children stranded?"

"Not the first time it's happened," Rob said. "When she came to church last Sunday, someone punctured all four tires and Ted Fenwick brought her home then too."

MY SWEET HAUNT

"Where's the rig now? At the Fenwick's?" Newt asked.

"No, your kin, Aidan has it so he can repair it," Rob said.

"Well, I'll go take a look at the truck and see what I can see," Newt said. "None of our folks did that to your gal. She's a looker and smart to boot. Got a lot of good ideas to bring back the town."

"And that will help most of us move on once we know our families are safe," the mayor said. "I'll go see if I can roust my great-grandson. When he's hoisted a couple beers, he can hear me just fine in his dreams."

"Thanks, Mayor O'Connell." Rob turned his attention to the three men in uniform. They'd passed on long before his war, but a soldier was a soldier and they'd come home too. "She needs protection when she comes to town. I can take care of her and the twins at the ranch. Could you—?"

"We'll watch over her when she's here." It was the ranking officer who spoke. "Sarge, go and round up the other vets. Get the women, too. They can follow her when she goes places that we can't."

She'd read two stories, one for each girl and tucked them into their beds. Lad opted to stay in their room with them, obviously afraid of the kitty family in the kitchen. Cat bent and petted his tri-colored head. "She'll figure out that you won't hurt her babies soon. It'll be okay, buddy."

Adjusting the blankets on each of the girls, Cat tiptoed from the room. "Sleep tight, sweeties. I love you. See you in the morning."

She headed for her own room to collect her robe and nightgown. She had a million things she could be doing around the house. She could clean, design websites and brochures on her computer, but not tonight. Right now, she needed some alone time.

Who was out to ruin her life? Why? Sure, other people had entered the essay contest, but it hadn't hurt anyone when she won the prize. And as far as she knew, no one held a grudge about it.

She went into the bathroom, piled her clothes on the vanity and turned on the shower. While the water warmed, she stripped out of her clothing. She stepped under the spray and only then did she let the tears pour down her cheeks.

Someone hated her and she didn't know why. What was she going to do? How could she keep her children safe? If she left here, where could she take them? No answers came. She cried harder.

By the time she shut off the shower, she felt better. Tears didn't solve any problem but being able to vent eased the emotional upheaval. She made herself a cup of warm milk and added a shot of peppermint schnapps for flavor, taking the mug with her to the bedroom. She sipped the drink while she read her murder mystery, trying to solve the crime before the detective could.

When she switched off her bedside lamp, she was back in control. She could handle this. She hadn't let a ghost drive her off the farm and she wasn't letting a live human do it either.

She wondered where Rob had gone. He'd disappeared hours ago and hadn't returned. She shook her head. Now, that was familiar. Did ghosts go to casinos to gamble the way that Frazer did?

Did his kiss wake her? Was it part of her dream? He was on top of the comforter and she rolled closer to him. She tangled her hands in his hair and brought his mouth to hers. His tongue took possession, starting a teasing duel. Then, he lifted his head for an instant.

His lips found her ear and he nipped gently. "Wildcat."

"Where were you?"

"Checking on your truck." His soft chuckle warmed the spot below her ear. "Purr for me, kitten."

"What?" She tried to push him away, but his mouth claimed hers in a fierce kiss.

No, he wasn't here. It wasn't real. She shook her head, woke herself up. She wasn't alone. He stood by the side of the bed, still a ghost, a shadowy figure in fatigues and combat boots. "How did you do that?"

"I can touch you when your defenses are down," Rob said, "but it takes a lot of energy, more than when I work around the ranch."

She reached over, turned on the bedside lamp. He was almost invisible and yet she knew he'd kissed her. She still tasted his mouth on hers. "You were here before. It wasn't my imagination."

He chuckled. "Not unless you have the same kind of imagination I do, cougar cub."

She pointed to the door. "I'm not sharing a bed with you. Don't expect me to fall into your arms. I won't." She couldn't feel his touch, but there was an odd sensation of warmth as if his hand brushed her cheek. "The answer is no, Mister Robbie. You can go now."

"Rob or Robert." He smiled down at her. "Robbie is what the twins call me, not you."

The next morning, she felt herself smiling while she dressed, made coffee, fed the mother cat and took Lad with her to the barn to feed the horses. The collie made little dashes after his tennis ball, bringing it back so she could throw it just one more time. And another time. And yet a fourth, fifth and eventually a tenth time as they started back to the house.

She glanced toward the bridge and saw a candy-apple red car coming up the drive. *Now*, what? She called Lad to her. The pup sat by her heel and she petted him. He was learning to be safe.

The driver parked and she recognized Dray when he opened the door. "What a beauty. Where did you get it?"

"Oh, it's not mine." He came toward her, swinging a set of keys. "Aidan sent it so you would have something to drive while your truck is in his shop. It's your Aunt Rose's Mustang."

"No way," Cat said, charmed by the classic vehicle. "I've never seen her drive it. Why would she leave a car like this in a garage?" Cat walked around the hood of the car, softly touching the brilliant red paint. "It's gorgeous. When did she get it?"

"It's mine." Rob said, behind her. "I saved my Army pay for two years and ordered it from the factory. I left it to Rosie in case something happened to me."

Cat caught her breath. "You know my aunt?" She looked at Dray but spoke to Rob as well.

"Sure." Dray passed her the keys. "Everybody in town does, but her husband isn't real thrilled when she drives this car because he feels like he's competing with her high school sweetheart. The guy died in Vietnam and he left the Mustang to her."

"Well, it wasn't like I could drive it anymore and I didn't want my brothers touching it," Rob said. "I'd seen them with my dad's tractor and that was just plain scary."

Cat stared at the set of keys in her hand, then looked at the two men, one alive and one dead. Why hadn't she put the facts together and realized that Rob was her aunt's former fiancé? Because the whole thing sounded far-fetched. She moved into a haunted house and discovered she could see ghosts. It wasn't just the ranch that was haunted. It was the entire town.

And she had two kissing sessions with the same man that her aunt had undoubtedly slept with. Cat shuddered. It lent new meaning to the saying, "All in the family." She adored her aunt, but sharing a man with her? No way!

"I'll go plant some trees," Dray suggested. "I only have three hours before Ted gets here. Mrs. Tommy said to tell you that she'd drive the kids today and you could take her turn tomorrow. She'll bring the town kids in the church van and switch out vehicles with you. She said not to worry. She'll park the Mustang in her carport."

"I'll need to check the garage here," Cat said. "We want to make sure there's plenty of room for this car."

"I'll sweep out the garage after I plant the trees," Dray said. "Where do you want the new ones?"

They walked toward the orchard, leaving Rob with the classic car. When she reached the orchard, she saw the saplings were sitting in a small plastic tub of water. When had he done that? It must have been earlier this morning. She hoped her smile looked genuine, and said, "I thought they were thirsty."

"Great idea," Dray said. "I'll pour the water on them once they're settled."

Cat glanced around the orchard. Whoever planned the area had more of an artist's eye than that of a true farmer. The trees were in clusters, not straight lines. Wooden park benches in strategic places invited visitors to sit and enjoy the peaceful view. She led the way over to the apple section. The first tree would be in the spot vacated by the dead one.

They examined the group, figuring out where each of the new fruit saplings would fit. "Maybe, I ought to stop by the hardware store and see what else they have on sale. It doesn't look like anyone has brought in new stock for the orchard in years."

"They had some leftover rose bushes too," Dray said. "And I know you like those."

"Definitely time to go shopping." Cat laughed. "Let's get you started. I need to feed the girls breakfast. It's French toast Wednesday. Have you eaten or would you like to join us?"

"He's a teenage boy," Rob pointed out, appearing out of nowhere, as always, and looking around the apple trees himself. "They can always eat."

"Thanks, but I had breakfast at the café," Dray said. "Mom had the early shift."

"I'll call you when the food's ready just in case you want some, but it'll be a while." Cat headed for the house. She'd send her aunt an email after the girls left for school. The two of them needed to talk. How was she going to bring up the subject of a dead Army hero, a haunted dude ranch and a town full of ghosts without sounding like a total nutcase?

PART II

"I died to buy this farm and I'm not going anywhere..."

ROBERT JACOB WILLIAMS

CHAPTER FIFTEEN

Between training horses, mowing the yard and rose garden with the self-propelled, lawn-mower from the garage and laying out a new pasture fence, the rest of the day zoomed by. Shortly after three, she headed into the house to make snacks for the girls since they would be home soon from school.

The telephone rang and she hurried to answer the kitchen extension. Instead of her aunt's cheerful voice, Cat heard a string of obscenities. She hastily replaced the receiver. What was that about? Had she been assigned a number that belonged to someone else, someone with a crazy ex?

The calls continued throughout the next hour. When Lad barked a warning that someone was approaching the house, she unplugged the extension, tucking the cord where the twins wouldn't see it. Then, they wouldn't ask questions or make comments about the broken phone. Pausing to unplug the phones in the living-room and den, she headed for the front door, expecting to see the van and her daughters.

Instead, a tall, older man stood on the porch. Broad shoulders filled out his blue uniform shirt tucked neatly into dark blue slacks. A belt around his waist held all the paraphernalia that an officer needed. Short black hair liberally sprinkled with white was barely visible under his western hat, modeled after the Canadian Mounties' version.

Behind him, a police cruiser sat on the gravel apron in front of the house.

Cat petted the young dog who stood between her and the door before she opened it. "Can I help you?"

"I'm Police Chief Dick O'Connell from Baker City." He held out his hand to shake hers. His polite smile didn't touch ice-cold blue eyes. "Pop MacGillicudy told me about your truck and then I went by Aidan O'Leary's to see it. I've filled out the paperwork and I'll send a report down to the county for their records."

"Thank you." Cat decided to opt for the friendly approach. "I appreciate the help."

The smile faded, as he opened a metal folder. "Aidan said he loaned you his sister's Mustang. I don't see it."

"Because it's locked in the garage," Cat said. Something about this cop grated on her nerves and she wondered what bothered her. "I didn't want to worry about the car. Someone has been siphoning my gas. Is that a regular problem in Baker City?"

"That's it," Rob drawled, suddenly appearing in the living-room doorway. "Take the battle to him, kitten. Now, ask him where the county clown is hiding."

Cat kept her focus on the police officer's weathered features. "Well, is it me? Or does your town have trouble with visitors too? If they do, the B.C. Business Association will have trouble promoting festivals to bring in visitors during the next two months."

A muscle twitched in Dick's jaw. "Are you threatening me?"

"Does it sound like a threat?" Cat folded her arms and met his gaze. "Or just a fact? I can't think the town will be safer if the city council contracts out crime prevention to the county sheriff. Their office is over two hours away in Everett."

The awkward silence lengthened between them. Then he finally asked, "Are you having any other problems I should know about?"

It was the use of a civil tone that earned her momentary trust. "I started getting obscene phone calls this afternoon."

"A teenage prank? Does it sound like a man? Or since I don't want to be accused of being sexist, a woman?"

Cat thought for a moment. "If it were teens, I'd hear somebody laughing in the background. No, this was a man's voice. I didn't recognize it."

Dick nodded and made notes on a pad. "I'll add this to my list of the harassment, but could I suggest that you get an unlisted number? I can have Ted Fenwick arrange for one. He'll get it faster than you will. The closest tower is between here and Lake Maynard so you can't count on cell service up here in the hills all of the time, especially when the weather is bad."

"That makes sense," Cat said. "Thank you."

She glanced past him as both a green and white sheriff's car and the church van holding her daughters pulled up in the driveway. "Did you expect the other officer?"

Dick looked over his shoulder. "I wasn't sure if he'd make it," he said. "You're not actually in the town limits and that's where my jurisdiction officially ends, but I'm not leaving a woman and two kids out here without protection."

"Okay, I appreciate it." Cat watched the van come to a stop and her daughters pop out. They waved to their friends and raced toward her. She stepped aside and allowed Lad to bolt past her. The collie ran to the girls, tail wagging. He barked and leaped, then circled them before sitting in front of Samantha for some petting.

Sophie hugged the dog too, before she eyeballed the two police cars, then hustled toward the porch. "Mommy, why are the police here? Did something bad happen to Daddy?"

"No, sweetie." Cat brushed her daughter's hair back from her face. "As far as I know, your dad's just fine. These officers are here about the things that happened to the truck and I need to talk to them for a bit longer."

"Then, will you ride with me and Sam?"

"Yes, after you change your clothes." Cat waved to Virginia as the woman cautiously backed the van out, turned it and headed down the drive with the rest of the elementary school crowd. "Come on, Samantha. Bring Laddie. It's snack time and you know how he loves that."

"Okay." The eight-year-old leaned down to rub the pup's ears, before the two of them ran toward the porch. "He wanted to do his job and woof at the other man, but I told him that you already knew we had company and that would be tacky."

Dick chuckled, his eyes warming a bit. "Now, I know you're Aidan's niece all right. His momma used to swear that there was nothing worse than 'tacky' and she could come up with punishments when we embarrassed her."

Cat held up her hand so the twins couldn't carry on the conversation any longer. "Inside, girls. We have a lot to do today."

Samantha tilted her head to one side. "Mommy, do we really get to ride in Mister Robbie's car? Mrs. Virginia said we could, but some of the boys said she was fibbing. No kids get to even sit in it, 'cause we're messy."

"It is a special kind of car," Cat said, "but if he has problems with you two riding in it, he'd better get over himself. I'm not putting my girls in the trunk or making you walk to town."

"Come on, Sam. He's right here and we can ask him." Sophie hurried into the hall, followed by her sister and the collie. "Mister Robbie—"

Cat stepped onto the porch and closed the door so the twins' one-sided conversation with the ghost couldn't be overheard. She watched as emotions slid across Dick's face—curiosity, wonder, concern and a trace of fear—before he took a deep breath. "What else do you need to know for your report?"

"This has nothing to do with that." He lowered his voice so the county officer lumbering toward them didn't hear. "Your kids have the O'Leary gift, don't they? They're mediums."

Cat nodded. "It takes a while to believe it."

"Not around here, but it's something we don't discuss with outsiders." Dick turned to the burly man mounting the steps that shook beneath his tread. "Ms. McTavish, this is Officer Paul Griffith who keeps the peace out here with me. Paul, this is Cat O'Leary McTavish. She's taken over the place and that's going to make your life a lot easier."

Cat studied the county officer. He was nearly as broad as he was tall. Thinning sandy hair was carefully combed to hide the multitude of bald spots. His plump, ruddy features weren't handsome, but for some reason she found herself smiling back at him. "How will it make things easier?"

"Kids party here and then call for help when things get weird," Paul Griffith said, with a cheerful grin. "Lights flashing on and off, music playing loudly and then cutting out, things being thrown at them, cars moving by themselves. It's just a bunch of wild stories, probably brought on by drugs and alcohol."

"Is that what they say?" Cat struggled to suppress a smile and didn't look at Dick O'Connell. "Or did they have another story?"

"Oh, they claim it's not them." Griffith shook his head. "I know they're lying. Their lips were moving." He laughed. "Like I believed there was a ghost floating around this place."

"And now you know why we called him Bigger when we were boys," Rob said, as he wandered out to the porch. "It was short for 'Bigger is Dumber.' He never did have any imagination."

That was downright mean, and she'd discuss it with him later. As it was, Cat contented herself by giving him a stern look. "Well, I appreciate you protecting the farm, Officer. It does have some property damage, but not as much as if you hadn't been here."

Dick nodded. "Good points. Let me bring you up to speed, Paul." He outlined the recent events. "It sounds like there's a problem we need to resolve before it escalates."

"Maybe so," Griffith said. "Some folks may think that busting up her rig and making funny phone calls isn't really serious."

Cat frowned. She counted to ten and then said, "Officer Griffith, I think you should do some research on stalkers and female homicide victims before you decide all of this is my hysteria. Now, as far as I'm concerned, Chief O'Connell can keep you posted, but I have two daughters who just got home from school and there are things I need to do before dark."

"The girls are fine," Rob said. "They were eating their snacks and naming the kittens when I left."

Cat nodded, eyed the two cops again and then said, "You have a nice day." With that, she stepped into the house, locking the door before she headed to the kitchen. Securing it wouldn't keep the ghost out, but it would at least slow down the two cops. She heard the girls talking in their room and went to check on them. "Ready to go riding?"

"In a few minutes," Sophie told her. "The momma kitty still worries about Laddie, but he promised not to hurt the babies."

"Someday, she'll believe us." Samantha pulled a sweatshirt over her head. "Are the police going to find the bad people who hurt our truck?"

"Chief O'Connell will look," Cat said. She wasn't as sure about Officer Griffith. "Now, how was your day?"

The police were gone by the time the three of them walked out the front door. They headed for the barn to saddle up. Lad charged ahead of them, eager for a new adventure. Cat took a deep breath and glanced at Rob when he floated across the yard. He looked a bit sheepish, and she said. "Don't you ever teach my children to call anyone names, especially not a police officer, or you'll answer to me. A two-hour time-out will seem like Christmas. Got it?"

"Bigger is an idiot."

"Are you pushing me for a reason? I'll bet next time I go into town, I can find somebody who knew your parents. I'll be able to ask your mother if she raised you to be a bully. Do you want me to go there?"

"No, ma'am! She'd skin me alive."

The man had been dead for decades and he was still scared of his equally deceased mother. Cat tried not to smile. "I'll expect good manners as long as you're here." She relaxed, tension finally slipping out of her mind and body. "What did you tell the twins about your car?"

"Of course, they can ride in it or their special seats wouldn't be in the back," Rob said. "You may not want to let anyone know that Rosie and I used to go to the drive-in and eat popcorn in it."

Cat laughed. "Okay, your secret is safe with me."

The next morning, she started earlier than usual since she was in charge of the carpool to the elementary school in Lake Maynard. Because she planned to do errands in the larger city, she opted to wear a blue denim shirtdress, made of a cotton and silk blend with a classic western yoke and large pockets. She rolled up the sleeves and buttoned them into place. When she added a brown belt and her favorite blue cowgirl boots, she was still comfortable, but didn't look like she'd just come from the barn.

Rob was nowhere in sight and she refused to admit she missed his reaction to her appearance. He was dead, damn it! And she didn't care. Yeah, right!

Once she'd dropped off all the kids, she drove to the bank to deposit the checks she had received from Frank and Ingrid. Then Cat headed to the hardware store.

Sure enough, Dray had been right about the end of the season sale on fruit trees, rose bushes and flower bulbs. When she stopped for a fast food taco, she went through the calls on her cell phone. She called her aunt and left a message for the other woman to call or email her. Then she was off to the grocery. Cat loaded up on staples like flour, sugar, cereal and canned goods. She'd wait to buy frozen foods, milk and ice cream at the mercantile in Baker City.

She finished off with a visit to her lawyer's office to check on the progress of the divorce. She only had to wait for ten minutes before the paralegal ushered her into the conference room. Blonde and slender in black jacket and matching slacks, Bree Hawke, the divorce attorney, came in with a handful of folders. Cat suddenly realized the lawyer bore a striking resemblance to the man she'd seen up in Baker City.

"Are you related to Durango?" Cat asked suddenly. "I met him at Pop's café."

"He's my older brother." Bree pulled out a chair and sat down at the table that took up the center of the room. "I haven't seen him in a while. How is he?"

"He looks fine." Cat shrugged. "The locals were giving him a hard time about fixing the boundary fences between the McElroy place and mine."

"He has more money than most," Bree said, "and a construction company, so make sure he does it." She flipped open a file. "Okay, so I had your husband served with the divorce papers. His lawyer hasn't contacted me yet. Has he called you?"

Cat shook her head. "I went through all the calls on my cell today while I was in town and I still haven't heard from him. What's next?"

"The judge wants a parenting plan from him. Failing that, we need to show you'll allow reasonable visitation."

"He gets busy at work and he forgets to feed the girls when he's playing poker, so any visits would have to be supervised by an intelligent adult." Cat picked up the cup of coffee the paralegal had provided her. "I'm not trying to be difficult, Bree, but there were some issues when I was out of town at a horse show this past summer."

"Been that, done there." Bree flipped pages. "My parents always made it plain that my father's political career came first. Okay, so we'll show that your expectations are reasonable, and the twins' dad may be hard to pin down. We'll keep moving forward with the proceedings."

Cat sipped her coffee. She hadn't thought of contacting Frazer until yesterday when Sophie asked about her father. It would be possible to call the casino and leave a message for him, but why bother? He hadn't called them either. *And I don't miss him.* They'd been married for nine years, almost ten. He'd been a big part of her life for so long. Why didn't she want him around?

Because of Rob. He spent more time with her in a day than Frazer did in a week. Rob talked to the girls. He was there if they had bad dreams. The twins said he comforted them when they were afraid of monsters. He could be counted on to help take care of the horses. He petted and played with Lad too. And Rob wasn't even alive. A dead man was more responsible than Frazer.

Cat glanced at her watch. "I need to go pick up the kids at school. I'll check in with you next week and call your office. Cell phones don't work consistently in Baker City."

"No worries." Bree smiled. "I know where your place is, so if I need anything in the meantime, I'll stop by the ranch. If I run into Durango, I'll remind him about the perimeter fences."

After she picked up the group of children from the elementary school, it took a little over an hour to reach Baker City and the church parking lot where parents were waiting to collect their kids. Cat transferred the groceries and plants to the trunk of the Mustang. She helped the twins buckle up and then they were on the way home.

When she pulled across the private bridge and into the driveway, she saw Rob and Lad driving the herd of horses across the fields toward the big corral. "What on earth are they doing?"

Cat cruised slowly up the driveway behind the herd. She hoped the horses would consider the car part of the team putting them back where they belonged. Trotting, Gambler led the way with Lucky and Stormy directly behind her, then Star, the two young geldings and finally the older ones. The group headed straight into the big corral and Rob closed the gate behind them. The horses drifted off to graze, none of them seeming upset by their adventure.

Cat parked and switched off the car. She went to play detective when Rob came toward her. "How did they get out of the barn?"

"It doesn't make any sense," Rob said. "I didn't want to put them out today because you were gone. When I came back from building the fence, they were all across the creek, grazing by the cabins. Lad helped me bring them home."

"I saw that." Cat watched the tri-colored half-grown pup barking and bouncing around the girls earning their praise for his collie heroics. "Twins, I need your help. Can you ask the horses how they got loose?"

Samantha and Sophie looked at each other, then went to stand at the gate. Their ponies jogged over to meet them. A few moments later, Samantha came over. "It was a mean man who chased them out of the barn. He tried to make them go down to the highway, but Lucky didn't like the big cars so he took the other horses where there was good grass to eat."

"And Stormy says the man saw something far away so he left," Sophie added. "They want apples for dinner, and I promised they could all have some. Okay, Mommy?"

"That's fine. We'll have apple waffles for dinner." Cat knelt and drew Lad into a quick hug. "You're a very smart puppy. I thought you'd need more training to learn how to do your job, but you're getting closer and closer."

She ducked away from his puppy kiss and rumpled his white fur ruff. "Come on, girls. We have groceries to put away, a barn to clean, and chores to do. Rob, how are we going to keep this from happening again? I refuse to be held prisoner in my own home."

"If I'm around the barn, I can keep the horses safe."

"Only if the person doing it has imagination enough to see you,"

Cat said. "I don't think most adults have the capacity, do you? Officer Griffith never believed a word the teenagers said about you."

"Hadn't thought of that." Rob floated beside her to the Mustang. "If I could feel my feet, I'd be able to really drive my own car again."

"I thought Officer Griffiths said the party kids complained about you moving their rigs," Cat said. "How did you do that?"

"By using my energy and thinking about it."

"Then, I guess you'd better *think* when you get behind the wheel."

CHAPTER SIXTEEN

Rob waited until the twins were tucked into bed and their mother came out to the kitchen. She'd changed from her 'go to town' dress and fancier boots to the regular clothes she wore around the dude ranch. A western blouse clung to her curves and tucked neatly into black jeans that left little to his imagination. "Got to thinking about how to keep strangers off the ranch. There was always somebody around when I was a boy, so we didn't have to worry."

"What's your idea?" Cat knelt and collected the scampering kittens, taking the mischievous bunch back to their box and patient mother. "I haven't come up with anything yet."

"Highway gates, chains and padlocks," Rob said, shrugging. "You could have the boy set the posts in the morning. Call Summer and tell her to bring down four metal gates along with the chains and padlocks to secure them. She can get those from Aidan. He really needs to re-open the hardware store."

"You're brilliant. I could hug you." She laughed. "Well, I would if you weren't dead."

"We'll make it work at some point." Rob started toward her, then stopped when the phone rang.

"Cedar Creek Guest Ranch." Picking up the receiver, Cat paused to listen, then smiled. "I've been trying to catch up with you, Aunt Rose. Is now a good time to talk?"

Women always took forever on the phone, so he'd leave them to it. He drifted through the walls into the living room wondering if Cat's aunt was the same one he'd known and loved. Yet the notion didn't bother him.

When had he finally let go of the idea that he and Rosie would be together forever? It wasn't after he died and came home, or when she married Mac McTavish. Rob had regrets; who didn't?

But he was also ready to return to enjoy life even if such a thing seemed impossible to some folks. He'd been lonely for so long, but things were different now. Glancing at the TV, he turned it on, choosing an old John Wayne movie.

Cat settled into a chair at the table, listening to her aunt talk about the miles she and her husband had driven through the Yukon Territory that day. When the conversation ebbed, she said, "Did you get my letter about winning this farm in the essay contest?"

"Yes. I'm thrilled for you. I remember how much you loved the place when we visited."

"What about you?" Cat asked. "Didn't you love it?"

"Oh, honey. It was a lifetime ago. I liked it, but I also wanted to have adventures, not be tied down to one place for eons."

"What?" Cat held the receiver away and stared at it. "The folks in Baker City still talk about the way you were engaged to Rob Williams."

"Oh, sweet little Robbie." A smile was obviously evident in Rose's voice. "He was such a cutie. Whenever, his mom had roses in bloom, he'd bring one to me each and every day, all through grade school, junior high and then high school. I'd never known there were so many colors."

"You dated him."

"Honey, Baker City is really small. It wasn't like there was a lot of choice for us kids when we were old enough to start eying each other. I think there were thirty people in my graduating class and there weren't even twenty in his. I wanted to get out of town to go to college, but I wasn't going to break my parents' hearts."

"You were engaged to him."

"Yes, but I don't know if we'd ever have gotten married. He wanted that farm more than anything and like I said, it really wasn't for me. It was a great place to visit, but that didn't mean I wanted the responsibility of running it. His parents never had a vacation. They worked every day including holidays and couldn't come and go."

Cat shook her head, not quite believing what she was hearing. "It doesn't sound like a life and death romance to me."

"It wasn't to me and then I felt horribly guilty when he didn't come back alive from Vietnam. He left me his car and told his parents how much he loved me, that we were going to have a houseful of kids. I always wished I could have told him that he was a wonderful friend and there was somebody out there who was perfect for him, but it wasn't me."

Cat hesitated, then deliberately said. "If I tell him for you, will you answer two more questions for me?"

"Wait a minute. Is he there? He died. I know he died. He's not missing in action. They sent home his body and we had a beautiful funeral for him. He's buried up town."

"Yes." Cat listened to her aunt sputter for a few more minutes. "He died, but he also came home. He was here when we moved in and he hasn't left yet. Why didn't you or Grandma tell me about the O'Leary gift?"

"Because your father threatened to keep me from seeing you if I shared anything about the family heritage," Rose said. "When you were little, you saw what my mom did. She told me that she thought you'd be stronger than any of us and worried about how she could train you."

"Why didn't she?"

"She died just before your thirteenth birthday. You were so upset that you ran away for three days."

"I don't remember any of that."

"Of course not. You had a concussion, a broken leg and broken ribs by the time Aidan found you in an abandoned gravel pit. In the hospital, you couldn't even remember your name. We didn't know if you'd live so when your dad started having meltdowns, we figured he was ballistic because you might die. We all agreed to go along with what he wanted."

Cat frowned at the phone. She'd suffered a severe trauma, and everyone hid it from her. She could believe it of her mother. Camille was the queen of denial, but why didn't Liam still bring up the accident at this late date? Her father never had been the soul of tact or discretion. Why did she feel like there was more to the story?

"I'm going to have to do some thinking about that," Cat said. "I've never been able to carry on a conversation with my father without feeling attacked. It surprises me that he worried at all."

"Well, he had a tough row to hoe as Mac says." Rose heaved a sigh. "Liam should have been the next O'Leary gift-holder. He was the seventh child of a seventh daughter and it passed him by. When everyone stopped treating him like the local crown prince, he couldn't handle it."

"So, he's jealous of me?" Cat leaned back in her chair. "Now, why doesn't that shock me?"

"Because you've always been a smart little cookie," Rose said. "I'm thrilled that you have the gift. My mother had it and my grandmother. And now, you. How are you holding up? Are you okay?"

"I'm fine, now that I know what I am." Cat leaned back in her chair. "Thank heaven, it's not Hollywood. No one I've seen has shown up covered in blood. The same goes for the twins. We may see the ghosts, but as the girls say, they're not icky."

Rose laughed. "I can hear them saying that. Are they still talking to critters?"

"Yes. I haven't learned how to do that." Cat paused, twined the handset cord around her finger. "This will sound tacky, but how serious were you and Rob?" She looked around, then lowered her voice to a whisper. "Did you sleep…?"

"What? No way! Honey, it may have been the 1960s, but we were from a small town. Robbie worshipped me and we just didn't do that kind of thing. Besides, I didn't want him that way. I figured things might change when he came home, but as far as I knew, he didn't. And I have the husband I want with me now and always. Are we okay?"

"Yes, we're fine. I wanted to talk to you about everything and I feel a lot better. When will you be back in Washington State? We're having a big festival in Baker City next month."

After a few more pleasantries, they hung up. The kittens had scrambled out of their box once more, so Cat picked them up and returned them to their mom before going to check on the girls again. She adjusted blankets and kissed each of them. Then she went into the living room where she found Rob and Lad watching John Wayne kick butt.

"Thanks for letting me talk to my aunt in private."

"You're welcome." Rob muted the sound on the TV, pushing back in the recliner, an interesting feat since he didn't actually sit in it, much less put up his barely visible feet. "Did you have a good visit?"

"An interesting one." Cat eyed him. He wore his favorite green uniform. "Did you know she married someone else?"

"Oh sure. I went to the wedding. I had to respect her choice. Quinn McTavish is a good sort and she waited ten years after I was buried. They brought flowers to my grave and he promised me that he'd take good care of her."

Cat sank down on the couch. "Didn't you mind that she chose someone else?"

"What was she supposed to do, kitten? Throw herself in the grave with me?" Rob gave a dramatic shudder. "She was alive, and I wasn't. It could have been different if we died together and came back together, but that wasn't an option. Now, can I watch my movie?"

"Sure. Turn it up so I can hear it. I'll make popcorn during the next commercial." She hesitated. "Do you think we have to worry about the stock tonight?"

"No. I'll check on them while you're microwaving your snack and I'll stay out there tonight. Then if someone comes after them, I'll wake you up."

"Before you raise a ruckus?"

He chuckled. "Now, I'm not promising that."

The next morning, she put his suggestion in effect. Dray found four of the biggest cedar posts under the huge evergreen tree. He toted the posts to the end of the U-shaped driveway. He dug post holes and set each one, using gravel to stabilize them. Summer would bring a bag of quick drying concrete when she hauled down the gates and the hardware to hang them.

Cat didn't stop there. She called Durango Hawke's construction company. The manager, Jeff Ransom promised to have a crew out to start rebuilding the property line fences by the next day. He apologized for not getting to her sooner, but Durango hadn't made it sound like a high priority before leaving town. Cat assured Jeff that it hadn't been until someone turned her stock loose the day before and asked about cyclone fencing.

Chores done, the twins off to school, Cat and Dray planted the fruit trees she'd bought the day before in the orchard. She went to the tool room for a bucket so she could mix the flower bulbs the way her grandmother taught her. When she returned to the porch with the shovel, rake and pail, she saw a car approaching. *Now what?*

She recognized the visitor when he parked the Cadillac and then came toward her, Herman MacGillicudy in a brown three-piece banker suit. Lad stepped in front of her, hackles raised as he growled. Cat didn't smile. "You're trespassing."

"That's not very friendly." Herman tugged at his yellow striped tie. "I heard you're having problems here. I wanted to tell you that my offer stands. I'll take this place off your hands."

"Problems?" Cat leaned on her shovel. "I don't have any problems. What are you talking about?"

"I'm sorry your tires were slashed and somebody's stealing the gas out of your pickup. I hear you've been receiving nasty phone calls. I guess this place isn't that much different than the big city."

"I wouldn't know about that." Cat straightened, tightening her hold on the shovel handle. "I haven't lived in big cities since I was a child. Why are you bragging? Do you want to show me that you're involved in trying to run me out? If you were smart, you'd keep your mouth shut and there wouldn't be any proof."

"Women can be so paranoid, especially when I'm just here to express my sympathy." Herman shook his head, a smile splintering out on his broad features. "And I'm sorry someone stole your battery and busted all the glass out of the windows on your rig."

"You're the sorriest excuse for a man that I've seen in a long time."

Cat heard Lad's growl grow louder. "You're still trespassing. Do I need to call the cops to have you removed from my property?"

"Like I said, I'm only here to make an offer for the land."

"It's not for sale. Not to you. Not ever. Now, get out!"

"What if I don't?" He stepped closer, the threat clear.

She laughed, refusing to let him see that she felt the least bit intimidated. She raised the shovel a couple inches from the ground, holding it in front of her. "How far can you come when I whack you with this?"

"You won't always have a shovel to back you up," Herman blustered.

"No. Next time, it could be a hammer. Or I could just feed you to my dog. I'm protecting myself. You're trespassing on my property and you're threatening me." Lad bared his teeth, lending credence to the claim that the six-month old pup was an ally.

"I'll go, but don't think you've won. I'll get this place sooner or later and that dog could get hurt."

"You don't want to go there." Cat lowered her voice and met him glare for glare. "If anything happens to my dog, I'll come looking for you." She glanced past him and saw his late-model Cadillac begin to roll down the driveway. "And right now, it seems like your car is going for a swim, so I won't have to look far."

He swung around and uttered a curse when he saw his car rolling away. He hurried after it. Soon, he was running, his jacket flapping around his beefy sides. He really was stupid, she thought. How did he think the Caddy steered around the curves in the drive? He caught up with the car, struggling to open the driver's door.

She waited until he was gone, and the car was out of sight before she dropped the shovel. She crouched down, pulled Lad into her arms and buried her face in his white and golden-brown fur. If something happened to the pup, how would she explain it to her daughters? How could she even explain it to herself? He whined, wiggled and tried to lick at her face. Tears crowded her eyes and flowed down her cheeks.

She felt a comforting hand brush her hair. "Don't cry, kitten. He's gone. He won't be back for a while."

"I don't want Laddie hurt and if Herman wasn't that kind of person, he never would have threatened a dog."

"So, we'll watch the pup," Rob said. "You'll put him in the house when you're gone, and we'll keep the gates closed and padlocked when you're not home."

"All right." Cat cuddled the pup for a while longer. Then, she took him in the house for a treat while she cleaned up. When she returned, she saw Summer parking the delivery truck near the barn. Cat went to meet her friend, Lad tagging along.

Summer jumped down from the driver's side of the cab. As usual, she wore jeans and a comfortable work shirt, brown braid swinging. "Hello there. How's it going? Aidan sent a couple different styles of padlocks so you could choose one."

"I'm okay." Cat drew a deep breath. "I just had a run-in with Herman MacGillicudy and I'm still a bit frazzled."

"Oh, that jerk." Summer planted her fists on her hips. "Let's just shoot him and hide the body. You don't tell and I won't either. If we get caught, we demand a jury of women who know the creep and we'll get off."

Cat laughed. "You make me feel better. Thanks. Tell me you have time for a cup of coffee."

"I'll make time," Summer said. "So, why are you installing gates before you have property line fences?"

"I came home yesterday and found the horses out of the barn and across the creek," Cat said. "I'm going with the theory that whoever is harassing me is lazy and if he has to walk a mile and a half from the highway to the barn, he won't bother."

Rob watched the two women work together planting the variety of daffodil and tulip bulbs in the flower beds in front of the house. They didn't talk about Herman MacGillicudy again, but they certainly chatted about everything else. Topics ranged from their kids to the festival in town to plans for the guest ranch and expanding the feed store. Since they seemed content with each other's company, he left them to it and went off to work on the new pasture. He had three more lines of posts to set before he could run fence wire. With any luck at all, he'd have the field ready for the horses by next week.

MY SWEET HAUNT

It took some adaptations to make the new chain fit around each pair of gates and to fit the combination lock into place, but she was finally satisfied with the result. Cat closed the second set of gates and locked it. She'd leave the main gates open until the girls arrived home from school. She turned and started for the Mustang, then stopped when a dark brown truck pulled off the road into her driveway. "Can I help you?"

The brown-haired driver introduced himself. "Jeff Ransom. I run Hawke Construction for Durango. I wanted to stop by and discuss the fences with you so I'd know where to have the crew start tomorrow. I tried calling, but nobody answered. Since I have to feed Durango's horses because he's out of town, I figured I'd stop by. Hope that's okay."

"It's fine." Cat stepped back. "If you want to park by my car, we can walk and talk."

When she finished her conversation with Jeff, Cat drove up to the barn. She had time to work Skyrocket before the twins arrived home from school. She turned on the radio in the tack-room. Classic country music filled the air. While she groomed the flashy bay, she hummed along with Patsy Cline who was singing about *"Walking After Midnight."*

Cat smiled when the song ended, and another classic country song started. Obviously, Rob hadn't liked it when she switched to a more contemporary station, one that played music from the past year.

Okay, so much for thinking I'm in charge. Just because I live with a dead guy, it doesn't mean I have power over the radio dial!

CHAPTER SEVENTEEN

"I saw you talking to a fellow down by the cabins," Rob said, stopping outside the stall. Lad plopped down in the aisle, ready for a puppy nap. "Who was that?"

"Jeff Ransom. He works for Durango Hawke. They'll have a crew here tomorrow morning to put in a boundary fence at the front of the property between the cabins and the highway. After that, he'll have the crew move onto the east and south boundary lines. We'll have to wait on the west side for a while."

"How are you going to pay Hawke to put up those fences? Did you win the lottery again last week?"

She laughed. "Not hardly. Anyway, this is the latest in the soap opera update I heard a little about when I was in town a while ago. According to Jeff, the McElroys were supposed to be maintaining the fences for the last few years and they haven't because the farm was tied up in some kind of inheritance squabble. So, Durango will have the fences repaired or replaced in order to keep me from suing his fiancée, Heather."

Rob came into the stall and began brushing the right-hand side of the horse in his unique way, the brush seeming to sweep over the brown hide on its own. "You wouldn't sue either of them anyway."

"That's true," Cat admitted, "but we're getting a fence out of the deal and that should keep Herman off the property."

"That works." Rob leaned on Skyrocket's back and grinned across at her. "What if we go riding together? I'll show you how much I've done on the new pasture fence."

"Wait a second. You're a ghost. Don't you have limitations? I know you said you've been riding Sky, but I don't understand how. Why hasn't he given you flying lessons?"

"Because I don't actually weigh anything," Rob said. "I'm dead, remember? I can't get bitten or kicked or stomped on. And I do have limits. I'm never hungry or thirsty so I don't eat or drink anything. I still lose time, but not as much as I did before you and the girls moved here."

"Lose time?" Cat began to comb Skyrocket's dark mane. "You mean like a blackout?"

"More like a fade-out," Rob said. "I didn't know about the essay contest, but I knew the house had changed from when I left it last winter. It was dark and empty inside. The outside was covered in snow. When I got back, it was summer and there was furniture in all the downstairs rooms. The upstairs doors were unlocked."

"Where did you go?"

"It doesn't actually feel like a place." He shrugged one barely visible shoulder. "It's more a gray, foggy area where we can congregate. I can hear waves crashing on the seashore, but I don't see that ocean either. When I get done there, I come home. If people are living here, I can stay longer and do more."

"Why?" Cat stopped brushing the horse. "You look more solid than what you did when I first saw you."

"Because you're not blocking me. I never need to actually sit or lie down or sleep, but the more people and animals here believe in me, the longer my energy lasts."

"So, when I said you weren't here, it made you go away?"

"It could have if you were here alone, but your daughters and the animals kept me around."

Hmm, in a strange way that made sense.

Cat glanced at her watch. "Okay. We have almost two hours before the girls get home. If you finish up Skyrocket, I'll do Pal."

They were on the trail a short time later. They rode through the big corral and out the back gate with Skyrocket trotting behind his buddy. He didn't appear to be concerned about Rob riding him bareback and Cat hoped that someday soon, the horse would be comfortable with a saddle too. Sooner or later, he had to figure out what his new job would be. She thought he'd be more comfortable as a western pleasure horse with Angie Barrett, than as a rodeo bronc.

The path circled through groves of cedars. Alders and maples with their multi-colored leaves marched alongside. Lad happily dashed off in pursuit of the occasional rabbit. He came back to check on the riders, then was off on another puppy adventure. Cat relaxed in the saddle. An autumn breeze brushed over her face.

She flicked a sideways glance at Rob. "Are we taking the long route? I hope there's a shorter way to get there when I turn out the horses."

"Actually, we're in the field right now, kitten." He chuckled. "We're just going to enjoy it for a bit longer."

Saturday afternoon, she was in the middle of working Tonka in the round pen when Jeff Ransom limped up to the fence. He wore a white shirt under his expensive black suit and an old-style black hat, one she remembered was called a fedora. "The crew finished the cabin line. Do you have time to inspect it with me now?"

"Sure." Cat collected on the line and brought the black gelding to her. She petted him and offered a piece of carrot. "Let me put him in the big corral with his brother and check on my kids and the dog."

When she came back from the corral, she found Jeff in the barn where the twins groomed the two fillies. Rob was with Pal and Jeff stood just outside the stall talking to the ghost. "We can extend the line to the western boundary to keep out intruders."

"What about the cost?" Rob asked. "Mindy MacGillicudy has had the place listed for ten years, but with the economy there haven't been any offers. She won't take chicken feed for it which is all that Herman's offering even if she's on a fixed income. She can't afford to pay half the bill for a new fence."

Jeff removed his hat to run a hand through his short dark brown hair, revealing a scar that circled his right wrist. "I'll tell Amarillo to send the bill to the new broker. When she sells the place, we'll pass on the costs to the new owner."

"Is that ethical?" Cat asked, still confused that the two men, live and dead were able to converse. "If your company will finance it, I can handle small monthly payments."

"Let's try it the other way first," Jeff suggested, amusement in his gravelly voice. "It'll give Amie something to..." He obviously glimpsed Samantha's curious look from the next stall, because he changed the comment. "She'll have something to snivel about and then she can tattle on me to her brother."

"Mommy doesn't like tattletales," Sophie warned him.

"I'll keep that in mind." Jeff chuckled. "I promise not to tattle, but Amie loves to rat me out whenever Durango comes into the office."

"You got to be careful when you get someone else in trouble or it's a double time-out," Samantha said. "Sixteen whole minutes. You got to sit still at the kitchen table. No talking or moving or looking bad at Mommy. You got to think the whole time. Mister Robbie had to go to his room when he was naughty."

"Wow, that sounds rough," Jeff said, trying not to grin.

"I'm not that bad." Cat told him, petting the pup that came to stand next to her. "I cut some slack for bleeding, barfing and broken bones. I want to know about those, but I don't like the twins trying to get each other in trouble." She flicked a glance at Rob. "And people who play games with the lights when I'm trying to get supper on the table definitely deserve to be sent to their room."

"Hey, I haven't done that since the first night," Rob told her. "A two-hour time out cured me of my mischief-making ways." He winked at her. "The girls and I will finish the grooming. Then, we want to go on a ride and explore the upper trails."

"Sounds like fun. I'll be back soon. Keep Laddie with you so he doesn't come out to the highway." Cat walked beside Jeff out of the barn, baffled by his behavior. "I don't get it. Why did you see Rob? He's—"

"Dead." Jeff shrugged. "So what? Everybody has issues."

"Well, that's one way of putting it." When she looked at him straight on, she saw a scar running down the right side of his neck. "But, why you? Nobody else sees him or even realizes he's here."

"Probably because I flew choppers for the Army till the last one went down," Jeff said. "I was captured. Spent two years as a prisoner in Columbia. Then Durango came and got me. My crew stayed with me."

She waited for him to open the passenger door of his truck for her. "So, he came and got all of you."

"Just me. They'd all been killed by then."

She wouldn't tell him that she was sorry for him. Very few people liked to be pitied and Jeff didn't sound like one of them. She waited as he walked around to the driver's side. When he slid into the seat behind the wheel, she said, "Rob died in Vietnam. Anytime you want to visit and talk to him, it will be fine. He probably gets tired of all the girly chatter, even if he's too polite to say so."

"Sounds good to me," Jeff said. "Not a lot of folks for me to talk to when Durango goes off on one of his quests."

"Where does he go?" Cat asked.

"He says he's looking for *La Capitana*," Jeff told her, "but it's been almost five years and he hasn't found Heather yet. He will one day."

The cyclone fence ran across the greenbelt that provided back yards for the six guest cabins. Despite his limp, Jeff barely used the wooden cane he'd brought along. He led the way down the path next to the thick wire mesh. It was approximately four inches off the ground and stood six-feet high with posts every eight feet. She knew she ought to think that the cyclone fence made the farm look like a prison, but instead she felt safe. She wouldn't have to worry about livestock escaping to the highway or being hit by the gravel trucks leaving Baker City.

"The fence should only be four feet tall on the other three lines," Jeff said. "Then, the deer can jump it, but your stock will still be safe. What do you think?"

They discussed the idea as they finished the inspection on the way back to the barn. It made sense. She didn't want to leave wildlife without access. She just wanted to keep her own home safe from whoever tried to harass her. When Jeff left, he promised to close the combination lock on the gates so she could ride out with Rob and the twins.

When she returned to the barn, she led the way out to the round pen. She checked the tack on the ponies and helped the twins mount up. Then she tightened Pal's cinch and swung into her own saddle. Rob opted to ride Skyrocket bareback again.

This time, they didn't go through the big corral. They rode beside it, then cut through a gate and headed up the dirt track that eventually led to the top of the ridge behind the buildings.

The land rolled down to Cedar Creek. No wonder Herman wanted the place, Cat thought. A developer could make a fortune on the view property after mining the gravel.

From her time here as a child, she remembered that each of the three rising terraces had its share of buildings, barns, storage sheds and even a cabin or two for the help. The main trail wound through more groves of giant evergreens. Alders, maples, and a few cottonwood trees occasionally joined the cedars.

Rob led the way since he knew the land better than the rest of them. The twins followed him on their ponies and Cat brought up the rear. Well, not really. Lad heeled behind Pal most of the time, except when a rabbit or grouse demanded the pup's attention.

Cat glanced off to the left and saw a large grassy pasture. She didn't know much about what was now her property, but she had time to learn. "What's that?"

"My dad always grew his own hay," Rob said. "If we get the equipment running, we'll be able to get one cutting and that would save on buying hay. We could also bring in some beef cattle and feed them up this winter. It'd give you a cash crop in the spring."

Cat added that to her mental list of interesting ideas to be explored. As they rode, she noticed repairs that needed to be made to fences. Two of the hay sheds had fallen down. Thistles and blackberry bushes tried to take over in a couple of the fields, but she could use them for pastures now and then cut hay next summer.

When they rode back to the barn, she saw the black Lexus down by the road, sitting outside the locked highway gates. She grimaced. What on earth was her father doing here? Hadn't one visit been enough? She guided Pal into the round pen. "Let's put away the ponies and Sky. While you unsaddle, I'll ride down and see what Liam wants."

Rob waited until the girls led their ponies into the barn. "Don't give him any money."

"No worries there. I learned that years ago when he helped himself to my savings account for one of his hokey investments." Cat petted Pal's golden neck. "I was going to buy a purebred Quarter Horse back then, but I couldn't until last spring when I got this fella and I finally had a horse of my own."

She reined the palomino toward the corral gate. "Keep the puppy and the girls busy for me. I'll be back in a few minutes."

Before Rob could offer to come with her, she rode down the path beside the driveway. The next time Zeke came, she'd have him put shoes on Pal. Then, she wouldn't have to be concerned about the gravel laming the gelding. She squeezed her legs and asked for a slow jog. He responded beautifully and they trotted down the grassy verge to the gate.

They slowed to a walk to cross the bridge over the creek. She continued to the end of the driveway and stopped. Her father wasn't alone in the Lexus. Someone, another man sat in the passenger seat. Who had Liam brought with him? Why?

She found out when her father opened the door and came around the vehicle, pasting on a toothy smile. "Look who's here."

"Who?" Cat asked, holding the horse still and keeping the locked gate between them, suspicious. "A friend of yours?"

The passenger door opened, and Frazer stepped out. Still six foot six, with thick black hair that curled to broad shoulders, he wore a tired black suit. He had strong handsome features, but he couldn't meet her gaze. Why not? What had he done now? Did she care? No, not really.

Cat sighed and shook her head. "What happened, Frazer? Did your job fizzle or did you just get fired?"

"I've missed you, honey." He came toward the gate. "I called your dad and he picked me up at the airport. I wanted to surprise you. Would you unlock this please?"

"No." She straightened Pal's white mane. "We're getting the

divorce you said you wanted last summer. You've been served. Go stay with Liam or rent a hotel room. We're not reconciling."

Was that calm voice hers? She couldn't quite believe it, but she wasn't angry or upset. She honestly didn't care. Letting him move in with her meant risking the farm and she wasn't going to do that. Since it was listed as her separate estate, he had no claim on it and she damned well wasn't giving him one.

"My attorney is Bree Hawke in Lake Maynard. Contact her if you have any questions or comments that you want to make." Cat collected up on the reins. "Anything else you two have in mind?"

"Catriona, you could let the man talk to you after coming all this way," Liam scolded.

"I could, but he doesn't have anything I want to hear." Then, she deliberately added, "Neither do you."

"Let's just take a few minutes to talk, honey." Frazer rested his hands on the gate. "Just let me in and afterwards, I'll call a cab."

"Hello, this is the outskirts of Baker City," Cat said. "There aren't any cabs, but we do have cops and if you stick around, you'll meet them."

She didn't wait any longer. Instead, she turned Pal and trotted back in the direction of the barn. It was time to clean the stalls and feed. Tears stung her eyes and she wondered why. She didn't want Frazer back in her life. She saw Samantha and Sophie throwing a toy for Laddie to chase and suddenly realized what had upset her. Frazer never asked about the twins. Supposedly, he'd returned to reconcile with her, but he didn't even mention the girls. They were his daughters too.

Now, she knew she was finished with him. They didn't have a future and she wasn't desperate to create one. He definitely didn't love their children, and nobody could force him to be a good husband or a decent father. So, why waste time and energy on the man? She rode Pal into the round pen, stopped him and swung out of the saddle. She led him into the barn, pausing outside the tackroom to unfasten the latigo.

"What did Liam want?" Rob asked, coming from the stall area.

"He brought Frazer from the airport." Cat unbuckled the breastcollar. She looked over her shoulder and made sure the twins were out of earshot. "Would you believe he never even asked about the girls?"

"Isn't he the same fellow who told them he didn't want to be their daddy?" Rob asked. "I think he's the one who should have a time-out, not me."

Cat laughed. "I did tell him to go rent a motel room, that he wasn't welcome here."

"Well, good. Then, I don't have to drive him away."

Did he sound pleased because she'd sent the other man away or disappointed that he didn't have the opportunity to protect her? Before she asked, the saddle and pads floated off Pal's back on a ghostly trip to the peg in the tackroom. Okay, so now she knew she preferred a dead guy to the living ones she knew. What cowgirl wouldn't?

CHAPTER EIGHTEEN

After she put Pal in his stall, she went into the house. She poured a cup of coffee and called Bree on her cell phone. The attorney didn't answer, but Cat left a message. If she didn't hear from the lawyer tonight or tomorrow morning, then it would be time to rearrange the carpool schedule. After dropping the elementary crowd at school, she could cruise by Bree's office.

Housework took up most of the evening. Once she had the twins in bed, she put in a load of laundry, washed the dishes and cleaned house. Before she started work on the website for the haunted town celebration, the phone rang. Cat answered it, glad to hear Bree's cheerful voice. "I called because Frazer is back in Washington State."

"Where is he staying?" Bree asked, suddenly concerned. "You didn't let him move onto the ranch, did you? That could cause problems with your ownership."

"I told him to go to a motel." Cat took a deep breath. "He never asked about the twins. Would you talk to my former boss and arrange for a deposition? She said she'd come to court for me and she was the one who took care of the kids when he neglected them last summer."

"Give me the number. I'll get her on board."

"Any other advice?" Cat asked.

"Yes. You'll want to document his visit today and make

arrangements to see a marriage counselor or even your minister. Ask him if he wants to come to any sessions with you. That shows you're serious, that this relationship needs work. He hasn't left any messages for me. Did you give him my number?"

"No, but I gave him your name."

"You have my card. The next time he shows up, give it to him. Ask him for the name of his lawyer or the marriage counselor that he's seeing. I know you filed for the divorce, but didn't you say he wanted one too?"

"He was the one who suggested it," Cat said. "I just followed through when he left me to go to Louisiana."

She listened to the rest of the lawyer's advice and then went to the den to start work on the website. Before she loaded up the prototype, she scanned her email. She deleted the sales messages, answered the ones from her aunt and her mother. Frazer hadn't sent anything to her and neither had Liam. That meant the visit today was the first time either of them had wanted to see her and she definitely didn't want to see them.

"What are you working on?" Rob sat down in the leather recliner across from her desk. Well, at least he looked like he was sitting, if she didn't pay attention to the fact that he floated about two inches above the seat. Lad curled up in front of the chair, chewing on the last puppy cookie she'd given him.

"Anything special for the ranch?" Rob asked.

"We're going to set up a block of haunted buildings in town to celebrate Halloween," Cat said. "It will promote the town and bring customers to the local businesses."

"Too bad they won't be able to see the 'real' ghosts," Rob said. "You'll have to hire help. What are you doing for costumes? Have you told people to start going through their attics for old clothes?"

"Not yet, but I will tomorrow at church." Cat made a note so she'd remember to speak to Reverend Tommy. "I'm surprised you're helping with this idea."

"Why wouldn't I? It sounds like fun. Are you bringing back the 'trick or trunk' on Halloween night?"

"What is that?" Cat asked. "I never heard of such a thing."

"Everybody brings their cars and backs them up to the sidewalks.

They have boxes of candy in the trunks. Then the kids go through and trick or treat. There are prizes for the scariest car, the funniest car, the most seasonal—you get the idea."

"That's great." Cat made more notes. "What else?"

Between morning chores, fixing breakfast and collecting her notes for the Halloween festivities, it took some hustling to get the girls ready the next day. Cat made sure that Lad was safe in the house before they left. When they reached the end of the driveway, she unlocked the gate, drove through and then locked up after them.

She'd deliberately used Rob's birthdate as a set of numbers on the combination lock. She was pretty sure most people wouldn't think of his information and now she was glad. If she used her birthday or anniversary or the date the twins were born, Frazer would figure it out and would be able to get onto the property. She didn't want him waiting on the porch for her when they returned.

There were already several cars in the lot when she parked the Mustang. She escorted the girls inside the church, waving to Virginia and Maxine. They came to meet her; Maxine was armed with a sheaf of papers. "We think the block with the school and hardware store would be perfect for the haunted town," she said without even saying 'hello.' "The service doesn't start for twenty minutes. Shall we go take a look?"

"The girls can stay with me," Virginia said. "I need help setting up the hall for the coffee hour."

Cat glanced at her daughters. "Do you want to help Mrs. Tommy?"

Samantha nodded. "When we help, we get to bake lots of our favorite doughnuts for later."

"And we get to choose the cloths for the tables," Sophie added.

"Okay. Well, I'll be right back." Cat hurried out of the church beside Maxine. "How many buildings are we going to use?"

Maxine turned left and headed across the street to the next block. "This year, we'll start small. Next year, Pop says we can expand to more of the town especially if we get Herman on board or we buy back his buildings from the bank. Most of his are private residences and we won't need them."

"That makes sense." Cat stopped and looked around, hoping the older woman would just take it as wanting to see the potential, not the fact that they'd collected an audience. There were three soldiers in antiquated dress uniforms, a vintage Army nurse who looked like she'd just stepped out of the old TV show *MASH*, her relative, Newt O'Leary, the madam and the former mayor. Talk about a party.

"Didn't we want to use the school?" Cat asked.

"It's on the other side of the church," Maxine said. "We'll look at it later. The school won't be a problem since Frank owns it now. He hopes that Angie will reopen it when she gets back from Afghanistan. Teaching jobs are so tight right now and she had to substitute for months after her first tour when she didn't get her position back in Lake Maynard."

"I thought it was the law that reservists couldn't lose their jobs if they went to war," Cat said. "Did that change?"

"The war's gone on so long, a lot of companies don't pay attention to it and there's not much enforcement or support for veterans unless they raise a stink." Maxine started walking and pointed to a large two-story building. "This was the hotel. We figure on putting in a sort of ghostly staff so you can see folks try to check in and things start popping when you get up to the rooms."

"Lights flickering on and off, music playing, running footsteps, suitcases being dropped," Cat suggested. "We can do a lot with sound and then add in the wanna-be guests."

"We'll do the sound effects," the mayor said.

"And the lights," Newt added, as Maxine scribbled notes, unhearing.

"I'm counting on it." Cat smiled and glanced down the street at the row of wooden buildings. "The hardware store is directly across from the hotel. If we had clerks offer to help and you could see through them that would definitely add atmosphere. We're going to need someone to coordinate employees and set up schedules for them."

"Summer and Pop say they can take care of the living ones." Maxine paused, then led the way to the post office. "What we need is someone with the O'Leary gift to handle the others."

Cat caught her breath. Everyone seemed to know about it—and her. "You believe in ghosts?"

"I may not be able to see them, but I can feel when they're around and I respect them. I grew up in this town and I knew your grandma. She had the gift. So did her momma. Your great-great-grandma set forth the rules for the spirits who come here."

"What rules?" Cat asked.

Maxine shrugged. "I'm not dead yet so I don't know all of them, but the big one was not to scare children. No blood or gore. Your grandma used to say that if they didn't act like it was a Disney movie set, she'd send them away. And there was no coming back if she evicted you."

"We only had to help her three times," the late mayor volunteered. "We don't cater to that kind of folks anyway. If nobody liked them when they were alive, why would we want them around when we're dead?"

Cat laughed. Maxine didn't seem to notice she was having a second conversation. "That makes sense. Okay, if I have help from the other residents in this town, I'll take on talking to the previous mayor and business owners about their schedules."

Maxine looked up and around. "So, you do have the ability to see what most folks can't. I suspected as much." She glanced at her watch. "Come on. We only have ten minutes and we need to have a plan in mind to get the repairs started after church."

"I need a minute." Cat turned to the ghosts. "Okay, I get why the mayor and a couple business owners are here. Why are the military here? What do you need?"

The three soldiers looked at her and each other before the nurse spoke. "I'm the ranking officer, Lieutenant McElroy, and we're following orders."

Cat studied the slender red-haired woman. Her friendly smile warmed dark gray eyes. "Heather? I've heard about you, but nobody knows you're gone."

"Because she isn't. She's my great-niece and she's back in Nashville. I'm Bridget." The smile widened. "And Sergeant Williams asked us to watch over you and the twins when you're in town, so we are."

"Who's minding my daughters?" Cat asked. "I thought they were safe with Virginia."

"Oh, they are, but the Colonel is just making sure they stay that way," Bridget McElroy said. "Now, we'd better hurry if you want to finish your inspection."

"All right." Cat glanced at Maxine who stared in obvious awe. "I'd introduce you, but I think they already know who you are, and they agree with you. We should get back to work."

"Sounds good." The silver-haired woman turned and marched down the sidewalk, reviewing her notes. "Now, if anyone has a problem, tell Cat and she can tell me."

"I don't think we'd dare," Newt said.

"She's like the sergeant who made me scrub the bathroom floor with a toothbrush during basic training," Bridget said in agreement.

Since everyone seemed to be on the same page and nobody was upset about it, Cat had time to think about Rob. She didn't know whether to be pleased, amused, or angered by his attempt to protect her. Granted, she wasn't sure what the ghosts would be able to do, but just having her own security detail was interesting to say the least. They could warn her of any danger and that would give her time to prepare a defense. The idea that someone cared enough to look out for her, and the twins was a new one and something she could grow to enjoy.

By early afternoon, Cat saw the haunted town taking shape. Ted arranged for some of his friends to use her design from the website to create signs up and down the block. Dust and cobwebs in the various buildings would be left to provide atmosphere. Meanwhile, falling doors and some of the missing siding would be repaired. Aidan and his crew replaced broken windows. He'd brought back her truck so Dray could drive it home for her at the end of the day. She'd keep the Mustang a while longer.

Cat finished sweeping up the trash in the post office and carried the black plastic bag to the door. She grimaced when she glimpsed her father, followed by Frazer coming toward her. She muttered a swear word. What would it take for them to get the message?

"Who are they?" Bridget McElroy asked. "Looks like your relations, Newt."

"Well, the older one is," Newt said. "Most of my kin are redheads, but we get a few black Irish now and again. Don't know about the younger one. He has the look of the Williamses."

"He's my soon-to-be ex-husband," Cat said. "I don't think he's related to anyone up here. His mother died when he was a teenager and he spent the next four years in foster care." She stopped talking to the ghosts when Liam entered the room. "What's going on?"

"I brought up Frazer so you two could talk." Liam returned to the entry and looked up and down the street. "What's going on? Why are so many people around?"

"We're having a Halloween festival and it kicks off next week," Cat said. "Everybody's getting ready for it. Want to jump in and help?"

Liam brushed a cobweb off the sleeve of his black jacket. "I'm hardly dressed for it, am I? What fool would come to this rundown, creepy place?"

Cat intervened before her ghostly helpers took umbrage. "Hello, Liam. Focus. Halloween is the biggest retail holiday next to Christmas. We're setting up a haunted town and we'd like to make some serious money. That will provide a kick-off to the Harvest Festival in November."

"And a Christmas holiday town in December?" Frazer asked.

Cat shook her head. "No. There's only one major road to Baker City and if the snow closes us down, we'd lose money. We'll start up again in the spring."

"With what?" Liam sneered. "Some kind of remembrance of the avalanche that decimated this place nearly a century ago in February?"

"Not a bad idea." Cat leaned on her broom. "I was going with Valentines' Day, but you're right. We should have a memorial for the people who were lost. Then, they'd never be forgotten."

"That's good, Cat, but it won't bring in customers." Frazer walked over to check out the back counter and the rows of boxes for mail. "This is amazing. You could have a postmaster standing back here and calling for the next person in line. And put out some donation cans for the memorial. It'll help raise enough money for it."

"And it also gives us another way to promote Baker City," Cat said. "We can connect with historical societies and groups."

For a moment, she remembered why she fell in love with Frazer. At times, when he looked beyond casinos and card games, he had a tremendous imagination. He wasn't dressed to help, but as she watched, he unbuttoned his suit jacket. "What's going on?"

"There's a squirrel nest back here. If you give me your broom, I'll help clean up."

"Probably isn't squirrels," Newt informed Cat. "It's rats. Tell him not to pick up the mess. You sure he isn't related to the Williamses?"

"I have places to go and better things to do than stick around here," Liam said. "Are you coming with me, Frazer?"

"No, I'll jump in and help for a while," Frazer said. "Maybe, Cat will talk to me then."

"Your choice." Liam left, letting the door swing closed behind him.

Cat allowed her gaze to wander over the tall, broad-shouldered man who wanted her attention. A sexy smile played over his lips, but it didn't make her long to kiss him anymore. And the charm left her cold. Okay, not cold. It just didn't affect her at all. She honestly had better things to do than listen to his practiced lines.

She walked over and handed Frazer the broom, dustpan and box of trash bags. "I'm still pushing on a divorce. Play your cards right and I'll let you buy me and the twins supper. You remember them, don't you? The eight-year-old girls you never ask about? The ones you don't want calling you 'Daddy?'"

He winced. "Damn, you carry a grudge."

"When you mess with my kids, you betcha." Cat sauntered toward the door. "I'm going to help clean up the laundry next door. Come on over when you finish here."

"Can I thump him with a two-by-four?" Newt asked, following along. "Picking on kids ain't suitable for a grown man."

Cat shook her head and walked out of the post office. "No. He'll get bored and leave. We haven't given him a reason to stay."

"Not even when you agreed to have supper with him?" Bridget adjusted her Army hat before stepping—or rather, floating—outside.

"He'll be long gone before then," Cat said. "He wants me right now, but his plans don't include our daughters."

"That's the problem when girls grow up to marry men like their fathers," Bridget said. "You'll have to make some changes if you don't want history to continue to repeat itself."

A definite zinger, it strikes straight to my heart.

Cat shuddered. Why didn't she ever realize that Frazer was so much like her father? Had she'd been so busy trying to win Liam's love and approval that she'd continued the same pattern as an adult? Bridget was right. She'd have to make some changes if she didn't want Sophie and Samantha to make the same mistakes.

She found her uncle Aidan making repairs to the counters. A rugged, outdoorsy type with silvered red hair, he seemed perfectly comfortable cutting pieces of plywood and talking to the twins at the same time. Virginia and Linda hung tablecloths from the overhead drying rack. Cat began to wipe out the first in a long row of sinks. "So, what's the plan for this building?"

"We're thinking to make it historically accurate and create a hand laundry, so it looks the way it did when the Sweeneys ran it," Virginia said. "Jassy is bringing down her grandmother's mangle. It's a wringer that was developed in the 19th century."

"It's two long rollers in a frame and a crank to revolve them," Linda explained. "Back in the old days, a laundry worker took sopping wet clothing and cranked it through the mangle. It got rid of the extra water and was much quicker than hand twisting."

Cat looked around the room at the rows of tubs. Some had handles that would move paddles inside them. In one corner she spotted a woodstove and three ironing boards. "Do we still have the old style flat-irons that have to be heated?"

"Not around here. They were stolen ages ago," Virginia said. "Jassy promised to look in the attic at the old Sweeney homestead for some. The rest of us need to do that too when we're hunting down costumes for our staff."

"We'll have a crew working here," Aidan went on. "When visitors come, Mrs. Sweeney will greet them and ask for their tickets if they want the clothes they left. She says she'll choose one visitor in each group to wash clothes or hang sheets or iron tablecloths for the restaurant."

"That doesn't sound too spooky," Cat said.

"Oh, it will be," Bridget said. "We'll have our folks showing them how to do each task. Even if they can't see or hear us, they'll see brushes and washboards working by themselves."

"Me and Sophie want to be ghosts with the other kids at the school," Samantha said. "Can we, Mommy?"

"I don't see why not." Cat grinned at her daughter. "It sounds like fun. Who is going to be the teacher?"

"Mrs. O'Sullivan," Sophie said. "She talks funny because she came from Ireland."

The three living adults stared at the child. Then Virginia asked casually. "What is she going to teach?"

"She says we'll sing the ABC song and the multiply songs like little kids do," Sophie said. "And the big girls and boys have to recite poems and speeches in front of the whole class. Me and Sam are supposed to find an old-time song. She says Mister Robbie can help, but it has to be—"

"She said, 'pro-priate,' Samantha finished. "If he's silly, he'll be cleaning the 'rasers for a week and once she visits him, his daddy will take young Robert to the woodshed."

"Oh, I remember those talks," Newt said. "She used to scold me something fierce when I acted up in class. I had to stay after school and write my lines, then chop kindling for the stove. When I was late getting home, my momma wasn't happy, so I had even more chores."

"And heaven forbid, you make fun of her accent. My grandma said Mrs. O'Sullivan would grab her by the ear and put her in the cloakroom until her daddy came," Bridget said. "He was terrified of Mrs. O'Sullivan."

"She'll definitely be an asset to the event," Cat said. "It sounds like she'll scare the visitors half to death."

"Only if they sass her." Aidan came across the room and hugged Cat. It was clear he had a touch of the gift too. "The O'Learys are back. We've missed having someone like you and your girls in town since my momma passed."

CHAPTER NINETEEN

An hour later, Cat finished wiping out the last of the metal washtubs. She glanced across the room as the door opened and Frazer entered, followed by Herman MacGillicudy. Fury filled the banker's face, making it ruddier than ever.

Cat sighed. "Now, what? Are you going to make an offer for this place too?"

Herman glared at her. "Nobody in town would have done this unless you suggested it. You need to leave here before you cause more trouble."

"Who died and put you in charge?" Frazer swung around and stared down at the shorter man. "Watch your tone when you speak to my wife."

Newt lounged back against the counter, folding his arms. "I'm starting to like this boy. You sure he's not related to the Williamses?"

Cat dropped her rag in the scrub bucket and opted for her sweetest tone. "We're only trying to make things better here for everyone, Mr. MacGillicudy. The festival will be so much fun. Wouldn't you like to be part of it?"

Herman narrowed his eyes and shot her another dirty look before he snarled, "Bitch."

Frazer grabbed Herman's collar and shoved him in the direction of the door. "You're leaving."

"Who the hell *are* you?"

"I already told you. I'm her husband. You can fight with me anytime, or do you just pick on women?" The door swung open and Frazer gave Herman an added push that sent him stumbling out onto the sidewalk. Frazer turned back. "He's the kind of guy I'd have escorted out of the casino. Cat, what are you into?"

"Finding a home for me and the girls." Cat watched Newt close the door. "Herman just wants to chase me off the farm so he can make it a gravel pit. Thanks for the help."

Taking a few minutes, she introduced him to the other people in the laundry. She didn't mention the ghosts. Neither did the girls who gave him a wide berth while he played his usual charming self. He and Aidan appeared to get along just fine. When her uncle mentioned needing more lumber, Frazer offered to make a run to the hardware store in Lake Maynard.

Cat breathed a sigh of relief and handed over the keys to her pickup. She didn't have to worry about the girls or their reaction to having supper with him. A little after four, the three of them headed over to Pop's café for burgers. After they ate, it would be time to head for home to take care of the horses.

Pop brought them menus and crayons for the girls so they could color their placemats. "Dray went with your husband to the hardware store."

"Good," Cat said. "Then, Dray can bring the truck back in the morning when he comes to work."

A short time later, she'd just finished the deluxe cheeseburger and sipped the last of her coffee. The twins still swirled French fries in puddles of ketchup when the door opened, and Chief O'Connell strode into the café. He crossed straight to the booth. "Got a minute?"

"Sure." She put down her cup. "You girls finish up. I'll be right back."

She followed him to the door and out to the sidewalk. "What's going on?"

"There was an accident. Who was driving your truck?"

Her lips suddenly dried. "Dray went with my husband to the hardware store. How is he?"

Worry made Dick's mouth a tight line. A muscle twitched in his jaw. "He was unconscious when we got him out. They lost him twice, but the medics brought him back. He had a pulse when they put him in the ambulance."

"And Frazer?"

Dick rested his hands on her shoulders. "Cat, I'm telling you about Frazer. It doesn't look good. I need to take you to the hospital now. Are you with me?"

"Dray? What about him? He's everything to Linda and her dad." Cat measured the officer's weathered features and the pity in his eyes. "I thought the truck was safe. Aidan just gave it back to me. And Dray drives it all the time."

"He wasn't driving today. Frazer was. The boy will make it, but it's touch and go for your husband."

Cat managed a step back. "I have to tell Linda."

"No, I do," Dick said. "It's my job. Do you have someone to look after your daughters? Or do you want to take them to the hospital with us?"

Cat shook her head. "No. They're not close to Frazer and he'll want me, not them. I'll ask Virginia if she'll look after them."

She started back inside, remembered that Rob might be at the dude ranch, but then again might have vanished for a while since they were gone. "My horses. Who will feed my horses?"

"I'll arrange for Ted Fenwick to do it tonight while you take the girls to the church."

Cat nodded and went back inside. "Come on, twins. Your daddy's been in a car accident and I need to go visit him at the hospital with Chief O'Connell."

"Are we going too?" Sophie asked, sliding out of the booth. "Or can we stay home?"

Samantha followed her sister. "We don't like hospitals."

"I know. That's why you're going to stay and help Mrs. Tommy tonight." Cat put an arm around each of her daughters. "As soon as your dad feels better, I'll take him to your grandpa's and then I'll come for you."

"We're still getting a 'vorce, right?" Sophie asked anxiously.

"That's right." Cat dropped a kiss on the top of the girl's strawberry blonde hair. "But it doesn't mean we can't be nice when he's hurt. Right?"

"Right," Samantha agreed. "We're sorry he doesn't feel good. Do you want to take him my picture from dinner?"

"That would be very nice," Cat said, although she was certain that Frazer wouldn't appreciate the gesture or the thought. However, she wasn't telling the little girl that. "Do you want to send yours, Sophie?"

She hesitated. "If he says it's not very good, will you bring our pictures home for Mister Robbie? He likes 'em."

"Yes, I'll bring them home if your dad doesn't appreciate your artwork," Cat promised.

The pup yawned and stretched. After he tilted his head and listened, he bounced up and ran to the windows, barking. Turning off the TV, Rob followed and saw the Fenwick boy's truck. Anger bubbled. Now what? Had someone hurt Cat or the girls? Had he busted up the Mustang?

He heard a key in the lock and followed the pup to the front door. The door opened to reveal Ted who leaned down and petted the pup. "Come on, dog. We're doing chores and then I have to put you back inside. Your people won't be home tonight."

"Why not?" Rob demanded. "What happened to them?"

No answer, of course. Rob tended to forget he was dead and that only a few people actually saw or heard him. He went after the two toward the barn. Ted hurried through the evening chores, mucking, putting in shavings, watering and feeding the horses. While he looked after them, Ted mentioned a car accident. No, it was a truck accident.

Something had apparently gone wrong with Cat's pickup. It had veered off the highway, rolled over a guard rail and tumbled down a hill. Cat's estranged husband and Dray were in the hospital at Lake Maynard.

"I'm going as soon as I finish taking care of you guys," Ted told Skyrocket, dropping hay in the manger.

"I'm going with you," Rob said. "She'll need me."

The waiting room was crowded with family and friends from Baker City filling the chairs and couches. Hands shaking, Cat accepted the cup of strong black coffee Pop handed her. "I'm so sorry."

"For what?" Pop sat down beside her and covered her hands with his. "My grandson loves working for you. Your husband is the one in surgery, not our boy."

"Frazer was, I mean, is a good driver," Cat said, worry filling her mind. She lifted the cup to her lips, smelling the slightly scorched odor of overdone coffee. "He hates wearing a seat belt."

"But he made sure Dray wore one," Pop said.

That was a good point. She blinked hard and looked around the room done up in antiseptic white and beige tones. Large windows overlooked the parking lot. Magazines dotted a few of the tables—not that anyone bothered to read them right now. They were holding vigil for the man Cat planned to leave. How kind of them, she thought again.

She glanced up at the sound of footsteps on the tile floor. It couldn't be the doctor. No, it was Ted. He came directly to her, Rob behind him. Nobody else saw the ghost, but she did. He stood behind her and she could almost feel his hand on her shoulder, giving her strength. He was the only spirit she allowed herself to see or hear currently. There were so many around a hospital and she didn't want to talk to strangers right now or try to help them.

"The horses are fine," Ted reassured her. "I watered and fed all of them. I walked the pup, then put him back in the house with his kibble. I cleaned the cat box and counted kittens. Everything will be fine until you're home. If you need me to, I'll feed them all in the morning for you."

"I should be there by then." Cat forced a smile. "Thanks, Ted."

He nodded, then went to talk to Linda. The buzz of conversation continued with stories about Dray. A sudden hush fell, and Cat looked up to see Herman plodding in their direction from the elevator.

Linda flew across the room, hands curled like claws. "You bastard!"

she screamed, looking very unlike the calm, cheerful woman Cat had gotten to know. "You tried to kill my boy!"

Herman blanched and cringed. "Not me," he squawked. "I wouldn't."

But Linda wasn't listening. Instead, she lunged for his face, her nails digging down his plump cheeks. Thin trails of blood sprang up even as he weakly tried to fend her off. "You hate him."

Dick O'Connell grabbed her arm, pulled her away. "Linda, stop it!"

Tears started, flowing down her face. "He was a grown man and he went after my baby whenever he got the chance, just because we adopted him, and he said he 'didn't want a stranger's kid' in our family." She wrestled one foot free and kicked Herman in the knee.

"Tell her, Dick," Herman repeated, bright scores of blood on his face. "I didn't do it. I wouldn't run her kid off the road, even if he is a snot-nosed punk."

"Nobody ran them off the highway, Herman. We'd have seen the tire tracks." Dick guided Linda across the room, pushed her into a chair vacated by another visitor. "We're having the truck towed to the county garage and the crime scene folks will go over it. Aidan says he'd swear all the mechanical work was fine. He'd done everything the rig needed because he knew his niece and her daughters would be in it."

Cat looked up from the depths of the coffee. "Then we were the ones he wanted dead, not Dray or Frazer. Did you really think killing us would get you the guest ranch?"

Darker red flooded into Herman's face as he struggled for air. "Don't you believe me? I wouldn't do this. I didn't."

"You were going to kill my dog," Cat said, "and he's only a half-grown puppy."

"I was joking." He held out his hands toward her, face going gray. "You have to believe me."

"I don't," Pop said. "You'd better go, Herman. We don't want you here."

"But, I'm *family*," Herman said.

"Not to me." Pop told him. "I don't think my daughter will agree you're a relative either."

Herman looked around the room, obviously searching for a

friendly face anywhere—and not finding one. He turned and stumbled away.

Just then, Cat saw a male nurse coming toward them. "We have Dray MacGillicudy settled in a room for the night. Is his mother here?"

Linda rose from her chair. "Yes, and his grandpa is here, too. Can we see him?"

"One at a time." The middle-aged man smiled. "He's going to be fine. He has a bump on the head, a few bruises, a twisted ankle and a cracked rib. He'll be going home tomorrow. He said to tell his boss he'd be back to work on Wednesday, but the doctor says he probably needs more than one day off."

Cat managed a smile. "Tell him he can come back when the doctor clears him, Linda. I'm not fighting with you over your boy. I like my face the way it is."

Her comment prompted anxious titters from the audience and then Linda hustled after the nurse. Cat clutched the foam cup tightly as a surgeon in light blue scrubs headed their way, a white mask on a string around his neck.

"Mrs. Hendrickson." The tone of his voice said it before the words came. "I'm—"

Her nails bit into the cup. She felt coffee drip onto her jeans. "No. He's not gone."

"I'm sorry. He didn't make it through surgery." The doctor came closer, explaining about the injuries and the treatment, but Cat barely heard or understood anything beyond the fact that Frazer hadn't regained consciousness after the operation.

Frazer was gone and it was her fault. She shouldn't have let him drive the truck. It'd been sabotaged before. Why didn't she suspect it could be again especially after he defended her from Herman? And that should have been suspicious in itself.

"I need to see him." Cat stood and the remains of the coffee splashed onto the floor. "Now."

She sat next to the hospital bed, looking more alone and fragile than he'd ever seen her. Rob wished he could touch her, comfort her. He couldn't hold her and let her cry in his arms. She was blaming herself for the accident. He knew that even if she didn't say so. He looked beyond her to the man lying in the bed.

It was like looking in a mirror. Okay, the man was taller than he was or that he had been when he was alive. But they both had curly black hair and their faces bore a certain resemblance. Hendrickson, Rob thought. Had he known anyone with that name? Nothing came to mind, but he had three brothers.

While Rob had gone off, fought and died in Vietnam, Ed and Adam grew up, married and had kids, none of whom were this particular man. If he had been related, Rob knew his brothers and their wives would be out in the waiting room. That left his brother, Devin who died from a drug overdose in 1981. He could have had a kid and not been there to raise him.

"How old is he?" Rob asked. But he wasn't asking Cat.

A shadow stirred by the window. It was Frazer, newly dead. "Ask me. She's beating herself up. She's not ready to talk yet or even admit I'm here. I'm thirty-three, or I was. Why? Who are you?"

"Rob Williams. She won the dude ranch where she lives from my younger brothers. And you are?"

"Frazer William Hendrickson." The other man eased forward to stand behind her, no longer bound by gravity. "Oh, Cat. You're blaming yourself and it's not your fault. Or mine, come to think of it. The brakes failed. How's the boy?"

"He'll be fine," Rob said. "He's going home tomorrow. Now, since you're not gone, why don't you get back into that body? Live, damn it!"

"Been that. Done there. I'm wondering what comes next."

Cat stirred in the chair. "Frazer, you're such an ass. Why couldn't you just grow up and be a man? A husband? A father? I loved you so much when we first got married."

Rob felt the words slice into him, sharper than a KA-Bar, the knife of choice for Rangers. He stepped close to the other shade. "Get in that body, boy!"

"You didn't listen, Williams. She's using the past tense." Wry amusement twisted Frazer's mouth. "She loved me once. She doesn't love me anymore. I lost her when I didn't want kids and she wouldn't get an abortion. Then, she kept them."

Rob shook his head. "You're an idiot. What kind of man doesn't want his own flesh and blood? And sweethearts like those little girls? How can you turn your back on them?"

"What can I say?" Frazer shrugged. "The apple doesn't fall far from the tree. My old man preferred drugs to my mom and me. Guess I'm just like him. I'd rather have a winning hand of cards in a poker game than a wife and kids."

Cat had closed off her senses when she entered the room. If Frazer was here, she didn't want to see his ghost. She'd undoubtedly start screaming at him. That wouldn't do either of them any good. She sighed, leaned over and brushed black curls off his face. "We could have had a great life if you'd just loved me and the girls, but it wasn't meant to be. When I loved you, that wasn't enough, either."

She stood up, kissed his forehead. "Goodbye, Frazer."

She stopped at the desk and promised to return to make the appropriate arrangements. She turned and started for the elevator. Out of the corner of her eye, she saw the door to Frazer's room open and the nurse enter. Then, she heard buzzers go off and the nurse called for help.

Cat stopped. What was going on? She watched three more medical staffers hurry into the room before the doctor arrived.

She had to leave. She had things to do. Instead, she went down the corridor and stood outside the door, peering inside. The nurses and doctor in brightly colored scrubs rushed around Frazer's body. They were all concentrating on something. And it was then that she saw it.

She saw Frazer's hand dangling next to the bed. And a finger moved.

Was it real? Or had a doctor or nurse done it, pushed the arm out of the way?

The doctor glanced over his shoulder. "Mrs. Hendrickson?"

"Yes," Cat said, coming closer, but not entering the room. She stared at Frazer.

"I never thought I'd say this, but it's a miracle. He's alive."

"No way." Cat stalked into the room. "How could he be dead moments ago and alive now? What did you guys do? If this is a joke, I'm not laughing."

"Don't, kitten." A hoarse whisper. "Don't go."

She crossed to the bed, saw the flutter of dark lashes. "I'm here, but if you die again, Frazer, I'm going home. Alone."

A whisper of a chuckle. "Stay."

Cat sank into a chair that one of the nurses pushed forward, beside the bed, and touched his hand. "Okay, I'm here for a while, but this is totally weird."

His fingers closed over hers. "You're telling me, kitten. You're telling me."

CHAPTER TWENTY

She stayed beside him for the rest of the night while the doctor ran tests. At dawn, when streaks of light painted the dark sky, Frazer had slept for more than two hours. She eased out of his hold, stretched her aching back. She had chores to do at home and she wanted some sleep in her own bed. She also needed to pick up the girls. She couldn't leave them with Virginia for much longer.

When Cat walked out to the waiting room, she found Pop MacGillicudy asleep in a chair. She gently shook his shoulder. "Hey, can you give me a ride home?"

He opened his eyes and yawned. "That's what I'm waiting for. How's your husband? He can eat free at my restaurant for the rest of his life. He saved my boy."

"You should know I've filed for divorce," Cat said.

Pop nodded. "Does that mean I can't feed him when he's in town to see the girls?"

"He never wanted kids," Cat said. "I don't think he'll visit often, but you can serve him when he does."

"Sounds like a deal to me."

They headed into Baker City first. Cat shared the good news of Frazer's survival and Dray's excellent prognosis with Virginia as they took the girls out to the Mustang. Reverend Tommy said that Aidan had gone over the classic sports car and it didn't have a single problem. She should be able to drive it anywhere. Cat promised to take suitable precautions and store the car in the garage.

When she arrived home, she put the twins to bed. Then she and Lad headed for the barn to take care of the horses. Chores done and the puppy walked, it was Cat's turn to take a shower before she pulled on a nightgown and crawled into bed. Just before sleep claimed her, she realized she hadn't heard anything from Rob. Well, she'd catch up with him later. He had to be around the ranch somewhere, or maybe he'd stayed in Lake Maynard for a while catching up with old friends, or perhaps he was in that zone where he lost time.

The next four days slipped by. She trained horses, did chores, got the kids off to school and took her turn driving the carpool. Rob hadn't turned up again and she wondered if ghosts went on business trips the way her father had or attended poker tournaments like Frazer. The twins asked about him a few times, but then got caught up in helping her make their costumes for Baker City's Halloween show.

Dray came home on Monday, the day after the accident. He sat in the café and whined because his doctor hadn't released him to work the ranch. Instead, he ended up peeling potatoes and chopping vegetables for his mother who kept Cat posted on Frazer's condition. He was getting better, passing all his medical tests with flying colors and running the nurses ragged.

Cat remembered her grandmother's lectures about being tacky and didn't say that she honestly didn't care about her soon-to-be ex. However, she did contact Bree Hawke and tell the attorney where to find Frazer, so the social workers could discuss a parenting plan with him. In her spare time, Cat worked on the town website. Halloween might officially be a month away, but the haunted town opened in less than a week.

There still hadn't been word about the truck. Uncle Aidan told her he'd follow up with the cops. Cat thought that was a good idea. He understood mechanical doo-hickeys and she didn't. Anyway, she had enough trouble getting the ghosts and the townspeople on the same page. The bottom line was building a customer base and that meant rehearsals galore. They had to scare the clientele, but not terrify them to the point that they wouldn't return to Baker City for upcoming events. The living help had more trouble with that than the spirits who lived by the O'Leary rules.

Thursday afternoon, Cat drove into town. The girls had the school rehearsal today, so she promised to meet the carpool at the church. She wished Rob would get home. She could use another ghostly liaison to help coordinate the actors. Right now, she needed an espresso so she went to the café.

Linda sat at the counter with a cup of coffee, a piece of Dutch apple pie and the Everett newspaper. She glanced up as the bell rang on the front door. "Hey, Cat. Tell me you don't have any kids and I'll be happy. I sent mine back to school. He's making me crazy."

Cat laughed. "I think that's the job description. I came for a mocha before today's rehearsal." She'd been in and out so often that she knew her way around the kitchen. "Don't get up. I can make it."

"Wonderful." Linda propped her elbows on the counter. "I took Frazer some clothes today. He wants to know when you'll be back to see him."

Cat poured milk into the metal cup and placed the plastic jug of milk back in the fridge. "What's wrong with that man? We're getting a divorce. He's been wanting one for years. The last time he demanded one, I agreed. I filed seven weeks ago."

"And they say women are flaky." Linda picked up her mug. "Maybe, it's because he died at least four times on Sunday, Cat. He could have had one of those moments that Dr. Phil talks about and decided there's more important things in life than a poker game."

Cat laughed and steamed her milk. "No way. Not Frazer. He's like one of those old-time guys who would bet on two flies racing on a window."

The bell over the door jangled. They glanced over to the door and saw Pop who was followed by Dick O'Connell in his police uniform. "Saw the Mustang in my lot," Pop said. "The chief needs to talk to you about the truck, Cat."

"What about it?" She continued to fix her mocha. "It's totaled. When the cops release it, I'll get my insurance agent to do her magic so I can buy a new pickup. Well, new to me. I won't spend a fortune on a farm rig."

Dick crossed to the counter, sat down on the stool next to Linda's. "Well, the investigation just took a different turn, Cat. Someone cut your brake line."

Worry edged Pop's voice. "Honey, unless you were a really great driver and able to think as fast as Frazer did on that two-lane mountain road, you and the girls would have died."

Cat stiffened, fear rocketing through her. "Nobody knew that Frazer and Dray needed to go to the hardware store. That was a last-minute change. Someone really meant to kill us."

Cat found it impossible to sleep that night. She finally brought her laptop to bed with her, popping in to make sure the twins were all right on the way back from the den. Leaning against her pillows, she finished designing the town website and sent off another round of promotional releases to area newspapers, TV stations and radio personalities.

She got up and went to check on the girls again, adjusting their blankets and stepping over Lad who didn't stir from his rug. When she went back to bed, Cat picked up her paperback and tried to read, but she couldn't face a fictional murder. Somebody had sabotaged her truck. Somebody tried to kill her. It wasn't entertaining anymore.

She went into the kitchen, made herself a cup of hot cocoa and added peppermint schnapps to help her relax. She checked on her daughters. Still asleep. Cat knew she ought to return to her own room, her own bed. She couldn't. She didn't. She sat in the rocking chair in the girls' room to watch them sleep. Where was Rob? How long did he plan to be gone?

The ringing of the telephone woke her four hours later and she stumbled out to the kitchen to answer it. "What?"

"Is this Mrs. Hendrickson?"

"Make that Ms. McTavish and you have me," Cat said, tired of using Frazer's name. "Is this Lake Maynard Hospital?"

"Yes, ma'am. I'm Penny, the morning nurse. It's 7:00 a.m. and your husband wants you to come get him. He says he has fences to build and work to do on the ranch."

"That man has never done hard labor in his life. I don't think the doctor wants him starting now."

Penny laughed. "You're right about that, but he woke up, demanded his pants and a ride home. We'd like him to stay in bed, but it's becoming more and more difficult to keep him there."

"Tell him that if he behaves himself, I'll be in this morning after I take the girls to school." Cat pulled out a kitchen chair to sit down. "Otherwise, he can walk to my dad's place. You could offer to call Liam for him."

"Is your dad a distinguished looking older man in a three-piece suit?" Penny asked. "If so, your husband kicked him out yesterday and offered to rearrange his face. I don't think a ride with him will work."

"That's strange. The two of them are terrific buddies. Well, tell Frazer I'll be there later."

Yawning, she replaced the receiver and headed for the shower. She had a lot to do if she planned to drive to Lake Maynard this morning. She needed to get the twins up and moving. While she took care of the horses, made breakfast and packed lunches for the twins, Cat considered her options. There still wasn't any sign of Rob. Had the ghost come home? Maybe, he'd already gone off to work on the pasture fence.

The truck accident hadn't been *an accident*. Frazer could have died. If he hadn't been such a good driver, he would have. And it shouldn't have been him. She was the one that someone wanted to kill. She shuddered at the thought. Okay, if he actually needed a place to stay, she could clean up one of the guest cabins for him, but there was no way she'd move him into her house. They were finished.

A little after ten, she breezed past the nurses' station and into Frazer's room. She stopped just inside the door. She almost didn't recognize him.

He stood across the room, gazing out the window. He wore dark blue jeans, a blue-checked flannel shirt and boots looking unlike himself. Were those some of the clothes Linda brought him? That was downright odd. Frazer never went for the country look.

Cat folded her arms and glared at his back. Did he think she was stupid enough to take him back if he dressed like a wanna-be cowboy?

"Wow, what's going on? Are you applying for a job at a casino in the boonies in that get-up?"

He turned, a smile tugging at his lips. "Oh, I think you're a big enough gamble, sweetheart."

She lifted her chin. "One you'll never ante up for again."

"Want to bet?" He strode to her.

Cat gasped when he pulled her against him, catching a brief scent of lime aftershave. "What are you doing? Let me go!"

"Not happening, kitten." He bent his head. "You're mine."

Before she wrenched out of his hold, his lips claimed hers. The fierce kiss surprised her. Stormy passion wasn't his style. She felt his hand twist into her hair, pulling back her head. Then his tongue swept into her mouth. And she surrendered, melting against him, but only for an instant.

That was all it could be. She remembered. The lying, the cheating, the humiliation, the way he hurt her babies when he ignored them. Fury rose in her. She bit down, tasted blood. "Don't you ever touch me again!"

"I haven't finished touching you, wildcat, but I can wait till you ask me."

She struggled to free her hand. God, she wanted to hit him. She glared up into his dark eyes, hating him. When he smiled down at her, she lost it. She kicked at him. He side-stepped and laughed. "You son of a—"

"Come on, kitten. You don't mean that." He feathered a thumb over her mouth. "Now, be nice. We'll shock these folks if I teach you to purr here. Let's go home."

She stared at him for a moment, her mind reeling. Frazer never played with her name, never used it as an endearment, never called her, 'kitten'. But, Rob did. She shook her head. "It's not you. It can't be you."

He chuckled. "Didn't you wonder where I was?"

"I knew where you were." She tossed her head, trying to clear her mind of its confusion. "You've been in the hospital since Sunday, Frazer."

"And you didn't come see me once so I had to get the nurses to call you." He lowered his head.

When she turned away, his lips brushed her cheek. She trembled. What if he was right? Could he possibly be Rob? No, she thought. She didn't know where the ghost was, but he'd turn up sooner or later, and she wouldn't allow Frazer to make a fool of her. Not again. He'd done it so many times.

She managed to pull away from him this time and stepped back. "If you want a ride somewhere, you'd better come now. Or you can stay here till you have a better offer. I don't care."

He walked over to the closet and picked up a small suitcase. "I'll make you care one day, kitten. I promise you that."

"Want to bet?"

"Not hardly."

Once again, she wondered, where was Rob?

He sat on the porch swing in the corner of the wrap-around porch, gazing toward the round pen. Cat had provided him with a blanket, made him a sandwich and filled an insulated cup with coffee that he could take with him to the porch. Then she stalked off to the barn, saying she had horses to train, and he was a waste of her time. He chuckled softly. She was a spitfire, but he'd been able to kiss her. What a thrill! He looked forward to repeating it.

Meanwhile, he enjoyed watching her longe the big palomino. He liked the way her tight-fitting faded blue jeans clung to the curves of her rounded hips and long legs. Then, there was the pink and black western blouse. He'd debated unsnapping it when he kissed her, but she'd probably have clobbered him before he caught a glimpse of her bra.

And her hair. She'd braided it back and the end bounced against her butt. He imagined the copper curtain spread across a pillow. How long would it take to get her in bed with him? It didn't matter. They had the rest of their lives.

Lad heaved a huge sigh and cuddled closer, his head on the blanket that covered Rob's lap, brown eyes blissfully closed. Rob stroked the tri-colored fur, the white ruff. "Did you miss me?"

The collie nudged him in a demand for more attention and Rob complied before he leaned back on the wicker seat and closed his eyes. A breeze from the creek filtered through the roses. He began a mental list of winter preparations from mulching the roses to filling the woodshed. He drifted off to sleep.

The stirring of the pup woke him. He glanced across the yard and saw Cat riding one of the blacks in the corral. It had to be the filly. She was shorter than her brother. A white van came up the drive. Was it already time for the twins to arrive from school? He looked at his watch. It was a little after four.

Lad jumped down and Rob stretched and slowly stood. This new body was bigger than his own, but he liked being taller and stronger, even if Frazer was twelve years older than Rob had been when he died. Well, he'd take care of himself and he'd last a good long while.

He followed the dog over to the porch steps and waited for the van to stop. When it did, Sophie was the first one out, then Samantha. As usual, they wore jeans, sweatshirts and tennies. They stopped when they saw him.

Backpacks slung over their shoulders, they slowly approached. One matching step, two, three. They saw their pup sitting by him. Sophie gaped at that, but not her sister. Samantha took one look, then ran toward him. "You're back. You're home."

He didn't know how, but the little girl recognized him, knew he wasn't her father. "Yes, I am." Rob dropped to one knee, caught her when she flung herself against him. "I missed you."

"Me too." Sophie joined her sister and hugged him. He held both girls tight. "Did you miss me too?"

He nearly choked on the lump in his throat. "You know it."

Lad circled them, tail wagging and yipping in excitement. Rob glanced past the dog and watched the van reverse, then turn to head back to the highway. He hugged the girls—*his girls now*—even tighter and closer. He'd watched the afternoon ritual for so long, he couldn't wait to take part. "Is it time for snacks?"

"Yes," Samantha said promptly. "Will you help us make some?"

"I'd love to."

The girls chattered while they put away their backpacks, telling him all about school. Together, they made sandwiches. He cut them into the triangles he knew they liked. Then, he sliced the apples into wedges, saving the cores for their ponies. It was his turn to be a dad and he loved it. Samantha put away the bread and jam, coming back with the plastic jug of milk. He heard the door close while he filled two glasses.

Cat came into the room. "Hey, girls. How was your day?"

"Good. It's better now that Mister Robbie's home," Samantha said.

"We missed him and so did Laddie," Sophie said. "Did you miss him too, Mommy?"

Rob put the milk away while he waited for her answer. She eyed him for a long moment, then asked. "How do you know he's not your dad playing a trick on us?"

It was lucky that Frazer was dead and gone. He'd really done a number on this woman and the children if they could even consider such an idea. No wonder the man wanted to see what came next. He'd done enough damage here.

Rob strode across the room, caught Cat's chin and looked down into the emerald green eyes. "I'm not him. I'd never hurt you or the girls."

"That's something he'd say."

Before she continued, Rob pulled her against him. At last, he had her in his arms and it wasn't a dream. "I'm sorry, kitten. So sorry he hurt you."

For an instant, she relaxed against him. "Well, he never once said that."

Samantha beamed at the two of them, a sunshine smile. "That's how, Mommy. Our old daddy never wanted to make snacks with us."

"Or hug any of us," Sophie finished.

CHAPTER TWENTY-ONE

Cat couldn't remember any of Frazer's kisses being so steamy. When was the last time he touched her in front of the girls? Never.

Lad followed this Frazer around the house. The dog liked him, really seemed to like him. When the man settled into a chair, the pup collapsed nearby. Twice, she'd seen him roll over for a tummy rub and wag his tail when he received one. The kittens seemed to think that Frazer's legs were perfect for climbing and he just carried them back to their box when they were done playing. He'd helped put dinner on the table and did the dishes afterwards while she supervised homework. He didn't act like it was brand new even though she'd never seen him do it before.

At bedtime, he read two stories to the girls making up voices for the different characters to the twins' delight. Even at his most charming, Frazer had never volunteered to spend time with their daughters. He'd always headed for the casino whether or not he was working. He claimed that kids bored him and so did their night-time activities.

She went into the living room. Frazer was stretched out on the couch watching an old John Wayne movie. She knew either she was going crazy or he was. Her ex didn't like cowboys. He preferred sports and betting on his favorite teams. She crossed to the recliner in the far corner and switched on the pole lamp. She needed to hem Sophie's dress for the Halloween festivities.

She threaded a needle and waited for a commercial. "Did Chief O'Connell visit you in the hospital?"

"No, but Deputy Griffith did. He said someone cut the brake line on the truck." Frazer kept his gaze on her, another new trait. "Dray and I were lucky to survive. I told Bigger I was glad you weren't driving. I don't think you could have pulled it out of the skid."

She stopped and stared at him. How would Frazer know the nickname that Rob had for the county cop? Her husband couldn't, could he? Whoever he was, he seemed to be waiting for an answer, so she said, "I'll agree you're a better driver than I am in hazardous conditions. How long do you plan to stay?"

"For the rest of my life, kitten. You may as well get used to the idea."

It wasn't going to happen, but the commercials ended, and the movie started again, so she didn't tell him that. He watched the show and she sewed the blue dress. On the next commercial break, she said, "Your doctor doesn't want you alone for the next week while you finish recuperating, but your *visit* doesn't include living in this house, Frazer."

"What game are you playing?"

"No games. I won this place with an essay that I wrote. It's mine and I'm not letting you screw this up."

He pushed his hands into the pockets of his jeans, stretching the denim across his flat stomach. "Are you trying to annoy me? I told you when you moved in that I'm not the kind of man to let you play mudpies with my guts. I'm here. I'm not leaving."

"Don't push your luck. I already told you that we're done."

He stood up, his eyes narrowing. "And your point is…"

"I don't love you. Hell, I don't even like you, Frazer, and I have no respect left for you. All you ever wanted was a piece of tail and I was stupid enough to marry you. You've been bitching that you wanted a divorce for years. I filed for one."

He stalked toward her. "I'm not him. I already told you that. I'm not stupid enough to risk losing you or the girls."

"You already lost us."

He laughed suddenly, but there was little humor in the sound. "I'm not letting you run or ruin my life, wildcat. And I'm sure as sugar not afraid of you. Pull any smart-ass trick you want. Irritate me and I'll cloud up and rain all over you."

"No tricks, Frazer." She lifted her chin and met him, glare for glare. "I'll clean up one of the cabins for you tomorrow and you're out of my house. In a week, you're off my ranch."

"Right." He stopped in front of the recliner, resting his hands on the arms of the chair and leaning toward her. "I had time to think in the hospital. I figured I'd marry you ASAP."

She blinked, surprised. "Marry me? What are you talking about? We've been married for almost ten years and you've been whining about it since the day after we left that chapel in Reno."

"That was *him*, not me." He leaned closer, his deep voice lowering even more. "First, we'll talk to Reverend Tommy about the ceremony. And if you don't push me, I'll wait to take you to bed."

He was too close. "I'll never sleep with you again."

"You're so gorgeous and I didn't have sleeping in mind." He caught her chin in hard fingers. "I love that fire in your eyes."

"No, you don't." She wouldn't give him the satisfaction of a struggle. "You hate it when I talk back to you."

He grinned down at her. "Maybe he did, but I don't, kitten."

"What do you have, an identity crisis?"

He chuckled. "Beautiful, wild and all mine."

"I'm *not* yours."

She trembled when he bent to brush his mouth over hers. "I'm not marrying you again. I'll see you in hell first."

"When I die next time, sweetheart, I know I'm going to heaven because I've already been to Vietnam."

She gaped at him. What? The Vietnam War happened years before either was born. Before she could move, he lowered his head and his lips found hers. His tongue swept inside her mouth, exploring, taunting until she joined in the sexual battle. He kissed her as if he owned her, as if they'd been apart far too long and there was no choice except her surrender. She kissed him back.

He trailed a leisurely line of butterfly kisses to her ear, along the side of her neck. She shivered when he unfastened the top two snaps of her blouse.

"Enough." She pushed against his chest. "Did you hear me? I'm not in love with you. I won't marry you and you're not staying here."

She felt his smile against the pulse in her throat before he straightened. She was still trapped in the chair. He must know how much she wanted him, but she wouldn't say it. "You bastard."

She squirmed deeper into the chair when he stroked the inside of her knee. She had on her jeans. He didn't know how hot he was making her. "Don't."

"All right then." He stepped back. "I'll give you the space you think you want, kitten. I'll move into the bunkhouse as long as you don't lock me out of this house. And if I have to drag you to the altar, believe me I will."

Cat breathed a sigh of relief when he returned to the couch to watch the movie. She'd choose her battles. She'd won most of this round, even if he didn't realize it. She would have the space she needed.

She shook out Sophie's dress. She'd finish hemming it tonight and then she could work on Samantha's pinafore.

The next morning, she still didn't know what to think or what to do. What was going on with him? He seemed very different than the man she'd been married to for so many years. The twins seemed to think he was someone special. The dog liked him. The cat and kittens did too. She suspected the horses would too when he finally went out to the barn.

How had this Frazer even known about the building he called the bunkhouse? It was a small cabin directly behind the house where she lived with the twins and she hadn't had a chance to give it a good examination. Well, no time like the present.

She'd left him to nap on the couch while the twins watched cartoons. She'd brought out cleaning rags, a mop and a bucket. She would scrub down the bunkhouse and then he could move into it.

She used the key he'd told her about at breakfast to unlock the cabin door. Another question. How had he known there were sets of keys in the cabinet adjacent to the antique cookstove in the kitchen?

Keys that apparently opened all of the locks on the dude ranch. *Was* he really Rob? Or was he still Frazer playing some kind of sick game?

If she broke down and trusted him, would he jump out and laugh at her for being a fool? And how could Frazer know about Rob for that matter? She hadn't shared anything about the ghost and neither had the twins. She just didn't know what to do.

The bunkhouse—the cabin—needed work, she judged as she unlocked it. The door opened into a kitchen with a pantry off to the right. A set of stairs leading to a loft cut the main room in half. On the other side of the staircase was a small furnished living-room that ran the width of the house. A dusty couch, a rocker in the corner and a small TV along with two bookcases filled the area.

The bathroom backed onto the pantry—well, at least the place had indoor plumbing, she thought. There was a tub and a shower, both of which needed scrubbing. So, Frazer could stay clean. One less thing for him to gripe about.

She returned to the kitchen, flipped a switch and the overhead lights came on. She nodded, satisfied. Okay, it had electricity and it hadn't been turned off. That was another plus. She glanced inside the pantry, noting the stackable washer and dryer on the other side of the hot water tank. She'd have to check and see if they were connected. Then, there was a small cabinet and shelves followed by the refrigerator. He could make his own meals if he chose or continue eating with her and the girls. The cabin was livable.

She wiped down the walls, the kitchen table and the cupboards. She took time to empty them and wash the dishes. She swept and mopped the linoleum floors. She put the small rugs into a basket to take over to her house. She'd wash and dry them there. She didn't want to risk breaking the machine here.

After she finished cleaning the bathroom, it was time for her to hit the upstairs. She climbed up, cleaning rags and bucket in hand. A queen-size bed took up part of the loft. She'd have to bring over sheets and blankets. The lamps on the bedside tables needed new bulbs. She added that to her mental list. It was a nice little place. It reminded her of the apartment where she lived when she first started working for Mario, back when she was an apprentice at his training barn.

"Are you here, Cat?" Frazer called. "The girls are making lunch and I told them I'd come find you."

"I'm upstairs," she answered. She saw his dark hair first as he mounted the steps, then his face and shoulders, then the rest of him. "I'm almost done cleaning. You should be able to move in here tonight."

He glanced around the room. "Needs some curtains. You'll find them in the linen closet where my mom kept them."

"Are you still claiming that you're not the man I know you are?"

He chuckled. "And I thought you were pigheaded when you moved in and pretended not to see or hear me." He shook his head. "Next week when the girls are in school, we could make some memories up here."

Heat flooded Cat's face. She stepped back as he came closer. "Didn't you promise to give me time?"

"Yes, but I've been waiting for hours to kiss you." He snagged her wrist. "Just one and then we have to go."

"All right." She dropped her rag in the bucket. She could do this. She slid her hands over his broad chest, up to his shoulders. She tiptoed up, touched her lips to his. "Okay, there you go. One kiss."

"Oh, I think we can do better than that." He lowered his head. "Or are you afraid?"

"I'm not scared of anything." She tangled her fingers in his hair, brought his mouth to hers and kissed him. Her tongue slid between his lips and she teased his into a darting duel. His big hands slid up to cup her breasts.

"Mommy? Mister Robbie? Where are you?" Sophie called from downstairs. "We made lunch."

Cat pulled away from him. "We're coming, honey," she answered. "We'll be right there."

She hurried down to the main floor of the cabin. He patted her butt and she felt her face burn. She hoped that Sophie hadn't seen him and since the little girl was standing just inside the door, that was a safe bet. "What are we having?"

"PB and J," Sophie said. "And potato chips and cookies and apples. But we need help cutting the sandwiches and apples."

"I can do that," Cat said. "After we eat, we need to go to Baker City for the dress rehearsal. The haunted town opens Monday night."

"Reverend Tommy says he's having a sleepover at the church tomorrow night to kick off the big event," Sophie said. "It's only for kids. Can me and Samantha go? Mrs. Tommy says we have to sleep on time because there's school on Monday and we'll be real good."

"You're good," Cat said. "Let me talk to them about it today. Then we'll take your overnight things with us to church tomorrow."

That earned her a big smile. When they reached the kitchen, Sophie asked. "Why are you cleaning the bunkhouse, Mommy? Mister Robbie has his room upstairs."

"Because even though I look like your dad, I'm not him," Frazer said, before Cat could fumble with an explanation. "Your mom and I need to decide if we love each other enough to get married. That's why you gals are going to live in the house and I'm going to stay out back for a while."

Samantha carefully filled two glasses with milk and carried them to the table. "Me and Sophie were talking. If we tell people that you're not our dad, then they'll think we're real strange. We got to pretend you are Frazer."

It was Sophie's turn for questions. "So, where did our dad go? Will he come back?"

"No, he won't be back. He went on to see what there is to do next. He said I could have his body because he was done with it."

Cat washed her hands and went to cut the sandwiches. "It's rather like one person moving out of a house and another moving into it. That's your story and you're sticking to it."

He nodded. "And the best part of the deal is I get to kiss you whenever I want."

Cat glanced at him. "Want to bet?"

Taking over in another man's body wasn't as easy as Rob had figured it would be. On the one hand, he could actually touch her and the girls. He tasted food and coffee had never been this good before. Still, there were times when he felt like he was driving an eighteen-wheeler when he was accustomed to a sports car since Frazer Hendrickson had eight inches and damn near sixty pounds on him.

Most of the other Army Rangers were comparable in size to what he'd been, five foot, eight inches, with a lean and wiry build. He hadn't felt short or skinny around them. Truthfully, he had no complaints, beyond the obvious. He wanted Cat to trust him the way she had before he landed in Frazer's body. The fear in her green eyes continued to cut deep into Rob's soul.

The girls led their ponies out to graze in the round pen. He haltered up Skyrocket. When Cat took Pal out of the barn to the big corral, he followed with the flashy bay. The former rodeo bronc knew him no matter what shape he wore. The horse nuzzled him, looking for apples and affection when Rob turned him loose in the paddock.

"He likes you." Cat sounded surprised, as she released Pal. "Skyrocket is afraid of men."

"I've been feeding him apples for almost a month," Rob said. "We'll have to see if he'll let me ride him now that I have an actual body. I don't want to break this one taking flying lessons."

Sophie giggled. "You're funny, Mister Robbie. Sky knows you want him to carry you like Pal does Mommy."

"That's right," Samantha agreed. "Sky likes his new job better. Nobody hits him or scrapes and stabs him with those sharp, pokey things on their boots. And he gets lots of apples. What are we going to give them when we run out of apples, Daddy?"

Rob stared at the little girl, feeling the word warm him. Pride mingled with joy and a new sense of responsibility. "What did you call me?"

"Daddy." Samantha sighed. "Weren't you listening at lunch? We have to stop calling you Mister Robbie or people will think we're crazy."

"So, you're our new daddy," Sophie added. "It'll be okay. Frazer never liked being called that, but you will. Right, Daddy?"

Rob nodded and dropped to his knees. "Come here, you two." When they ran into his arms, he hugged them tight. "I promise to be the best daddy I can. I've never been one before so if I make mistakes, tell me."

He waited for a scathing comment from their mother, but she

didn't say anything. She just looked at the three of them, then turned and headed back to the barn, Lad trotting behind her.

She still didn't have a lot to say when they headed for town, but she did let him drive the Mustang. Maybe, she was starting to figure out that he wasn't Frazer.

Rob hoped so. Anyway, what had he expected? It'd taken ages for her to admit that she was living with a ghost when she moved onto the farm. She was downright stubborn.

He pulled up by Reverend Tommy's house. "We're still parking in his garage, right?"

Cat nodded. "And he's still locking the door when the car is here so nobody messes with it. I thought I'd ask Uncle Aidan for help finding a new pickup. What do you think?"

"Sounds like a good idea to me," Rob said. "Then, he can give it a once-over and make sure we don't have any mechanical problems starting out."

She hesitated. "I was also going to do it so he didn't feel bad about the brakes going out on you and Dray. He'd know that we still trusted his judgment."

"Makes sense to me. No mechanic should be blamed because someone sabotaged a vehicle he repaired."

CHAPTER TWENTY-TWO

In the restroom at the church, Cat helped the girls put on their matching blue dresses from what they called the *olden* days. Then came the pinafores that looked like miniature aprons. She'd done their hair in braids so they fit in with the other children in period costumes. She walked them over to the school where a dozen kids raced around in the playground. She waved to the ghost of Mrs. O'Sullivan who stood on the porch, an old-fashioned golden bell in her hand and the teacher waved back.

Reverend Tommy was lining up their audience outside his church, townspeople, press and even the local politicians who would be the first to tour the haunted town. When they finished seeing the sights, Virginia had organized a reception at Pop's café for the guests to fill out surveys about what worked and what didn't at the Baker City event. Cat had arranged for the ghosts to be in the adjacent cocktail lounge so they could hear the comments too.

Cat bypassed the church and glanced at the cemetery on her way to the haunted hotel. She spotted a few teens dressed as ghouls and zombies. They mingled with some actual ghostly loggers and a few volunteer firefighters who were still alive. The plan was for them to chase the guests, but only the ones healthy enough to run. She'd told the kids not to let anyone have a heart attack. They'd laughed and agreed.

A tall blonde walked away from the crowd and Cat recognized her lawyer. "Hi, Bree. This is a surprise."

"My father decided it would be a good publicity op," Bree said with a smile, "and I came so he couldn't screw up anything."

"How could he do that?" Cat asked, flicking a glance at Frazer when he came to join them. "This is a town event so we don't need county permits. Pretty much everyone is on board from the business association to the city council."

"Except my dad's good buddies, Herman MacGillicudy and Liam O'Leary," Bree said. "Those two scumbags are trying to get him to use his influence to shut you down."

"How do you know they're scumbags?" Frazer asked. "I know it because the cops suspect someone of cutting the brake line on Cat's truck and I damn near died last Sunday. How do you know it?"

"Because they're friends of my father's and my dad doesn't have great taste in friends." Bree pointed to a tall, gray-haired man in a black suit who wore a white cowboy hat and chatted with a lovely blonde about his age in a tailored blue dress. "Only Floyd Hawke, better known as Tex to his thousands of adoring, stupid supporters would come in a suit to a haunted house."

"Haunted town." Cat frowned thoughtfully at the politician. "Would you be majorly upset if I tell you I always vote against him?"

"No, I like smart clients. And I always work for his opponents." Bree held out her hand to Frazer. "I don't think Cat introduced us. I'm Bree Hawke, her divorce attorney. And you are—?'

"Going to talk you out of pursuing the divorce until Cat and I have a chance to work things out." He shook hands with her. "I'm Frazer Hendrickson."

Cat eyed him, wondering why he didn't use Rob's name if he was claiming to be him and then realized he couldn't. If he claimed to be a dead man, everyone would think he was crazy, just like her kids had come to the same conclusion.

Cat focused on the lawyer. "He's dealing with a concussion and some other medical issues since the accident last week. The doctors said they lost him a few times, twice before they got him in the ambulance, again in the ER and then again in the operating room."

"They also found me each time, kitten." Frazer put an arm around Cat's waist. "Dead only counts when you don't come back. Stop fretting. I'm fine."

"I heard about the truck's brake lines being cut. So, what do you think of him now?" Bree asked.

"To be honest, I don't know what to think," Cat said. It still felt strange when he acted affectionately. "He's not the same person that he was last summer, and I'd swear he actually doesn't remember what a jerk he was then. He even suggested we go for marriage counseling."

"And I'm even standing right here listening while you talk about me." Frazer teased. "Reverend Tommy just signaled to you. They're about ready to start. He's sending the first bunch to the school, another group to the hotel and a third to the bordello."

"I haven't checked the rest of the town and I want to see the girls sing their song."

"Don't worry, Catriona." Newt hustled up to Cat, his form passing through the crowd. "The mayor just asked me to tell you that everything is hunky dory." He glanced at Frazer, then did a double-take. "Well, I'll be hornswoggled, young Williams. How'd you get in there?" He noticed Bree and added. "Never mind. Tell me later."

"It looks like everything's okay from here," Frazer said, looking around. "Let's go watch the fun at the school."

"So, you're letting your kids be part of the show?" Bree walked beside them in the direction of the two-story school. "Was that Cat's idea?"

"Actually, it was theirs," Cat said. "They've been practicing with the teacher and the other kids for the past week."

"Let's go see. I can't wait to be scared to death, especially since I heard there's hot chocolate at Pop's when we finish," Bree said, smiling.

"And frosted Halloween cookies." Cat slipped closer to Frazer.

No, she thought. It's Rob. Newt wouldn't lie to me. It's really Rob. Now, we just have to work out everything. They heard the ringing of the bell and Cat wondered how many of their guests saw Mrs. O'Sullivan's spectral figure in her white shirtwaist blouse and black skirt.

The children raced to line up in two rows, one of girls, a second of boys. As they marched into the school, they sang what the twins called the 'ABC' song. Once they finished it, they went onto the multiplication tables. The guests followed, lining up along the back wall of the classroom.

Chalk squeaked as Mrs. O'Sullivan wrote her name on the board.

Bree leaned close to Cat and whispered. "How did you do that?"

"Do what?" Cat asked, waiting for the actual show to start.

"Make the chalk move by itself and write a name."

Cat glanced at her lawyer and realized the other woman was serious. "Okay, I told you we've been practicing and it's a trade secret."

She needed to see what their company saw, so she took a moment to block the ghosts from view. Now, she'd experience what most people did. She still heard the teacher and suspected others did too.

"You big boys in the back know what to do when we have company. Stand up and give those ladies your seats."

As Cat watched, the chairs at the last row of tables began to move, apparently by themselves. She felt a breeze brush by her face and heard a teenage boy speak, but she didn't see him. "You can have my seat, ma'am."

"Thank you," Cat said.

The offer of chairs was enough for two of their guests. They didn't take them. Instead, the women backed up to the door, clutching their escorts' hands. Bree sat down next to Cat. "Now, what?"

"Whispering in class isn't appropriate," Mrs. O'Sullivan chided, the chalkboard visible through her. "Would you like to write that on the board, young lady?"

Chalk waved in front of Bree and she shook her head. "No, ma'am."

"Very good. Let's do attendance."

Roll call succeeded in scaring a few more people in the audience when invisible children answered to the names the teacher called. They were visible to some of the audience and not to others. Then, it was time for the pledge of allegiance. The American flag moved to the center of the room, but only Cat knew it was the ghosts who carried it. Chairs slid across the floor and everybody stood, the living and the spirits.

Afterwards, it was time for different children to recite their lessons. Two of the older boys moved to the front of the room and began with a Sir Walter Scott poem. Cat heard Bree's sigh of relief since the two of them were part of the living cast and looked real. Nothing scary there...

"Breathes there the man with soul so dead." The boys pointed toward an empty corner and the ghost of a man in a naval uniform floated into view.

A scream erupted and the school door banged as one of the girls from the audience fled. Cat looked over her shoulder and murmured. "I do hope she stays out of the graveyard."

"What's there?" It was obviously a friend who asked.

"Just a few zombies and a crazy logger with a chain saw." Cat focused on the boys and the poem was acted out by the ghost, ignoring the slam of the door. Next were the twins. Samantha and Sophie stood side by side as they took their places, looking angelic in their old-fashioned dresses. Mrs. O'Sullivan sat at the piano. Only her hands showed translucent as she started to play a familiar melody.

The girls sang. *"Oh, beautiful for spacious skies..."*

At first, it was just the piano and their voices. Then the sound of a harmonica joined in, followed by the strings of a violin and two flutes when other children slipped up behind the twins. Cat enjoyed the concert until Bree elbowed her.

"How are they doing that?" she whispered. "How do they make the instruments play by themselves?"

Cat smiled as sweetly as she could. "Trade secret."

Three hours later, the first guests converged on Pop's café. Cat handed out surveys while Linda and Virginia circulated with refreshments. Bree caught up with Cat and she smiled at the lawyer. "What did you think?"

"You have a hit on your hands," Bree said. "The school was eerie enough, but when I got to the hotel and saw the desk clerk, I totally freaked."

"Why?" Cat asked. "He was in the appropriate uniform, wasn't he?"

"It was a woman," Bree corrected. "And her head was on the

counter while her body stood behind the counter. I know you're going to tell me it's a trade secret."

Cat flicked a glance at the spectral mayor who was nearby, and the ghost shook his head, looking confused. Apparently, it wasn't one of his people. "Well, you can ask her when she gets here. The cast will be along so they can hear the comments. We may have had some glitches that we'll need to smooth out on Monday."

"Were we a glitch, Mommy?" Samantha asked, clinging to Frazer's hand on one side while Sophie clung to the other. "Daddy said we were perfect."

"You forgot part of the third verse, and I had to sing by myself till Claire sang too." Sophie passed her sister a frosted cat-shaped cookie. "And Daddy thinks everything we do is perfect."

Cat sighed and shook her head, meeting Frazer's—no Rob's amused gaze. "When the two of you have meltdowns over who gets to share her list with Santa first, he'll know you're not angels."

"So, which one is Claire?" Bree asked, looking around. "I only saw the two of you singing."

Sophie and Samantha eyed each other, before Sophie said. "Claire plays the violin and it's a secret why you can't see her."

"There you go, counselor." Frazer—Rob winked at Bree, before turning to Cat. "Kitten, I'm going to take a run home and feed the horses. I'll come back for you ladies."

"No, you can't." Fear raced through her veins. "Last time—"

"Don't." He dropped Samantha's hand and framed Cat's face. "Don't worry. The car is safe. It's been locked in Reverend Tommy's garage since we got here."

She trembled, unsure if it was the touch of his hands on her skin or concern about the Mustang. "You died—"

"I'm not dead." He leaned down, brushed his lips over her forehead. "Stop fretting. I'll find your uncle and have Aidan run a safety check before I head home."

"It will be all right, Catriona," the ghostly mayor intervened. "I've had Bridget and her patrol guarding the car since you left it. The last report was no one had entered or left the garage in the past four and a half hours."

Cat nodded, looking up into Rob's eyes. "You'll really have Aidan look at it first just to be sure?"

"I really will. I have a lot to live for." He turned and headed for the door, exchanging greetings on the way with a few of the locals, the live ones. Aidan waved at Cat before following Rob.

"He'll be okay, Mommy," Samantha said, before she chased after Sophie to connect with their friends.

"He'd better be." Cat glanced at the spectral mayor as he too watched the newly alive Rob leave.

"I'll send the Garvey loggers to watch him." The mayor started for the other room, then turned back. "When Williams has a rigging fit because the trap he plans to use to catch the fellow who sabotaged your truck fails, you'd better tell him that we allied with the O'Leary mediums more than a hundred years ago. We do what you want."

"Where did the accident happen?" Bree still stood next to Cat, unaware of the additional company. Any curiosity as a local about the haunted town was rapidly being replaced with that of a lawyer intrigued by an interesting case. "Between here and the ranch?"

Cat shook her head. "On the highway. A few miles past the farm on the first set of 'S' curves."

"There have been several fatalities there," Bree observed. "He's lucky he survived."

"And my son made it too." Linda paused on her rounds with a tray of cookies. "Pop and I have decided that Frazer can eat here free for the rest of his life and it had better be a long one. If Herman or anybody else goes after him again, I'll be the one needing a lawyer."

"Well, you know how to find my office." Bree glanced across the room. "I'll let you get back to work, Cat. I want to talk to Chief O'Connell. I suggest you put the divorce on hold while your husband recovers from his injuries. No judge is going to want to push this forward if one of the parties is impaired. Once the doctor agrees that Frazer has recovered, we can pursue the case."

Her anxiety over Rob's safety began to subside as Cat considered the offer. "Thanks, Bree. I've been reconsidering it since he saved Dray and nearly died in the process."

"Four times," Bree reminded her, "but I hear he's not taking it seriously because they brought him back each time."

"Men." Cat sighed. "They do have to be macho."

"Only some of them." Bree gazed across the crowded room. The current senator, Bree's father, was being a politician in a crowd, shaking hands and favoring everyone with his typical plastic smile.

"What's wrong?" Cat followed Bree's gaze. "What's going on?"

"My father is definitely glad-handing possible voters. He and his weasel, Elijah Robinson have never gone the machismo route."

"Weasel?"

"My term for his campaign manager," Bree said. "I have family issues too." She brightened as the door to the café opened and two men entered, Durango Hawke and a smaller version. "I don't believe it. My brothers made it. I'll catch up with you later."

Cat smiled and returned to her own task. She continued handing out the written surveys and collected the completed ones. Midway between her tasks, she talked to the press, offering up the promotional one-liners and sound-bites she and Frank had written. Most of the comments about the haunted town were positive with a few critiques about things that could be fixed by Monday. She'd have to make a list before the meeting tomorrow.

Sunday morning, Rob woke early. Sun streamed through the gauze curtains of the bunkhouse. This was what living was about, all over again. As a ghost, he hadn't needed to sleep. He just faded in and out if he wasn't paying attention. Waking up to sunshine was a definite plus for the living.

Cat, he thought. He couldn't wait to see her, but if he showed up without clothes on her doorstep, he'd never hear the end of it. He rolled out of bed and headed for the shower. When he arrived at the house, Lad met him at the back door, and he let the collie out to take care of puppy business.

He checked the twins first. The girls weren't awake yet. He picked up Sophie's pillow which seemed to spend more time on the floor than on her bed. After he eased it under her head, he adjusted Samantha's blankets. When he left the kitchen, he saw a light in the den. He walked into the room and found Cat asleep in a chair behind the desk.

MY SWEET HAUNT

He went to her, scooped her into his arms. She turned her face into his neck. "Rob?"

"Yes, it's me. Time for bed, kitten."

"The girls?"

"I'll take care of them. You get some sleep."

"Church today." She yawned but didn't stir in his hold. "Have to be ready."

"Services don't start for another five hours. I'll take care of things now and wake you up in time."

At nine, he brewed a fresh pot of coffee. The girls and Lad watched cartoons in the living room. Before he could wake her, he heard a knock on the door. The pup trotted to the hall and barked. Rob petted him on the way to open the door. "Stay with the twins."

He found Herman MacGillicudy standing on the front porch.

"Why are you here?" Rob asked.

"You have to tell the truth." Herman's voice rose. "*I* didn't do anything to the truck. How could she leave town if she didn't have anything to drive?"

That was a good point. Rob folded his arms so he wouldn't slap the man. Herman didn't deserve to be punched. "You insulted and threatened my wife."

"She was supposed to get scared and leave. My family turned against me. Dick O'Connell kicked me out of Baker City. He said I had no business there. I own property in that town. I have a perfect right to be there."

"Sounds like a personal problem." Rob glanced past him to his car parked in front of the house. "How did you get onto my land? We locked the gate last night."

"You couldn't have. It was open when I arrived. You have to tell people that I didn't do anything to her."

Rob took a step forward. He caught Herman's tie in his fist. "You're on my land."

"I'll leave."

"And not come back." Rob tightened his grip for an instant, long enough for Herman to choke for air. "Got it?"

Herman managed a nod.

Rob released him and watched as the banker scuttled to his

Cadillac. Rob turned back inside, locking the door after him and pausing to glance in the living room. "Okay, girls. Time to turn off the TV and get ready for church."

CHAPTER TWENTY-THREE

A short time later, Rob took Cat a cup of coffee. She carried it with her to the bathroom, heading for the shower while he checked on the twins. Once they had dressed, they'd started packing for their overnight as Lad lay on the rag rug in their room, watching them, his tail gently wagging. The doorbell rang and the pup stood. He stretched, then wove his way through sleeping bags and backpacks to go bark at the intruder.

Rob chuckled and followed the collie to the front door. After his doggy guard duty was done, Lad turned and headed back to the girls. Rob opened the door. This time Liam O'Leary was on the porch. Rob stepped out and looked down on the shorter man. "What?"

"We had a deal," Liam said. "How long are you planning to play house with my daughter?"

"The rest of my life." Rob leaned against the doorframe. "Get used to it."

"You can't. We made a bargain."

"I don't remember that." Rob folded his arms and waited. "Tell me about it."

"Get serious." Liam glared at him. "You'd lost your job, your car, everything in a poker game. I sent you a plane ticket. I got you here.

You're supposed to take her away and I get this place to turn into a gravel pit."

"Sounds like a no-brainer to me," Cat said from the hall. She was in a robe, her hair wrapped in a towel. She stood beside Rob—Frazer as far as Liam was concerned. "Only you and Hermie screwed up when one of you cut the brake line on my truck. Frazer doesn't remember your deal because of the accident."

Liam's jaw dropped. "You can't believe that nonsense. He's gaming you."

"That could be. He has done that before during the last nine and a half years." Cat cuddled closer to Rob. "The doctor said the dissociative amnesia was probably caused by the trauma inflicted during the accident." She slid her arm around him, pleasing Rob to no end. "In other words, Daddy dearest, you should choose smarter friends. My husband doesn't have a clue what the two of you planned. So, I'm keeping him and throwing you off the farm."

Rob watched as the words made an impact. "Guess I win, and you lose, O'Leary."

At first, Liam paled as if he'd been sucker punched then he changed his focus. "Catriona, you need to think. I know you had mental problems when you were a child. Making up stories, hallucinations, blackouts, acting up and even running away from your problems eventually landed you in the hospital."

Rob felt Cat tense beside him. He straightened. "Do you think we haven't talked about the way you abused her, O'Leary? I may not remember everything I did in the past couple weeks, but I certainly haven't forgotten that."

Liam opted for the voice of reason. It came across as oily. "Check his cell phone. You'll see I'm telling the truth. We talked every day for a week before he came here."

Cat shook her head, heaved a sigh and then said, "Liam, you are the dumbest man I've ever met. Do you actually believe his cell phone survived a crash through a guard rail and a rollover accident down a mountain side before hitting a tree? The truck was totaled, and it was a miracle that both Frazer and Dray survived. You really need more competent minions. Now, go."

Liam gave them one final glare before turning away. "You'll beg to sell this place to me. And I won't give a top price now. The price keeps going down the longer you put it off. Think about it."

"Since it's not for sale, I won't be thinking too hard. It doesn't matter how many times I say it. You're too stupid to understand the legal terms of the deal I made. This place was a destination resort once and it will be again." Cat rose on tiptoes and nipped Rob's ear. "Now leave, Liam. We have plans for today and they don't include you."

Rob chuckled and followed her inside. He enjoyed the sway of her hips under the golden-brown material of her robe. "Keep me happy, kitten, and tell me that you have high heels."

"You know it." She paused to look in on the twins. "Hustle up, ladies. We're out of here in fifteen minutes."

When they reached her room, Rob asked in a low voice, "How can you forgive me for plotting to steal your home with Liam?"

"Because it wasn't you," Cat said. "Frazer would do something that rotten, but not you, Robert Williams. There is no way that you would ever let my father turn your family home into a gravel pit. You're too smart to trust him to keep his word on anything. Frazer wasn't."

"It's too bad the cell phone's wrecked. You could check up on me."

"It's not," Cat said, opening the closet door. "I have it. I lied, but we don't need to check it. Do you know how to use one?"

Rob blinked. "No, but it can't be that hard. You just dial the number you want."

"Oh, you have so much to learn." Cat laughed, searching through her clothes.

He grinned and went to pull her into his arms. He tipped up her chin, lowered his mouth toward hers. "Kitten, you can teach me anything you want."

They spent the day acting like a family from an old TV show and she loved every minute of it. It was nothing like she and Frazer had ever done when they had been together. First, they went to church, then brunch at Pop's café, the haunted town meeting and a cartoon movie at the theater in Lake Maynard followed by dinner at a fast-food restaurant. During the meeting, Rob had run home and put new padlocks on the gates so the farm would be safe. He reported that he'd checked the livestock while he was there, putting the horses out in the corral for the afternoon, and allowed Lad some run-around time.

After the movie, she'd taken the kids up to the church for their sleepover while Rob did evening chores under Lad's supervision. When she returned to the farm, Cat headed for the kitchen. She opened a bottle of white wine, poured two glasses and carried them into the living room, stepping around the sleeping young dog, sprawled out in the middle of the floor.

Rob was choosing music. The afterlife wasn't much for cell phone technology, but he apparently knew how to put a CD in the player.

"Make it country," she suggested. "I have it on the best of authorities that if it isn't country, Mister Robbie says it's not music."

He chuckled. "Will you dance with me?"

"You know it."

She put the glasses on the coffee table in front of the couch. "Come here, Laddie. Let's move you so you don't get stepped on."

The collie didn't move. She snapped her fingers. "Lad, come."

No response. He didn't lift his head, move a paw or even twitch a black-rimmed ear.

"Lad?" She dropped to her knees beside him. She put a hand on his side and felt the slow, almost ragged breaths. "What's wrong, buddy?"

Rob swiftly joined her. He tried lifting the young dog, but the pup was totally limp. He collapsed onto the rug. "We need a vet. Get your purse and keys."

"It's Sunday night. How can we find one? Everett's at least two hours away. He'll be dead by then."

"We're going up town," Rob said. "Doc MacGillicudy."

"Herman threatened him. How do we know we can trust his relatives?"

"Because we don't have a choice." Rob's tone hardened, became more authoritative, sounding like the soldier he'd once been. "Come on, Cat. Throw me that blanket off the couch."

She hesitated at first. Then she grabbed the afghan, tossed it in his direction. She hurried into her room, grabbed her keys, coat and purse and slid her feet back into the shoes she'd kicked off moments before.

He met her at the front door, carrying the dog wrapped in the afghan. "You hold him, and I'll drive."

In the Mustang, she cuddled the pup on her lap. He weighed just over twenty pounds and wasn't that big, but this was the quietest she'd ever seen him. He was such a furry bundle of joy. How could this have happened? How did Herman get to him? Lad spent so much of his time with them and recently when they weren't at home, they made sure the dog was locked inside the house. A tear trickled down her cheek and landed in his fur. She clutched him tightly. "Laddie, I'm so sorry."

Rob stopped long enough to unlock and open the gates. He drove through, then locked up the farm again. "Tomorrow, call Jeff and have him get on the other three fence lines. We need to be able to keep trespassers off the farm."

Cat nodded. "Did you find what happened to the padlock on the entrance gate?"

"It was missing. I replaced it with a reinforced one, the kind that's almost impossible to cut with bolt cutters," Rob said. "We'll call Dick from Doc's."

She stroked the pup's head. "I had really planned to seduce you tonight, not spend it saving the kids' dog."

"Oh, we'll have a lot of nights together." Rob signaled for a right turn. "We're just getting started, kitten."

He parked in front of a neatly restored Victorian on a quiet corner in town. Lights shone in one downstairs room.

"How do you know this is where the doctor still lives?" Cat asked.

"It's where all of them have lived for years. Mike went to 'Nam with me. He was always going to med school when he got back."

"You said med school." Her heels tapped on the front walk. "Is he a vet or not?"

"He's a doctor. He can save the pup." They reached the porch and Rob pounded on the door. "I'm not letting the girls break their hearts over this dog."

"All right, I'm coming," a deep voice bellowed from in the house. "There better be blood, barfing or broken bones."

"None of the above," Rob yelled back. "Get your backside moving, Mikey."

"What do you want, Williams?" The door yanked open. What looked like a mountain man in black pants, a red flannel shirt and orange logger suspenders loomed in the doorway, beer bottle in hand. Silver hair hung to his shoulders. He eyed them. "You aren't who I thought. Sorry. What do you folks need?"

"Dog's been hurt," Rob said. "He's paralyzed. I'm thinking poison."

"I treat humans, not their pets."

Tears crowded into Cat's eyes. "We'll never find a vet on Sunday night. Please."

"Lady, I don't know a damned thing about animals. What if I kill him?"

"He'll die without you," Rob said. "And your dad was a vet. Let's get this done." He shouldered past the other man. "Where do you want him?"

"Shoot fire. Don't you ever take, 'no' for an answer, Williams?" Mike MacGillicudy blinked, then followed Rob. "Sorry, been drinking a bit too much tonight. Something about you reminds me of a guy I knew in high school. Take the dog into the dining room. Put him on the table."

Rob kept walking, Lad a crumpled heap of gold, white and black fur in his arms.

"Who is he?" Mike asked. "For that matter, who are you?"

"Cat McTavish. I won the Williams' place in an essay contest. I've been trying to refurbish it so we can open in the spring."

Mike jerked his head toward Rob. "And who is he?"

"My husband," Cat said, taking a moment to think before she combined the names of both men. "Frazer Robert Williams Hendrickson."

Mike spread a white sheet on the dining table and then helped Rob straighten out Lad's body so he lay prone. The doctor listened to the collie's heart and lungs. He went to his desk and came back with a laptop that he passed to Cat. "I need you to do some research."

"What am I looking for?" Cat asked.

"The drugs used to euthanize large animals," Mike said. "That may be what the problem is here. My granddaughter just started as a veterinarian at the clinic in Lake Maynard. She told me that if wild animals find a dead horse or cow, ones put down by a vet, the drugs can kill them. A few months ago, some eagles died from an overdose when they got to a carcass. I need to know the symptoms so I can treat this little guy."

"All right." Cat turned on the computer.

She was in the middle of the first search when she heard a key turn the lock in the door. She glanced over her shoulder and saw a young red-headed woman in jeans and a Washington State University sweatshirt.

The girl came into the house, smiling. "Hi, I'm Robin. What's going on? I didn't know you were having company tonight, Grandpa."

"Wasn't planning on it, but things change." Mike gave her a swift look. "How was your date?"

"Okay." Robin paused, but only for an instant when she saw Lad on the table. Then, she was across the room and inspecting the puppy. "What happened to him? What did he get into?"

"We don't know for sure," Cat said. "We think he was poisoned."

"Of course he was," Robin peeled back an eyelid to check Lad's pupils. "Looks like a phenobarbital overdose. How long has he been like this? Ataxia? Drunk acting, lethargic, sedated, unable to stand?"

"We found him an hour ago and he was almost comatose," Rob said. "He must have found whatever he ate during one of his trips outside sometime today."

Robin nodded. "Okay, well I can't induce vomiting when he's like this. Let's get him on a saline drip."

"What are you thinking?" Mike asked.

The two doctors launched into a discussion that Cat barely understood. She caught something about possible liver and kidney damage. Then, Mike went for a plastic tub and Robin said, "We're going to pump his stomach. After that, we'll introduce activated charcoal to pull the phenobarbital out of his blood vessels. It's going to take at least a few hours to stabilize him."

Cat turned off the computer, since they didn't need it now. She went to the table and stroked Lad's golden shoulder. "But, can you save him?"

"We can try," Robin said. "There aren't any guarantees. The fact that he's young and strong is on his side. We'll do our best."

Mike returned with the basin. "Roberta's best is damned good. She was named after her father and I named him for my best friend who died at Hamburger Hill." He looked at Rob. "The same guy that you're named for, right? You're Devin's boy, aren't you? You look a lot like him."

"Who is Devin?" Cat kept petting the collie, glancing between Rob and the older man.

"Devin Williams," Rob said. "One of—." He paused. "He was Ed and Adam Williams' younger brother."

"What happened to him?" Cat asked.

"Died of a heroin overdose back in the 1980s. Sad case." Mike opened a medical bag and began to pull out surgical tubing. "Okay, Robin. What's first?"

It was after one in the morning when they arrived home. Lad remained at the doctor's place. Rob sat down on the couch and pulled her down to sit beside him. He passed her a glass of now warm wine. "Drink up."

Cat leaned her head against his shoulder. "Who do you think it was? Who poisoned Laddie?"

"Either Herman or Liam. They both showed up here yesterday." Rob stroked her hair. "I'm going to slap the crap out of both of them till one of them talks."

A smile trembled into life. Cat kissed his cheek. "We don't do things that way anymore, Rob. There are laws against animal cruelty. We turn him over to Deputy Griffith and Chief O'Connell."

"Okay, you do that. I'm slapping the crap out of them for hurting my kids' dog."

"He's our dog too."

"He sleeps in their room." Rob put an arm around her shoulders. "So, I'll slap them around for us too."

Cat swallowed more of her wine. "If I'm being barbaric, I'd prefer it if you punched them."

Rob smiled. "I have been in fights before. What Army Ranger hasn't? I've hit my share of men, but you don't *punch* guys like Herman or Liam. They aren't worthy of that much respect. It's why I'll slap them a bit."

Cat finished her wine, trying to hide a smile. "You're just a fun guy, Rob."

He chuckled. "Incidentally, I liked my new name. Frazer Robert Jacob Williams Hendrickson. Good job."

"When people ask, you could say that you're using 'Rob' now and drop the 'Frazer'. I've known lots of people who don't use their first name. Eventually, you could talk to Bree about legally changing it."

"Works for me."

Cat leaned forward, put her glass on the coffee table. "I never shared the details of my childhood with Frazer. I got into my share of trouble when I was a kid, but how did you know Liam was lying about me?"

"Because of all the stunts he pulled when he was a youngster. I only shared a couple of them with you, but he was a real stinker." Rob drew her back beside him. "And maybe twenty years ago, I was minding my own business floating around the farm soaking up energy during an electrical storm. I heard a little girl screaming, terrified of the thunder and lightning."

"Why didn't her parents comfort her? I always go to the girls when they're scared."

"Her mind was screaming, kitten, not her mouth. Nobody else could hear and her father had threatened to whip her if she made any noise after she was sent to bed."

"You came and told me to snitch cookies when I was locked in the pantry," Cat said slowly, cuddling closer. "And you told me stories until the thunder went away."

"Yes, and I made you a promise that night."

She nodded, trailed a finger down his cheek. "You said that nobody and nothing could ever hurt me at Cedar Creek Guest Ranch."

"And nothing ever will." He caught her hand, held it to his lips. "I won't let it."

"Promise?"

"Always."

CHAPTER TWENTY-FOUR

Cat sighed when he drew her across his lap a short time later. She felt the muscles of his legs under her, the warmth of his chest against her cheek. Her dress hitched above her knees. She gasped when he slid a hand under the cloth, up her thigh. "I do have a bed."

"And we'll get there later." His lips trailed down her neck to the pulse in the hollow of her throat. "Kiss me."

She threaded her fingers in his night-black hair and brought his mouth to hers. It felt oddly familiar to be in his arms and yet oh so different. He wasn't her former husband and kissing him was such a sweet adventure. Her lips parted beneath his and his tongue tangled with hers in a passionate duel. One kiss led to a second, then a third. She pulled back a fraction when his hand cupped her breast. His thumb tormented her nipple and she moaned.

He smiled, lowered his head. "And we're only getting started. I can't wait to make you purr."

She surrendered to the steamy kiss. She was barely aware that he'd unfastened the buttons on her shirtwaist dress. She pressed closer, feeling him harden beneath her. Payback was hell. She'd get to his shirt at some point, but only if he stopped kissing her. She couldn't think when he touched her.

He opened her dress, unhooked the front closure of her bra. Her breasts spilled out and he bent his head. She stifled a groan when he strung kisses over her skin. Her nipples tightened under the teasing flicks of his tongue. "More. Rob, I need more."

He laughed softly. "Oh, I'll give you more."

She gasped when he pushed up her skirt, stroked her through the panties she still wore. She squirmed on his lap, relishing his muffled groan. "Oh, I'm so getting you for this, Rob."

"Promises." He drew one of her nipples into his mouth and sucked.

She reached for his shirt, undid the snaps and slid her hands inside over his chest. She felt his heartbeat quicken. He liked her touch as much as she did his. She caught her breath when he cupped her through her panties. "It's my turn."

"Not yet, but soon. I've wanted you far too long."

One finger slid past the silken cloth and inside her. At the same time, he found her other nipple and sucked. A second finger joined the first and he began a slow rhythm that drove her crazy. In, out, up, down. His thumb rocked into her clitoris and she fell apart. When he laughed against her breast, she yanked his hair in retaliation. "You're not funny."

"Sure, I am." He lowered his head and kissed her again.

She twisted, tried to evade his mouth. He followed, anticipating every move until he captured her lips with his. When he deepened the kiss, she surrendered. How could she help it? She moaned when he released her, and his hand slid between her thighs. "Not again."

"Yes. I told you that you're going to purr for me." A finger eased inside her, then the second and his thumb joined the dance.

It seemed like forever before their clothes ended up on the floor. They kissed, explored each other's bodies with their hands as well as their mouths. He rolled on top of her, parting her legs with one of his.

"You're mine."

She arched against him. "And I want you, Robert Jacob Williams."

He slid into her. They moved together. The slow, steady pace seemed to shatter every wall between them. When they kissed, it was only part of the magic. Her nails dug into his shoulders, urging him on. He groaned and she knew he enjoyed her touch. He alternated short shallow thrusts with long, deep ones. She met and matched them, unable to help herself.

She heard him whisper again. "Mine. You're mine, wildcat."

She didn't answer. She couldn't, not when the storm swirled around them and they rode it together. She stared up into his face, drowning in the black heat of his gaze. They went on and on until she reached the stars and flew among them. And he followed her to the ends of the universe.

Afterwards, she lay in his arms, content. She couldn't imagine fighting with him again. Soft butterfly kisses landed on her face, eyebrows, ears. She slowly smoothed a hand over his chest, a muscled arm. "That was nice."

"Just nice?"

She sighed when he kissed the spot under her ear. "Very nice."

He dropped a kiss on her cheekbone "I'm going to kiss you until morning, wildcat."

"You can't." She tangled her legs with his. "I'll die."

"No, but you may want to." He pulled her closer and she felt as if she'd melt into his body. "Say you belong to me and I won't kiss you a hundred times before I take you again."

"It's not happening." She murmured when he kissed the line of her jaw. "I won't say it."

"Next time, I think it will be against the wall, but that may be the third time. We may just end up on the floor now." He nipped her ear. "And it may not be tonight, but eventually I'll have you in every room of this house."

"You're a bit of a bore, Rob." She traced a line down his nose. "All you do is talk."

He kissed her forehead. "I'm having you soon, so I think I'd better start counting."

"You'll never get there."

"Want to bet, kitten?"

When she awoke, the sun shone through the master bedroom windows. She was in the middle of the big brass bed. She felt the warmth of a long body next to hers, the weight of an arm on her hair. She opened her eyes, turned her head so she could look at him.

Oddly enough, her husband.

He sprawled across the queen-sized bed, taking up more than half of it. She studied his relaxed, sleeping face. Gently, she brushed a lock of coal black hair from his forehead. No wonder he was tired.

He'd made love to her two more times in the living room before they made breakfast together. Then they'd gone to the barn and done the morning chores. He'd searched the back yard and found a meat-laden bone. He said it looked like it'd come from a dead horse. It was possibly a leg. They'd take it to Mike MacGillicudy and either he or Robin could arrange to have it analyzed.

When they came back to the house, they showered together and made love again. Then they'd gone to bed. She propped up on an elbow, tugged her hair out from under him. She glanced at the clock on the nightstand. It was after eleven. Suddenly, she realized they hadn't used any protection. She kicked him. "I could be pregnant."

Opening his eyes, Rob reached for her. "Well, give me a minute, wildcat."

Now, she knew he couldn't be her former husband. Frazer complained about the twins. He complained when she got pregnant and he certainly never suggested having more than the two girls. They had always used protection, but when she filed for divorce, she hadn't worried about running out of birth control pills. She grabbed her pillow and whacked Rob with it. "You macho pig. I've already gone the pregnancy route. Once was enough."

Before she could bop him again, he wrested the pillow from her and tossed it to the floor. "I always wanted a houseful."

"In your dreams, Robert Jacob Williams." She squealed when he snagged her wrist and pulled her to him.

"And you? What's your full name?"

"I changed it to Catriona Rose McTavish when I turned eighteen." She snuggled close and felt him respond, his erection pushing against her. Ah, that was very nice. "I never got along with Liam so I didn't want to use his name."

"He always was an embarrassment to the O'Learys." Rob leaned back enough to cup her breast, his thumb and finger rubbing the nipple. "Let's not talk about him. I haven't done everything I want to do with you.

"Really?" She nipped his ear and felt him catch a breath. "What did you have in mind?"

"Seeing how long it takes to make you scream when I have my mouth on you."

"Nobody's ever done that." She nibbled along the strong column of his neck. "It's not necessary. I don't know if I'll like it."

"Wildcat, you're going to love it." He kissed the hollow of her throat. "You'll beg me to do it every time."

An hour and a half later, they were in the kitchen. Cat wore a checkered blouse and her usual jeans. She laid strips of bacon in a frying pan, then stirred the hash browns in a different skillet. He was supposed to be setting the table, but he couldn't help staring at her. She was perfect and all his. He couldn't help it. He strode across the room and laid claim to her mouth, tongue sweeping away all resistance.

Finally, she pulled her lips free. "Food, Robert Jacob Williams. I need calories."

"We can eat anytime."

"Yes, and we're going to do it now."

"Fine." He pulled her rounded hips back against him. "Then, I get to choose the next activity and guess what it's going to be?"

She laughed, pushing back against him. "I already know what you want. We have horses to train. You wanted me to talk to Jeff about the fences too."

"Okay." Rob kissed the back of her neck. "We'll take a couple hours for work. At two o'clock, ready or not, I'm hauling you to the nearest bed."

"All right, but remember we have to be up town at four to meet the girls and get ready for the first night of the haunted town."

The telephone rang and he answered it. "Hello?"

"This is Mike MacGillicudy."

"How is—" Before Rob finished the question, he heard barking.

"Is that—?"

"Yes, it is. He's urinated and I gave him more saline. He's eaten a bit and slept. He's moving fairly well, but he'll need more rest." Mike turned away from the phone to holler, "I'm on the phone with your family. Be quiet and let me talk."

More barking ensued.

Rob chuckled. "Tell him we'll come get him after the girls do their routine at the school for the haunted town. I don't want him home by himself tonight."

"Sounds good. Did you find what poisoned him?"

"I think so," Rob said. "I'll bring the bone to you too."

"Fair enough. Do you know who gave it to him?"

"I'm not sure." Rob saw Cat frown and added. "Both Herman and Liam O'Leary were here yesterday before the dog got sick."

"I don't think it was Herman," Mike said. "I can't stand my cousin, but he's not sneaky enough to poison an animal. It takes too long, and the owner might be able to save the pet. No, if Herman did it, he'd have shot Laddie or drowned him or tortured him in another way."

"Good to know," Rob said. He'd watch Herman a lot more closely now. "Would you please let Dick O'Connell know the latest developments?"

"Be happy to. I have results from the tests I can pass onto him too. But, I'm not a vet. Robin wants to take Laddie to her mentor's office and run a few more tests. If you bring it by, we'll give her the bone today too."

As soon as he replaced the receiver, Rob said, "Lad's fine. We can bring him home tonight. Mike and his granddaughter are going to watch him until the girls finish up."

"Really?" A big grin spread across Cat's face. She put down the spatula, ran to him and threw herself against him. A fierce hug and then a kiss that made his head reel.

He slid his hands over her rear, scooped her up. He cupped her butt in his hands and held her tight against him. "Did you turn off the stove?"

"No." She laced her arms around his neck. "I have two hours, remember?"

"I was afraid you'd say that." He lowered her feet to the floor, looked at the clock. "Okay, but time's a-wasting. And you're wrong. Now, you only have an hour and fifty minutes."

It was almost time to leave for town. While Rob cleaned the barn and put out the supper hay for the horses, Cat cut roses to take to the cemetery. She'd meant to visit the graves yesterday, but she'd forgotten. There'd been so much to do, and they were running late for church. She carried the bouquets over to the car and put them neatly in the back seat beside the plastic wrapped bone for the vet.

The first stop in town was at Mike's place. He led them into the living room where Lad was curled up sleeping in a blue recliner, the afghan from home draped neatly over him. Cat smiled at the sight of her sweet puppy and went to pet him. He yawned, wagged his tail and licked her hand. "He's not moving like usual."

"Not yet." Rob wrapped an arm around her waist. "He will be before long. He just needs to get the rest of the drug out of his system."

Cat stroked the puppy's head. "Well, he'd better not get used to sleeping on the furniture. He stays on the floor at home."

"Yes, ma'am." Rob drawled. "We'll give him a memo."

She glowered at him. "Do you think I didn't see him on the porch swing napping with you?"

Rob chuckled. "You didn't move him."

"She probably didn't want to wake you up," Mike said. "Dick O'Connell told me that you just got out of the hospital from a car accident. I can have your records sent here and then you won't have to go back to Lake Maynard."

Before Cat helped the girls change into their costumes, the three of them took flowers to the cemetery. It didn't take long to put roses on the family graves. On their way back to the church, the twins ran ahead of her. Cat followed them until she saw Rob standing in a quiet corner of the graveyard. She went to join him. "What are you doing?"

He shrugged. "Just looking."

She followed his gaze to the headstone that read: *Robert Jacob Williams. Beloved son and brother. June 10, 1948 – May 15, 1969*

He hadn't even turned twenty-one. Just a boy. He hadn't been old enough to drink and the 26th amendment to lower the voting age wouldn't have passed for another two years. He'd been old enough to fight and die for his country, but not old enough to elect the politicians who sent him to war or to drink.

And she was twenty-eight, soon to be twenty-nine. Cat laid the last three roses against the marker. "We need to talk when we get home."

He put an arm around her shoulders. "Is this when you come up with another excuse, Catriona Rose McTavish?"

"An excuse?" Cat glanced up at him. "What are you talking about?"

"You're afraid to trust me." He dropped a kiss on her forehead. "Your father taught you to fear men when you were too young to defend yourself. Frazer kept up the lessons and now I want you to love me. That's a risk you're unwilling to take."

"I haven't said that."

"You don't need to when you're constantly showing it."

She took a deep breath. She wouldn't argue with him, not here and not now. She slipped out of his hold. "I'm going to help the girls get ready for tonight."

"All right. I'll run home and take care of the horses. I'll be back later. Where should I meet you?"

"We'll be at Pop's by nine," Cat said. "The twins leave the school at the first break. The older kids and adults do the second show."

"You're a wonderful organizer."

She met his gaze evenly. "Are you trying to charm me?"

"I wouldn't dare." He caught up with her in two strides, grasped her shoulders.

"Rob, I need time and space."

"I'm not letting you drive me away, kitten." He bent his head.

Their lips met, but only for a moment until she wrenched free and hurried after her daughters. She needed to make a decision. Why did she feel as if she was taking advantage of a boy so much younger than she was? He wasn't a boy, not really. He'd been a ghost and seen everything that happened in the world for decades. And it wasn't because she didn't trust him. In fact, she cared more about Rob Williams than she had ever cared about any other man.

So, what was the problem? Could he be right? Was she afraid to trust herself and her emotions? Wait a moment. He'd died as a boy and never had the chance to grow up. Now, he was in the body of her former husband, but that didn't make him a man either. She'd enjoyed having sex with him. Still, that didn't mean she could plan her life around or with him. Rob deserved more than to be tied down with her and the girls.

They had a good turn-out for their first official night in the haunted town. Guests paid at the church and then divided into groups to begin the tours. The school seemed even more eerie in the twilight and the show the kids put on seemed spookier tonight. In the lamplight, Samantha and Sophie looked adorable in their matching dresses and pinafores. Their invisible classmates played instruments behind them. It mesmerized the audience, especially since the twins acted unaware of anything special about the musicians.

After the performance, they finished up at Pop's café. Cat checked out the donation jar for the memorial on the counter, pleased to see it was already a third full of bills. When the girls finished their cocoa and cookies, they headed for the car with Cat and Rob. She hesitated, then said, "On our way home, we need to stop and pick up Laddie. He's visiting the doctor."

"Why? Was he sick?" Samantha asked.

"Yes," Rob said. "And when we put him outside, we need to go with him for a while. He found a snack yesterday when we weren't looking, and it wasn't good for him."

Sophie heaved a sigh and shook her head. "I've told him and told him that he's only s'posed to eat the food we give him."

"And he's not s'posed to trust strangers," Samantha finished. "Or the food they give him."

"But, he's barely six months old," Cat said. "We need to keep teaching him that lesson and watch him to make sure he stays safe."

"And the kittens too," Samantha said. "The momma already knows to be careful of the food she gets."

CHAPTER TWENTY-FIVE

When they arrived home, Rob took Lad out to walk around the yard. Meantime, Cat helped the girls unpack. After their baths, they were in nightgowns and tucked into their beds. She started the first story. Before she was halfway through, they were sound asleep. Lad walked in slowly, turned three circles and collapsed on his rug.

Cat stood up and tucked the chapter book back on the shelf. She covered up Samantha, kissed the girl's forehead, then did the same with Sophie. "Sleep tight. I'm glad you're home."

"We're glad," Rob said, from the doorway. "We missed you."

Cat tiptoed from the room and led the way to the kitchen. She opened the refrigerator and removed the partial bottle of chardonnay along with a beer and handed it to Rob. She poured one glass of wine before she turned to him. "We need to talk."

He lowered the beer. "Let's go in the other room if you're going to yell at me."

"I'm not yelling." She drew a deep breath, then followed him. "I didn't know you were only twenty when—"

"I died." He sat down in the recliner, putting the glass on the table beside him. "Does the forty plus years I've haunted this place count at all?"

"I'll be twenty-nine in October. I'm almost ten years older than you are."

"Or you could add up all the years I've been around and I'm more than thirty years older than you are." He chuckled. "Or how about the fact that Frazer had used this body for a while. You could say that we're right for each other."

She advanced on him. "Will you stop making fun of me and listen?"

He held out his hand. "Come on down here and let's just be together for a while. You can fight with me tomorrow."

"Will you admit I'm right and you're wrong?"

"Maybe." He grinned up at her. "Then again, probably not."

She smiled and put her wine on the table next to his bottle of beer. "At least you're honest."

She slowly closed her fingers over his and let him pull her down onto his lap. She sighed, relaxed and pillowed her head on his shoulder. "You could turn on the TV. There might be a John Wayne movie."

"Sounds good." He reached for the remote.

Hours later, the movie he'd been watching came to an end and he turned off the television. She'd fallen asleep half an hour before. He cuddled her close and she didn't wake. Rob could spend the night here in the recliner with her. That meant both of them would be stiff and sore the next day. Still holding her, he slowly rose to his feet. He carried her from the living room to her room and lowered her onto the bed.

Rob debated leaving her dressed and decided she would be more comfortable without her jeans. He unbuttoned her pants and slid them off her hips, over her butt and down her legs, but left her underwear and T-shirt on. *I should be nominated for sainthood.*

He hadn't awakened her or thought about making love to her more than a half-dozen times. With a sigh, he pulled a blanket up over her and left the room.

He stopped to check on the girls. First, he picked up Sophie's pillow and tucked it back under her head. Then he collected Samantha's teddy bear and slipped it under the covers beside her. The puppy slept on his usual rug, emitting soft little snores. So, Lad was definitely on the mend.

Rob turned around and stopped. Cat stood halfway across the kitchen. "What's wrong?" he asked.

"You left me."

"You were asleep."

"I'm awake now. Will you stay with me?"

"I'd love to." He crossed the kitchen, picked her up and carried her to the bed.

"What if I said I didn't have sex in mind?"

"Neither do I." He held her tighter. "Making love, yes."

She laughed and shook her head. "What am I going to do with you, Rob?"

"A lot I hope." He carried her into the bedroom, closing the door with one booted foot. "Okay, wildcat. Let's see what it takes to make you purr."

She peeled out of her t-shirt tossing it onto the floor before she pulled him down on the bed with her and kissed him. He rolled next to her. His tongue swept into her mouth, taking possession. He kissed the tops of her breasts. She shifted against him. "Hurry, Rob."

He unhooked the front closure of her bra. "Oh no. We're just getting started."

She bit his shoulder. "Hurry."

"No." He drew her nipple into his mouth, sucked. He found the other one with his thumb and finger, rubbing it to a peak.

She moaned, tangled her fingers in his hair. "Faster."

He chuckled against her skin. "I already said, no. My rules. We do it my way."

His control didn't last when she unbuttoned his shirt. He shuddered as she slid her hands over the warmth of his skin, over his chest to his arms.

She gasped when he rubbed the silken panties against her. Then, he slid one finger inside her.

She writhed, moaned when a second finger joined the first. He probed gently and then his thumb sought her clitoris. "Oh God. Please, Rob."

"Soon, kitten." He smiled down at her. "Hot, wet and so tight. You want this."

"Yes." She arched against him, moving with his hand, unable to help herself. It went on until she came, convulsed in what felt like a hundred pieces.

Afterwards, he pulled off her panties. He eased between her legs. Then he lowered his head. His mouth slowly traveled down to where his fingers had been.

"What are you doing?" Cat struggled to demand, but her voice sounded so weak.

"What do you think?" His hands slid beneath her bottom and he lifted her. His tongue teased her as he licked softly.

She arched against his mouth, tangled her fingers in his hair. "Please, Rob."

He laughed against her. Then, he lifted his head, blew gently on the small bit of flesh. "Oh, I will, kitten. I will. Now, purr for me."

Morning felt as if it had come all too early. Cat wished she could roll over, curl up next to Rob and sleep for another three or four hours, but she couldn't. It was her turn to drive the local kids to school and that meant she needed to get the girls moving so they'd be at the church on time to pick up the van. Yawning, she pulled her hair out from under his arm. She would let him rest a while longer.

She glanced at the clock as she stepped over scampering kittens on her way to plug in the coffee pot. Almost seven. With the coffee brewing, she went to wake the twins. "Good morning, sweeties. Rise and shine."

"Okay." Samantha pulled the blanket over her head.

Sophie grunted something and buried her nose in the sheet. At some point during the night, Lad had managed to climb on the bottom bunk. Cat wasn't going to shoo him off at this point, which was just as well since he didn't shift either, just snuggled closer to the little girl.

"We can skip the haunted town tonight if you two are so tired," Cat said from the doorway. "Then, you can come straight home after school, do homework, have supper and be in bed before dark. What do you think?"

"No, we want to do our song." Sophie sat up and stretched. "We're coming, Mommy."

"All right. Pancakes for breakfast in twenty minutes." Smiling, Cat swung around and headed for her own shower.

The savory smell of bacon frying brought Rob out of a sound sleep. He heard clattering dishes from the kitchen. Breakfast was under way and he should be too. He tossed the blankets aside, stood and started for the bathroom. He stopped when he saw the stack of his clean clothes on the rocking chair. She was amazing. How did she do so much?

He made it to the kitchen ahead of the girls. He took the cup of coffee Cat offered and leaned down to kiss her. "Tell me you left something for me to do, Superwoman."

She laughed, flipping pancakes at the stove. "The horses. Will you take care of them so I can drive the girls to school after breakfast? But, first things first. Will you watch Laddie while he takes his outside run?"

"You bet." Still carrying the cup, he went to get the collie.

The twins were pulling up the blankets on the top bunk when he entered the room. He spotted the pup hiding in the covers on Sophie's bed. "What's going on?"

"Laddie has to go potty but he's scared that the bad man may have left something else to make him sick," Sophie explained. "He slept with me 'cause he was having bad dreams."

Rob put his coffee cup on the dresser. "That's why I'm going out with him. I'll keep him safe."

Samantha climbed down from her end of the bed. She sat on Sophie's bunk, beside the tri-colored pup and hugged him. "Okay, I'll tell Lad."

Cat had grown accustomed to the routine of driving the van down the winding mountain road from Baker City to Lake Maynard. The cluster of kids in the vehicle was fairly well behaved most of the time, but after their nightly adventures in the haunted town, the younger ones dozed most of the way to school. The older ones talked quietly to each other. It gave her time to think about the way her life had changed in little more than a month.

She had what she'd always dreamed of, a real home for her and the girls along with a loving husband. There were friends, a town full of people who accepted her for what she was, so why couldn't she accept herself? What was missing?

No, not missing. She just had a sense of overwhelming dread, like there would be another avalanche and this time she would be buried under tons of snow and rock. *Get over yourself, Cat O'Leary McTavish. The leaves haven't even finished falling off the maple and alder trees. Winter hasn't arrived yet and this time you aren't alone.*

She took a deep breath and signaled for the last turn onto the street by the Thompson's house. She'd park the van, pick up the Mustang and head home. She'd take Pal out for a ride and clear the mental cobwebs. Horseback riding always made things better.

Cat headed through the backyard to the side porch so she could trade out the sets of keys. She came to a halt when she recognized the plump gray-haired woman sitting on the swing in the corner, knitting needles flashing in the sunlight, a pile of yellow yarn on the seat. Or rather, Cat saw through the ghostly image to the slats of the swing. The insubstantial form of a golden collie lay on the deck nearby.

"It's been a long time, Grandma," Cat said, wishing she could hug the woman and pet the dog. "I've missed both of you so much."

"Well, you finally got here to Baker City even if you haven't made it to my house yet." Her grandmother put the knitting to one side. "Not that I blame you after you were almost killed there at my wake."

"What?" Cat gaped at her, feeling like someone should scrape her jaw off the floor. "I don't get it, Grandma. What are you talking about?"

"It's time to remember everything, Catriona."

Folding her arms, Cat struggled to control the tension that flowed through her. "You knew that I really could see ghosts when I was a child?"

"Of course. And we were having a nice chat in the kitchen when you came to my wake. I was telling you what to expect in the next few years, how you'd grow in strength and what a medium does to help people, both the living and the dead."

"I don't remember that." Tears filled Cat's eyes and she felt sobs rise in her throat. "I'd love to remember that, but I don't. Grandma, why can't I *remember*?"

"Because I told you to forget." Her grandmother rose, drifted toward her. "Honey, I was trying to protect you, but now you need to remember everything or this time he'll win."

"Who? Herman MacGillicudy?"

"Herman?" Her grandmother sighed, shook her head. "He's a conniving sort, but he isn't as vicious as he wants to be. You need to look closer to home."

"Frazer? My husband?"

"Oh, you don't need to worry about him either. He's moved on to as peaceful an end as he could want. He may not have lived well, but he made up for it at the end."

"By saving Dray?"

"And by stepping aside so Robert Williams could love you and your daughters. That took honor and grace."

"Can Rob still see you and the other ghosts around here?" Cat asked. "Or did he lose that when he took over for Frazer?"

"Oh, Robert hasn't lost the power to see the unseen. He's just been busy living these last few days. And he can help with everything you have to face."

"Then, who is our enemy?"

"I can't say it, Catriona. You need to remember on your own. I can tell you that I came to see you in the hospital and told you to forget everything I'd taught you over the years."

"The hospital," Cat repeated. "Aunt Rose told me that I ran away at your funeral and Uncle Aidan found me days later in a gravel pit."

"You didn't run away. Not then. That was the story cooked up to explain your disappearance."

"Who made it up?" Cat heard a dog whine and almost felt the coolness of a canine nose nestle into her hand. She longed to stroke the soft thick fur when the collie pressed against her leg. She closed her eyes for a moment. "What happened to you? How did you die?"

"Now, you're remembering. You're old enough to handle it, brave enough, strong enough. You're not a little girl anymore. Remember, Catriona. Remember it all."

Cat opened her eyes, saw the empty swing. It swayed in the morning breeze and she spun around. She was alone. Dimly, she heard her grandmother's voice again. "Remember."

The autumn sunshine faded and a teenage girl that Cat somehow knew was a younger version of herself stood in an old-style kitchen decked out with red-checked curtains at the windows and a matching tablecloth on the small round table. A refrigerator hummed in one corner and a golden collie sat nearby, tail wagging as it waited politely for the dog treat in Cat's hand.

Her newly dead grandmother sat at the table, a plate of Oreos and glass of ice-cold milk in front of where Cat had obviously been sitting across from her before she went after a doggie snack.

Thirteen-year-old Cat handed the treat to the dog that crunched the bone-shaped cookie in less than a moment. Petting the collie, she asked, "So, what if I find a mean ghost, Grandma? How do I get rid of it?"

The back door slammed open, striking the wall and her father stormed inside. "How many times have I told you not to tell lies, Catriona O'Leary? How dare you tell Aidan that our mother is still here?"

"She had things to say to me," Cat said, glaring back at him. "And I don't care what you say. You're the liar. I know she's real."

"Oh God no!"

Enmeshed in her vision, the grown Cat watched Liam backhand the teenage girl. He knocked her into the basement door which flew open. The dog rushed forward, barking. It lunged for Liam, teeth sinking into his arm.

He kicked it in the ribs. The blow sent the collie spiraling into the basement and Cat heard it howling in pain when it crashed onto the concrete floor a story below.

Teenage Cat scrambled to her feet, reeling, one hand pressed to a swelling cheek. She spat curse words at him. Then, she turned toward the basement and the stairs, obviously intending to go to the injured dog.

"Watch out!" Cat yelled at her younger self, even though she knew the girl wouldn't hear, wouldn't be able to save herself.

Liam shoved the teenager from behind, sent her tumbling down into darkness.

A short time later, Cat parked the Mustang in front of the O'Leary hardware store. The bell on the front door tinkled as she stepped inside. The wooden floor creaked beneath her boots as she headed for the office where she found her uncle sitting at an antique rolltop desk, ledgers spread in front of him. "I have questions, Uncle Aidan."

He turned on the swivel chair to face her. "Depending on what they are, I might have answers."

"Why does my father hate me?"

"Because you have what he always wanted and could never get."

"The O'Leary gift? Was it that important to him?"

"Power over the dead? It was all he ever wanted." Aidan ran his fingers over an old accounting sheet. "He'd lie, steal—"

"Kill?" Cat asked.

Her question hung in the air until Aidan slowly nodded. "I always wondered how you'd ended up in that gravel pit. It didn't make sense for you and Goldie to be there. You hadn't explored the area and it was miles from where you were last seen at the house."

"Because he dumped us there. He didn't think anyone would find us and we'd die," Cat said. "How did you know?"

"I took him when the dog came and got me after she died," Newt O'Leary said. "I had to wait until he was falling down tired from hunting for you before he heard me."

Cat gazed at her older relative. "Does he hear you now?"

"Most times, but not always. We get by."

Cat nodded again, eyeing both men, the living and the dead. "I'm not a child anymore and I'm not afraid of him, but he doesn't get to ruin any more of my life." She paused. "Or anyone else's, so I'll be watching out for him."

CHAPTER TWENTY-SIX

She stopped at the mercantile to pick up fried chicken and a container of potato salad from the deli counter. At home, she added chips, fresh fruit and bottled water to the menu, packing the food into her saddlebags. She took a few minutes to get Lad out from under the twins' bunkbed and walked the pup but opted to leave him inside again.

Then she headed for the barn and saddled up Pal. Skyrocket wasn't in his stall so she figured Rob had ridden him out to the field to work on the fence. Her hunch proved correct. When Sky whinnied a greeting, Rob turned around. Leaving his tools, he started toward her.

"I brought lunch," Cat said, when he was close enough to hear. "And we can talk."

"That sounds worrisome." He snagged the rein close to the bit and held Pal while she dismounted. "Don't tell me you're still fretting about my choice to be here with you."

She managed a smile before untying the saddlebags. "Actually, I'm better with that, but I want you to know I'm not a total idiot. I've made mistakes too."

"Who hasn't? It's part of being human." Rob removed the bridle and stepped back so Pal could wander off to graze with the other gelding. "I'm not the one to judge you, kitten."

She measured the sincerity in his dark gaze and nodded. "All right then. Let's eat and I'll tell you the story of my life. It sucked way before I married Frazer. I thought he'd rescue me from my parents' drama. I didn't know I'd be trapped in another loveless desert."

With Cat and the girls settled in the house for the night, it was time for his last walk-around. Rob didn't turn on the barn lights. He didn't need them. The moon shone through the windows. He saw Pal pacing, then Skyrocket stomping on the right side of the aisle. The ponies were in the first two stalls on the left. Both old-timers were restless. What was going on out here?

Normally when he walked through the barn at this hour, the horses were sleeping. The older ones would be standing up, but the fillies would be lying down in the next two stalls. Their half-brothers might be down or up, depending on whether they had hay left.

Tonka wasn't quiet tonight. He tossed his black mane, stomped, snorted. Then he reared in the stall and slammed against the back door. Why wasn't it open to his private paddock? And why was Lucky Charm in the adjacent stall? He liked being out in the cool night air. Rob glanced at the back of the young bay's stall. Yes, his back door was locked too.

Rob caught a sharp scent, the same thing the Morgans had to be smelling. What was it? And he knew. Gasoline.

In his barn? No way!

A shadow was ahead of him, tipping what looked like a five-gallon gas can. Rob leaped forward. He slammed the guy into the wall. He collapsed. He wasn't alone. Another man came out of the darkness waving a two-by-four. He swung it.

Rob caught the board and propelled his opponent against the black's wall. The horse apparently decided to join in the fray, lunging forward and sinking teeth into the intruder. The man yelled but before he recovered, Rob punched him in the ribs and followed up with a blow to the jaw.

He swung around to head for the tackroom, but someone was there first. The lights came on. He saw two barely visible men in logging clothes. Some of his former compatriots in the spectral world, Rob realized. "Who are you?"

"Part of the Garvey crew. The mayor sent us to keep an eye on you." One of the ghosts pointed to an intruder sprawled on the ground. "That guy's coming around. You'd better get a cap back on the gas if you don't want this barn going up in flames."

Rob nodded. He backhanded the first stranger who promptly hit the wall, knocking him unconscious again.

Now, for the gas can. Rob closed it up, screwing on the lid as tightly as he could. "I need the hose to soak this down. And I'm putting the horses out tonight just in case."

"And you should call the cops too." One of the ghosts came forward with three lead ropes. "Tie those bums up and we'll keep an eye on them while you do."

The hose floated toward Rob. He took it, flipped the nozzle and soaked down the aisle way. Some of the water hit the second man, but he wasn't awake to complain. Once the hallway was thoroughly wet, Rob tied the man's hands together, then the ankles. He ran the rope between the two, binding them tightly together. After that, he tied up the other stranger. "I have to get Ted Fenwick out here and have a phone installed in the tackroom."

"That will wait till daylight." The older logger walked to the end of the barn and leaned against the wall. "Go call. We'll be here."

The sound of sirens woke Cat. Was that an alarm clock? It couldn't be. She tossed the blankets aside and stood up. She couldn't see the barn or the driveway from the back of the house. She picked up her jeans off the chair, pulled them on and grabbed a pair of socks.

When she reached the front porch, she saw lights in the barn. Fire trucks and two police cruisers were parked in front of the upside-down 'L' shaped building. She hurried down the steps.

Lucky and Stormy nickered to her from the round pen. She saw other horsy shapes out in the big corral. Deputy Griffith had just finished muscling a scrawny looking guy in a plaid shirt and ragged jeans into the back of his car. Beyond them, she saw a ghostly cluster of loggers looking on and discussing the situation among themselves.

"Who wants to tell me what's going on?" Cat asked the living; in this case, the police chief of Baker City.

"These guys were hired to burn down your barn with the horses in it." Dick O'Connell shoved a second man forward. "You should be pressing civil charges too. Call Bree Hawke. We'll file the criminal ones when we get them to town."

Cat frowned at the young man's bruised face. "Who hit him?"

"Your husband took umbrage when this fellow tried braining him with a two-by-four," Dick said. "We'll be adding attempted murder to the list of charges. You'll want to take Rob to the doctor in the morning."

"Rob?" Cat asked, astonished that the chief actually knew his name.

"He told us that he preferred it to Frazer. Can't blame the guy. I always knew I was in trouble when my mother yelled, 'Richard.'"

Cat managed a weak laugh. "Where is he? Is he all right? He's barely recovered from that car accident. Now someone's trying to kill him again?"

That brought forth a response from the thug being shoved toward the second police cruiser. "Lady, if he hadn't swung on me, I wouldn't have had to defend myself. The guy's a giant. I'm more hurt than he is."

"Where is he?" Cat repeated.

"Talking to my cousins from the local fire department about how to clean up the gasoline spill and odor, so the horses can move back into the barn." Dick propelled the would-be arsonist into his car. "So, like I said, I'm pretty sure the district attorney will be talking attempted murder, arson and animal cruelty. That's just for right now. When we roll in the other charges, these fellas will be in jail for quite some time."

There was more squawking from the guy, but Dick shut the car door on that. "I think we'll get him to talk and tell us who is paying for all the harassment. Then, I'll arrest whoever is behind it and your troubles will be over."

"I certainly hope so." Cat heaved a huge sigh. "And to think I wanted this place so other people could come and enjoy it the way I did when I was a kid. I always saw it as a dream come true."

"It will be again." Rob came out with the volunteer firefighters and waited while they loaded up their equipment. "As my grandfather said, 'Never shout whoa in a bad place.' And we're going forward, kitten."

Cat mustered up a smile. "I'll give you a hand with the horses. Will the barn be safe?"

"It had better be since my family built it."

"We'll keep an eye on it." One of the ghosts sauntered forward, the details of the building clear through him. "Don't worry, ma'am."

"Thank you." Cat headed for the hay-room. She picked up two flakes of alfalfa and Rob carried six more. "Should we call their owners and have the horses picked up tomorrow?"

"No," Rob said. "You contact Durango Hawke and get his crew out here instead. Thieves are lazy. If they have to hike miles through the woods to get here, Herman or your dad will wind up doing their own dirty work."

"That makes sense. How did they get in here?"

"They came around the fence—which is why we need more of it."

It didn't take long to spread piles of hay around the corral and add a tub of water. Dick had closed and padlocked the gates on his way out. He promised to bring back the witness statements for Rob to sign the next day. With the police on their way, Cat and Rob left the ghosts to guard the barn and headed for the house. Luckily, the twins had slept through the entire thing so she didn't have to worry about their reaction, Cat thought.

The next morning, Cat waited until after breakfast and the girls were picked up for school before she asked, "What's the plan for the horses? I know you have one."

Rob nodded. "I already threw them some hay and refilled the water buckets out in the paddocks. Now, I'll repair the stalls on the short wing of the barn while you put in shavings and feed. We'll move them in there while I clean up the gasoline spill. The O'Connells told me how to do it. I just need to make a run to the mercantile for laundry soap, trash bags and other supplies. But, horses first."

"That's great." Relief crept into her eyes. "It's easier having someone to work with during emergencies." The phone rang and she answered it. She listened for a moment, then said, "Hi Jeff. We need to get those other fence lines in as soon as possible. The barn was almost set on fire last night."

Rob drawled. "And if I hadn't been out for my usual walk-around, we'd be in trouble."

She passed on the message and then paused. "We appreciate it, Jeff. We'll see you in an hour with the fence crew. Please thank Durango for us." Another pause and then she said, "Well, all right if he wants to rent it, he can. We'll work out the charges when we figure out the costs for the fence lines. The police suspect Herman MacGillicudy is behind all of the harassment. Yes, the banker in Lake Maynard."

When she replaced the receiver, she eyed Rob. "I don't know what's going on. Durango wants to rent the party barn. He says that the second floor has two dormitories and he has friends coming into town. Then, Jeff wanted to know who the police suspected. What's up with that?"

"I would guess that Herman is about to have a run on his bank in a little bit of Baker City style justice," Rob said. "He's caused a lot of harm over the years and folks are getting mad. It was one thing when he vandalized your truck before the accident. Now, it's escalated to people and animals being hurt. He's definitely crossed the line and payback's coming."

She smiled, then went to the cupboard by the woodstove to get the keys to the party barn. "Good. It's his turn to suffer." She glanced around the room. "Where's Laddie? Let's get started."

Rob frowned. He hadn't seen the pup since breakfast. He started by checking the twins' room. No collie in sight, but he glimpsed the black tip of the young dog's tail protruding from under the bunk beds. "All right. Come on, boy."

The tail vanished under the bed. Rob glanced over his shoulder. "Well, I found him, but he's still scared to death."

Cat hesitated. "He does need to rest, but I don't want him to get in the habit of hiding. Let's take him with us for a bit and then I'll bring him back inside." She turned around, headed into the kitchen, then came back with a dog biscuit. She dropped to one knee and tried to coax the pup to her. Whimpering and reluctant, he belly-crawled her way, nonetheless.

When he was within reach, Rob scooped up the collie, petting him for comfort. "Okay, let's go."

Lad whined constantly as they went out down the hall to the front door. When Rob put him down on the porch, the pup piddled all the way across the wooden deck.

Cat winced. "Maybe, we'd better put him back inside."

"He's only six months old. He has a long life ahead of him," Rob said. "Do you plan to let him live under the twins' bed for the rest of it?"

"No." She lifted her chin. "We all have to face our fears. Come on, Laddie. If Herman shows up on the property, I want you to bite him."

"Makes sense to me." Rob put his arm around her. He whistled to the dog. Lad trembled and reluctantly followed them in the direction of the barn.

Halfway there, they saw an old red pickup making its way up the drive, followed by a new brown truck since the gates were left open after the girls were picked up for school. Both rigs came to a stop in the driveway. Durango Hawke climbed out of the first one. He wore faded blue jeans and a sleeveless light blue chambray shirt. Lad took one look, yelped, then bolted for the front porch.

Cat and Rob watched the young dog hightail it for safety. "Do you think he—?"

Rob shook his head. "No. Durango wasn't here that day. Lad will get over it."

"I hope so for his sake." She obviously struggled to paste on a smile. "Good morning," she said to Durango who approached, glancing after the half-grown collie.

Durango nodded and raked a hand through tawny blond hair, concern in his navy-blue eyes. "Heard about the would-be fire. How are you? Was the dog hurt?"

"Not from the fire," Rob said as Lad cowered up on the porch. "Somebody tried to poison him."

Durango winced. "I hate scum like that." He nodded at the shorter man who came toward them. "My little brother Laredo has a house-warming present for you. Hope you like it."

The younger man eyed Rob warily as if he expected a blow. Like his brother he wore jeans, but his western shirt actually had sleeves. He cradled a cardboard box in his arms. Something in the container growled, then yipped a warning.

"Oh, let me see." Cat hurried forward. "Is it a puppy?"

Rob watched as she oohed and aahed over a small black and white furball in the box. "What breed is it? She's stuck on collies. How old is the dog?"

Durango smiled, but the amusement didn't touch his steady gaze. "Twelve weeks. Border collie and purple heeler. She's a toughie, the oldest of her litter, and she's aggressive as hell."

"Well, she'll fit in just fine with the rest of the womenfolk around here then." Rob glanced over his shoulder. "Let's take her over by the orchard so she can do her potty business and see if she can lure Lad off the porch. Being sick really scared him."

They watched Lad while the female pup explored her new territory and marked it. He crept closer and closer until the newcomer spied him. She bounced forward, barked and then pounced on him. Capturing Lad was just the first event. She rolled him over in the grass while he sniffed her and then tried to evade her attempt to chew on his white ruff. By the fierce tail-wagging going on, he seemed delighted with the new doggie companion.

Rob chuckled as he watched the canine duo run laps around the orchard in a rough and tumble game of chase; or was it puppy tag? "This was a good idea. Thanks."

Cat passed over the set of keys to the party barn to Durango. She beamed at the men. "We'd talked about another dog, but I hadn't even started to look. Thanks, Laredo."

He hesitated and then asked in a low, almost frightened voice. "Did Zeke Knight tell you about me?"

"No," Cat said, looking surprised at the mention of the old shoer. She tucked her hand into Rob's. "What was he supposed to tell us?"

"He said I could apprentice with him if it was all right with his customers."

"Sounds fair to me." Rob kissed the top of Cat's head. "We don't tolerate meanness toward any of our animals. You follow that rule and we'll get along just fine."

Cat tilted her head. "I thought I was in charge of training the horses."

"You are." Rob pulled her close. "Got anything to add?"

"Nope." She leaned into him. "What Rob said. Okay, Laredo?"

"Yeah. I can handle it."

"Fair enough." Rob glanced at Cat. "Do we want to schedule Zeke in to shoe Sky and Pal?"

"Yes, so will you tell him I'll be calling him, Laredo?"

He nodded, then looked at his watch. "I have to meet Zeke in town at Pop's for lunch. Let me say goodbye to Lassie and I'll visit her when we come to shoe."

Rob chuckled. "Lassie, huh? The girls will love her."

"Then, you won't be changing the name?" Laredo asked, anxiously. "It's what I've been calling her. If it doesn't work out here, I can come get her."

"No need to," Cat said. "She already knows her name. She answers to it and she fits in with the dog we have. They're buddies and Laddie needs a friend. I'll come with you so she knows she has a new home."

Rob waited while Laredo and Cat went to pet both dogs. Lassie ran up to be petted and fussed over. Lad followed, getting over his anxieties, and bounced up to lick Laredo's chin. The man laughed and scooped up both pups to hug them.

"Somebody's done a number on that boy," Rob commented. "He's the walking wounded."

"My old man," Durango said, with a lethal tone. "He and his campaign manager really enjoy setting Laredo up to get the crap kicked out of him. He never stays down, and it means he ends up in the hospital a lot. I've told both of them if they come anywhere near him again, they'll be the ones who get busted bones and heads."

"I see." Rob studied the other man. Something about the brawny blond man screamed prior military. "You served. Which branch?"

"Marines." Durango nodded toward the black van coming up the drive. "My crew. We do private security too so they'll be on the lookout while we're building those fences. They're just back from Iraq and Afghanistan. They'll clean the party barn and cook for themselves. They bunk separately. Men in one room. Women in the other. No fraternization, but they know it. They have their own weapons. What do you want them to do with intruders? Trespassers?"

"Don't kill them," Rob said, glancing at the other man. "A few bruises are do-able. Tie them up and we'll turn them over to the cops."

"Works for me," Durango said. "We'll post the place with 'No Trespassing' signs and they'll divide into patrols now. We've got it covered twenty-four, seven."

"Why?" Rob asked. "This is my family and our place. Why are you guarding it?"

"Angie Madison Barrett is my fiancée's favorite cousin. Your wife is training her horse and Angie's in Afghanistan until next spring. Her dad doesn't want to have to tell her that Skyrocket died in a barn fire while she's overseas. He'll pay for security and then take the money out of Herman MacGillicudy's hide."

"Works for me," Rob said.

CHAPTER TWENTY-SEVEN

She was in the middle of bedding the second stall with pine shavings when the double dog alarm went off. She laughed as she recognized Lad's bark and now, Lassie's. Thank goodness, the male dog was feeling better and back on guard duty with his new girlfriend.

Cat headed out to the parking lot and saw Frank Madison's pickup. She was surprised to see him. He didn't have the trailer, so did that mean he wasn't planning to take the horses? He didn't look upset. He was petting both collies and fussing over them.

She went to meet him. "Hi, Frank. What's up?"

He reached for her hands, squeezed them. "Are you okay, honey? Dick called and told me what happened last night. You must have been scared to death."

"I was," Cat admitted. "The horses are fine, Frank. Rob put them out in the corrals so the smell of gasoline wouldn't affect their lungs and respiratory systems. We're prepping the far end of the barn for them while we clean up."

"And how is Rob?" Frank asked. "Dick said the arsonists tried to attack him."

"All guy. He insists he's fine." Cat heaved a sigh. "Dick wants me to take him to Doctor MacGillicudy, but Rob says he has too much work to do around here. Unless I tie him up and throw him in the trunk, I don't know any other way to get him there."

Frank laughed. "Invite Doc and Robin down to the farm," he suggested. "She could look over the horses when she gets off from the vet clinic and Doc could check out your husband."

"That's a great idea." Cat hesitated. "I wanted to get the horses settled before I called and brought you up to speed, Frank. I wasn't hiding anything from you or Ingrid."

"Oh, I know that. I'm just not much for standing around and waiting." Frank removed his hat and fiddled with it. "I was at the bank when it opened to close my accounts. Herman had barely finished with that when Amarillo Hawke showed up to move all of Durango's business. Then, the Baker City Council arrived."

"Oh, my word. Will he have a bank left by the end of the day?"

"I have no idea and I don't care," Frank said. "There are other banks in Lake Maynard, and they'll be happy to have our money. Meantime, I have fifty pounds of organic carrots in the truck. I wasn't sure if you had any apples left."

"They wanted to kill the horses," Cat said, "so they were setting the fire at that end of the barn first. They hadn't hit the tackroom or feed room before Rob found them."

Frank frowned. "There's nothing worse than an animal abuser. I hope Frazer—I mean, Rob—busted their heads."

"He did." They walked over to the truck and Cat took a handful of carrots. Then they headed over to the corral where the horses trotted up to meet them. They doled out the treats over the fence. "Do you want to see me ride them?"

Frank began to smile. "I would. Are you riding all of them now?"

"Yes," Cat said, smiling again. "They're doing beautifully. We've made a deal with Skyrocket. No spurs or whips, just lots of carrots and love."

"Good. Angie will appreciate that." Frank looked past the machine shed to the party barn. "Did my security team get here?"

Cat stiffened. "What security team? Durango wanted a place for his friends to stay while they're in town and he rented the party barn for them."

"Great." Frank said, leaning on the fence. "I'm glad they got here safe. Durango retired early from the Marines, but he's still a warrior. He does retrieval work for Nighthawke Security."

"I've heard about them," Cat said. "They're private contractors who spend a lot of time in the Middle East."

"Not just there. Nighthawke has people in South America, Africa and anywhere else we need mercenaries," Frank agreed. "Nobody will be trespassing here again."

Frank left after watching her ride Tonka, Lucky Charm and Skyrocket. Cat turned the flashy bay gelding back in with the other horses. She headed toward the parking lot when Summer pulled in with a delivery from the feed store. The dogs escorted her, tails wagging, Lassie settling in quickly. Dray climbed out of the passenger side of the pickup.

"What's going on?" Cat asked.

"I brought more hay, shavings and replacement water buckets," Summer said. "Had an early morning visit from the O'Connell boys and they told me they were out here last night to deal with a pair of would-be arsonists."

"And I have the supplies to clean up the gasoline spill," Dray added. "I'm a volunteer firefighter so normally, I'd have been with the guys last night, but Mom won't let me go on the late calls except during school breaks. After Herman's latest stunt, she said I could help you folks today. She and Grandpa were on the way to his bank in Lake Maynard to close their accounts."

"I didn't have to do it because I never did business with him in the first place," Summer added. "I didn't like the crap he gave me. Same goes for Maxine."

Cat nodded. "Makes sense to me. I didn't either, so I went elsewhere too."

"So, who was the guy who stopped us at the bridge?" Summer asked.

"Frank Madison hired some of Durango's people to provide security for a while." Cat glanced at the barn as Rob joined them. Lassie followed him, sniffing around. "Do we want to put this hay in the other wing near the new stalls?"

"Works for me." He bent to pet the black and white puppy while Lad demanded the same attention from Cat. "I can open up the pasture gates so Summer can pull closer to the barn if you get these two out of the way."

For an instant, Cat admired his broad shoulders and lean build in the plaid flannel shirt and jeans. She remembered the way his thick coal black hair felt in her hands. She smiled. "What if I go throw together some sandwiches? We can have lunch before you guys get started on the gas spill. Summer, would you like to join us?"

"Sounds great. Let me park this rig and I'll come help you for a change."

"Okay." Cat called the dogs and began walking toward the house. Lassie bounced along beside her, occasionally chasing after Laddie's tail. She piddled a couple times along the way which made it easier to take her inside. The mother cat took one look at the second dog, picked up a rambunctious kitten and carried it into the pantry.

"Not a bad idea." Cat picked up the box by the woodstove and followed the adult feline. There was room in the corner behind the door. So, the first kitten went into the cardboard carton. Cat returned to the kitchen and gathered up the rest of the litter, carrying the fur babies to join their family. Then she moved the dishes of dry food and water. The sandbox was already by the back door.

Lassie and Lad sat by his food bowl and watched. Obviously, the little border collie already knew better than to chase cats and Lad had learned that lesson too.

"I'm here." Summer called as she came down the hall. "Where do I jump in?"

"I'm in here," Cat said. "I was dealing with the kitty family that Dray brought me. The momma wasn't impressed with the puppy that Laredo Hawke gave us."

"Well, I think she's adorable," Summer said. "My kids will want puppies too. I know he raises border collies and heelers. Did he have more?"

"Durango said Lassie was the oldest of her litter," Cat said. "It'd be worth asking Laredo when you see him, or I will when he comes to shoe the horses with Zeke."

"Sounds good to me." Summer washed her hands at the sink. "What kind of sandwiches are we making?"

"Roast beef."

While Summer pulled the makings out of the fridge, Cat put a scoop of kibble in the dish that Laredo provided for Lassie and topped off Lad's too. The dogs could eat now and then she'd take them out while the humans did. She felt much safer with the veterans patrolling the place. With everything underway, Cat called Mike and arranged for Rob to see him. The doctor agreed to drop in for a visit that afternoon when his granddaughter arrived home from the veterinary clinic.

That settled, Cat called Ingrid and brought her up to speed on the aborted barn fire. The woman said she and Mandy would be in to see the Morgan fillies after school. The horses moved into the short wing of the barn shortly after lunch. Summer had headed back to the feed store so she could make her next delivery. While Rob and Dray worked on the other wing of the barn, Cat groomed Starlight, then Gambler. She took the fillies out one at a time to work them. Both were coming along really well.

She saddled up Gambler first and warmed her up on the longe line. After walking, trotting and loping both directions, the bay filly was ready for riding. She stood quietly while Cat swung up in the saddle. With a soft squeeze of her legs, she cued the young horse to walk. Gambler flicked her ears and then trotted off to circle the round pen.

Cat sighed. She dropped her heels down, sat deep and tightened her hands on the reins. Back to working on the stop and slowing down, not the filly's favorite thing. She tossed her head, black mane flying and jumped sideways.

"That isn't what I want either." Cat repeated the cues for slowing down and added a soft pull on the reins. When Gambler finally slowed her pace, Cat relaxed, and the filly trotted forward again. Back to the drawing board. Disengaging the hindquarters so they stopped, slowing each time she trotted and requesting the walk again. They kept working on the walk for the next hour, much to the bay's disgust. Mandy and Ingrid arrived just as the filly finally gave up and stayed on the rail at a nice pace.

"I don't believe it," Mandy exclaimed as the two of them got out of the car. She jumped up and down beside Ingrid. "Look, Mom. She's a riding horse. Isn't she beautiful?"

"Definitely." Ingrid smiled at Cat. "I'm impressed. How is Star doing?"

"She's calmer than her sister, so she's further along." Cat reined Gambler to a stop and used her seat and legs to ask the filly to back up. With a toss of her head, the bay complied. "But this one is constantly testing me. You have to be really alert so you don't go flying. Do you want to ride her, Mandy?"

"You bet. I'll get my helmet out of the car." Mandy hustled toward the driveway.

Cat slid her hands down the reins. She rested her left hand on the brown neck in front of the saddle, put her right hand on the pommel. She stood up and slowly swung her right leg over the filly's haunches. Standing in the left stirrup, Cat waited till Gambler listened and stood perfectly still. Then, she finished sliding down to the ground.

"I'm going to add the halter and longe line," Cat said. "Then, I'll have the control while Mandy rides her. You hardly have to touch with your legs to get Gambler to move."

Ingrid nodded. "Will you have time to show me what Star can do today?"

"Yes. I've arranged for the vet to come take a look at the horses." Cat rubbed Gambler's neck while she waited for Mandy to join her in the round pen. "I think they're fine. They barely inhaled any of the gasoline and Rob got them out of the barn right away when he realized what was happening."

"That's what you said on the phone and Frank Madison called to tell me about the security team he hired." Ingrid leaned on the corral fence. "I think you're doing everything possible to keep the horses safe, Cat, and I don't plan to move them. I can give you cash for this month's training, but if you want a check, it will have to wait until next week because I opened a new account today at Cascade Mutual in Lake Maynard."

"Cash is fine," Cat said, grateful that she wasn't losing any customers. "And after Mandy rides Gambler, there may be time for you to ride Star."

Time for a break. Rob left Dray to finish moving the rest of the hay and shavings from the longer wing to the shorter wing of the barn. He found Cat supervising a lesson in the round pen. The twins led the way at a steady walk while the owners of the two fillies followed. He couldn't decide which of the riders looked happier, the girls, the teenager, or the adult.

Cat spotted him. "Time to stop now," she called out. "Turn your horses in to the center of the pen and face me. Then, stop them."

"Now, we back up four steps," Sophie said.

"That's right." Cat stepped over to the bay filly and talked to the teen, explaining how to complete the maneuver. "Rob, will you come hold Star while Ingrid dismounts? I don't want the horse to move and this is still a learning activity."

"Happy to." Rob opened the gate just wide enough for him to enter. He didn't want the horse to think escape was possible. He walked over to the black filly and caught hold of the left rein. "She'll stand whether you vault out of the saddle or do a proper dismount. It's your choice."

"At my age, I prefer a regular dismount." Ingrid collected on the reins, then swung out of the saddle, jumping down to the ground. "Have we met before?"

"I don't know." Rob opted for the explanation that Cat gave her father. "I was in a truck accident a week and a half ago. It's affected my memory. I know my girls and Cat, but if we met prior to today, I don't remember, Ingrid. I'm sorry."

"I'm not." Ingrid smiled at him. "We'll go with today being our first meeting. Okay?" She held out her hand to shake his. "I'm Ingrid Nielson and that's my daughter, Mandy on her horse, Gambler."

Rob shook hands with her. "It's nice to meet you. I'm Frazer Robert Jacob Williams Hendrickson, but I prefer Rob to that long handle."

Ingrid laughed and took the reins. "I don't blame you at all. Thank you for saving my horse last night. I know Mandy's grateful too."

"You're both welcome." Rob grinned at her. "Think you could tell

Cat that punching out the wannabe arsonists is okay with you? She's afraid I've hurt myself and wants to drag me up to see the doctor."

"I am truly glad you punched them, and you look fine to me," Ingrid said.

Once the horses were back in the barn, unsaddled and groomed, Ingrid and Mandy left with promises to visit soon. Mandy dashed to the car and came back with a container of homemade chocolate chip cookies that she gave to Rob. "Mom made these today, but I'll make you a batch for saving Gambler."

"Tell Daddy that he gots to share," Sophie said. "We love cookies."

"I don't know," Rob teased. "If I have to share these, then don't you and Samantha have to share the present that Laredo Hawke brought you two?"

"What present?" Samantha asked, her eyes round. "We didn't find no present."

"Then, you'd better go find Laddie and see what he's done with it," Cat said. "It's time for him to go on a potty run before we head for the haunted town."

"He was really tired so he's sleeping under our bed." Sophie ran for the house, Samantha right behind her.

"And what's the present?" Ingrid asked, light blue eyes amused.

"You're about to see it," Rob said. "I'll share my cookies with the girls and Cat, but not with Laddie and Lassie."

The twins came charging from the house, Lassie in Samantha's grip, Lad right behind Sophie. "Mommy, look. Did you see Laddie's friend?" Samantha called, holding the black and white puppy tight. "He's so happy."

"And he's not scared anymore." Sophie bent down to hug the tricolored collie pup. "He really likes having his own puppy."

"Everyone does." Cat petted the new addition. "Her name is Lassie. Why don't you girls take them over to the orchard to do their puppy business? Then, Ingrid won't have to worry about having them around when she starts her car."

"Okay." Samantha carried Lassie toward the trees, the border collie trying to lick her face.

Sophie and Lad raced after them, the older pup yapping excitedly.

Rob glanced at the pickup pulling into the parking lot. He recognized Mike MacGillicudy and his granddaughter in the cab. It was hard to believe that the guy he drag-raced with, played football with, went to Vietnam with was a grandfather. "All right, kitten. 'Fess up. What rotten thing have you done now?"

Cat tucked her arm in his. "Well, *darlin'*. You wouldn't go to the doctor so I had him come make a house call. And Robin is going to check out the horses. I know they're all right, but I want a second opinion."

Rob tugged gently on the copper red braid that hung to Cat's hips. "You do realize that my cookies could be in jeopardy. If I lose any to Mike, you'll owe me an entire batch."

"Mandy's already promised you cookies," Cat pointed out. "You're good to go."

"A guy can never have too many homemade cookies," Rob said. "We'll stop at the mercantile and get some chocolate chips when we're in town tonight. It's payback."

"I am not making you cookies."

"Want to bet?"

Robin examined the horses and pronounced them in fine shape while Mike looked over Rob. When Cat came in the kitchen, she found the men sitting at the table bonding over the cookies. She pulled the deep-dish casserole out of the oven and popped in the tray of drop biscuits. "If you spoiled your appetites for dinner, gentlemen, you'll both be in trouble."

"Shades of my mother." Rob put the lid on the plastic container, then set it on the counter. He stood. "I'll get the plates. Mike, there's a salad in the fridge."

Between the three of them, they had supper on the table by the time the oven timer buzzed for the biscuits. Cat dished up small helpings of *Tator-Tot* casserole for the twins. "I want them to have dinner before we go up to the haunted town."

"I'm hearing great things about it," Mike said. "Robin and I are going tonight since she's not on call. It'll be fun. Dray tells me the best part is his mom's hot chocolate and frosted cookies afterward."

"That's the part the twins love too." Cat smiled as the girls came into the room, followed by Robin and Dray. "Wash up. Let's eat. We have places to haunt tonight."

CHAPTER TWENTY-EIGHT

After dinner, Cat helped the girls change into their costumes. Rob and Dray cleaned up the kitchen. It was another way to prove that Frazer was truly gone even if she hadn't heard that from her deceased grandmother the day before. Cat didn't remember him ever helping in the kitchen, let alone doing the dishes in their almost ten years together.

She finished braiding Samantha's hair. "I think we're ready to go, ladies."

"You look amazing," Rob said.

"Oh, Daddy. You say that every night," Sophie told him. The twins had settled in quickly to having a father who liked being one.

"And it's always true."

Cat glanced around the immaculate kitchen. Scrubbed counters, swept floor, dishes put away; she could so get used to living like this. "Coats, girls. Otherwise, you'll be cold coming home."

Rob headed into their room and came back with her gold leather bomber jacket. "You'll need yours too," he told her. "We've already walked the pups and fed the cats. Did you know they moved into the pantry?"

"Yes. M.C., Momma Cat wasn't too enthused about another

canine." Cat smiled over her shoulder at him as he held the coat for her so she could slide into it. "And it really worked for me."

"Fair enough." He put an arm around her. "Let's go. I definitely don't want Mrs. O'Sullivan mad at me if you girls are tardy. It would be hard to explain if she sent me to stand in a corner."

Samantha giggled. "She's so nice. I wish she was our regular teacher. She never mixes up me and Sophie like the playground teacher does at our 'real' school."

They dropped Dray at Pop's café. When they reached the school, Cat climbed out with the girls. "Are you coming back soon?"

"Right after I put the Mustang in Reverend Tommy's garage." Rob winked at the twins. "Don't sing without me."

"Then, you'd better hurry," Cat said. "We don't want to mess up Mrs. O'Sullivan's schedule." She walked the girls over to the playground and they ran ahead to join the games with the other kids. She waved at the teacher standing on the porch with her bell. Dusk had started to settle on the distant hills, but it wasn't dark yet.

When she looked across the cemetery, she saw the gang of teenage zombies. They still seemed to enjoy terrifying the guests. It hadn't become a bore or a chore yet. Of course, they were only in the first week. As Halloween approached, the event might become dull for them.

However, she wouldn't say that to anyone. At the meeting next Sunday, she'd suggest they adjust the schedule so people could start having the occasional night off and they would alternate who played the ghostly roles. For now, she needed to walk through the town and see how things were actually going. She spotted Virginia coming toward her and went to meet the older woman.

"Hey," Cat said. "How are the numbers tonight?"

"Going upward, ever upward." Virginia looked toward the cars filling the church parking lot. "We have five hundred dollars toward the memorial and Pop is talking about opening up the back half of his restaurant again. He hasn't had enough business to keep it going so he pulled the partitions across. He told Durango that if Heather ever comes home, he'll reopen the lounge and have live music."

"Do you think she will?" Cat asked.

"I don't know. She spent a lot of time talking to Tommy before she packed up and called it quits with Durango. She really doesn't like him working for NightHawke. Going after captured soldiers or mercenaries is a dangerous business."

"Can't blame her there." Cat walked past the church toward the block of haunted buildings. "I'd have issues if Rob went off to be a mercenary. On the other hand, the farm feels a lot safer now that Durango provided a dozen of his folks to guard it."

Virginia smiled. "You should have seen Herman's face today when Julie Fenwick and I went to get the money and close out all the church accounts. He was almost in tears and kept saying that he hadn't hired those boys to burn you out."

"If he hadn't nearly killed Rob and Dray in that truck accident, tried burning the horses alive, and poisoned my pup, I could feel a bit sorry for him." Cat led the way into the hotel to see if everything was ready. The living desk clerk waved a cheerful greeting, then opened the register on the front counter. A ghostly bellman rolled a cart forward.

Smiling, Cat left the building and headed next door. "As my Aunt Rose used to say, 'what comes around, goes around.' And Herman's been asking for this for a long time. I can't be the only one he's harassed."

"No, but you have the O'Leary gift," Virginia said. "I didn't realize how much we all missed it until you moved here with your girls. Granted there are a few folks who could sense when the ghosts were here, but nobody else can talk to them the way you do."

"I didn't know how much I missed having a home until we came here," Cat said.

"That's nice." Virginia hugged her. "Come on. You have a lot left to do before you head for the school and the girls."

They continued the tour. Cobwebs draped the windows of the hardware store. Tinny music poured from the saloon. Scantily clad girls, living and dead, hung out on the porch of the bordello. Everyone looked ready for a haunting good time.

Cat turned and started back for the school. She was even with the laundry when Newt O'Leary rushed to her side, concern written on his spectral features. She smiled, but he didn't. "What's wrong?"

"Mrs. O'Sullivan sent me. The girls are missing."

"What?" Was that croak hers? It couldn't be. Cat gaped at him, shaking her head, causing those around her to stare while she spoke to the ghost. "No. They were playing with the other kids."

"Yes and Mrs. O'Sullivan called them inside. And when she took attendance, they didn't answer."

Instinctively, Cat grabbed for his arm, but her hand went through him. "Find them."

"The mayor's organized a search party. We're tearing the place apart."

"Cat, what is it?" Virginia asked. "What's wrong?"

"My girls are missing." Cat spun, started toward the church and the school beyond it. "Go round up a search party. Find Herman."

The townspeople of beyond got to work. Wind howled through the buildings. Doors slammed open. They banged closed. Shutters crashed. Windows rattled in their frames. Car alarms wailed.

Cat ran past the first group of live customers. No sign of her girls. One of the teenage zombies raced from the cemetery, sliding to a stop in front of her. "What is it? Why are the ghosts going nuts?"

"Someone took my daughters. Have you seen them?"

"No, but I'll get everybody looking."

Cat nodded and kept running. Halfway through the parking lot, she heard someone shout her name. She whirled.

Herman MacGillicudy staggered toward her, blood streaming down his ruddy face. "You gotta stop him."

Cat froze. "Stop who? You? Where are my daughters?"

"He has them." Herman pointed toward the trees bordering the far end of the lot. "Won't get far. I slashed his tires."

"Who?" Cat demanded. "Are you crazy?"

"Liam."

"What?" Cat advanced on the stocky man. "My *father* took my girls? Am I supposed to believe that?"

"He wants the land for that gravel pit. I told him we're not going to get it, not after the Williams family came flat out and said it was against the rules, just like you've been telling him. It's not worth killing anybody, but he lost his shirt in some kind of money-lending scheme and his investors are threatening him." Herman wiped at his face. "This whole thing's gotten way out of hand."

"And you had *nothing* to do with it?"

"I wasn't saying that."

Cat looked at the cemetery, the rows of headstones, some old and moss-covered, others newer. "I need help," she called. "I'm the O'Leary medium. If you're here, will you please help me find my girls?"

"We're here." It was a woman who answered, as soft as a summer breeze although she couldn't be seen. "We'll find them, and we'll bring you word."

Herman paled and fell back a step. "You're calling up the spirits?"

"I have news for you." Cat headed for the parking lot. "They've been here a lot longer than you or I have. I just talk to them. And right now, I'm turning them loose. If Liam has my daughters and you sabotaged his Lexus, he'll need another rig to get them out of town."

Rob raced toward her. "Cat, I just heard. Where have you looked?" He spotted Herman. "Where are my daughters?"

"I told her. Liam has them. He said he was taking one, but he has both of them."

"Thanks to Herman, he's stuck in town," Cat said. "Everybody's looking for him." She paused as the ghostly mayor hurried forward. "Where is Liam?"

"In the cocktail lounge at the back of Pop's. He's going to swap the girls for the Williams' farm."

"Like hell." Cat glanced at Herman. "Go get Chief O'Connell and tell him what you told me. Rob and I are getting our kids. And you'd better hurry."

They reached the café before the police and other first responders. She walked into the bar. Rob was right behind her, but they weren't the only ones there to rescue the twins. The room was full of ghosts, led by a furious Mrs. O'Sullivan, surrounding the three living people in the back of the room.

The girls were pushed into a corner booth, clutching each other and eyeing their grandfather.

"He took us away 'fore we gots to sing our song," Sophie announced.

"You have the whole rest of the month to sing your song," Cat said. "Samantha, are you okay, honey?"

"She's mad," Sophie said. "She bit him when he grabbed her, and he hit her."

"I only slapped the brat." Liam glared at Cat. "I should have smacked you a lot more when you were young, but your mother wouldn't have it."

"I've got to invite that woman for dinner more often." Cat said. She drew a deep breath. Her daughters were alive and apparently unhurt. She could deal with him. "What do you want, Liam?"

"The farm." He pulled out a fistful of papers. "Sign off on it and my lawyer will deal with the Williams bunch. Then, you can have your brats."

"I can't do that, and I don't like that choice." Cat stared at him. "I remember everything, Liam. Everything you did to me." She couldn't tell the twins that he tried to kill her. If he'd succeeded, none of them would be in Baker City. "Here's a different option. Mrs. O'Sullivan gets to whack you with her bell because you stole my kids when they were in her care."

"There are two kids," Rob drawled. "She gets to hit him twice. And after that, I'll clean up the floor with him."

"And you think that's going to stop me?" Liam demanded, reaching into his briefcase to grab a pen.

The bell materialized and crashed into his hand. He yelped and jumped sideways, looking around. Before he could do anything else, Mrs. O'Sullivan, still unseen by him, swung again and this time the bell hit the side of his head.

Rob took advantage of the distraction. He grabbed Liam's shoulder and threw him against the bar.

"Men," Cat said, rolling her eyes. "I'm not paying for the damages, Rob. And if you want him to go straight to jail, don't bust him up too much." She walked over to the booth and held out her hands. "Let's go, young ladies. You have a performance and you can't do it here."

The twins slid out of the seat and into their mother's arms. "Mommy, he's not a nice person," Sophie said.

"No, he's not." Cat guided her children into the café. "You will never have to see him again. Are you hurt, Samantha?"

"I'm okay. I was just scared when he said that he'd make you give up our home to get us back. He says he's gonna 'doze all the barns and buildings and find lots of rocks. We like living on the ranch just the way it is."

"I told you that we weren't going nowhere. Mommy and Daddy won't let the bad man wreck it," Sophie informed her twin. "It's our 'forever' home. Mommy said."

"And you know my rules," Cat said. "I'm the mommy and what I say is what happens."

A group of visitors came into the café. One of the teenage boys grinned at Cat. "This is the best haunted place ever. We were just in the saloon when this guy covered in blood came in and yelled that an O'Leary had called up all the spirits in the graveyard and they were gonna get everybody in town."

"We'd better stop on the way and let them know we're safe." Samantha wiped at her eyes. "Else, they'll be up all night scaring everybody."

"Good point." Cat ushered the twins out the door, and they strolled up the sidewalk, passing revelers, who seemed unaware of anything not festival-oriented. She nodded to Dick O'Connell. "You may want to get into Pop's pretty soon. Rob's kicking the crap out of my father for taking the girls. Herman sabotaged Liam's car so he couldn't take them out of town."

"Yeah, that's what Herman told me while Doc MacGillicudy patched him up." Dick sauntered toward the lounge. "I'll go arrest Liam. He'll probably be ready to confess and if he's not, I'll let Rob knock him around a bit longer."

"Remind Rob that he needs to come hear the girls sing," Cat said. "If he's late, Mrs. O'Sullivan won't be happy."

Dick chuckled. "I'll pass the word."

"I knew he was jealous of your gift and the fact that you could talk to everyone in Baker City, but I never would have thought it was your old man making trouble." Stretched out on the couch, Rob nursed a beer. He cuddled Cat close beside him. "I was sure it was Herman."

"So was everyone else in town, but Liam was the money guy for the new gravel pit." She put an arm across Rob's broad chest and snagged the bottle. "I was serious. I am inviting my mother to come for dinner."

He waited till she took a swallow, before reclaiming the beer. "Well, she can help you plan our wedding."

Cat sighed, sliding her hand inside his shirt, then kissing his throat. "I already told you. We've been married for nearly ten years. We don't need a wedding."

"Okay, then let's renew our vows in front of the whole town. Reverend Tommy can perform the service." Rob tangled a hand in her copper red hair. "And I can spend the rest of my life making you purr."

"Promises. Promises." She smiled down at him. "Why don't we just go to bed? We love each other. That's enough, isn't it?"

"Not for me."

"Want to bet?"

THE END

THANK YOU FOR READING

Did you enjoy this book?

We invite you to leave a review at your favorite book site, such as Goodreads, Amazon, Barnes & Noble, etc.

DID YOU KNOW THAT LEAVING A REVIEW…

- Helps other readers find books they may enjoy.
- Gives you a chance to let your voice be heard.
- Gives authors recognition for their hard work.
- Doesn't have to be long. A sentence or two about why you liked the book will do.

ABOUT THE AUTHOR

Josie Malone lives and works at her family's riding stable in Washington State. She's taught children to ride and know about horses for so long that she often discovers she's taught three generations of their families. Her life experiences span adventures from dealing cards in a casino, attending graduate school to get her Masters in Teaching degree, being a substitute teacher, and serving in the Army Reserve - all leading to her second career as a published author. Visit her at her website, www.josiemalone.com to learn about her books.

Contact Josie at:
josiemaloneauthor@outlook.com

Find her on Facebook at:
www.facebook.com/JosieMaloneAuthor